EyeCue Productions
Presents

CLASS FOUR

Those Who Survive

DUNCAN P. BRADSHAW

Daniel Marc Chant and J.R. Park, my Sinister Horror Company brethren, there aren't two people in this world that I would rather be on this journey with.

Ash Williams and Stuart Park for beta reading this and pointing out things I've missed or elements that need sorting, lucky to have you both do this for me.

Paul Feeney for his advice on a particular section and Hannah Lockett for the inspiration to an entire set piece, thank you.

All of those people who volunteered to be characters in this book, I appreciate your enthusiasm, I hope I've done you justice.

Adi Stone and Paige (Madame Grotesque) for the covers and Penny Gaff illustrations respectively. I can't draw for shit and your work gives this book a real added dimension, you rock.

Adam Millard, proofreading this badboy in three days and transforming it from a seven stone weakling into a sand kicking beach bully. Your kind words for the back cover are thoroughly appreciated.

For Debbie, the balance in the Force, your unending support gets me through the days when all of this seems so impossible.

Mum, Dad and Stuart, I wouldn't be the person I am today without you.

To all those lost along the way, the hole you've left never leaves us, but you're always alive as long as we remember.

And finally to you.
These words only come alive thanks to your imagination breathing life into them.

ZOMBIE OUTBREAK CLASSIFICATION

Class One - Low-level outbreak, usually Third world or rural First world, numbers of infected range from one to fifty. Time of infection before 'correction' is between 24 and 48 hours

Class Two - Urban or densely populated area infection, numbers between twenty and one hundred. Casualties could reach around seven hundred. Time elapsed can be about the same as a Class One outbreak.

Class Three - Zombies measure in the thousands and infection could last several months if not dealt with immediately.

Class Four - The undead now rule the world. Society and civilisation has collapsed, humans are scattered to the wind. Survival is the only option.

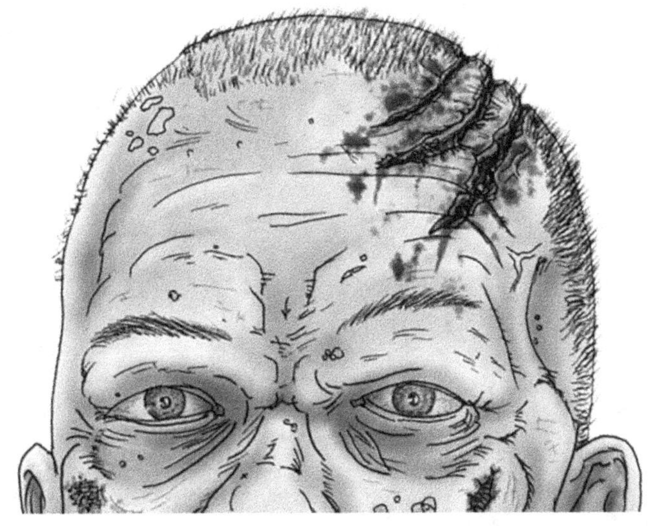

'People were always getting ready for tomorrow. I didn't believe in that. Tomorrow wasn't getting ready for them. It didn't even know they were there'

- Cormac McCarthy 'The Road'

'It is necessary to do (useful?) violence to oneself, to induce oneself to speak of the fate of the most helpless'

- Primo Levi 'The Drowned And The Saved'

'If history were taught in the form of stories, it would never be forgotten'

- Rudyard Kipling

INTRODUCTION

Nice watch huh?

No, it's not broken, not at all. It's meant to be like that; serves as a welcome reminder. The world we live in today holds so few certainties anymore; some things fade away, whilst others endure.

For instance, the memories I have of the times before the end are like a disjointed slide show, or a shoddily edited old 35mm film reel. You know, the ones we see with all the glorious conquests these days.

Random scenes with people I can no longer recall the names of, in places I couldn't give you directions to. All existing in a world which lives solely in the stories that the survivors, us, tell.

I have but three images of my mother. Whether time or grief removed the others, I haven't the slightest clue.

One is from my seventh birthday. I was crying for reasons unknown, she pulled in close to me and whispered soothing words, I wiped the tears from my eyes and blew the candles out. She smelt of cake mix and her skin was as smooth as a sharpened blade.

Another is from the final morning we had together. My reluctance to eat breakfast was testing her, I can remember the strain in her eyes. I had no idea why we had to leave so quickly that day; it would be years before I was able to understand the look she gave me that fateful morning.

The last image is the one I like to dwell on the least. I used to think she was wearing a red scarf, but time and adult eyes revealed the awful truth that it was her blood.

She had come back as one of *them* by then. The face I snuck a glimpse of as the man told me to look away, whilst similar to the other pictures of her, looks the least like her.

I remember the man striking her with the baton, I ignored his warning and watched as she died.

For the second time.

These days such horror seems so distant, so utterly alien. The things I have seen since then and over the course of so many years have withered away the ability to baulk at such sights.

But whilst my senses have been dimmed, one thing burns brighter than ever. The wish to keep alive those voices that were silenced in those days, months and years. We had plenty of false dawns in the struggle to reclaim our place in this world and, for many, they never got to see the world we live in now.

After *them*.

Those early days almost extinguished all hope we had. Some withered away, whilst others took evil into their hearts and used those dark times to create private fiefdoms or empires based on suffering and blood.

These places were the last to conquer, the hardest. Where *they* were found, they held no claim, other than to the body they were spawned within, they acted on instinct and impulse alone.

The others, though, were there because they felt they were owed something. They took advantage of the zeitgeist and acted out their depravity to every unimaginable whim.

This story, or at least the one that I can relay, is to speak for the silenced.

His is not the only one I have heard and remembered over the years. The other story I'll impart with his, is from another who felt equally compelled to remember those he shared time with.

In life, there are no coincidences, no fate, no master plan; there is only a choice.

Many of us are able to make our own decisions; for some, that privilege was taken away, but it was a choice to someone nonetheless.

Sometimes though, lives, both in the past and present become intertwined. This is nothing more than chance.

So please, stay a while. The lights will remain on a little longer yet, this zone has been cleared of the last of the risen dead. We'll get no further interruption.

Let me tell you a story.

This is not how he died.

This is how he lived.

MAY 14TH 2014

18:17

The black and white security monitors flickered. Aside from a stern looking woman locking up at Warchuck's, the wide angled shots showed no signs of life.

Francis sighed and looked back to the crossword: *five across, eight letters, one that returns after death or a long absence, R at the beginning and an N next to last.*

Hmmm.

His pondering was broken by 'If Love Is A Red Dress' singing from his phone. He looked at the caller:

Diane

"Hey sweetie, what's up?"

"Woah, woah, woah, slow down, breathe, okay? Go on, tell me. Slowly."

"How long for?"

"Okay baby, calm dow—"

"I know, okay, get yourself down there, I'll—"

"I know, I gotta call up Rob though, get someone to cover for me. I'll do that right after I finish speaking to you."

"Of course I do sweetie, don't say that. You know I'd do anything for you."

"That's okay, nothing to apologise for, you just go now. I'll call up Rob and get someone in here."

"No idea baby, hopefully within an hour or so, okay?"

"It's going to be fine, probably just last minute nerves before coming out and meeting us I guess, eh?"

"Ha, yeah, things are going to be okay. I'll see you real soon. I love you."

"Okay baby, bye."

"Bye."

CHAPTER ONE

"Who do you think they were?" Nathan asked softly. Try as he might, he couldn't see much of the body which Francis had covered up with the sleeping bag after its initial discovery, and the now compulsory check for zombie vital signs. The missing top half of the woman's skull confirmed quickly that she wouldn't be getting up again.

Francis stopped reading the scavenged pamphlet and looked from the shrouded, withered cadaver to the young boy sitting at the table. He looked miniscule compared to the large oak table, which took up a good portion of the log cabin. Strewn over its surface were all kinds of rotten food debris and other flotsam.

Nathan's hand was suspended in the air. Grubby fingers clutched a fork halfway down the handle, a piece of tuna balanced precariously on it. "I don't know kid, looks like it was a woman. Been there a while I'd say. Eat your breakfast up, we're not staying long."

The flakes of fish were shovelled into the kid's mouth, and he chewed slowly. A big gulp signalled its transition into his guts. "Is everyone dead now?" he asked reluctantly, looking into the can as if it might provide an answer.

"No, you know they aren't, Nate. Just because most of the folks we meet these days are like them, doesn't mean that everyone is dead." Francis folded the pamphlet up and shoved it into his rucksack. He scratched his burgeoning beard with dirt-encased fingernails; the once clear delineation between intentional moustache and smooth cheeks were long gone.

Nathan weaselled another morsel onto his fork. "But we haven't seen anyone alive for *ages*, and when we did, you—"

"We have to be careful these days, kid. People aren't what they used to be. We need to be one step ahead of them, make sure we can see them, and…" Francis looked over at Nathan with an expectant stare.

"And to make sure they can't see us," Nathan replied, forcing another mouthful of tuna down.

Francis nodded. "Good kid. That way, we can stay out of trouble. That's how we'll get through this, by staying out of trouble."

"But…" Nathan trailed off.

"What is it, Nate?"

Nathan ran the fork around the inside of the shallow tin, herding the remnants into a heap. "Why can't we stay somewhere? I'm tired of walking. I want to sit down for a while and read my comics." Faux innocent eyes looked at his guardian.

Francis laughed. "Nice one, kid. I'm not going to fall for the ol' poor puppy dog, 'woe is me' routine. Only one person had the power to make that work and, well, you ain't her."

Small shoulders sagged. The fork finished its duty and rested against the rim like a miniature diving board.

"Don't sulk, kid. Hey, if it's any consolation I think you're right. We just need to find the right group of people to be with. I was told to look after you, and that's exactly what I'm going to do." Francis wiped an arm across the detritus covering the map on the table. "Here, let's have a look, see what's around here."

Nathan rubbed a grubby sleeve across his mouth and let out a fishy burp. "'Scuse me."

Francis laughed and shook his head. "Shame we don't have any toothpaste left, that stinks."

Nathan laughed, pulled himself onto the table and looked at the map. To him it was just lines and circles; he pulled a puzzled face. "Where are we, Francis? Are we there?" a small filthy finger plonked down onto a large green area of the map. Francis took his hand and slid it a few inches diagonally towards him.

"Not bad, kid. Lucky guess. We're in this rather large forest. I reckon we find this train line here and follow it out the other side. We can see where we fancy going after that, *deal?*"

"Deal," Nathan nodded furiously and held out his pinky. Francis mirrored him and the two linked digits shook on it. The child scooted off the desk and landed on the wooden floor with a thud. Francis peeled the map off the table, which was only a matter of weeks away from becoming one with the furniture, and tried to fold it up. His many attempts ending in guffaws of laughter from the watching Nathan. "You're rubbish at folding," he offered. Francis scowled and eventually managed to get it back into its original shape.

The mildewed parchment was stuffed into the rucksack and Francis dug out a half packet of Tuc biscuits, wormed a few out of their plastic bondage and put them back. "Don't even look at me like that, kid. These are mine. I won them fair and square, remember?"

The reply was a mumble of inaudible consonants and grunts. "What was that, Nate?" Crumbs of fake cheese and biscuit were spat out as the question was asked.

"I said you cheated. I'm only eight, your thumbs are way bigger than mine. It's not fair," Nathan grumbled.

Francis smiled. He shoved the last Tuc in whole and started to do the bag up. "As I recall, you had the choice of game, could've been anything, Paper, Rock, Scissors, I-Spy, but you went with Thumb Wars. Anyway, I get to put up with your fishy burps if it makes you feel any better?"

The child's smile nearly split his face in two. Francis slung the backpack over his shoulder and ruffled Nathan's greasy unkempt hair. "C'mon kid, let's get a move on. It's light enough now, let's go and find that train line, yeah?"

Nathan jumped up, shouted, "Yeah!," and ran to the front door. He had to use both of his hands to heave it open. He jumped off the top step and into the leaf mulch which surrounded the cabin's porch.

"Slow down Nate, check before you head out, okay?" Francis called after the boy.

Tired eyes looked round the cabin one last time. Where the map used to be now showed the table's true colour, a light brown, like deer-hide. Where it ended there was grime and muck. Francis took a last look at the covered body in the corner, its legs cradling the spent useless shotgun. He gave a brief nod of understanding and headed back into the forest.

CHAPTER TWO

A red, scaly finger traced a line down the scar which ran from the top of his right temple, skirted the eye socket, over his prominent cheekbone, (which his mother always said was his best feature) and ended just below the middle of his jawbone. The depressed ravine had healed into a severe crease. It had taken four months to get to this stage. In the wan light, he turned this way and that to study his new unrequested facial feature.

Satisfied that he would no longer be able to stick his tongue through the deep incision which had been made, attention turned to his right arm. This looked the same as it did the day after it happened; the skin from shoulder to finger was a red, cracked oil painting, white hairline tendrils formed a patchwork quilt effect. The thinner skin over his scratched crimson wrist pumped like a turned up speaker cone playing a slow, monotonous drum beat. His fingers curled into a claw. All meat, and no nail.

He raised his left arm, which by contrast to its limb-sibling was a slab of new pink skin. It looked like his forearm was a Blobfish; the smooth skin stretched from the elbow to his knuckles. It was still puffy, tender to touch and hurt like a bastard.

Dry, crusted red digits squeezed a blister which had come up overnight. The thin skin bulb burst and dribbled clear acidic pus over his pink flesh. He gritted his teeth in delight and revelled in the burn.

He flexed the stubs where his fingers once lived. He swore he could still feel them when the lights were out; his thumb gripped his palm, missing its pals. His remaining digits on the other hand pressed the round stump dimples of skin. A crimson finger pushed into the fleshy abscess and he could feel the tip of his finger bone scratch against the inside of his knuckle. The pain shot up his arm like a lick of lightning. He closed his eyes and savoured his suffering.

He turned the ruined hand over and looked through the perfectly circular hole in the middle of his palm. The flesh inside had been cauterised and vitrified, like a skin coloured marble. Ends of the (now missing) middle finger metacarpal bones were separated by thin air.

Vision returned as he focused through the hole in his hand and onto the reflection in the mirror. He leant in closer to study his right eye. They had saved it, for what good it had done. The scalpel had sliced through the lens, and had gone so deep that the blunt end had scraped against the retina, whilst the point had invaded the lair of the optic nerve.

At least *he* had been creative and made it into a cross; for that he was grateful. Malky had volunteered to pluck it out, be done with it.

Cut out the weak.

That's what he had said to Malky.

What he said to everyone, including his brother.

No.

He wanted it. He needed it to be left there, to remind him of his own hubris and where it had led him.

To here.

To today.

The time when the final bandage had been removed, the ravages of the devilment at *his* hand were shown. Not just to him, but to the world, they were his stigmata.

He ran a fingerless hand across the crown of his smooth head; the cold water he had applied to soothe the razor rash was displaced and ran down his face, using the fresh scar as a shortcut.

A dark shadow appeared behind him. "Your Grace, I apologise for the intrusion, but it is time," a deep voice growled, the words thick with anger and frustration.

The visitor surveyed the naked flesh in front of him. The back was pock-marked with burns, misplaced lumps and bobbles of fused bone and skin. The visitor held out a thick red cotton unzipped hoodie. Devin turned, took it and slid it onto his toned but battered body. His digitless hand fumbled to hold the bottom of the runner as he struggled to pull the zip up through the toothed track. He opened his cracked lips, and a near hoarse voice crackled, "Thank you Malky, let us begin. Show me to the penitents."

Rebirth.

Malky bowed shallowly, turned and walked out of the bathroom. Devin followed close behind. As he reached the doorway he cast a glance to a large glass laboratory beaker sitting on a shelf at head height. The sound of laughter filled the room as he pulled down the hem of his hoodie and left the room.

The dead eyes of the severed head turned and watched him leave; the rictus grin seemed to guffaw in the formaldehyde. Wet flaps of skin around the neck rippled as the floor sprung from the men's departure. The bone from the remnants of the spinal column scratched against the glass bottom. Grey hair waved in the light green miasma.

The front door opened with an ominous creak and the two men walked out into the frigid morning air. The fields were covered in frost, like a watercolour painting. The herd of people kneeling on the floor stood out stark in comparison. They were surrounded by eight men armed with a variety of weapons, both makeshift and scavenged. Each guard was wearing the same red hoodie as Devin and his second in command.

To one side stood a hunched man. His black straggly hair led to an equally rough and shaggy beard; the glint had disappeared from the man's eyes weeks ago, resigned to his course of action.

The two men ignored the throng of captives and made a beeline to the forlorn looking man. He snapped out of his introspection as he saw them loom into his cone of vision.

He braced himself just as Devin's one remaining working hand grabbed him roughly around the throat. With apparent ease he lifted him in the air. Feet kicked out where his shins were a moment earlier. "I asked you for the plans to the infidel's camp. Do I have to tear you apart to find it?" Devin asked. His voice still sounded like he had just been found in a desert; it cracked and gutted like a bad telephone line.

The hoisted man looked down into eyes which burned with a resolve forged in a crucible of faith and unimaginable terror. One eye was pared like a tomato, the edges of the wound were curled up. As the eyelid closed, it formed a lump. His hands held onto the vice which was choking the life from him. "I…I…I have it….your Grace, please…"

Unsteady legs landed back on terra firma with a painful jolt. A bolt of agony ran up his bones and into his skull. He rubbed his hands around his neck, trying to invoke life back into his core again.

The morning sun hung low over the horizon; rays of light washed over him, intensifying the pain. Devin formed an eclipse by transitioning in front of it. "Well?" he snarled.

His breathing was still shallow, but it was returning. His hand switched from resuscitation mode and into his jacket pocket, fishing around momentarily before holding a folded piece of lined paper aloft. As Devin went to take the document, he stopped and turned the paper over, revealing the man's hand. "It would seem as though we share a similar disability."

As the page was snatched from his grasp, he instinctively held his hands together. One hand massaged the place where the little finger had been removed. He nodded in deference and lay on the floor, unsure of his fate.

Devin unfolded the paper and studied its contents. His brain ran over the map scrawled in black biro, assessing the security and potential avenues of attack. "Thank you, Mister Mystery Man. I'm not sure why you volunteered to help us, but I am a man of my word. Both of our intentions form a synergy, for now at least." The map was tucked into a trouser pocket and a scabrous hand was extended to the stricken man, which was accepted, reluctantly. "I'll honour our agreement."

As he was drawn up to full height, Devin whispered in his ear, "If I discover that this is a ruse or a play on your behalf, you can be assured that you will suffer the same fate as the penitents over there. But not before Malky has had his fun with you."

Mystery Man nodded meekly. "Trust me, I want what you do."

Devin patted him on the back. "Then you have nothing to fear. Friend."

He spun on his heels and headed back to the group of sorry creatures being held under guard. Malky followed him, his thick lamp-post arms folded across his skyscraper chest. They stood over the disparate wretches. "That one, put him in the coffin cage first. He has enough meat about him. Please don't forget to begin exsanguination before we leave this time. It was quite frankly an embarrassment when we started collection for that last camp."

Malky traced the gnarled finger to a sullen half-naked man. He gestured to one of the guards who picked him up roughly and frogmarched him to an RV which was parked up a short distance away.

Devin stood over the group and announced, "Ladies and gentlemen, my lucky fifteen. We begin the collection today, and you are the chosen ones. Please follow these men into the Securicar over there. I don't need to remind you what will happen if you opt to disobey me."

He gestured to an upside down body strapped to an old mill wheel on the outside of the building. A gore and filth covered burlap sack hid the face. The violated ribcage looked as if it had been pulled open like a bag of crisps; several ribs were missing and a number of internal organs were hanging down from meaty pipes of viscera. Beneath the figure was a puddle of half frozen offal and congealed blood.

The guards forced them to stand and herded them into the back of an old Group Six security van. Devin walked over to the back of the RV where Malky had just managed to get the half-naked man into the human shaped metal cage. The cage swung a few feet off the ground from a winch which had been welded onto the roof. The man sobbed gently, and a dark patch appeared on the crotch of his jeans.

Malky withdrew a box cutter from his pocket and slashed the soles of the man's feet, causing him to howl in pain. A steady trickle of blood started to pitter patter onto the frozen earth.

Dank, acrid breath smothered the man's tear-strewn face as Malky spat out, "Please, make as much noise as you can. We will need every last ounce of your screams."

"We'll take the route as planned. Let us hope that *She* has blessed us and that her flock are numerous. If this map is accurate, we will need as many as possible to ensure that we can bring Rapture to these heathens," Devin said raspily.

CHAPTER THREE

Steve wiped his glasses with the bottom of his t-shirt. Holding them up to the shaft of light which pierced the grimy window, he saw that all he had achieved was making a bigger smear.

He wiggled the metal arm which was still poking out at a most peculiar angle. He wrinkled his nose in annoyance and squished the piece of sticky tape which was barely holding it to the frame. Satisfied that it would hold, for now at least, he looked around the room at the other five occupants.

The room itself looked like it used to be a small storage unit. Judging by the oil stained floor, Steve assumed it used to hold spare machine parts for the factory which took up most of the footprint of the site. Whitewashed brick walls were lined with a wallpaper of fine brown dust and muck. The windows, streaked with filth, peered out onto the bleak concrete loading bay.

Steve cleared his throat, gingerly placed the glasses back on his face and addressed his unwilling congregation. "Good morning all, my name is Steve. Before all this…unpleasantness, I used to be a therapist, helping people deal with all sorts of everyday issues. The Gaffer asked me to set these weekly meetings up, so that we can hopefully help you come to terms with certain…events which you have all gone through."

"Hey dick-knot, go fuck yourself," growled a man whose entire head, with the exception of his eyebrows and the odd nose hair, was completely shaven. He leered at Steve, and the scar which watermarked his left eye socket opened up like a hungry shark's maw.

Steve crossed his legs, carefully opened his notebook to a blank page, withdrew his ballpoint pen emblazoned with a picture of Young Einstein on it, clicked the end to extend the nib and looked across at the man. "Good morning Sir, you are?" he asked in a level voice, hiding the fact that a boulder of sweat was now crashing down his back and his balls had withdrawn into their internal cavity.

The man scowled again, he was hunched in the plastic chair like it was his dominion, forearms rested on his stained jeans. "Well hello there, Doctor Dick-Knot, my name's Anton. I have only one thing to say to you mate."

Steve scribbled in his book; the pen scratched against the page. As he wrote, he maintained eye-contact with Anton. "Yes Anton, and what would that be?" he enquired.

The response was abrupt. "Go fuck yourself. I ain't saying shit to you." With that, he folded his arms, and looked round the rest of the group, almost begging someone to start on him.

The pen scratched some more and came to a halt. Steve was still evaluating Anton as a woman's voice, with a Lancastrian accent, gate-crashed the building silence. "Erm, you what? Are you fucking kidding me? Why don't you have some manners, pal, before I put my foot on your windpipe and crush the life out of ya.”

The woman was locked into a staring competition with Anton. As he tried to glare back, the woman increased the power to her death stare and he acquiesced. She continued to bore holes into the side of his head until Steve spoke again. “And you are?”

She turned to face him. Her dark brown hair swished and brushed the nape of her neck; her gaze switched to a more playful tone. “I’m Dee. Used to be a copper when this all kicked off. Wouldn’t have taken crap from this kind of a-hole then and I won’t take it now,” she stated bluntly.

Steve resumed writing duties. “Hello Dee. A policewoman eh? I bet you’ve—”

Dee interrupted with a raised hand. “Listen, pal. No offence, but I believe this is as much use as a cock on a trumpet. I don’t need therapy, I’m fine. It hasn’t happened again for ages, so I don’t really see the point of sitting here when I could be out there doing something useful.” She thumbed to the window behind her.

Steve looked at her. His hand autonomously continued to scrawl in his notepad.

“What do you think you’re writing now?” Dee snapped.

The scratching continued.

“Seriously, pal, you need to stop writing. *Now.*” Her voice had hardened and slapped across the circle at Steve.

He stopped.

“Interesting,” he muttered. Dee sank back into her chair, flashed one last demeaning glance at Steve before investigating her immaculately manicured fingernails. Steve turned to the man to his right. “Hello there, who are you?” he enquired.

The man shifted uncomfortably in his seat. His hands were clasped together in a white knuckle grip. The fingernails had gone translucent with the pressure. “Tristan, hi.” his mumbled words were barely audible to some of the group who leant forward to hear them, only to return to the upright position upon the brevity of his sentence.

A brief period of scratching caused everyone to wince slightly. Steve looked to the chap to his left. “Hello there, who are you?”

The man stirred slowly as if he had been dreaming. His lank, blonde straggly hair, which looked like it hadn’t been washed since Day One, hung down. As he lifted his head, it hit his face and parted like a pair of theatre curtains on opening night. Glazed eyes, sunken into black lined sockets, nervously looked round the group. “Wotcha, I’m Matt. I had Weetabix this morning, three of them, which was odd as I haven’t had them since I was a kid. Is it me, or were they bigger when we were younger? Used to think they were as big as my dad’s hand. His hand…they…” He trailed off, his head flopped forwards again and he stuffed his hands under his legs.

Steve turned the page, and looked across to the last remaining anonymous member of the cabal. A woman in her late forties. Previously dyed auburn hair now betrayed its true colour, with a growing layer of pepper grey sprouting from her scalp. “Sylvia,” she answered nervously.

“Hello, Sylvia,” Steve said softly, matching her tone of voice automatically. “How are you today?” he asked with seemingly genuine concern. Sylvia shuffled uncomfortably in her chair. Her right hand slowly moved across to hold her left wrist; her thumb gently rubbed the arm of her jumper.

She took a moment to answer. Lost in a memory, she forced a half smile. “I’m okay thank you, Steve. Getting better. I think. Just all gets too much sometimes, eh? And then before you know it, something silly has happened and all these people fuss about nothing and then you realise that you're a failure. A ruddy great failure." As she finished, she clenched her jaw. Her eyes reddened as she fought to maintain control over her fluctuating emotions.

Steve held the notepad to his chest and slid the pen into the coiled metal binder. "It's okay, Sylvia, you're not a failure—"

Anton tutted loudly. Dee whipped round to glare at him once more. Steve raised a passive hand for silence, and then used it to stroke his beard.

"Sylvia, perhaps you would like to be the bravest of everyone here and start us off? With it all being so fresh in your mind, and after recent events, it could be a very cathartic thing to do. It'll help you. No one here will judge you. No one *here* can." As he said the last words he cast a withering look around the group. Each member recoiled back into their plastic chairs and settled down.

Her thumb continued to stroke up and down her inner forearm. Sylvia looked up, nodded gently and began.

- 14 -

SURVIVOR

TALES FROM THE ZOMBIE APOCALYPSE

The NETZACH'S Series

ISSUE # 1   HOME COMFORTS

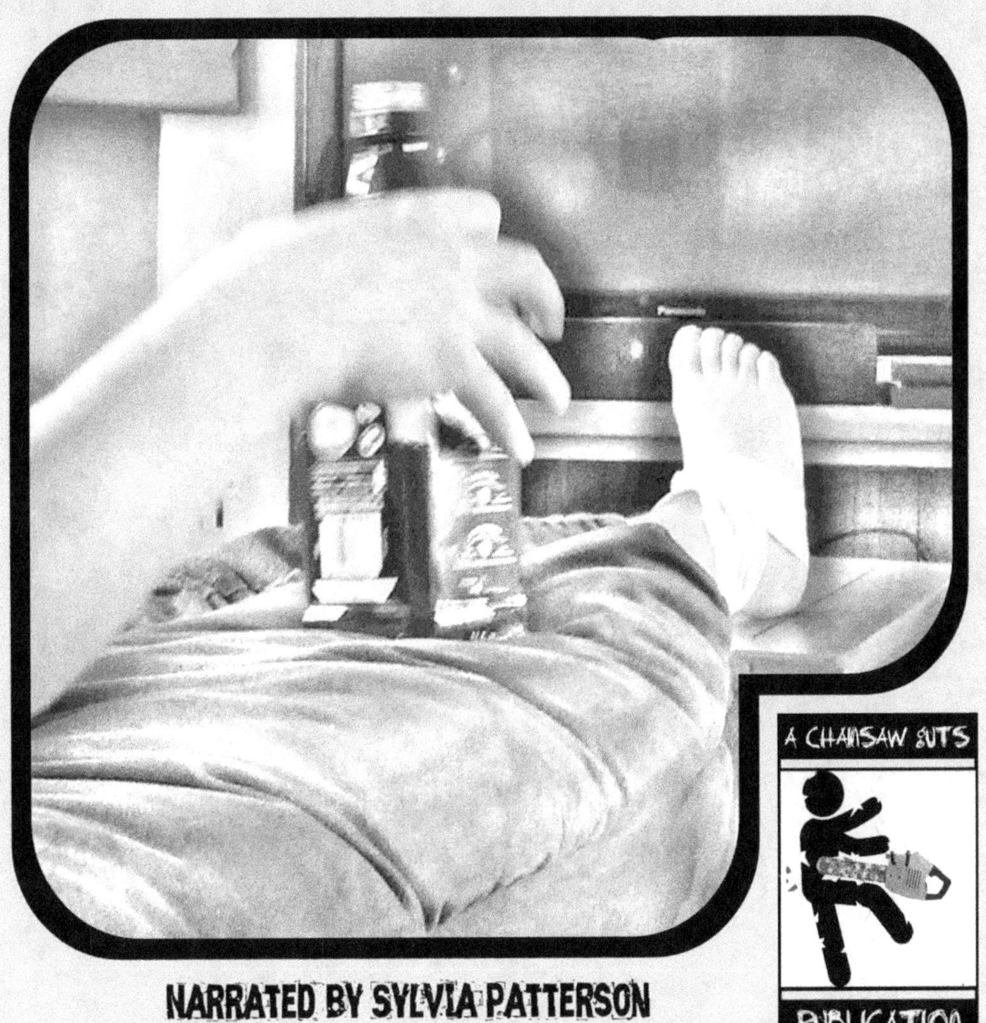

NARRATED BY SYLVIA PATTERSON

HOME COMFORTS – PART ONE

It was only a month ago now since…*it*.

But well, first off, my husband, Donald, and I had been holed up in a holiday cottage on the edge of the forest. It was perfect. We had been there every year since we were married. It was visit number sixteen. When this all happened, those many months ago, we were out there celebrating our anniversary.

The sixteenth.

I remember *that* night. I think everyone does now, like you always knew where you were when the Twin Towers were hit, or when Princess Diana, God bless her soul, was tragically stolen from us. I met Donald the night she died. We were in a pub on a night out; separate parties of course. We just talked the night away. Before I knew it, we were out on the dancefloor. Just something about my Donald.

It was the way he looked at me I think. The moment I first saw those magical baby blues looking across the bar at me, oohh, gives me goosebumps now even thinking about it.

He walked over and I will never forget the line he opened with. 'Are you tired?' he asked me. The pub was so loud, but his voice just cut through it all.

I didn't have a clue what he was on about, and after flapping my mouth open and shut for what seemed like forever, I managed to stammer out a 'What?'

The corner of his mouth rose slightly. He has…*had*, a lovely smile; used to make any trying day seem brighter.

Anyway, he leant in closer, and whispered in my ear, 'You must be tired. As you've been running round my mind all night.' He gave me a little wink and that was it. I was hooked. I giggled like a schoolgirl, and he bought me a drink, one of those Smirnoff Mule's.

Sorry, I'm rabbiting on about stuff. So, it's *that* night. Donald took me out to a fancy restaurant, one of those where you get lost with all the cutlery. Always got terribly worried if I was doing things wrong, you know?

I *always* seem to do things wrong.

The taxi took us back to the cottage. Donald paid the driver and gave him a generous tip. He was always like that, always made sure he looked after people that gave good service. He was such a gentleman. I walked through the house to the decking at the back. I thought it'd be nice to have a hot-tub to round the night off, you know? Show my appreciation for a good evening.

As soon as I opened the back patio doors, though, the sky just seemed to, well, *bleed*. The light blue and orangey sky just turned red; it was like someone had a great big roller out and painted the sky. Donald had joined me by now, and we were both standing there, looking out at the ungodly scene. He took my hand, held it so tight to stop me trembling, and said, 'It'll be okay, Syl. It'll be okay.'

We never did get into the hot tub that night. It all unsettled me so much. It may have only gone on for a few hours, but it scared me. We sat on the decking with a bottle of red, a nice Rioja if I remember correctly. He had his arm around me the entire time, and we just sat there in silence.

The morning came round. I had slept in fits and starts, kept getting the same dream over and over again.

Hmm? You want me to tell you, Steve? But it's terribly boring; these people won't want to hear it.

Okay then, if you're sure.

I'm at a train station, and I'm waiting for my train to come in. I look up at the clock, and see that it's due any time now, so I check my ticket and pick up my bag. It's only then that I look up at the announcement board and see that I'm on the wrong platform.

I start to panic. I look to one side and can see a train coming in. My train. I can feel my heart beating faster and faster. I turn towards the stairs and try to make my way to them, but there are so many people in the way, and I'm trying to fight my way through them, but they just won't move.

So many of them.

I weave this way and that, and eventually, somehow, get through, but as I reach the stairs I realise I'm already on the other platform. The train doors are shutting though, one by one, starting from the far end. I run to the nearest door and catch it just as it is about to close. I get on the train, put my bag on the floor and breathe a sigh of relief.

It's then that I look around and notice that the train has no walls, and as it pulls away from the station, it starts going really fast, so much so that people who are sat on their chairs, reading newspapers or checking their phones, are just falling by the wayside. I feel this gust of wind start to pick me off my feet. Just as I'm about to fly off, I wake up.

What does that mean do you think, Steve? Hmm ? Okay, I'll continue.

Sorry.

So, the day after, we're packing up. It's a couple of hours drive back to our house, and we hear this thudding from the decking outside. It gave me quite a start. Donald put his arms around me and calmed me down, said he would go and see what it was, that I was not to worry and things would be okay.

I continued packing, I remember I was putting all the vitamins and tablets back into one of my bags when I heard Donald curse. That in itself was odd; Donald never swore. Well, only twice, but that Doctor really was being quite nasty to me.

I called his name but had no reply, so thought I best go and see what had got him so angry. Donald never normally got angry with other people, it just wasn't in his nature. Well, there was that time with that Receptionist, but she was a nosy busy-body.

I walked through the cottage and, as I reached the living room, I could hear Donald, well, *grunting*. It was unsettling. So I picked up this walking stick which always lived in the umbrella stand in the hallway. No idea whose it was, but every year we went, it was always there. We used to joke, 'The old man is still here then, watching us from the wardrobe.'

Clutching the stick I walked into the living room and looked towards the patio doors and there he was, my Donald.

Except, he wasn't alone. There was another gentleman there with him, outside. The door was wide open and we were losing all the heat from the radiators. As I got closer, my eyesight isn't the best, another useless thing that doesn't work properly, I could see they were fighting.

I shouted something. Think it was, 'Excuse me, leave my husband alone or I'll call the police,' or something, I can't remember. The other gentleman didn't seem to pay any attention, and I thought he must be one of those Polish people we read about. The ones that Donald always talks about.

You know the ones.

Donald grunts again, and I edged my way towards them. I remember then it sounded like Donald was gasping for air, like he was being choked. Well, it put the fear of God into me, so I held the stick tighter and moved past the little coffee table and headed for the doors.

He saw me then, my Donald. His eyes seemed to ignite as if he was a boiler and a little pilot light had come on. He balled his fist and punched the man on the side of his head, which made him release his hold on him. Donald's face, which was nearly the same shade as the sky the night before, started to turn back to its normal colour.

The man spun from the impact and knocked into the little patio table and chair set on the decking. He must have landed awkwardly as his arm caught the table and the rest of him folded onto the floor. There was this terribly loud snap, like someone had just pulled a big Christmas cracker. He just lay there on the floor.

Donald rubbed his throat, and his knuckles; he used to do that when…

Anyway, he walked across to me. I asked him who the man was, and he said that he didn't have a clue. He saw I had the stick, though, and took it from me. I remember I must have been holding it really tightly as it hurt my hands when he took it.

He started to circle round to the other side of the table where the other gentleman was lying. I walked out onto the patio. The garden and fields looked so beautiful; morning dew was making the tall crops bend over so that they looked like tiny little catapults.

It was then I looked down at the gentleman that had attacked Donald. His arm was still resting on top of the table, but as I looked down to the body that joined it, I saw a large point sticking out where his shoulder should be.

I got closer, and could see that it was the bone from his arm. It was glistening in the morning sun, like the dewy crops. I thought that it was very strange, at least until I looked down at the rest of him.

He was trying to stand up. He seemed drunk or something; his legs were wobbly and unsure, his boots kept slipping as he tried to get purchase on the decking. He was wearing a tracksuit top, silver I think, but there was a gaping hole in the side. Through the tear, I could see lines of red running down his body.

It was then I saw the gentleman's face. It was the same colour as we had just painted the study in. Garden Folly, I think it was called. It looked most unnatural, but it was his eyes that put the willies up me.

They were white, except for a small black fleck in the middle. His face was dirty and bruised, he didn't look very well at all.

Donald was standing over him by now, demanding to know what the hell he was doing and why he had attacked him without warning. The man didn't say anything, he just kind of growled. Those Poles, eh? Don't bother to learn our language. Or that's what Donald said at the time.

Donald was shouting at him so much that he didn't see the man's free hand reach for him. By the time he knew, it was too late. I've never…

…never…

Sorry, just need to compose myself for a moment.

Ahem.

I'd never seen someone bite another person. You'd think it would be the same as when you bite into a roast chicken.

Which we always had on Sundays.

But it's not. The man grabbed Donald's ankle and pulled him to the ground. He seemed so strong.

Donald was caught off-guard and landed with an almighty thud on the wood. I was in shock I think, just a watcher. It was like it was on television. You know, that show they have with that Sheriff and his son, fighting those monster things. The man pulled Donald's leg towards him and just bit into it, trying to chew through his socks; the man's jaws locked onto his ankle and just tore away.

The first couple of bites came away with nothing but mouthfuls of white fluff. The fifth I think it was.

Yes.

The fifth.

That was when I saw the blood. Donald screamed again, worse than before. The man, the *thing*, chewed on whatever he had torn away. He had barely started when I saw the stick smack against his skull.

The force made the thing spit out whatever he had, then the second smack came, and I heard the crack again. From then on, I remember hearing the sounds and the cracks, but I don't remember what I saw. Or if I did, I can no longer recall the images. I think that's a good thing.

Yes. A good thing.

I came to, with Donald yelling at me, telling me to help him get his belt off. I didn't understand, so he yelled some more until I did what he asked.

It was always easier if I did what he asked; I couldn't mess things up then could I?

I took his belt off. His hands were covered in these little flecks of blood. It was really noticeable against the white of his skin.

So white. Just like this room really, I suppose. I passed him the belt and he tied it tightly around his calf, said it would do as a tourniquet for now.

Silly me, I should've know really. I don't know what else he would've used the belt for, hmm?

He crawled back inside the house, told me to lock the doors, and to call the police. As I reached the phone, he turned the television on, flicked through the channels onto one of those dreadful twenty four hour news programmes, you know the ones. All lies and nonsense, that's what Donald says.

Said.

It's still strange saying it like that.

I tried calling the police, but I just got some message on repeat, over and over again.

When I went back through to tell Donald the bad news, he had managed to haul himself onto the armchair and was just watching the television. He looked down at his leg, then at me, and shook his head. He said, 'The bleeding has stopped, Syl, don't worry.

It'll be okay, but I don't think I'll be able to drive home just yet, plus, it sounds like there's more trouble everywhere anyway.'

I looked outside at the gentleman who was lying in a big puddle. Donald saw this and said I better close the curtains; it'll help to keep the unpleasantness out, he said.

After that, I felt much better. So I made us a pot of tea, sat down on the sofa, and we just watched the news reports, over and over again.

HOME COMFORTS – PART TWO

I'd only heard the word *zombie* before on the television shows or films that we used to watch. Never really liked horror films; don't like all that blood and gore. I seem to be so scared of real life that Donald said it would be silly of me to watch something which would do the same thing.

A few days had passed since Donald had been attacked. His leg was still sore, so he told me. We had discussed driving home, but I'd only taken a few lessons, back before we met, so I wasn't comfortable with driving all that way, and neither was Donald.

Donald had started to work his way through the drinks cabinet by then. His mood had gotten dark, like he was prone to from time to time. He said that it helped numb the pain from his leg, but when he was drinking the cooking sherry in the second week, I knew that he had just fallen back into old habits.

The cottage had enough food for a few weeks; the owners always made sure that it was well stocked. With the regular power cuts they experienced out there in the middle of nowhere, we had those cartons of UHT milk for tea. It wasn't too bad. Plus, the news channels were now telling people to stay put if they could, and if not, to make for the nearest safe zones that were being set up.

Donald said that it would be pointless to make a move to our closest safe zone as it was too far away. That was in the early days when he was on the whiskey.

That was the worst. That stuff always made his mood darker. There were days where I didn't dare be in the same room for too long, not unless he was shouting for food or for more bandages for his foot.

I remember when the news stopped. Day sixteen, just like the amount of years we've been married for I thought. We had just had breakfast, dry crackers I think it was. The news channel now was just a couple of people, more or less repeating the same information over and over again. We had put the television on mute by then. It was becoming boring listening to it and Donald said it made his head hurt even more.

So we were watching, and it just went off, like a switch had been tripped. Nothing but blackness. Donald tried going through the other channels and aside from some show about a man fighting food, or something, there was nothing else on. He muttered some more, and got back to his drinking.

I had to tell him a day or so later that we needed to go out soon, as we didn't have much food left. I never ate much anyway, especially after that time with the hospital, when, you know, oh of course, you don't. Well let's just say that something stopped working.

Women's things.

Sorry.

Donald was only eating in the mornings now, and sometimes at night, but even then it was just some pasta with tomato ketchup on. He said that the pain made him not want to eat. He said his ankle was better, but it still caused him trouble. Helping him get to the toilet was becoming nigh on impossible, so he told me to find a bucket, and he just did his business in the living room.

Hmm? Yes, I did have to. Usually only once a day, but sometimes, it was two or three times. Almost like looking after a child I suppose, though we never had children.

Well, because of…you know.

Those women's things I mentioned.

Day twenty two. That was when the food ran out. Always prided myself on being able to cook on a budget; had to since we got together. Donald used to give me a weekly allowance which included all the food for both of us, so I had to make it last.

I never worked, not after we got married, Donald said it wasn't befitting of a woman, that I was his princess and deserved to stay at home and keep the place all nice for him.

For us.

Sorry.

I crept in that morning. The sherry had gone. I knew the cabinet would be bare, so thought that he might be having one of his…migraines. I saw he had done his ablutions already. He was asleep. As I got near, he stirred, and an empty bottle of mouthwash fell out from his cardigan.

Poor Donald. Never was able to stop once he got the taste of it. Well, there was that one time, where he had to go away for a few weeks, but we don't like to talk about that.

Hmm? Where did he get the mouthwash from? Hmm. I don't know; never thought about it really. It would've been in the bathroom cabinet upstairs.

You don't think?

No.

He wouldn't, he could barely move.

He couldn't have got it. I must've brought it downstairs for some reason.

As I snuck away carrying the bucket with the…you know, in, he stirred, asking me what I was doing. I told him that I was just going to tidy up. He grunted and started to nod off. I knew there would be no better time, so I said that we needed to go somewhere and find food, that if we stayed there much longer, we were going to go hungry.

He nodded, said we had to get out of the cottage, find some more supplies. Said his ankle was much better. I had tried to change the dressing over the past week, but he didn't let me. It did smell funny.

Like marzipan.

There was a little village shop about five miles away. I cleaned him up the best I could, but he still couldn't walk properly. I loaded our cases in the car, and Donald got in the driver's seat. Ten minutes later, and after trying to put the gearstick into number one, he got out and said that I'd have to do it.

I wasn't very happy about it, but smiled and said I would give it a go. Took a bit of doing, but I managed to get us moving. Donald said to keep us slow. There was no one around at all, so I didn't get beeped once, which was a relief. Wouldn't want to be holding people up.

We drove into the village, and it was like something off the television. There were a few cars around, just left in the middle of the road. Some had their doors open and there were these, erm, trails leading off. I thought it was blood, but Donald said to not look and keep on driving.

One of the cars we went by had a couple of people in. They looked like the gentleman that had attacked Donald; he stared at them as we drove past, and he looked angry, but also a little afraid. They were pawing at the glass like a puppy locked in a car on a hot day.

That was silly of me too, wasn't it?

We finally got to the little shop. Well, it had a post office inside, too. Something for everyone. It looked quite dark inside, so I parked up, though I did stall the car whilst doing so. Donald didn't even seem to notice. He was breathing heavier. I had to prod him to tell him that we had arrived, and he jolted like he'd been stung. He always preferred touching me rather than the other way round.

I opened the car door for him and I helped carry him towards the shop. I tried the handle and was relieved when I found it wasn't locked. I pushed the door open and we walked into the gloom.

HOME COMFORTS – PART THREE

The shop was in a frightful state; there were bits and pieces strewn all over the place. I rested Donald on a stool which was behind the counter, just by the entrance. Donald said, well, *panted*, that I should close the door. He didn't look very well at all; I wondered if I should've just left him at the cottage and gone on my own. He wouldn't have liked that though.

No.

I closed the door and said that I'd have a look around, but I don't think he even heard me. Thought there wouldn't be much left. Luckily for us, though, as Middle Hazeltree is so out of the way, most people hadn't had a chance to strip it bare. I was filling up a basket rather nicely. Looked like there had been a struggle of some kind, like a rocket had gone off.

The back of the shop opened up to a flight of stairs and a door. Looking through the window with that criss-cross wire glass, I saw it led to a storage space out back. I could see big boxes of Cheese and Onion crisps on some shelves. I know I shouldn't have, but I was curious what was upstairs. I stuck to the edge of the stairs; learnt that from…well, anyway, managed to get to the top without making a peep.

Up there was a little two bed flat. I had a check in each room, but there was no-one there. It looked like whoever lived there had left in a hurry, as there were clothes on the floor of one of the bedrooms, and the picture frames were empty.

I looked out of the window, and thought how wonderfully quiet it all was. There were no cars, no alarms, not even a bird in the sky. I closed my eyes, just for a moment. And then…then…and then I heard a loud thud and a whimper; it sounded almost pathetic.

I dropped the basket on the floor. It sounded so loud. I stood at the top of the stairs and called down to Donald, but I didn't hear anything except a mewling, just like the puppy made when he was lying on the policeman's coat.

You know, after they broke the car window.

Hmm. Poor thing.

Anyway, I made my way downstairs, stuck to the edge of the stairs again, needed to be really careful. The mewling was getting louder. There were these smaller thuds as things bounced onto a hard floor. Crashes of glass. I got to the bottom and peered into the shop, to see if Donald was okay. I couldn't see his silhouette by the counter.

I was getting scared now. I heard the sound again and it was coming from behind me, in the store room. I was sure the door had been closed, but there it was, wide open.

Silly me, must've opened it earlier and not even remembered.

I took off my shoes and tiptoed really quietly into the room. A light was flickering on and off, like it was a candle. And that's when I saw him.

He must've been trying to reach the box of Bell's Whiskey from the top shelf. The silly so and so didn't pull it right and as he tried to get the box down he pulled too hard and a crate of Newcastle Brown Ale had landed on his head.

Oohh, it was terrible; there was blood everywhere. He was sort of kneeling against the shelving unit. The crate had bounced off his head and landed on the back of his legs, pinning him to the ground. I could see his bandage was bulging from his ankle, and this thick black goo was coming out.

I did chuckle, as to one side lay the box of whiskey. Looks like that had been the final straw as it was all smashed on the ground, and he was looking at me, like he was drunk.

You know, like the night we met.

He had this big cut on the top of his head and one of his hands was trying to feel where it was. Ha, you should've seen it. He was patting his head and it kept slapping against the wound and this blood would fly up into the air. The only thing missing was him rubbing his tummy.

Awww. He looked so silly.

By now, he must've worked out I was there, but his breathing was becoming more shallow. He stopped patting his head and just looked at me. His mouth was moving, but I couldn't hear what he was saying. I moved closer and could see that it was an effort for him to breathe now. I tried to move the crate off his legs, but it just made him worse.

He beckoned me with a finger covered in blood. It nearly made me retch. You know I don't like blood and gore. So I get closer, and he looks at me, well, tries to. He managed to get three words out: "You. Silly. Cow."

And then he sort of shook, his eyes went up and his head fell down against the shelf with this sort of wet slap. I remember that noise. I'll never forget that noise. Heard it before. Hope I don't get to hear it again. Well I did recently, though, didn't I, Steve? Hmm, guess that's why I'm here.

I just knelt there for a bit. I felt lost without my Donald. I remembered how I felt when Princess Diana, God bless her soul, went, and I closed my eyes really tight and I prayed to God.

The strangest thing happened.

All those years, when…when I was silly, and Donald had to show me that I was silly, all those years I prayed that I would stop being so silly and Donald would be like he used to, and *He* never listened. Not once.

But this time, he did. I heard a little moan.

Barely believing my luck, I opened my eyes and there he was. My Donald. Alive again. His eyes were like the gentleman's we had seen, but I didn't mind, he was my Donald.

He would be like he was.

Better.

The man he used to be.

I knew what he was, though; I'm not *that* silly. But I knew that I could look after him properly now. I would be his princess and keep the place nice for him. Just like I promised I would that day, in front of all of our friends and family.

You know, in the church.

And the hospital.

That one time.

So, I locked the door to the store room, found the keys to the front door and locked them up good, too. Pulled the blinds down and made the place all nice for him.

For us.

Sorry.

It was all so perfect until *they* turned up. Until *they* came along and took my Donald

from me. We were just fine. Why did they do that to me?
     To us.
     Sorry.

CHAPTER FOUR

Steve placed a conciliatory hand on Sylvia's shoulder as she finished speaking. She closed her eyes and leant in, nuzzling it against her neck. "Thank you, Sylvia, that was beautiful. I really think we got a window into your life today, I want—"

"Yeah right, that her husband was a complete and total wanker to her," Anton snorted, his harsh features bristled. Steve looked across and peered down the rim of his glasses at him. Anton held his hands up in deference.

"Well, fuck-a-doodle-doo, that was magical Steve. Don't mind me if I don't come back again," Dee cooed. Steve slowly retracted his hand from Sylvia's shoulder; she remained motionless, lost in the physicality, stroking her inner arm.

Steve walked back to his chair, but remained standing, hands across his chest, the notebook held tight to his bosom.

A strange smile birthed across his face. "Okay people, let's get one thing straight. This meeting is not voluntary. You *will* be here, each and every goddamn fucking week until I get told that it's not required. And you know what? I get the distinct impression that I'll be doing this until those walking bags of shit and guts break down the fucking fence and eat every one of you sorry sons of bitches."

Dee realised her mouth was open the same shape as a Cheerio. "Erm, you fucki—" she began to say. The notebook flew through the air and slapped firmly against the side of her face, silencing her. She was left trembling at the sudden spike in violence. Where the pen and binder had caught her eyebrow, a small trickle of blood ran down her face. She made no attempt to staunch the flow.

Steve removed his glasses slowly, rubbing a lens with the bottom of his t-shirt again. "You think you're so fucking important, huh? Well, you're not, that's why you're here. Why you're *all* here. You are a liability to this entire camp. You've all done things which necessitates you being here. With me. And I want you to know that I wish you weren't. You think I don't have better things to do than nursemaid a bunch of gimps?"

Steve peered through the lens. "Finally, looks like I'm not in stage one of Macular degeneration." He slid the glasses back on and walked over to Dee. As he bent down to retrieve his notebook, he shot her a look that told her what would happen if she were to speak right now. He nodded and smiled.

"Let's not get off on the wrong foot. Just…I didn't want to go back to doing what I did before the dead started walking again. I was done with it. I've got my own baggage to deal with. But, of course, *he* asked me to, and if The Gaffer asks, well, you all know you don't get a say in the matter," Steve said solemnly. He walked and stood behind his chair before casting a glance at his wristwatch.

He looked back up quickly, beaming. "Wow, good session today guys, really well done. I'm glad we all know each other now; even in a camp this size, you never truly know anyone, eh? We're done just in time for us to all head over to the floor for the public Remedial session.

"Shall we?" With that, Steve bowed his head and held his arm out to the door. The group started to stand from their chairs. As they filed out of the room, Steve called out, "See you all next week."

CHAPTER FIVE

A throng of people stood shoulder to shoulder at the far end of the factory floor. The machinery had long since been sold. 'Netzach's Biscuits' had gone tits up during the '08 recession. Too many lines with dubious chocolate quality, coupled with the rather unsavoury Bexley Heath Cub Scout poisoning incident, sounded the death knoll for a company that had been around since the reign of Queen Victoria.

Once the administrators had picked the bones clean and sold anything of use, including every single plastic cup used for the imbibing of cooled water, the building was locked up and sealed behind its barbed wire-trimmed stainless steel fence. Its location did nothing to appeal to prospective investors.

Netzach's factory was in the middle of nowhere. The train line that it used to take advantage of had closed in the sixties. The town it supported had withered away to a puckered up old hag's teat.

Yet, the reason why it didn't appeal to those looking to make money became a beacon when the dead stopped staying dead.

The world had gone to hell in a heartbeat, and those who were left were exceptionally keen on staying out of built up areas.

Netzach's was a godsend.

The military had set up a safe zone in each county, utilising the many mothballed bases which had been closed down over the years due to budget cuts. But those who couldn't get to them, or who wanted to remain…independent, needed to find alternative accommodation. One such man now looked out of the manager's office windows, across to the forest, which straddled the concrete road leading from the main gate like a pair of hairy legs.

He looked down to the imposing bastions of metal, the sole thing keeping *them* out. He saw a number of shapes bump and scrape against the chain-link fence. A cough from behind him jolted him back into the room. "Gaffer, it's time," Jones reported, not wishing to disturb, but realising that timekeeping was as important to this man as keeping *them* out.

The Gaffer turned to Jones, who looked to the floor, unsure whether he had caused displeasure. It seemed an eternity before he spoke. "Andy, thank you. Tell me, who is on Heads-Up detail today?" His cockney accent was laden with honey on the surface, yet an undercurrent of venom bubbled beneath.

Andy looked up. One hand rested on the rapier tucked into his belt. "Is something wrong, Gaffer?" he asked cautiously.

The Gaffer turned his sizeable frame back to the window and gestured for Jones to come closer. "We have stragglers, Andy. Heads-Up is responsible for ensuring that we do not have a build up at the gates, because if we have a build up at the gates, Andy, where does that leave us?"

Andy mumbled a reply into his hand.

"Pardon?" The Gaffer asked forcefully. His round, well-built face turned to look at Jones directly.

Andy cleared his throat and replied, "It leaves us at home to Mr Fuck Up. Gaffer."

"Precisely. Now, I'm going to ask again, and you know I hate repeating myself. Who the fuck is on Heads-Up detail today?" The Gaffer's eyes seemed to emit a shrieking sound which burrowed into Andy's skull.

Andy's eyes rolled up and to the left. "It's Jackson and Coates today, Gaffer. They're new, though. They don't know about the rules, do they?" No sooner had the words left the safety of his oesophagus, his brain demanded that they were taken back; his buttocks clenched in disapproval.

A T-bone steak of a hand rested on Andy's shoulder. The digits closed on his scapula like a multitude of adjustable pipe wrenches, the pressure started off slight and rose, seemingly with no effort exerted by the operator.

Andy's sphincter was clenched so tight that not even a quark could have escaped. He felt the hot, clammy breath being expelled on his cheek. He stared at the floor, hoping it would deposit him into a bottomless pit of doom.

A hearty hand slapped him on the back. "Ha, this is why you're my number two, Andy. Good man. I think I'll let them off this time. Besides, I'm sure after Remedial, Jackson and…"

"Coates, Gaffer," Andy spat out, followed by a small squeak of happy gas from his relieved cheeks. The Gaffer waved a hand and turned his nose up.

"I thought you were lactose intolerant, Andy. Stay off the milk, okay?" The Gaffer patted Jones on the shoulder again and turned towards the door which led to the factory floor. He pulled a sheepskin coat from a hook on the back of the door and swung it on. Andy followed in quick pursuit.

The hubbub on the factory floor fell to an instant silence the moment the formidable form of The Gaffer strode from his office and onto the top of the balcony which crested the stairs leading to his office. He had a bandolier of shotgun shells over one shoulder; over the other was a leather strap which was affixed to the top and bottom of a parking meter, the coin end of which was scratched and pitted.

"Good evening everyone. I trust your day has been one of joyful servitude for our happy little camp, down here in the spleen of our fine country." The Gaffer's voice carried out easily into the vacuous space, enveloping all who craned their necks up to see him. He turned and started to walk down the metal staircase. Jones followed five paces behind, his face a welt of concentration on not tripping up.

The small procession made their way to a small raised concrete area just in front of the floor where the inhabitants of Netzach's biscuit factory stood and shivered. The raised area was flanked by four men dressed all in black. They wore masks, body armour, and each cradled a double-headed fire axe.

The Gaffer reached the middle of the concrete stage and looked out into the crowd. His voice boomed around the masses. "Friends, we all work hard to keep this place safe. We grow food, we wash each other's clothes, babysit our neighbour's children, keep watch and make sure that the chompers don't tear down the wall and rip asunder all that we have worked for."

He gave it a moment to let the words sink in. "But with that safety, with this FREEDOM, we must have a code, one that is unyielding, yet fair and true. So if your neighbour steals from you, if they fail in their given duty, if they do not keep the chompers from forming en masse at the gates or if they FUCKING FALL ASLEEP WHILST ON SENTRY DUTY, then they know they will be punished."

Hushed murmurings ran through the crowd. People covered their mouths and talked to their friends, trying to work out who was missing and who was in deep shit. It didn't take long before they were revealed.

"Grimm, if you please, bring them out, let them look the people in the eye who they could've gotten killed. Bring them out *now*," growled The Gaffer. He moved to one side. His fists cracked as they formed into orbs of rage.

At the bottom of the stairs, a red windowless door opened into a forbidding chamber. From the murk skulked two men covered in sweat and soot; it looked like they had been left in a toaster for too long.

Pushing them out into the pallid light of the factory floor was a rotund man, his bulk barely able to squeeze through the doorframe. He wore a black jumpsuit, a silver mask similar to the guards, and two lump hammers tucked into the front of his belt.

The two men were forced onto their knees. Both looked on the edge of exhaustion. The transition from dark to light forced squints into their eyes. The Gaffer moved behind them. "Both of these men were caught sleeping when they were supposed to be keeping watch over *you* and your neighbours. We all know that all it takes is one lapse and those bastards will get in here. Some of you here will remember when we first made this our home, and what Douglas' neglect of duty caused." The Gaffer pointed to a makeshift memorial on the wall behind him.

"We lost seven people that day. Seven people who would be here, standing with you now, if only Douglas had done his goddamn MOTHERFUCKING JOB." Strands of spittle laced his lips.

The Gaffer cast a steely gaze around the room. Nodding to some of the old guard who remembered those times, he continued. "Since that day, I decided that if anyone, no matter who, was remiss in their duty, they get one strike. If you get three strikes, then, well, to coin a phrase from our friends across the pond, then you're outta here. Luckily we don't get too many of these little Remedial sessions anymore."

Some people started to clap and holler. The Gaffer raised his hands to stifle their excitement.

One of the kneeling men was hauled to his feet. His weedy dirty arm was held up by an uncaring gloved hand. The Gaffer turned to him. "Ian, this is your first strike, you know what that means don't ya?"

Ian nodded weakly. "Yes Gaffer. I know what it means. I'm sorry. Everyone, I'm sorry," he stuttered. A tear cut through the grime on his face, making his pale skin show through in one small streak.

The Gaffer turned to the room. "Some of you newbies here won't know the punishments we have. Ian here does. Strike one means you get to spend a week out there, in Chomperville. On your journey to the gate, you might have seen a coal scuttle next to the path. Some of you might not have done. It's not the biggest thing in the world. If you fuck up, strike one means you get put in there for a week. You'll get a blanket and two meals a day, reduced rations of course. If you feel like you want to break out and stretch your legs, be my fucking guest. I remember Lana thought that and made it all of fifty feet before she got turned into gut-sushi."

Ian began to cry in earnest, his face scrunched up. "Shhh, don't worry, Ian, you'll be safe, as long as one of these fine men remembers to lock the scuttle, or, well, you might not be. But don't go just yet, my friend. Let's see what you could win if you fuck up again." The Gaffer gestured with two fingers, and Ian was dragged to one side. His legs and bladder control both gave way.

Two of the guards hauled the other dishevelled man to the centre of the dais. The room fell silent. Even Ian suppressed his crying. The Gaffer sighed and pinched the bridge of his nose with his forefinger and thumb.

He regained his composure and looked at the second man. "Strike Two, however, well…Yohann here, he also thought that instead of being his brother's keeper, he would be his brother's sleeper. This will not do. Grimm, if you please."

The two men turned Yohann around. His naked back glistened with beads of sweat. A guard grabbed hold of an arm each and twisted them at the shoulder, so that Yohann's head was bent over. Grimm stood off to one side and reached a hand behind his back. It reappeared brandishing a barbed riding crop; he swished it in the air to emphasise the effect.

"Ten strokes for Strike Two, and one day on the angel outside. Grimm, if you please…" The Gaffer ordered. The blubberous mass of Grimm shuddered as each strike resonated throughout the factory. Only the cries of pain from Yohann came out. The crowd held its breath and waited for it to finish.

The Gaffer ran a hand through his slicked-back, black hair and looked on, impassively.

CHAPTER SIX

The jawbone, propelled by a small child's foot, flew through the air, bounced off a rusting railway sleeper and landed in a clump of nettles, which had sprouted amongst its brethren.

"Weeeeee," Nathan squealed as he lined up his next punt. The second shot thundered a piece of collarbone down the long abandoned train line. "Choo-choo," he shouted and ran after the nub of greyed bone.

Francis picked through the remnants of a corpse draped over the tracks as if it were wrapping paper. The body itself was nothing more than a collection of bones held together with bits of sinew the maggots couldn't be bothered with.

Fingers peeled open the dirt covered dark red top and peered through the ribcage and into the inside of the clothing. A family of disgruntled beetles scattered upon the intrusion and trotted up and over the coccyx, before they disappeared into the pelvic region, no doubt forming a bad review of the accommodation.

Turning out the trouser pockets yielded nothing except some low grade grit and a tissue which had been through the wash cycle once and dried into a firm lump of useless matter. He scoured the area and rolled over some spent shotgun shells, a sign of the violence that happened here a while ago. "Hey, Nate, don't go too far," Francis shouted.

Nathan booted the hacky sack bone once more and it sailed through the air before its journey was brought to an abrupt conclusion by a chain-link fence. "Francis, look," he shouted. A finger, which had just stopped a preliminary nasal cavity search for dried mucus, pointed to a large building.

Leaving the skeletal remains behind, Francis walked over to the boy, who was still indicating the building, the only thing in the entire area which wasn't defined wholly as 'Nature'.

"Can we go in? Please, please, please, can we go in Francis?" Nathan beseeched, bouncing up and down with the combined excitement of Chris Rabbit on a pogo stick.

Francis peered at the foreboding building and its surroundings. Patches of long grass and weeds suggested that it hadn't been visited for some time. "Fine, but you know the rules. Stay behind me, okay?"

Nathan nodded furiously. "Yay," he shouted and ran to the fence. "How are we going to get in, Francis. I can't climb over this, and it looks like it goes on for *miles*."

Pulling the rucksack up higher, Francis pointed through the fence to a gateway in the distance. "Looks like only one way in, kid. Over there, see? Stay with me, don't run off. There could be anything in the forest that we can't see, okay?"

A loud sigh answered him in the affirmative, and Nathan grudgingly trudged by Francis' side, running his fingers along the fence making dull thuds and clangs as he pulled on it. "What do you think it is, Francis? Is it a hospital or something? Did men work here? Why was it near the train track? Wh—"

Francis raised his finger to his mouth. "Slow down, kid, too many questions. Sometimes you need to just take your time and see for yourself, okay? It ain't going anywhere. It's not as if we'll get to the gate and it'll disappear, eh? Just relax, have a look around, try and get a feel for the lay of the land, you know?"

Nathan rubbed his hands together to get rid of the rust flakes he had collected thus far. He grinned inanely and nodded. Francis smiled.

"So who do you reckon lived here? Do you think there are any comics here? Is that a dead man over there? Do you reckon he was dead-dead or just dead?" Nathan gibbered.

Francis sighed and picked up the pace.

"Why is that skellington tied to the gate door, Francis? Is he like a Halloween man to keep the baddies out?" Nathan asked.

Francis looked over the pile of bones lying at the base of the closed half of the gateway. He picked through the macabre collection, but couldn't find anything of use. "There were a couple of people here, look." He pointed to two spinal columns; one still with a skull atop was affixed to the fence with twine, another lay on a mound of bones.

A pair of wrists and the withered remains of hands were bound to the fence with cable ties. Teeth-marks were visible as little indentations in the black plastic. "Stay close to me, Nate. There might still be some around, okay?"

Nathan nodded solemnly and looked through the open side and pointed to a scorched patch of ground beyond. "Look over there, Francis."

The pair walked into a barren area of ground. A large blackened patch of concrete was the picnic blanket for yet more bones. Francis walked to the epicentre and surveyed the scene.

A charred, chipped metal bar lay atop a ragged and weather-ruined sheepskin coat, which covered a pile of scorched bones. What looked like metal teeth were embedded in the ground. It was as if they stood in the retort of a crematorium.

"I've got a bad feeling about this," muttered Francis.

Nathan tugged the man's sleeve. "Come on, let's go inside and have a look, pur-lease, you did say."

Francis flicked the police baton and it extended swiftly. "I did, but I still don't like it. Come on, let's get this done." A rub of the beard and Francis cautiously edged towards the front double doors, which swung lazily off the latch.

Inside looked like an ossuary. From the entrance, looking down towards the far end where haphazard rows of foldaway beds lay dormant, it was clear that a feasting frenzy had gone on here.

Clumps of gnawed bone and rags of cloth formed cairns which were dotted around in a seemingly random pattern. There were clusters here and there, mainly towards the side doors; the draught made the tattered flags flutter gently.

Even Nathan's youthful enthusiasm had been left at the door. The musty smell of broken bone, rotten meat and death was all pervading. Not even an overdose of Vanish would purge the stench from their clothes.

"I'm scared, Francis," Nathan whimpered and held out his hand to his protector. Francis closed his hand over it and held on tight.

"Let's have a look up here, see if we can find anything. This place is giving me the creeps." Francis sidled over to a metal stairway, taking a moment to stare at a collection of photos and handwritten notes on a wall. It seemed to be some kind of memorial. Upon looking at a picture of a sleeping child, with an emotional eulogy scrawled into the paintwork beneath, he led the way up the stairs, the baton held out, ready.

A door opened into an office. A large chair faced out towards the window, as if a game of football was going on outside. Another decomposing body lay on the floor; its limbs were splayed out like a starfish amputee. Where the head should've been was a mass of congealed blood and jelly. Chips of skull and assorted head bone were arrayed around the impact site. "Go and check the desk, Nate. I'll have a look through these cabinets."

All of the drawers were bereft of useful items; some held bushels of yellowing invoices on official looking headed paper. A faded cherubic angel grinned back. Within another, he found partially completed performance reviews. He wondered what a Mr Squire had done to merit so many HR 'discussions'.

"Francis, do you know who Mr Daniels is?" Nathan asked, barely visible behind the desk.

"No, what have you got?"

"I think Mr Daniels left his drink at work. It's got his name on it. Jack Daniels, do you think he worked here?" Nathan held up a square bottle of bourbon, the label was badly faded except for the name.

"Ha, no, I haven't spoken to Jack Daniels in a long time now," Francis said, looking down at the floor and rubbing his beard.

"Did you and Jack have a falling out? Is he not your friend anymore?" Nathan asked, turning the bottle round in his hands. Taking the lid off, one whiff made his nose scrunch up and he screwed it back on. "Smells horrible."

Francis took the bottle and held it up to the light. "Yeah, you could say we don't see eye to eye anymore. How about we leave this here, in case Mr Daniels gets back and looks for it, yeah?"

Nathan nodded, took the offered item and put it back into the hinterland of the drawer where he had found it. "Nothing else here, except some pens and these little metal faces." Small fingers held up the item for inspection.

"Paper clips, they're paper clips. You never know, though, they might be handy. Put them in your pocket. Could make fish hooks at a push," Francis said distractedly. "Did you hear something?"

Francis got to the office doorway and looked into the guts of the building. There was a scraping sound composed with a familiar moaning melody. Across the far end, there was a folding bed being taken for a walk. Well, it was being dragged by the feet of a figure that didn't look quite right. In the sense that their head was tilted at an angle which would only be of use if you wanted to look round a corner whilst standing flush to a wall.

One moan became legion as shapes loomed from shadowy corners of the building. The room was alive with the sound of undead music. "Nate, get here now, we gotta leave," Francis hissed. He ducked down, but his guts, and their rapid loosening, told him that they had already been spotted.

Nathan scooted across the office floor to Francis, taking a detour round grey dead person, past the brain goo roundabout and over to the one and only exit which didn't end in face-planting concrete.

With optional pirouette and screaming.

"Right kid, here's what we are gonna do…"

CHAPTER SEVEN

"You clear, Nate?" Francis asked breathlessly. The sneaky peeks he'd taken over the railing into the building had merely added to the picture that they needed to get out of Dodge.

Sharpish.

The kid nodded slowly, his arms wrapped around his legs, held tight to his chest. "Good, let's go." Francis crept down the stairs.

Before he'd made it to the bottom, a chap with an arm missing, dressed in black with a blood-flecked mask lunged at him and tried to grab hold with his one remaining hand. Francis recoiled in time and the zombie head-butted a stanchion.

The baton swung and connected with the zombie's head. The ballistic face mask repelled the blow with ease. The reverberations ran up Francis' arm, through his funny bone and into his shoulder. A muffled growl signalled the walking cadaver's displeasure and pawed at him again. It was easily dodged and Francis swung low, sending the attacker crumpling to the floor with a smack to the back of its knees.

With a small escape window open to him, he trotted to the front double doors. "Come on, kid, let's—" He looked around to see a Nathan-shaped hole where he expected a child to be. He frantically looked around the dusty building. "Nathan!" he bellowed. A whimpering from above him was the kid's locator beacon.

Francis ran to the bottom of the stairs, kneeing the rising masked zombie in the base of the skull as he made his way past. Sent back into the concrete, the zed's one arm restarted the pain in the arse process of lifting himself off the floor again.

Between Francis at the bottom of the stairs and Nathan cowering at the top was a young slip of a man; tall, wiry, dressed in low-slung jeans which showed off his heavily stained undercrackers. A leather jacket covered a gore encrusted YOLO t-shirt and a baseball cap sat at a jaunty angle on his head.

Francis wanted to stove his head in even before noticing the tell-tale signs of reanimation. Black lumpy veins ran like industrial run-off rivers over his outstretched hands.

YOLO looked from Francis and then up to a smaller, yet more sumptuous, looking meal. Like a slinky in reverse, he clumped up the stairs with a regimented regularity. Francis bounded up the stairs and grabbed hold of the dead yoof by his pant elastic. With a side step and a mighty heave, he slung the zombie down the stairs. It landed face first, causing a number of teeth to chip and ping off across the floor. Its jeans, though, held firm, still showing off a band of gaudily stained pantaloons.

"I thought you were gonna follow the plan, Nate?" Francis said as he thundered up the staircase. Nathan was still in the egg position. Unblinking eyes stared straight through Francis' sizeable frame and onto the wall beyond.

"Kid, hey kid. It's alright. I'm here, come on, we have to go. Like now."

Francis picked up Nathan. The kid's body felt as if it was wrought from iron and incapable of suppleness. Only when he was cast over the shoulder did he relax and allow himself to fold over his saviour's grasp. "Let's roll, kid," Francis whispered and turned around, ready to begin the descent.

"Balls."

A congregation of now useless organ donors were milling around the base of the staircase. YOLO slapped a dead hand on the bannister and began to haul himself back up. Broken rows of gnashers chomped on thin air in anticipation. Behind him, it was now three deep, with more and more of the ravenous dead descending on them from seemingly never-ending hiding spots.

With a heavy sigh, Francis placed Nathan back onto the floor behind him. He instinctively readopted his sitting foetal position and thousand yard stare. Francis removed his rucksack and placed it next to the inert child. "Look after this, Nate," he muttered.

In a mini re-enactment of the Battle of Thermopylae, Francis stood defiant at the top of the stairs, funnelling the dead towards him. At most he reckoned they could manage two abreast. White knuckles clenched the baton. He braced his legs like a baseball player and awaited the first of the zombie Persians.

"Molon labe," he growled.

YOLO lumbered forwards and was met with a violent smack across the temple which rocked his skull against the collarbone. When he looked back, Francis could see that the frontal bone had cracked down the coronal suture, and had partially sheared off. The baseball cap stretched where the bones had separated like a door being kicked open. The force had torn the skin from the top of the nose down to the corner of his lip; an eye slipped through the hole and hung in his open mouth.

An autonomic response to seeing food in front of him, YOLO's jaw chewed down and bit into his own ocular device. There followed a crunching sound as if a heavy foot had stood on a cockroach, making Francis' gorge rise.

He swung again with a powerful backhand and the force knocked the zombie across to the bannister. A forceful meeting with the sole of his boot sent YOLO flying over the edge and crashing into the floor. The zed twitched twice and was then becalmed; a half bowl of skull weebled its way across the floor, followed by a tide of black and grey sludge.

The sense of victory was short-lived as doleful moans from below him brought him back to reality. "This is going to be a long day..." Francis readied himself again as a female zombie sous chef dragged her broken and twisted leg up the stairs towards him, with all the grace of a concrete laden milk float.

With four flat tyres.

And a penguin driving.

Yyyoooooooaaaaaaauuuuuurrrrrrgggghhhhhhh

The sound from the back of the building made every single thing, living and dead, stop and turn in its direction. At first there was nothing. Just as the sound faded into memory, something wailed again.

Yrrhhhuuuyyyy!!!!!!iiiiinnnn

COUGH, COUGH, COUGH.

"Fuck me, that's gonna leave a mark. Mental note, find some motherfucking Lockets," a man's voice echoed out.

A robed figure staggered out of a back storeroom, holding a staff aloft. An atrophied zombie which had an arm tied to the floor by a length of frayed rope went to reach for him, mustering a less than scary "Gahh."

The figure stopped and brought the staff down with a quick flick of the wrist. The zombie's head, down to its neck, split in two. Discoloured meat and built up fetid fluid spilled onto the floor.

Most of the undead host were now focused solely on the enigmatic stranger on the horizon. Sure it had more wrapping on it, but they were drawn to the sound like sailors to a siren's song.

The man walked towards them, his weapon now held in one hand, the grey robe still covering his features.

So enraptured was Francis that he only saw the sous chef pounce at the last moment. He bobbed back and her momentum made her overreach. Francis took advantage of his good fortune with a vicious downward smash onto the back of her head. Her face bounced off the stairs, leaving chevron imprints on her necrotic skin. Her nose had been completely flattened and one of her eye sockets was cracked. Withered skin was folded inside the split, pulling her skin taut.

As she rose, he kicked her under the chin and sent her careening through the air. Her whirling backflip was ended as velocity faded and she collapsed to the floor in a mass of broken bone and ruptured tendons. She elicited a pathetic whimper and her unlife evaporated.

The undead horde advanced upon the now stationary figure. Francis checked the stairs, relieved he was finally bereft of zombie guests. He rested his elbows against the railing and prepared to watch the show.

"Nate, get up, get ready. We'll make a move in a minute. This guy must have a death wish." With no popcorn and odds of twenty to one against, he didn't think it would last too long.

He was right.

The dead throng formed a loose semi-circle in front of the lone ranger. The grip on the staff had changed from the middle to one end; it looked like he was holding a giant sword. As the first of the gang made their move, Francis saw two things flash.

The first was a glint from either end of the staff; each a foot long beam of shimmering silvery light.

The second was as the man tilted his head back, and the robe rose enough to showcase a beaming smile.

In precisely one point three seconds, the staff had been pulled back behind the figure to shoulder height, and then swung round at full extension in a 360 degree rotation.

By the time he had returned to his starting position, what was left of the cognitive functions of the group had been extinguished. A crudely efficient mass lateral craniotomy was performed with breathless ease.

It was as though they all had their marionette strings cut at the same time. The zombies dropped like dominos around the man. He shook the end of the weapon to remove the cling-ons, regarded his handiwork, and then stepped over the dead-dead bodies towards a dumbfounded Francis.

Nathan, who had watched the massacre through the railings, looked up at Francis with a faceful of queries. "Wh—"

Francis raised a hand. "No questions, Nate. None. Let's go see who this is. If things go bad, remember the doors are below us. Just run, okay? Follow me this time." He glared at the child who swallowed his inquisitiveness for now and shadowed him down the stairs.

The staff was slung over the man's back and held in place by a leather strap across his chest. He dusted his hands together and walked towards the man and boy. "No shit. It can't be, can it?" he chuckled.

Francis stopped at the bottom of the stairs, shielding Nathan, who peeked from behind his protector's legs. "Do I know you, slim?" he asked cautiously.

The figure continued on his path. Calloused hands reached up and pulled the hood down. "Alright Cissy."

CHAPTER EIGHT

The fire crackled and spat, the wet wood resisting immolation as long as it could. Francis looked across at the now de-robed man and smiled. "Philip, so, how you been? Your brother okay? Did you find your folks? What are you doing here?"

Nathan looked up from his charred rat on a stick. "You ask lots of questions, Francis," he said between smirking and chewing.

"We got to our parents, but it was too late. Mum's dead and Dad, well, let's say he's on a tour of the culinary delights of those still breathing. Kinda why I'm out here to be honest." Philip peeled strands of meat off the flash-cooked rodent.

"I'm sorry, slim. Seems like everyone has lost someone these days," Francis offered, staring into the fire.

Philip nodded his thanks. "Jim is doing alright. He found Sophie, they're doing okay. Probably the best thing that could've happened to their relationship was the dead coming back to life; they've never been happier."

The wind picked up its howling, screeching through broken windows. Rain lashed the building like it was trying to scour it from the earth.

Philip lay dinner down on his robe. "As for me, well, I'm looking for someone." He plunged a hand down his Palehorse t-shirt and pulled out a key on a chain, which he passed to Francis.

"A mad bird gave me this, told me that I had to find a place which it would open. As is the way with deranged crones and quests, the clue she gave me was a little on the cryptic side." Philip warmed his hands against the heat kicking out from the blaze.

Francis turned the key over in his hand. It was a normal plain brass key. It looked more like a locker key than a normal front door one. Aside from a few nicks and scrapes, it had no symbols or writing on it. "What's going to be there? When you find this place?" he asked, squinting at the object.

"Some*one*. I hope. They're going to help train me to deal with the zombies. Sounds crazy, huh? Just…I've got something left to take care of, someone I need to see," Philip replied. His eyes welled up before the moisture evaporated.

"Your dad?" Francis asked. Philip nodded. "Fair enough, pilgrim. You gotta do what you gotta do."

"What about you two? You find Shortround here recently or what?" Philip pointed at Nathan who was wrestling with a stringy bit of rat tendon.

Francis huffed. "Well, he kinda fell into my care after his mum…came back. Was a few hours after I left you guys actually. I headed into town and…had some demons to deal with. I genuinely didn't care if I lived or died, not after what happened."

Philip poked the flaring embers. "What did happen, Franny?"

"I don't want to talk about it. As I said, we've all lost people. My pops always said that your actions determine the person you are. That's all I can do now, keep moving, keep

Nathan here safe. I made a promise to that woman, I intend to uphold it, even if..." Francis trailed off.

"I know." Philip patted Francis' shoulder. "So, you guys keep moving? Never stay anywhere? Must be tough."

Nathan piped up, "I just want to be able to read my comics somewhere, and have Francis read me a story without having to sit up a tree."

"Why don't you head over to Rhayader? We've set up a camp there, and it's growing every day with new survivors. We have people going out now to find other survivors. We've even blagged a CB radio, and it's helping to build up a network of all those who have survived," Philip said, taking the proffered key and chain.

"Jim's there, plus some other kids about his size," Philip added.

Francis scratched his beard; morsels of cooked meat flicked through the air. "How far away is it? Would be good to have somewhere to call home after the past few months."

Philip placed the chain round his neck and dropped the key down his t-shirt. "A couple of weeks walk, I reckon. Not much more than that. If you've got a map, I can show you the way? Point out a few places to stop at, if you need some respite."

Francis pulled a chunk of meat from the stick with his teeth and rooted around his rucksack. He dropped the map onto the floor and opened it up, smoothing down the creases.

"Weird meeting you, Philip. Found your little survival guide earlier," Francis quipped, searching the map for their current location.

Philip smiled. "That's good. Crops up the damnedest of places I'll tell ya. One of the pathfinders must've been round these parts. Glad it's out there. Just hope it saves a few lives and brings people together. We'll need everyone we can to take things back. Here ya go, Francisco."

Francis battled with the map again as he sought to decrease it back to its pocket size form. "Thanks, slim. Gives us something to aim for. What do you reckon, Nate?"

The two men looked across to the sleeping child, whose eyelids flickered and limbs twitched. "Ha, guess we're staying here for now. Let's go secure the place, you big bastard," Philip whispered.

Boots scuffed against the dusty concrete floor. Trails of viscous fluid led from the scene of the zombie cleansing to a collapsed pile of zombie Jenga. "So what are you looking for then, Philip?" Francis asked.

"A legend."

 CHAPTER NINE

EEEEEEEE

………………...

………………..

………………..

EEEEEEEE

………………...

………………...

………………..

EEEEEEEE

………………..

"Paul, mate, when we get back, you have to get some WD40 on that wheel. It sounds like WALL-E trying to have sex with a cat flap," Dean whinged. His breath misted in the early morning chill.

Paul looked across and smiled. "Actually thought it sounded more like you porking a cat flap." He cast a glance behind him onto the half laden trailer attached to his mountain bike. "Slim pickings, mate. Think Galthorpe has been well and truly pillaged. We'll have to let Andy know, see where we should hit up next," he added, his hands pumped his burning thighs, trying to keep up the momentum.

Dean nodded in agreement and pointed. "Ahh, home, sweet home. Least you know when you see this road and the scary bastard forest that in around eleven minutes time we can finally have a cup of tea and a sit down."

The two men turned up the concrete road, past a flaking, rusty sign proclaiming 'Netzach's Biscuits'. "Tell you what, Deano. You gotta wonder how many more waifs and strays The Gaffer is gonna take in. If we can't find more than we did on this run, this'll last, what, three days, at best?" Paul panted. The end in sight, he forced his calves to one last act of exertion.

Dean wiped a gloved woollen hand across his nose, leaving a trail of snot and mucus ingrained within the thick, grey weave, "And then how much further do we have to go? Galthorpe was what? Seventeen miles? It's no bother getting there, but getting back with some of the supplies these bastards ask for is an absolute killer."

"Just be grateful we don't have a blacksmith and the sod wants a new anvil. Some Mark three-point-oh model, with a hit-o-meter and a dark matter glove. Wouldn't put it past some of these little—" Paul managed to force out through sharp intakes of breath before a shout from Dean interrupted him.

"What the fuck? Paul, you see that? Over there, on the left, the edge of the forest, is that…"

Paul squinted and scanned the hemline of the forest. "I can't see a…oh shit, let's get a wriggle on, that don't look good." The two men picked up their pace.

EEEEEEEE

. . . .

. . . .

EEEEEEEE

. . . .

. . . .

Thomas ducked under the decomposing arms of one of his attackers. The lazy lunge had left ribs exposed. He took advantage with a solid blow to the solar plexus with a section of lead pipe. The zombie paid it no heed and looked down at breakfast with a black hanging tongue. Its bottom jaw had long since been ripped off; the ragged tear suggested a sudden and violent removal, rather than a precise and clean one.

"Oh, for fuck's sake," he muttered and rolled sideways, missing a clumsy arm sweep from another of his undead muggers. He climbed to his feet and looked at his assailants. No-bottom-jaw zombie had swivelled round to face him, his dry tongue smacked against his face like a rubbish swing ball.

Lunging zombie realised that his morning sweetmeats were going to be a bit more work than hoped for, and was turning around with all the speed of the Exxon Valdez navigating the Prince William Sound's Bligh Reef.

For now, they concerned him the least. For reasons known only to Mother (un)Nature, the one that was causing him the most consternation was 'Lofty'. At least that's what the blood- and bile-encrusted enamel badge pinned to the very dead chest of a circus dwarf purported his professional name to have once been.

Thomas swayed and, for a moment, his head was filled with only one question.

What was his real name?

The lapse in concentration was nearly paid for in body parts. Lofty reached out a part hand, part claw and latched onto Thomas' jeans, somewhere around the knee. He started to pull, and with his low centre of gravity, seemed to be winning.

Snapped back into reality, Thomas began to shake his leg like a dog suffering with a bad dose of arse-worm.

Clive?

The hold was firm. He pulled his arm back and brought the pipe down onto Lofty's head.

The clown bowler hat, with its secret compartment of unsoiled and undiscovered tied multi-coloured hankies, absorbed the blow with ease. Lofty latched his other badly burned hand onto Thomas' other leg.

Perhaps Daniel?

Thomas recoiled from the failed blow and pulled back to his favoured Nadal backhand.

Orville?

His next strike was full and true, catching Lofty just below the chin. There was a loud crack and splintered jaw-bone pierced his cheek in two places; fragments of tooth and dead tissue flew into the air.

Karl?

Lofty stumbled back and chewed the air. His face had the appearance of a fleshy surf wave. One side of his mouth worked as before, the other a mishmash of exposed bone and congealed blood. Still, though, he maintained his grip, determined if necessary to gum the meal instead. If it worked for guppy fish, it could work for him. The other two zombies were now nearly within reach of Thomas.

Thomas exhaled sharply and brought the pipe down onto Lofty's shoulder. It broke the clavicle and made the associated arm judder upwards. The blow also caught his name badge which splintered and the 'ty' fell to the floor.

Got it, he looks like a right Clint.

Thomas dragged his free leg backwards and repeated the process on Lofty's other arm. Freedom reigned, though he was still none the wiser about the clown dwarf's true identity.

He regained his posture and prepared to fight the others, when from behind him, he heard a strange noise.

Is that Johnny Five trying to procreate with a cat flap?

EEEEEEEE

....

EEEEEEEE

....

Thomas looked over his shoulder and saw two men pedalling for their lives on mountain bikes with aluminium trailers being pulled behind them. One of the men had what looked like a wooden beam tucked under his arm. As he charged the No-bottom-jaw zombie, an expletive laden guttural yell bellowed above the sound of blood rushing around Thomas' head.

Deano held the fence post firmly in the crook of his arm. He'd seen it on telly, days before the outbreak, and had been waiting for a chance to try it out. The squat, square, blunt point connected just below the armpit. Given the zombie's level of decomposition, it smashed into the mushy remains of organs that called the ribcage home and completed the process of turning them into pulp.

The only resistance the impact faced was when it smacked against the spinal column. The zombie was cleaved in two. As the torso separated, the pulverised remains exited the gaping hole like a grisly sluice gate. Both halves slopped to the floor with a wet shucking sound. The lack of firm resistance caused Dean to brake and skid, flipping over to one side.

Slightly dazed, he still had the forethought to stand up and plant the fence post through the zombie's skull before it had a chance to slither across the ground.

Brain matter—decayed away to a grey, gone off minced-beef colour—sprayed up the white fence post before dribbling down in a thick gravy. He looked down at the multi-coloured gore tableau, retched and added to the paste with his own concoction of stomach lining and partially-digested hot dog and beans.

Paul, witnessing the unorthodox and slightly ungraceful way his mate dispatched his allocated zombie, opted for the safety first approach. He brought his bike to a controlled stop. EEEEEEEEEEEEEEEEEEEEEEE

He dismounted and casually slipped the length of chain from his sleeve. It dropped two foot and then bounced up as it reached its limit. Paul stalked towards Exxon Valdez and swung the chain towards its face. Attached to the last link was a titanium hook which swished round the circumference of the zombies head, sinking inside its ear canal.

Paul tugged gently to ensure that it was secure, and as it reached its sallow appendages towards his face, he yanked on the chain as if he were spinning a top.

The hook opened up the top three-and-a-half inches of the undead skull as if it were a carton of chopped tomatoes. The creature stayed rooted to the spot, arms outstretched. The bottom half of its head remained, but the top half came apart in a seam of black slime and doughy tissue.

As he tugged, the skin sloughed off the bone and plopped to the floor with a loud squelch. Paul spun the chain round his fist and in a move, well-practised since the undead started to walk, smacked the zombie square in the face.

The metal-encased fist ploughed through the exposed, brittle nasal cavity and came to rest somewhere just past the medulla oblongata. The cadaver twitched involuntarily and slowly slumped to the side. "Timber!" Paul shouted triumphantly.

Invigorated by the graphic violence which had happened either side of him, Thomas jammed the pipe into the gaping hole where Lofty's mouth used to be. As it rested in-between broken jaws and cracked teeth, he remarked to himself how it looked like the zombie dwarf clown was puffing on a metal cigar.

He chuckled to himself and brought the palm of his hand down firmly onto the pipe. It acted like a crude face-jack and split the clown's skull into two distinct and very separate hemispheres. Lofty crumpled to the ground. The top of his skull, sans hat, rolled round on the floor like a hairy salad bowl, bereft of brain.

Thomas retrieved the pipe and slid it back into his belt. He went to walk away and then remembered something. He crouched down by the dwarf's body and began to rummage through his clothes.

"You alright, Deano? Look like you lost your lunch there, mate. I knew I should've had that can, bloody love those little hot dogs." Paul reached his hand inside his jacket sleeve and pulled the chain back up into its housing.

He cast a glance over to Thomas, who was rooting around in the dead clown's costume. "Erm, mate, what are you doing? Isn't opening him up like a Kinder Egg enough for you to get your kicks on Route sixty-six?"

Thomas ignored him and continued to search. His hands fell onto a tough square object. He shouted, "Ha ha," and pulled out a wallet from the many folds of the clown outfit. Flicking through pictures of cats and vintage cars, he pulled out a driving license. His face turned up like he had just smelt an open drain, "What? His name was *Shirley?*" He gazed at the remains of the head, looked around, and then peered down the clown's shirt before recoiling in disgust.

"Fuck me, shrivelled up zombie tits, not good," he gasped, sucking in lungfuls of cool, morning air. Through watery eyes he looked up at his two saviours, who were staring at him intently. "Cheers, lads, much appreciated," Thomas said breathlessly. He gave them two thumbs up to highlight his gratitude.

Paul offered Thomas a hand, and the three men exchanged manly grunts, pleasantries and first names. "What the hell are you doing out here then, Thomas? You could've just left those three chompers, you know? Didn't have to try and be Bertie Big Bollocks and kill 'em," Paul demanded, rubbing his wrist.

"Ah, in the excitement, I almost forgot. I couldn't…I couldn't leave him." He pointed to a ditch a few feet behind the slops of the zombie remains and Dean's overturned bike and trailer.

Dean and Paul looked at each other quizzically before following Thomas' pointed finger to a drainage ditch where they saw a crumpled figure. As they got closer, they could see that it was a man, and he had taken one hell of a pasting.

Paul's muscles grew taut. He turned to Thomas. "This your handiwork, Rocky? Looks like this bloke's been half beaten to death. Look at him. I've seen more life at a Leonard Cohen gig."

Thomas raised his hands in defence,. "Hey, not me champ, you really think I'd kick the shit out of him, attract the living dead and then not leave him to them? Not likely, mate."

Dean went off to right his bike and trailer, and started the process of placing the spilled items back in its hold. Paul eyed Thomas cautiously, and then nodded. "I guess, you go off with Dean, he'll get you inside. Pretty sure The Gaffer will want to hear your side of the story, mate." Thomas shrugged and walked across to Dean to help with the repacking.

Paul inched closer to the beaten man, and could see that his chest was rising and falling with some regularity. "Jesus, wondered if you were alive or a chomper. Come on, mate. Let's get you out of there and inside. The doc can fix you up." He looked him and up and down. "Well, maybe she can. Have to see if she's filled her miracle quota already today. You look as fucked as my marriage."

He leant down and offered the man a blood-speckled hand which was weakly grabbed. "Hey pal, what's your name?" Paul enquired, hauling the man up on shaky legs.

The man mumbled something through fat lips. "Huh? What was that, mate? Didn't catch it," Paul asked, offering the man a shoulder.

"…Bartholomew…my name is…Bartholomew." The words fell through the small crevice of the man's mouth. He hoiked up a wad of blood and spit which he gobbed on the ground. Paul cradled the man and walked him to his bike.

"Hey, Dean, what is this place?" Thomas asked, surveying the building. He could make out a large sign looming over the forbidding exterior.

Dean pushed his bike along; the wheel was buckled and it took some effort to keep it straight. "This, my friend, is, *was*, Netzach's Biscuit factory, home now to survivors and sanctuary to all. Providing you can do stuff and don't piss The Gaffer off."

Thomas made an involuntary, "Huh." He peered closer at the sign. Next to the name of the company, he could make out a large cherubic figure made out of a stainless steel lattice frame. "Tell me, Deano. Why is there a man tied to that angel up there?"

CHAPTER TEN

The lock crunched and the door swung inwards. Andy looked inside the small ex-janitor's cupboard. Thomas was sitting on the middle of a foldaway bed, supping on a bowl of soup. "The hospitality has been pretty lousy, but this onion soup is not too bad."

Andy grimaced. "That bloke you came in with…"

Thomas stopped mid-slurp and gulped. He rested the spoon on the bowl's rim. "Is he?"

Andy shuffled his feet and looked down. When his features were visible again, he was wearing a cheeky bastard smile. "Ha, nearly got you. He's fine, on the mend, doesn't remember much about what happened, but he does remember that you tried to save him from the chompers. Means The Gaffer is satisfied that you're not some Patrick Bateman. Finish off your lunch, I'll show you around."

In one motion, Thomas tipped the dregs of the soup down his throat, ran a sleeved hand across his lips and jumped up. "Let's rock and roll. There were some rats in here that were starting to give me the eye."

Standing to one side, Andy let Thomas leave his gaol. He kept one hand on the rapier's handle. "This way, mate," he said jovially.

The two men walked to the far end, by the concrete dais and the metallic staircase. "Up there is The Gaffer's office and personal quarters. You really do not want to go up there without an invite, otherwise Grimm, one of his lackeys, or *me*, will politely remove you."

Thomas stood on the raised floor and looked at the bottom of the stairs, where one of the armoured guards stood watch, statuesque. At the top of the stairs, he could hear a heated discussion between two men, but the words were indiscernible. His gaze swept the floor, noticing some brown spots flecked on the monochrome concrete. He knelt down and ran a finger over them. "Nice place you got here," he mumbled to himself.

"Look here, mate. We learned the hard way that without order you have nothing. Without rules, you have nothing. If you do your duties and your fair share, you won't get any problems; that's a Netzach's guarantee." Andy offered a smile. Thomas cocked his head to one side and took in the man's features.

He was around six foot tall, well-built, and he wore thick padded clothes, not too dissimilar to those favoured by martial artists. His receding hair was bordered by a pair of glasses. His hand seemed to be glued to the sword hilt. "Nice toothpick," Thomas quipped, nodding towards Andy's weapon.

Andy chuckled and, with a grace and speed which surprised Thomas, whipped the rapier out and held it en garde in the time it took the average mayfly to pass through puberty. "Toothpick maybe, but while you're wasting energy flailing around with whatever piece of crap you've foraged from a bin, this little stinger will have already lobo'd the chomper that disturbed you. In. Twist. Out, and rinse, obviously."

"Fair play, mate. Though I'll reserve judgement until I've seen you in action. Met enough people who talk the talk, walk the walk and who think they're some kind of undead killing badass. It's only when they've been turned into finger food by a group of those bastards and are begging for mercy, whilst drowning in their own fluids, that they tend to admit that perhaps they were a little on the over-confident side," Thomas chided.

"C'mon, this here is the floor where the public Remedials take place and any announcements. If you don't fuck up, you won't be standing there looking out at the rest of the camp. Over here..." Andy walked past Thomas to a large noticeboard, where pictures and graffiti were haphazardly laid out.

Thomas pulled himself to his feet and followed. As he got closer he could see that each picture was of someone unique. Under most were scrawls and messages. "What is this?"

"This here is the memorial wall. Not everyone we've lost is on here, but most. Since we got this place set up, we've lost eleven men, women and children. The worst was seven in one night. Trust me, don't ask about the Night of Douglas, you really don't want to know." Andy looked over the wall; his eyes rested on one picture longer than the others. "Let's go," he said brusquely.

They walked around. Andy pointed out the toilet blocks. With no running water, they consisted of a number of buckets filled with sawdust, rubber gloves and bleach.

They walked past the kitchen and a motley collection of plastic furniture which formed a makeshift dining area. "Does everyone have jobs here?" Thomas asked, eyeing up the chef who was skinning a squirrel.

"The Gaffer tries to get people to do what they're skilled at. We're lucky that we have a couple of decent cooks. A few ex-army types, they make up Grimm's guards. Most others though were office workers, shit, we haven't actually made anything in this country for twenty odd years. Everything was offshored. People here are skilled at photocopying and bitching at the water cooler." Andy pointed to various people. Some were sweeping, others helping to clean clothes and pick up the used paper plates from lunch.

Thomas looked around. "So what duties are there then? If you don't have a very particular set of skills?"

Andy picked up a snapped plastic fork and put it in one of the drone's bin bags. "Mostly tasks around here. Bit of gardening, though being winter, it's more about preparation for spring right now. Otherwise, it's sentry duty on the main roof, and two on the sign, by the angel."

"Ahh, the angel. The one that doubles as some kind of punishment crucifix, yeah?" Thomas retorted.

Andy looked Thomas in the eye. "Yes, that's right. Strike Two, ten lashes and a day on the angel. If you don't learn to do your duty, you're on the slippery slope to Strike Three."

"Which is?" Thomas enquired.

"We've only done it once, no need to tell you. Most people learn after Strike One and a week in the coal scuttle out front. One hundred and sixty eight hours feels a lot like a lifetime or three when you're in a six-by-eight box. Especially if we get real popular with the locals and chompers are banging on the lid. Trust me."

Thomas rubbed his stubbled chin. "So what else do you have as duties around here. Sitting and looking out for trouble don't really float my boat."

Andy turned and walked towards the foldaway beds, arranged in equidistant rows. "Well, there's always Heads-Up detail. Pairs walk the perimeter and deal with any build-up of chompers. Sure, we've got a lovely metal fence here, but if those dead bastards congregate in any sort of numbers in one place, it'll be as much use as a cocktail dress on a pig. There's some sharp bits of broken rebar we use to deal with them. Once in a while, we go outside, drag the bodies into a heap and burn them. Gets them out of sight; unfortunately, not out of smell."

The pair walked over to the nearest bed. "This one here is yours, mate. Just make sure before you sleep, you put this on your arm." Andy held up a looped rope, pinched in a slipknot. The other end ran to a metal loop embedded into the floor at the head of the bed, where it was firmly tied.

"Didn't realise I'd walked into Camp Kinky. What's next? We all rub each other down with baby oil and tug ourselves off to the strains of Kumbaya?" Thomas toyed with the rope. Andy shot him a look of disdain.

"Tell me something, champ. It's the dead of night, everyone's asleep, and old Mister Heart Attack croaks it. Except, these days, people don't stay dead do they? So he gets up, walks over to his neighbour dreaming of better days next to him and starts to have himself a midnight snack, and so on, and so on. Before you can recall Pi to two hundred decimal places, most of the people in this place would either be reanimated or a human feedbag."

"Hmm, not a bad idea. Sounds like you guys have thought of everything," Thomas said, testing the reach of the rope and seeing that it provided ample room to sleep, but not to wander.

Andy nodded. "As I said, we've learnt the hard way. C'mon, let's go see your pal."

They trudged over to a long narrow room, which was contained behind a door to one side of the factory. Ten immaculately made beds were laid out, each with a loop of rope by the pillow. Only one was occupied. A woman, dressed in blue scrubs, was standing with her back to them, leaning over the patient.

"Chopper, this here is Thomas. He was the one who made sure Bartholomew here was still breathing," Andy called across. The woman reverently placed her patient's arm back on the bed and turned around, removing her surgical mask as he did so.

The woman was around five and a half foot tall. She had shoulder length curly black hair, olive skin and a face that made her look like she had just finished her child labour shift for Cucci or Bolex.

"Charmed." Chopper extended a limp-wristed hand towards Thomas, who shook it vigorously, just to see if it would fall off.

Thomas shot Chopper a look of utter bemusement. His mouth gawped open. Chopper rolled her eyes and said in a posh accent, "Yes, yes, I have the demeanour of a choirgirl, but the handshake of a serial killer, and let me guess. You want to know why a woman of such standing is called Chopper, not Doc, or Bones, hmm?"

Thomas nodded absently. His jaws chattered against each other. "Os…gwelwch…yn…dda…fyun"

"You'll like this," Andy said, and rested back against the wall.

"In the early days, when people weren't too sure how the virus was transmitted, we believed that in order to arrest the development of Necro-Activation, the afflicted appendage had to be removed. Immediately. Post haste. Usually with something as delightful as, say, an axe. There was one chap back in Ingleby, I had to remove his leg with a length of cheese wire. Barbaric perhaps, but it was a work of art," Chopper simpered, stroking hair from her eyes.

"But, everyon—" Thomas started to say.

Chopper raised a hand topped with French polished nails to stop him mid-flow. "Yes, yes. As I said, this was in the early days. Andrew here and *him upstairs* found me knee-deep in hands, legs, arse cheeks and a few, *ahem*, old chaps, if you know what I mean. Not sure I wanted to know how it came to pass that their...*Johnson*, had happened to be exposed to a zombie's mouth. Ask no questions. Hear no lies."

Andy nodded towards Bartholomew. "Chopper, how's he doing?"

Chopper turned to her patient, smiled and then looked back. "He's doing rather well now. A few hairy moments in the first few days, some confusing contusions which would simply not go down. But most disappointingly, nothing to chop orf." She flashed Thomas a big perfectly toothed smile.

"That's good. Least I didn't get locked up in a broom cupboard for nigh on a week for nothing," Thomas added. Spotting something unusual on a tray of surgical implements, he asked, "Hey, what's that triangle thing?"

The sound of rapid clapping filled the room. "Oohhh, Andrew, he is simply divine is he not, a real keeper. You sir, have a good eye. This is a little invention of mine; hoping to patent it, when...well, the world sorts its bloody self out. This, my learned friend, I call a vert-chock." Chopper picked up a palm sized plastic plectrum with a blunt metal tip. "Please, I implore you, ask me again what it does."

Thomas shifted uncomfortably. He looked across to Andy, who was trying to stifle a laughing fit. "Okay. Chopper. What does it do?"

Chopper closed her eyes and emitted a sound like an octopus was using all of its tentacled arms to pleasure her in a way she had never experienced. "Mmmmm. That's good. Well, as you know, if you die, then you come back as one of the untreatables, those blasted cads out there. Well, we had a chap in here a while back who was terminally ill. The Gaffer fretted for ages as to the most humane way to stop him coming back. So, I made this. The chap passed one afternoon, Andrew here rolled him onto his front, and I applied the vert-chock between the fifth and sixth vertebrae. With a firm strike from a hammer, I was able to sever the spinal column and prohibited him from coming back. I was exultant."

Andy coughed. Chopper looked down nervously. "Yes, okay, so it wasn't a complete success, the head did regain some...motor function, did become a bit bitey, but I'm sure Bill Gates didn't strike it lucky with Gates-box number one, or whatever he did first time round."

"We best finish up. See ya later Chopper." Andy pushed away from the wall and bid the doctor farewell. Thomas followed quickly.

"Zan," she said loudly. Thomas turned around with a puzzled look on his face. She smiled sweetly. "Doctor Eva Zan, pleased to make your acquaintance." The two men walked back out onto the factory floor.

"She's…erm…"

"Yes. Very," Andy agreed, and the two headed towards a door beyond the beds.

"What's in there, mate?" Thomas asked.

Andy stopped and peered through the window into the storeroom. "Ahh, this is the new group The Gaffer started up, for some of our more…mentally delicate brethren. Sure you'll meet them later on. Come on, I'll show you around the perimeter."

Thomas looked into the room and nodded slowly. "No worries, I can see you and your toothpick in action, let's go. First off though, are the bogs over there? Need a quick piss first."

MAY 14TH 2014

19:51

The car edged into the bay slowly. Francis just managed to brake in time to stop it clunking the one opposite. He was still transfixed by the sky. It had begun a few minutes ago; he guessed it had started in the east, a wave of red sweeping across the sky. The clouds took on a pinkish hue, and everything was bathed in a blood-soaked glow.

Given the hour, the hospital car park was relatively empty; with the day visitors gone and simple procedures completed, the only residents now were those called here through accident or tragedy.

"Do you work here?" the receptionist asked, pointing a chewed biro at Francis' security badge.

"No, ma'am, just came straight from my work. I'm here to see my partner, Diane Webber. Can you tell me where she is please?" Francis asked gently. The lady disappeared within the PC, tapping out the name with her index finger in a slow, rhythmic beat. Her lips moved in mute sync to the letter she was typing.

"Says here that Diane Webber is in Maternity and Neonatal, that's Beatrice Ward. Take the stairs to level one, turn left and it's signposted from there on in sir," she said, pointing to a stairwell behind a set of doors.

Francis nodded his thanks and followed her directions.

CHAPTER ELEVEN

Francis woke with a start. Nathan sat at the foot of his sleeping bag, watching him. "You were having those dreams again," he mumbled. Sleep had only just lost its claim on the boy, too.

"Skip it, kid. Everyone has dreams." Francis rubbed his slumber encrusted eyes.

Nathan shifted uncomfortably on the unforgiving ground. "Who was she?"

"Doesn't matter, Nate. Let's get some breakfast. We got to make a move; got a bit of a journey ahead of us if we want to get to that place," Francis grumbled, looking around at the misty interior.

"The man's over there," Nathan said, pointing to a side room. Francis got up uneasily and walked over to the room.

A half-open door led to a narrow chamber which looked like a disused medical bay. Well-kept beds covered in a blanket of brown dust were lined up against one wall. A silver tray glinted with the morning sun as it streaked through grimy windows. Surgical tools lay untouched on its surface.

"Someone lived here," Philip said distractedly. He had his back to the entrance and was crouched down by a large ventilation cover. "Come here, look."

Francis squatted down and looked into the shaft. Empty cans and stained bandages were strewn around the entrance. "How long since they left?" he asked, nose buried inside a can of beans. Remnants of tomato sauce had long since dried and left a thick brown-ridged skin on the inside of the tin.

"A while. Not much has been disturbed around here. They could have been one of the skinjob's we met yesterday." Philip nodded at the building behind. "It's a damn shame about this place too. Used to love their Chocolate Crunchy Crème's," he muttered as he fished through a pile of rubbish.

Philip retracted his arm, groaned, and flicked a yellowing bandage onto the floor which had been affixed to his sleeve. "Fucking gross." The pair walked back out to the burnt-out fire, where Nathan was reading.

"Ooohhh, what ya reading, kid? The deconstruction of metaphysical constructs?" Philip asked sarcastically, plonking himself down with a thump and an eruption of dust.

Nathan tore himself away and showed him the cover. "It's called *The Red Mask from Mars*, about this man who went to Mars—"

"Woah, woah, hang on mate. You gotta let the ol' King of Deduction, Phil 'Genius' Taylor, have a crack on this. I'm gonna hazard a guess it's about a man who went to Mars. I also reckon he had a red mask. Am I right?" Philip interrupted again.

"No, silly, he was an astronaut, but then this thing got stuck to his face, and now he is like a superhero. Look, he's beating up this alien with a hammer and all this goo is coming out of him." Nathan displayed the page showing the titular character indeed beating the crap out of an alien, DIY implement in hand.

"Fuck me, he's a handy bastard, eh?" Philip took the comic from the boy and flicked through it.

Francis loomed over him. "Mind your language slim."

Philip glanced up. "Sure thing. Thuck me, this motherthucker don't take no thit huh?" He flicked to the end, examined the back cover and flung the comic back to Nat. "Well, don't know about you chaps, but I've got to make a move. Must've messed up with the last clue. Best have a mooch about and find out where next. You cool on the directions Cissy?" Philip picked up his weapon and checked the blades on each end.

Francis nodded. "Sure are. Think we're gonna go through the forest, though, rather than follow the train tracks. Big ol' clearing the other side which might be worth checking out. Nate, get your stuff together." He tapped the kid with the toe of his boot. Nathan reluctantly started to pack away his stuff.

A brisk breeze blew through the factory, sending a chill down their backs. A faint odour of decaying meat and mustiness carried along with it. Francis slung his bag onto his back and held out his hand. Philip took it firmly. "Thanks for the help, slim. Not sure we would've made it out of here if you hadn't shown up."

Philip let out a sharp chuckle. "No bother, mate. I seem to recall you did the same for Jim. Least I can do, and it was good to see you. Tell my bumder of a brother I'm fine, yeah?"

The two men stood immobile like Roman statues; their weary stares conveyed more than words could share. "Good luck finding your door. Hope to see you back in…"

"Rhayader," Philip finished off Francis' sentence. "Cheers, I wonder some days why I'm bothering. What are they going to teach me that I don't already know?"

Francis released his grip and pulled the other strap over his arm. "That's the thing, pilgrim. There's always something to learn, especially these days. Take care."

With that, Philip nodded and trudged towards the back door. As he got to the frame he paused, saluted, and then disappeared into the morning mist.

Francis ran his thumbs under the shoulder straps. The motion soothed a nagging feeling scratching away inside his skull. Nathan broke the spell. "That man says a lot of naughty words."

Stirred from his thoughts he looked down into the boy's eyes. Through the grime on his face, they shone back like two headlights. "That he does. Hey, let's get moving, eh? With some luck we'll be through that forest before the end of the day."

The pair took one last look round the derelict building and headed to the main double doors, passing the pile of bodies they had dragged into a heap after the run in the day before.

Grey appendages, with black lines traced over their surface, grew out of the macabre pile. Bowls of half skulls were stacked in each other, some vestiges of brain matter still clinging to the sides. Nathan took one last look, shrugged and walked off. Francis lingered a moment, looking from the kid to the stack of cadavers. "What world will he inherit when all of this is over? What will he tell people of these times?" he wondered aloud, before walking out into the grey morning.

CHAPTER TWELVE

The teaspoon tinged and tanged its way around the bowels of the 'I Heart Mondays' mug. Dee stared, lost in its sepia contents; the stirring created a whirlpool within the tea. Dee's imagination spawned narwhals and whaling boats spinning in the wake.

"Do I know you?" The words brought the beverage vortex to an abrupt end; both beast and boat sunk beneath the tannin seas.

Dee looked up and saw Sylvia's crumpled sad face studying her. She scowled and grunted a swift, "Don't think so," in reply. Placing the spoon on the worktop, she moved away hurriedly, holding the mug to her chest with both of her hands. Sylvia looked on with a mix of half-recall and wistfulness. Steve walked into the room, her face lit up like a bonfire.

A squawk of squeaking chairs later and a rough corral was formed. Tristan was the last to settle, still forlorn and hushed. "Good morning all. Hope you've been alright since the last session? Yeah? Good. So, last week, Sylvia," he flashed her a smile, "very kindly told us a bit about herself and a bit of background as to why she's here."

Anton coughed the word "Bullshit" into his hand. Dee shot him a look she hoped would maim or at least disfigure him some more.

"Sylvia, is there anything further you would like to add?" Steve sat back, opened his notebook and readied his scratchy pen.

Sylvia looked around the room at the disinterested and disengaged people she was stuck with. She pondered for a few moments before answering. "No thank you Steve. Some of it is still too painful to talk about right now. Particularly, you know. The end. I am feeling better though and I'm starting to remember more about those last few days, and the…other days. Here. When I was. You know. Silly." She giggled nervously.

Steve gave her a comforting smile and a subtle wink. "No problem, Sylvia. You take your time; we'll all be here. None of us are going anywhere. When you're ready, you tell us, okay? So, who's next? Do we have a willing volunteer?"

He scanned the room. Anton turned away, folding into himself. As he crossed his arms he stuck his middle finger up. "Sorry pal," he muttered. Tristan was still incommunicado and Dee had kept some of the intensity of her stare just for Steve.

"Matt, how about you? Are you ready to share with the group?" he asked softly. Matt stirred from his floor-gazing, fingered his greasy hair behind his ears and began.

SURVIVOR

TALES FROM THE ZOMBIE APOCALYPSE

The NETZACH'S Series

ISSUE # 2 — CONSPIRACY THEORY

NARRATED BY MATT MORLOCK

CONSPIRACY THEORY - PART 1

Ha, so, me then, huh? Wow, that'll be cool. I don't mind too much, though my tongue is a little swollen today, like it's been stung or summat.

Imagine that, though. Being stung on the tongue by summat, or like a little critter crawling in your mouth when you're like watching summat or thinking about, I dunno, how much dust there is in the world. And then it crawls in and just goes *chomp*, and then you'd be all like, huh?

Well, I don't have much of a story really. Don't even know why I'm here. Not as if I've done anything, not since I did that test at school.

That was a good day.

I got to stay behind after class, and then the teacher gave me this special test, and then gave me some Rolos and a can of Fanta. It was dead cold, too. But he said that we had to keep the test hush-hush.

So, don't you be asking about what I had to touch or play that afternoon, cos it was some kind of new recorder, or summat. I blew and blew, but just couldn't get it to play 'London's Burning'.

Sounded like he had to go to a school later, though, as mum was reading the paper one day and said that he was on the register, which was strange as he was really old.

My mum and dad only had me, said that I was all the children that they wanted, which I always thought was dead nice of them. My dad used to be in the air force. Had to leave though, after thinking it would be a good idea to load up and try and bomb Russia. He was always worried about those Russians. It's why we had the shelter.

Out back.

In the garden.

Any time he saw summat on telly that looked a bit iffy, that was it, off we went into the bunker. I remember when he saw the telly pictures of the missiles in the first Iraq war, he got it into his head that it was live pictures from Basingstoke.

I remember we were eating minced beef Crispy Pancakes, crinkle cut oven chips and baked beans.

Well, that came on the telly and Dad had us all down in the bunker before you could say Saddam Hussein.

A fortnight we were down there for. We only came out cos mum forgot to restock the toilet paper from the last time and we had to use the pages out of my diary.

That was awkward, wiping my bum-bum with the pages I had written about Emily on. When I saw her next I had to check to make sure she didn't have a big brown line down her.

From my bum-bum.

When I think about it, we did spend a lot of time in the bunker. Dad got scared a lot I think, but I don't blame him. He said that the aliens had done stuff with him. He didn't want to say what, in case you know. They were listening. But he told me one day they put summat…you know.

Eh?

No, don't be silly, they put it up his bum-bum.

I remember after the Twin Towers fell over, we spent about four months down there, I think. Only came out when Mum said that the water tasted funny.

Thing is, and this is a secret, so if you see her ghost, you can't tell her. It was all of our wee-wee. That's what Dad said, something about Phil Terr cleaning it, but I never met him and he must've cleaned it while I slept, cos there were only ever three of us in the bunker.

Well, three humans. Patches was in there as well. We didn't use Phil to clean and drink his wee-wee, though. Dad said it tasted like Gran's, so we never drank it after England got knocked out of the World Cup in 1998 and we were in the bunker again.

About three weeks I think. Dad always went a bit funny over those penalty shootouts.

Do you like it when you get tickled? Like when you're not really expecting it, you're just sat there, I dunno, reading Simon's Cat, and then Patches snuffles up to you under the table. His little wet nose rubs on your foot and then, as you aren't ready for it, your foot kinda goes KAPOW, and kicks out. I knocked over my cherryade once. Mum didn't like it as the carpet was beige and she said it looked like Gorbachev's head rash.

She cleaned it up well quick, said that dad wouldn't have liked seeing that on the floor and we might have had to go to the bunker again. Irrespective of all the glass knots that Gorbachev brought to the world.

Or summat.

Eh?

Glasnost?

What's that Steve, is that a music festival?

Mum said it was best if I stayed with them when I grew up and left school, because of, the, well, I don't want to say it, but Dad basically. Said that it was safer for everyone if we were all together.

I don't think that had anything to do with the fire.

I was eating a Toffee Crisp, and Martin had just called me a bellend cos of the mixtape I made Emily. I had to follow her for ages to find out where she lived.

So, I remember we were having tea. I had pork chops, mash and peas. Garden peas, just like Mum, only Dad had the marrowfat ones. I used to like them, but Mum said garden peas make you really clever, so I ate them.

We're watching the telly and it starts going on about the people in Manchester and how they were attacking other people, and some were like eating them, or summat.

Anyway, I had just cut up to the pork chop bone. Always like to save the strip of meat next to the bone till last, except for the bit right up in the corner, that's my favourite bit.

What's your favourite bit of pork chop, Steve?

Ha ha, yeah Anton, I guess I should shut the fuck up, but I'm telling a story, so if I shut the fuck up, you won't get to hear my story.

Are too.

Dee too?

Ha ha, no, you haven't said your stories yet have you? You're silly.

We got to the bit where the news reporter in Manchester was talking, just before that zombie thing got hold of him by the neck and was making him bleed everywhere and he was asking for his mummy.

Dad threw down his knife and fork and off we went again to the bunker. Before we got outside, he asked Mum if she had remembered the toilet paper this time, and she said yes, of course she had.

Patches always got there first. I think he was more excited than we were to go back down there. Though he was getting quite old by then, and used to just eat pasta, because his kidneys were all wrong.

Ha ha, he used to eat his pasta, and then go for a poo, and then he used to eat the poo which made him throw up, and then he used to eat that too. Sometimes he went round and did the same again, but without the pasta.

I thought it was funny, but Mum said that it wasn't. She said that it was all down to Reen Alfailure, but I never met her either. If so, I wouldn't have liked her very much as she had made Patches ill, and that wasn't very nice. I probably would've spat in my hand and then shaken her hand.

Yeah, reckon so.

It wasn't the biggest place ever, but we had our own little bedrooms. Patches was in my room. There was a living room and kitchen, a little bathroom and that was it.

We used to play Monopoly, cards, dominos and Risk, but we didn't play that much as Dad had cut out Russia from the board and eaten it one day with some French fries and Mexican refried beans.

Every hour one of us used to wind up the radio. Dad said we shouldn't listen to it for too long, though, as that's how propaganda starts. He used to say as well that the, *ahem*, you know what, in his bum-bum, used to itch if he listened to the radio too much, so we did Dangermouse jigsaws instead.

CONSPIRACY THEORY - PART 2

We put the radio on one day, though, and nothing came out. Dad wheeled through all of the numbers and there wasn't anything there except static. He scratched his bum-bum and said how odd it was, then he got that look in his eye. I remember it as it was the same one the picture in the papers showed of him just before he tried to get into his plane.

Before they had to tell him that he wasn't allowed to bomb anyone.

I think he just worried that people were getting all chilly through the Cold War, so wanted to warm them up.

Ha ha, do you get it?

Warm up.

EXPLOSIONS.

Cold War.

Well, Dad and I thought it was funny.

So the radio went quiet and Dad's eye went all boggly, like someone inside his head was pumping it up. He didn't say anything for a while. Mum said it was best to leave him. When he spoke he said that it probably meant that the Russians had won and they had invaded. He said the zombies were the first wave of troops, that we were all alone now and had to accept that we might have to stay in the bunker.

Forever.

Patches didn't like what he had to say. Mum put his pasta down that night and he didn't even get up. When she stroked him, she said he was all cold and hard.

Something about Ed and a doornail.

Dad's eye went all funny again, except this time it was his other eye. I knew something was wrong, but I had my tomato soup like a good boy and went to sleep.

I tucked Patches into the end of my bed, where he always used to lie. He didn't lick my face like he used to, and he smelt funnier than normal. I didn't mind though, Patches was my friend.

In the middle of the night, I remember Mum and Dad having an argument, worse than ever, shouting and saying rude words. Mum even said that he was a complete and total count.

Which was odd, as I didn't think dad was a vampire, though he did become a...well, I'll get to that bit in a minute.

I heard her say that she couldn't put up with the pair of us anymore. I didn't like it. I hugged up with Patches and we stayed hidden until my alarm went off.

Mum was always first up. She'd knock on the side of my doorway, by my curtain, and say, 'Morning pumpkin, time for breakfast. Better be quick or Patches'll be sick and you'll have to make do with porridge'. But my alarm went off and Mum wasn't there.

I waited for ages, thinking perhaps she was just playing a game of hide and seek with Dad, and was doing really well, so didn't want him to find out.

So I stayed under the blanket and me and Patches played Beg.

Except he didn't do as well as he used to. Poor thing must've been dead tired as he didn't even open his eyes or wag his tail.

A few hours later, I realised that Patches must be ill. I remember one time when we went to the vets, the animal doctor had to take his temperature, but instead of putting the thermometer in his mouth, he put it into his sticky-out sausage-hole.

You know, his bum-bum.

Patches made an awful crying sound that day.

So I thought I'd go and be like an animal doctor. I would put my finger in his sticky-out sausage-hole. I must've been good, as he didn't even make a sound.

I had to push quite hard too. I broke off a finger nail and lost it inside Patches. He was very cold then.

I got up to tell Mum and pulled my curtain open, and I saw there was light shining down on the bunker stairs. I was terrified. I thought the Russians must've found out where Dad was hiding and had come to get him.

But they hadn't.

Mum and Dad's curtain was pulled closed and I could hear a moaning sound. Mum always said that if the curtain was closed, and there was moaning to be heard, then whatever you do, do not disturb.

I had looked once before, and that was enough. It was like they were wrestling; Dad was winning, I think. He had Mum pinned down and she was obviously hoping for some help, as she was saying, 'Oh god, oh god, that's it.' Dad saw me and told me to go back to my room. I didn't want to see that again, but I had to tell Mum about Patches.

The curtain started bulging out, but it looked like a foot. I don't remember their feet kicking the curtain last time, so I shouted out loud that I was going to open it and pulled the curtains apart.

There wasn't any wrestling, but there was still a moaning. I opened my eyes and I was staring at Dad's winky. I'd never seen his winky before. It was like mine, but it was all grey. I looked at the rest of him and saw that he was hanging from the light grill by this rope round his neck, and that he was all grey.

Guess he had suffered his mid-life crisis in the night huh?

His head was all tilted, like he was playing the 'look at me sideways' game. I laughed and told him that it was a good one, but his eyes looked all weird too. His arms kept trying to grab me, but I know the rules: one hand is fine, but to win you need two, and then you have to say 'Gotcha'. I had a look on the bed, but couldn't see Mum anywhere.

I made myself some breakfast. I had strawberry Nesquik with a can of peaches. I felt good, as already I'd had two of my five a day. Mum would be proud of me, except I couldn't see her.

Patches didn't touch his pasta, and that went cold, and Dad didn't seem too fussed about his rollmops. He was still hanging there, and kept trying to grab me when I tried to feed him the stinky fish.

He obviously didn't know that the game was over cos I called 'Quitsies' when I was stirring my condensed milk and wee…I mean, Phil's water, to make my Nesquik.

I got bored of Dad keep on trying to play the grabbing game, so I thought, as the door was open, it would be okay to take Patches for a walk.

Wow.

He was *not* keen.

I had to drag him up the stairs when he was on the lead. He wasn't as stiff as the night before, but he still wasn't well.

Why are you laughing, Dee? Do you have stiff things in your bed at night, too?

Oh, sorry, please don't force the lungs out of my body by kicking me in the stomach with your army boots.

I managed to get Patches outside, but he didn't want to play fetch. I lost count of how many times I threw the ball; he didn't chase after it once. Then I remembered what else the animal doctor did, and I put my head to his chest and listened for his heart-drum.

I couldn't hear anything.

I spent ages trying to listen. I even opened his mouth up and tried to look down into his tummy, to see if I could see his heart, but I couldn't. His eyes wouldn't stay open either. That's when I realised that poor old Patches must be like when I saw Nana the last time. I tried to remember what Mum said, but Patches didn't look at all like brown bread. I hugged him again, and kept the flies away.

Stroking his fur didn't feel the same, so I knew I hadn't made a mistake. It's weird though isn't it? Those times when bad things happen, and people seem to always be there for you? I didn't hear anything, but as I held Patches that last time, I felt a cold hand on my neck. There he was, my Dad. He'd come up to say goodbye to Patches.

Though he looked like my Dad, but a bit more grey, like those aliens we used to watch from olden times, when the doctors cut them up. He looked funny. He was still playing the 'look at me sideways' game, even after I told him 'Quitsies'.

Summat wasn't right.

Summat wasn't right *at all.*

His neck was all purple and swollen. He still had his winky out as well. I remember it made this little slapping sound as it hit my coat. All he wanted to do was hug me.

To begin with anyway.

I moved out of the way so that Dad could hug Patches and say goodbye to him, but instead of doing that, he just kept following me, and I told him to stop it, but he just wouldn't listen. He was making the moaning sound again, and was still trying to grab me. I stayed ahead of him, but only just.

When I was walking round the garden, that's when I realised. He was one of those zombies from the television.

He had gone Russian.

I started crying. If they had got him, they could get *anyone,* damn bastards. He'd fought all his life so that me and Mum were free of their embrace, and now, well, his name was probably Ivan or summat.

This must have been why Mum left; there would be no way she could stay with someone from there. Dad did all this stuff for her and me. To see him become the very thing that he hated must've been too much for her.

Me and Dad were always the strong ones.

I pleaded with him to stop. I even tried in Russian, though one of the only words I knew was 'ot'ebis". He didn't even understand that. They must've got him good. The radio said that if you had to take the zombies on, you had to do so by removing the head or destroying the brain. Dad was the cleverest man I met, so I knew his brains would be difficult to destroy.

Luckily, though, in Mum's hurry to leave Ivan, she had left the rotary washing line in the garden. I pulled it out of the ground and just about managed to get away before he grabbed me. I knew that I'd only get one shot at this, as I could hear some more Russian moans not far from me. Who'd have known, even when he was gardening and pushing the daisies up, that Patches would save me?

Dad came for me again, but didn't see my trusty pal. His foot caught on Patches and he went flying, landing on his front. I never realised dad had such a hairy bum-bum.

Those aliens must've had to trim loads away before they got anything up there.

I stood over him, and he looked like that turtle I had when I was younger. I used to put him on his back and his little arms and legs thrashed around, but they couldn't help him stand up. Dad's neck looked even worse. There was a bone or two sticking out of this hole just above his shoulder, and you could see raw pork chops inside.

His hands were grabbing the lawn. He was pulling clumps of dirt up with his hand. Mum would be well mad when she got back and saw what he done. Those hands...

I pulled the rotary line together and clipped in the arms; it was like a pole I held in my hands, it felt so big.

Why are you laughing, Dee? Have you held a big pole in your hands before, too?

Sorry, please don't pull my tongue out of my head and what?

Beat me to death with the wet end?

I'll remember that when I'm fighting the Russian zombies next, thanks!

I looked down at him. He looked so strange. His moaning had changed, probably because he was eating dirt. I froze. I couldn't do it. Then he kinda growled 'nyet', and that's when I knew that he was gone. Cos that's Russian, he knew what I was going to do.

So I did it.

He would've been proud of me. I did it in one go, and didn't cry. His hands stopped digging straight away. His legs kinda kicked out a bit and then he stopped, like someone had turned him off.

I don't really remember what happened next. I could hear the moans nearby. I think I ran. The next thing I know these men had stopped me in the street, said they were going off to a biscuit factory to get away from the zombies and said they'd look after me. I said if they were going to a biscuit factory, I'd love to go with them.

I miss my dad.

And my mum.

But most of all, I miss Patches.

CHAPTER THIRTEEN

Steve removed his glasses carefully, rubbed his tired eyes and said, "Thank you Matt, that was…a real eye opener. I hope that you feel better after sharing your tale with the group?"

Matt stared gormlessly at his inquisitor, shrugged as a clump of slick matted hair slipped from its cordon behind his ear and swung in front of his face. He looked around the group and raised a cautious hand. "Yes, what is it Matt?" Steve asked.

"Do you think we'll get fish fingers for tea tonight? I love fish fingers. Mum used to cook them for me after I did something good. Ha. Which wasn't much, she said. I think I've only had them four times. Each time I had potato wedges, normal ones, and baked beans. Once I put brown sauce on the beans, but they tasted well funny, so I didn't do it again." Once the words were expunged, his head disengaged social protocol and dropped to look at the floor again.

"What an absolute bellend," Anton quipped, scratching the scar around his eye. "If I have to put up with any more fucking sadsack stories, I think I might just top myself."

Sylvia winced at his words. She started to stroke the inside of her arm again, trying to calm herself down.

Steve hastily put his glasses back on. The arm broke off and got embedded in his hair. He knelt down by her and whispered calming words.

Dee's eyes darted from Sylvia to Anton in a hummingbird's heartbeat. He raised his hands. "Woah, calm down mental bird. Didn't mean nuffin' by it, till next time, yeah?" With that, he stood up and made his way out of the room. Matt and Tristan stirred and followed suit.

"It'll be alright, Sylvia. You're safe now. No one is going to hurt you, shhh." Steve looked over to Dee and nodded towards the door. She gratefully took the cue to leave.

She was so preoccupied that as she left she bumped into a man standing in the doorway. "Steady on, Dee," Andy said. She looked at him with disdain and stomped off into the factory.

Andy gently rapped on the open door. "Steve, sorry mate, Chopper needs you. Our new guest has woken up. Could do with you having a little chat with him. Just to make sure he's not a policeman short of the Village People, cheers mate."

He headed back into the factory, walking past people going about their daily tasks. With some he exchanged nods of greeting. *Best get Thomas, assign him his duties. He's quite handy but bloody hell, he must have a bladder the size of a walnut.*

CHAPTER FOURTEEN

The garage door slid down rusty runners; a sound like a hundred mice having prickly pears inserted roughly into a usually outbound-only orifice made the hair on the guards' necks stand on end.

"Man, that was one mental day," one said to the other. "How much longer is it until we attack?"

Guard number two sneezed. "Fucking dust. Not sure. Feels like forever right now though. Still, better to be doing this than what the other chapters are doing. You heard about the Reverend didn't ya?"

Lackey number one nodded solemnly. "Yeah, man. That was all kinds of wrong. I heard they found his head still reciting chapter and verse from the Book of Ishtar."

"His devotion is an example to us all, Brother, that much is true. Still, we keep his fire burning through the work we do now, the camps of the unrighteous that we cull, the heathens we bring to Rapture. Did She not say—"

A sound like a blocked vacuum cleaner gasped behind them. The two guards jumped and looked at the source, calming when they realised it was the penitent who had been interred in the cage that morning.

"Hey, Malky, this one's still breathing, a regular Duracell bunny if ever I saw one," guard number one said, the panic still in his voice.

Malky made his way round the side of the RV and looked at the man in the cage. He had lost a couple of fingers after passing out holding onto the frame. One of the undead groupies had managed to clamp down on the back swing and remove them clean from the joint between the middle and proximal phalanx. He had learnt then he'd better stay awake, or he would be eaten piece by piece.

The hulk surveyed the whimpering husk and looked down on the floor. "Perhaps he is still with us, because the person who put him in there this morning did not commence bleeding before we set off." The guard gulped as the imposing figure loomed over him.

A pause followed which seemed to bookend the Palaeolithic and Neolithic time periods. "No matter. He will provide us with a distraction before we leave in the morning. Make sure the penitents are fed and that we are secure. We don't want any visitors in the night." Malky turned and headed into the gloom of the building.

"How many do we have?" a voice asked from the shadows.

Malky stopped and bowed. "Estimates are just over a hundred, your Grace. A few days in so far, it appears that we have not been as blessed as we had hoped."

Devin manifested from the murk. "It matters not, we don't want too many first off. It's the second week where we will be going through the larger towns; we should attract quite the following then. Though sleeping in the vans with them outside will test the initiates resolve. As long as our Brothers have prepared the refuelling and safe zones, we have nothing to fear."

Malky nodded in agreement. "Everything will be as you asked, of that I am sure."

"Of course it will. They know the price of failure," Devin replied succinctly. He regarded the two guards who were bowed in deference. "I also think it best that acolytes do not make assumptions as to the fate of the other chapters. Speculation and hearsay are the work of the unbelievers. These poisonous and seditious words will infect our harmony, do I make myself clear?"

The two guards saluted Devin with a hand to their chests. "Of course, your Grace. We meant no disrespect. We are Her children, and guided by your hand," they stuttered between them.

Devin nodded and allowed them to return to their evening tasks. "Malky, a word if I may?"

"Your Grace?" Malky asked softly.

"The Apostle has signalled to our scouts that he is in place and knows when to strike. He has gone dark, we will soon be able to remove another feeble bastion of resistance," Devin said fervently.

"That is excellent news indeed, your Grace. The snake is within their midst, coiled and ready to strike. It is truly a beautiful sight to see the heathens take the Apostle in as one of their own. Matched only by his blade being the first to be held against their throats," Malky said whilst smiling.

"Indeed it is. Come, we need to rest. Ensure the acolytes have read chapters eight through to ten; it will gird them for the days ahead."

MAY 14TH 2014

20:05

"No problem, Mr Davidson. Ms Webber has the doctor in with her at the moment, but you should be fine to go in," the nurse said, pointing to the closed door barring access to Room Three. Mumbled voices could be heard beyond.

As he gained entry into the room, he caught the end of a sentence. "...orry Ms Webber, but we should be able to do an ultrasound in the next ten minutes or so. We've been having problems with the power in the last half hour—" the Doctor stopped as Francis entered, and raised his hands in apology.

Diane looked across and smiled. Though it broke a face which was red as a result of crying.

The doctor saw his opportunity and left the room in a hurry. Francis walked over to Diane and held her hand. "Got here as quickly as I could, baby. You should see the sky out there, it's—"

His story was interrupted by his hand being crushed and a flood of tears. Diane pulled Francis into her and bawled, "Something's wrong, Francis, I can feel it. It just doesn't feel *right*."

"Shhh, it's okay baby, I'm here now, it'll be okay," he assured her, gently rubbing her back and kissing her forehead. "How doesn't it feel right?" he asked softly, still trying to stem her crying with his soothing.

Diane looked up, sniffed back a chunk of spit and mucus and swallowed it, coughing after it went down. "When I was ha…having dinner, he was just going crazy, kicking out, almost thrashing about. You know how he likes listening to Crosses? Well, it just didn't do anything. Even when I got here he was still flailing around. I must've been to the toilet five or six times. He's playing havoc with my bladder."

Francis pulled a tissue from a box next to the bed and passed it to Diane, who took it and blew into it with a noise akin to an elephant saying 'hello, how are you today?'. "Thanks baby," she said, wiping the dripping tissue across her nose.

"About five minutes ago, though, when the doctor came in, he just stopped. He's not doing anything now. I'm *scared* Francis. Something has happened, I know it," Diane whimpered.

CHAPTER FIFTEEN

"Are we nearly there yet?" Nathan whinged, his feet dragging along the sodden ground. Clumps of dead leaves and moss stuck to the toes of his trainers, leaving them looking like the prow of a Roman bireme.

Francis grunted and pushed on through the skeletal bushes. The buds of new life were just beginning to burst out of the finger-like ends. The going had been tough; they'd had to camp in the bough of an oak tree having failed to escape the clutches of night and nature the previous day.

"Not long now kid," Francis muttered, almost willing the words to be true rather than having any actual belief in them. His stomach growled in rebellion at him. The past two weeks of canned fish and soft Ritz crackers were not providing the fuel needed to traverse the bleak, seemingly never-ending terrain.

Nathan grumbled under his breath, huffed, and continued to half walk and half slide through the mulch underfoot. "Do you miss her?" he asked. His breath formed a cloud in front of his ruddy face. Francis turned and looked down at him, causing the child to walk into the back of his legs.

"No idea who you're talking about, kid," he mumbled. A hand moved from its temporary home of armpit and rubbed his nose. A trail of snot glistened like a comet trail. Francis turned and plodded onwards, head down; branches scratched and pawed at his face, but he paid them no heed.

The boy galloped for a few steps to catch up. "You were talking about her in your sleep again last night. You mention her a lot more these days, never used to," he said, matter of factly.

Francis plunged his hands back between his armpits, trying to hug the warmth into the fabric of his body.

"Was she like my mummy?" Nate asked softly. He had picked up a small stick and was poking it into small muddy hillocks as they clomped forwards. The mist hung like a thick pair of net curtains around them.

"I never knew your mother," Francis sniffed. "Only spoke to her briefly, before, y'know, she turned. I can't honestly say if she was like her."

Nathan trotted forward to walk by the man's side. "I get scared some days, Francis."

Francis wilted slightly and looked down at the boy. "Scared of what, kid? I'm gonna look after you. Nothing is going to hurt you. I promise."

The boy gave a toothy grin. "I know, that doesn't scare me. I know you'll always look after me."

"Then what are you scared of, Nate?"

Nathan sighed and started to swish the stick into patches of rotting leaves. "That I'm going to forget her. Forget what she looks like, what she sounded like. When I go to sleep at night, I close my eyes really tight, so tight that they go all stingy sometimes. I lie there and I try to remember her face. She's all hazy, like looking through this fog."

Francis stopped and knelt down. "Hey kid, don't worry, come here." Nathan planted the stick into the ground like a flagless pole and sauntered across to the man.

"Close your eyes, Nate. Not too tight this time, okay. They closed? Not too tight?"

Nathan nodded wildly.

"Good, okay. I want you to think about your last birthday for me, okay? Think back to when all of this didn't exist. You there?"

The nod was more subdued.

"Okay, kid. So what did you get for your last birthday?"

The boy's eyes flickered under their lids, chasing the memory down like a cup trying to trap a rolling ball.

"I didn't get my presents until after school. Mummy had to work late sometimes, and that meant my Grandad had to look after me in the morning. I got back from school, and went into the dining room. Mummy was there with my Auntie Sue, Uncle Ken, and my cousins, Karen and Brian. Nanny and Grandad were there, too. They were all stood around a table where there was a cake with candles all glowing."

Francis placed his hands on Nathan's bony shoulders. The contact made the boy shudder slightly, before relaxing; his eyes, still closed, lazily looked around the memory he was back in.

"They all sang happy birthday to me, and then said I had to blow out the candles and make a wish. Mummy lifted me up and stood me up on the chair, and I started crying. I don't know why. Mummy hugged me and said 'don't cry, Nathan, for the wish you make today will come true, just keep it close and tell no one'. She smelt of cake and her skin felt so smooth and soft. I wiped the tears, made a wish and blew out the candles." As he finished, Nathan opened his eyes as if waking up for the first time that day. They were red and welling up with water.

"Hey kid, don't cry," Francis pulled him in tight and held him. He felt the boy shudder against him; muffled words intermingled with heavy sniffs rocked his body.

"What was that, Nate?"

Nathan withdrew from the embrace and rubbed his tear-laced eyes. "It didn't come true, my wish. I don't want any of this. I want my mummy to still be here."

"Kid, there is nothing I want more than for that to be the case, honest. But life now doesn't work that way. Hell, I don't even think it worked that way *before* all this happened. We've all lost someone, people so close to us that it hurts to think about them now. But we have to. We have to remember them. They are always alive as long as we remember them. Your mum, my Diane, it hurts like hell to think of them and that they're not here anymore, but we have to, okay?" Francis hugged Nathan again. Little arms held onto the man.

The forest held its breath; the mist matched the mood and lifted a little. "Thank you, Francis," Nathan said, before coughing up thick nasally phlegm. Francis nodded back in acknowledgement. "So her name was Diane?" the boy asked.

Francis smiled, just a crack. "Yes, her name was Diane, and she was my world, much like your mum was yours. I remember her. In my way. But some things are too painful to talk about, kid. You know what, I'll make you a deal."

"What's that?" Nathan asked, wiping his tears with his coat sleeve.

"When I dream of her again, I'll tell you what happened, okay? Some of it will be as difficult to hear as it is to say, but…" Francis reached into his pocket and pulled out a small crumpled packet of Polo mints, "by telling you, you can keep her alive too, in case anything happens to me, yeah?"

Nathan looked puzzled for a moment and then nodded. "You're not going to leave me are you?"

"I'm sure as hell not planning on it kid, but the world is all messed up these days. You never know what you're going to bump into next, eh?" Francis dropped a mint into the kid's hand and chucked one into the abyss of his own mouth. "Come on, let's get going."

An hour or so later and the fog lifted its skirt to reveal the lip of the forest. Standing atop a small hill, the pair looked out over more forest opposite and a strange sight below.

"What's that down there?" Nathan pointed to a Big Top sat in the crescent of a clearing; another long narrow tent ran off the back of it, disappearing into the woodland. A scattering of vehicles of various shapes and sizes were parked out front.

"Looks like a circus tent or something. Come on, let's go have a look, but be on the lookout okay?" Francis cautioned.

The pair carefully picked their way down the muddy embankment. Roots jutted out, forming straggly handholds which made the descent manageable. They dusted themselves off at the bottom and made their way through the assortment of parked cars and vans. In front of the entrance was a once white minibus, sprayed with mud and detritus. From behind the van they could see a small plume of smoke being cast into the air.

A man, dressed in a red morning jacket, remarkably white trousers, a bow tie and black riding boots stood with his back to them, Francis moved the boy behind him and coughed. The man spun around as if he was on a roulette wheel.

His face was the colour of milky tea. A thin waxed moustache curled around his nostrils. At first glance it looked like it had been drawn on with a fat marker pen. His black hair was slicked to one side, his eyes wide with surprise, the man's puckered mouth was clamped down on a cigarette.

Thin fingers extracted the cigarette, poise returned, and a wisp of smoke drifted from parted lips. "My, my, you gave me quite the fright," the man enunciated. He placed the cigarette to his lips once more and inhaled deeply. The cherry flared angrily and ate into the remainder of the stick, stopping as it met the border to the filter. It was flicked away, sent cartwheeling through the air like a flare, before landing in a muddy puddle, a mini moat around one of the tent moorings.

A hand reached behind his back and pulled out a velvet disc the size of a plate. With well-practised alacrity, he bowed and the disc expanded into a top hat with a loud PUFF. With a showman's deep bow, he donned the hat and stood up, one hand behind his back, the other straight forward, fingers splayed.

"Good day to you fair travellers. I bid thee welcome to this site of wonder and astonishment. Where you will witness such sights which you thought were never possible. Some have fainted as they crossed this very threshold, the mere thought of what lay beyond too much for their brains to comprehend. I give you…Trevor Norman's Penny Gaff." The man bent to one side, his arms displaying the entrance as if it were a giant, priceless vase.

"Erm, what now?" Francis asked. "Do you want money or something?"

The man sighed and sagged, disappointed. "No, good sir, money is of no use to man or beast these days. I provide entertainment and sustenance, for man cannot live on adventure alone, hmm?"

Nathan appeared from behind Francis' sizeable frame. "Is it a circus?" The words squeaked out of him.

"Pah!" the man scoffed. He did a little shanty which brought him closer to the pair. Francis instinctively reached for the baton in the bag webbing.

"This is no circus, young man. Pray tell, have you ever seen…a man who lives as a scorpion? Hands ending in claws, a tail, which yields no poison, but arches over him in the same manner as the skittering desert insect?" The man bowed over again, one arm extended to the tent entrance, the other across his chest.

"Have your innocent eyes even seen a boy who looks like a shark, a denizen of the deep, yet lives on land and plays just as you?"

Nathan shook his head vigorously, his eyes bulging with wonder. "No sir…"

The man stood up, hands clasped behind him, one eyebrow raised in an upside down V. "Then please, come with me, enter my Gaff, see such sights as these, and *more*, for we are mere entertainers trying to do what we can in these days. There is such sadness now, so much sorrow. We try to bring only joy. Why, a party has just entered, the show is about to begin, come, come, we have room for two more. You won't believe your eyes. I just need any weapons from your person…"

Francis stepped into the man's personal space. "Listen, slim, we're just passing through. We don't want to see your freakshow, now just mo—"

The man shrieked, "FREAK SHOW? How dare you, sir. HOW DARE YOU! Those that dwell within are no freaks, they are wonders, nay, they are *marvels*, do not denigrate their existence with such vulgarities."

"Woah, I don't mean no offence, pal. Just we're trying to get somewhere, and this isn't helping." Francis raised his hands in supplication. The man stroked out the ends of his moustache against his lip.

"But of course," he simpered, "this interlude will not take you long, an hour at most. We have food and drink for when the show is over. Please, it's all we have these days."

The man turned around and his body started to fall and rise. Francis realised he was sobbing. "Hey, I'm sorry. I didn't mean to hurt your feelings. Why not, sure, if it won't take long, we'd love to, hey kid?" Nathan nodded enthusiastically, gripping Francis' sleeve.

"Wonderful!" The man spun around and wiped a bulbous tear from his cheek. "Come, come, this way. This is Goliath, please be gentle. He lost his twin brother a few months back and has been mute ever since."

The man led them to a large flap which served as the entrance to the Big Top. A dwarf dressed as a clown held open one side. A chipped hand-painted enamel badge confirmed his identity as 'GOLIATH'. Though he was stationary, his body leaned forward unnaturally, as if he was an extra in the Smooth Criminal video.

As Francis and Nathan were ushered in, it looked like the dwarf tried to make a move to grab them, but one hand was firmly affixed to the opening. His shirt collar was pulled up over the bottom half of his face. "Is he—" Francis spluttered as he was hauled inside.

"He's fine. He will be, anyway. Just needs time to grieve. So many lost these days, eh? Come hither, the others will be eagerly waiting for the show to start. You won't want to miss a single second," the Ringmaster said smoothly, "I promise."

"Others?" Francis asked. "What others?"

"Good sir, I have just returned from a recce of the local area in my van. Saving the unfortunate souls within who were travelling on foot, or too weary to carry on. I offered them the same as you: sustenance, both of the body and soul. Come, come, you'll see that this is nothing more than altruism," the Ringmaster said enthusiastically, cajoling them through a draped entranceway.

The interior smelt of mouldy canvas, wet grass, mud and eucalyptus oil. The gloom wrapped around them like fumes from a chain smoker's living room.

"TAA-DAA," the ringmaster announced. A column of light bathed the pair, and they shielded their eyes with their hands. Like mice to a lump of cheddar, Nathan and Francis staggered from the murk and towards the chamber beyond.

As they left the tunnel, the heavy tarp was released and swished back into place, rendering the outside world a thing of myth. Francis took a few steps inside and looked around the arena.

At first glance, it didn't seem as big as he thought it would be. As a child, he had spent the best part of a school half-term holiday nagging his parents to take him to the circus. Five solid days of sulking and throwing tantrums resulted in them agreeing to the blackmail.

He had hated it.

The clowns scared him, the car they drove in seemed like a death-trap, the way it fell apart and honked like an angry sea lion. Trapeze artists only made him hide his face with sweaty, clammy hands, not bearing to see them crash to earth with no safety net to break their fall.

It was the animals he liked least of all. He'd seen many of them in a zoo and whilst they looked bored, the circus ones were bored and slightly odd looking.

Tufts of fur were missing from the lion and tiger; the elephant had a missing tusk and a mournful face which hinted at serial abuse. Francis spent the entire time whinging to his parents to go, but they were oblivious to his protestations and delighted in the spectacle of whimsy.

Ahead of him was a small walkway, enough for two people to walk down abreast. Four rows sprouted out from this, five chairs on each side, looking at the other spectators. He figured there would be more than enough room. He counted fourteen. A few groups stood apart from each other, eyeing up the establishment and muttering to each other.

As they trudged into the room, Francis noticed the floor was covered in a thick layer of sawdust. His guess was to counter the moisture seeping through the ground. The Big Top must've been here for a while. It wasn't as if there were many able bodied people left to pack everything up and go on a grand tour of the country.

Walking though it was like traipsing through thick snow; after a few steps, they both had to pick their feet up to make their way more easily into the high domed area. The sodium lamps overhead produced a gentle glow, bathing everything in an orange light. It also gave the flooring the appearance of popcorn, but with no sound effects.

The compere strode down the walkway effortlessly, seeming to glide over the thick uneven floor.

"Ladies and Gentlemen," he beseeched. Everyone turned and looked at their host.

"Thank you for accepting my humble offer, to experience the wonders of nature and appreciate the many varied forms of humanity. Please take a seat. Don't be shy, get yourself comfortable, for the show shall start shortly." He bowed deeply and turned to a raised wooden stage at the end of the chamber. A canvas skirt surrounded the entire area, but a pair of thick ruby curtains barred the way to the back.

"When we getting grub?" demanded a burly man, seemingly already well fed.

"Why, after the show my dear fellow, as promised. Please, take your seats ladies and gentlemen, I shall be but a moment." With a flourish, he flitted between the curtains and disappeared within.

The disorientated crowd shared puzzled glances before finding a seat and waiting for the performance to begin.

The lights fizzled out. A spotlight clicked on from behind the audience and fixed on a point in the middle of the curtains. A tannoy crackled into life, and a voice boomed out…

TREVOR NORMANS PENNY GAFF
PRESENTS
THE SCORPION KING

HAIL TO THE KING !
FROM THE NEW KINGDOM
TO THE UNITED KINGDOM

'LADIES AND GENTLEMEN, BOYS AND GIRLS, WELCOME TO TREVOR NORMAN'S PENNY GAFF. HERE YOU WILL BE DAZZLED BY SIGHTS YOU'VE NEVER WITNESSED. ASTOUNDED BY THE POSSIBILITY OF HOW HUMANITY'S TEMPLATE CAN BE ALTERED. SHAKEN TO YOUR VERY CORE BY THE MALEVOLENCE OF NATURE.

OUR FIRST WONDER IS CALLED THE SCORPION KING. RAISED ON THE BANKS OF THE RIVER NILE, HE WAS SHUNNED BY HIS VILLAGE, BUT SAVED FROM AN UNCARING ORPHANAGE BY MY FATHER. HIS HANDS ARE SNAPPING CLAWS, WHILST HIS VESTIGIAL COLUMN BOWS OVER LIKE A SCORPION'S TAIL.

BE NOT AFRAID, FOR HE CANNOT STING YOU. BOW DOWN AND PRAISE... THE SCORPION KING, FOR HE IS HUNGRY.

FOR YOUR FLESH.'

The audience shuffled uncomfortably and looked at each other. Puzzled faces shook at the sheer preposterousness of the words. There was a loud clang from behind the curtains. The spotlight's beam widened to take in the whole of the stage. Following a ripple of awkward applause, the curtains parted…

The crowd collectively held their breaths. The sound of their hearts pounding in their heads the only thing they could feel. From beyond the curtains, there was only blackness, a fetid smell of decay, halitosis and damp meat. It was as though they had been transported to the outside of a fast food sandwich shop.

From the nothingness came a shuffling of boots, scuffing dusty divots into the floor. Two fleshy hands, formed into claws, pierced the void. Eyes recoiled at the appearance of fingers fused together and smoothed into larger parodies of the vile repugnance of nature. As rag covered legs strode uneasily into the ring of light, a now familiar sound rumbled from the innards of the approaching being.

A low baritone moan, which every single person in the room had become somewhat accustomed to over the past nine months of living in the apocalypse, covered them like margarine.

The margarine of the UNDEAD.

Not available in shops or via stockists.

"Everyone. Get back," shouted Francis, instinctively shoving Nathan behind him. The Scorpion King staggered into full view. His torso was bared, showing lines of ridged scar tissue running from his shoulders down towards his groin where they disappeared from sight behind his feculent trousers. They looked like thick black leather braces.

His arms were badly atrophied; flaps of grey skin hung from his humerus like carrier bags fished out of a canal. As he stumbled forwards they swung like half-filled water balloons. The claws themselves snapped idly. There was no visible thumb or stump where one had ever been, just the top and bottom two fingers stuck together and bound by skin covered Clingfilm.

Another moan rolled out and smothered the audience. A goatee formed from the crust of dried blood, surrounded rows of broken teeth. The Scorpion King convulsed causing a chunk of blackened meat to fall from his maw and plop onto the floor. The familiar black-flecked eyes scoured the panicked masses in front of him. What was left of his curtained hair stuck to his grey forehead through dried bone marrow and spinal fluid.

One of the punters in the front row was watching agape at the dead monster thudding its way towards him. He had straggly brown hair, and a bushy beard, dressed only in a 'Kleptophobia – Cow Circus' t-shirt, once black combat trousers and a pair of hiking boots.

The Scorpion King stepped off the stage area, and while everyone else in the tent was trying to find a way out, or back away from the monstrosity, Beardy sat there, catching flies. A claw snapped and clamped onto his neck. Finally in the here and now, he squeezed his hands around the strangling appendage and started to thump it.

Seemingly displeased with the show of rebellion, The Scorpion King pulled the man up and out of his seat. Despite his arms being nothing but bone, pooled blood, and decaying muscle, the man was hauled up to the King's face with as much effort as it takes to roll your eyes at a My Chemical Romance video.

Beardy pawed at the King's face, trying to make him cease and desist. The Scorpion

King pulled him in and took a bite out of his face. As he tore away, the man's head pinged backwards, his upper lip, nose and skin up to the bags under his eyes had been ripped away. Masticating on Beardy's face, the man started pleading. With no top half of his face, flecks of blood and spit were sprayed over the monster's face.

Annoyed with the facial hair which ruined the first bite, and the liquid he was being covered in, The Scorpion King brought his free arm across at a clip, smacking into the man's head. Between the impact and the vicelike grip, his neck snapped like a Cadbury's Flake and the body fell limp in the clawed grasp.

Regarding the flaccid body impassively, The Scorpion King dug his teeth into the exposed throat, ripping out the jugular and sending an arc of blood over the first two rows. He chewed it lazily, staring blankly at the bedlam in front of him.

"It won't open, it won't open!" a woman with stick dry hair and a tie-dye dress shrieked as she tried to open the thick canvas flap which led back out to the entrance walkway.

"You're trying in the wrong place, Shirley!" shouted a man wearing a leather jacket and flared trousers. The mullet gave him the air that he had been born into the wrong decade. "The entrance was over here." He frantically heaved the draped fabric to one side, only to find a second skin beyond, a thick material membrane which looked waterproof and idiot-proof.

The Scorpion King had worked its way through the meat of the neck, and was now covered in a thick, red soup of blood. Beardy's head, complete with death throe scream, fell to one side. With no foundations to support it, the skull rolled around in the claw so that dead, mad, startled eyes were looking out over his own back and into the screaming masses.

With a slurping tearing sound very much like a plaster being pulled off a pus-filled wound, the head detached from the neck and hit the floor, rolling around like the worst marble ever. Displaying a dexterity its dead shambling form could never hint at, The Scorpion King rooted around in the remnants of the throat with its free claw, fishing out delectable morsels and tidbits. When it was satisfied, it tipped the body up like a fleshy goblet and drank from the ruin of Beardy's neck.

The still-twitching body landed on the floor and on top of its previously attached head with a dull thud. The Scorpion King ran its blood-stained claws across its mouth, and, remarkably, let out a burp.

The screaming stopped, and the audience once more looked to the stage. The Scorpion King belched once more and then, as a follow through, regurgitated the freshly chewed remains of its appetiser over the body whence it came.

Following this thoroughly disgusting sight, the wailing and gnashing of teeth resumed. Mullet Man was now by the stage, though in-between the tent and the outer shell, feeling around for some way to freedom. The Scorpion King caught a flash of movement and trudged over to it, coming to a standstill before a bulge in the auditorium's wall.

"Hey everyone, I think I—"

A pummelling claw lashed out at the lump and the words ceased. Like a boxer working a speed ball, The Scorpion King flailed at the protrusion over and over again. Words turned into mumblings, and then into half-hearted protestations. The wall sagged into the room as Mullet Man lapsed into unconsciousness.

After more wild thrashings, The Scorpion King stopped and looked at the deformed wall in front of it. Bending down, it grabbed hold of a foot which had slipped out of the bottom of the canvas. Mullet Man got stuck at the knee, and rather than delicately teasing out the next dish in feeding time, The Scorpion King moaned angrily and lifted the leg up.

One stomach-turning crack later and the leg now bent upwards. The Scorpion King started to twist the bottom half of the leg round like it was a tough wine cork. Like a cheap Beaujolais, the leg popped and the beast turned the half a leg around in its claws.

The rag which was the trouser leg slipped off the leg and fluttered to the floor. The Scorpion King began to work its way up and down the leg, as if it were a chicken drumstick. The body behind the canvas slipped out and landed on the floor in a heap.

Tossing the meat shorn tibia towards the cooling corpse of meal number one, the beast knelt down by the unconscious man and sized up where to begin. Its claws chattered in anticipation.

A woman in her early thirties, with shoulder length blonde hair, picked up a chair and tiptoed over to the hunched figure. Members of a nearby group were hissing at her to stop; like an irate snake, she paid them no heed.

Francis turned to Nate. "Stay behind this chair, kid. Whatever you do, whatever you see and no matter what happens, do not move from here until I come get you, am I clear?"

The child nodded slowly, entranced by the grisly sight just outside of the spotlight's glow.

The woman flinched as Francis placed a steady hand on her shoulder. Her initial get up and go had got up and gone; she still clutched the chair as if it was mooring her to reality.

"Hey, we can get it together," Francis said calmly. "How about you go over there and distract him, and I'll...y'know."

A furious nod from the woman reignited her killer instinct. She crept around in a circuitous route. As she made her way round, Francis picked up a chair and edged towards the abnormality.

Mullet Man had gone from unconscious to barely breathing. The Scorpion King had torn away the leather jacket like an irritating chocolate wrapper and had breached the ribcage. Its claws latched onto organs like a fat pair of chopsticks. A piece of liver slipped through its grasp and was ingested back into the body.

As Francis got closer, he could see the vestigial column which elevated Mr Scorpion King to a cooler name than Lobster Man. A hole in the back of its trousers, just above his exit-hole, had been cut and a hem stitched, for comfort, in better times. The tail curled out and over its spine. It was completely covered in grey skin with black and purple roads criss-crossing underneath. It seemed to be immovable and didn't flex or waver.

"Hey, numbnuts!" The woman's shouting tore Francis' gaze away from the bizarre sight. The Scorpion King, who had a mouthful of lung, looked across at its rather rude dinner guest. Francis seized the opportunity and charged at it from the rear, trying to bring the chair down onto its skull, to finish it off nice and quickly.

A howl akin to a chimpanzee touching an electric fence crashed through everyone like an amp turned up to non-conforming Health and Safety limits. The strike had not connected with the head, but struck the tail, causing the tip to buckle like a bendy straw.

The Scorpion King's eyes rolled in its head, and the lung dropped from its mouth and splatted against Mullet Man's ashen face, giving him the appearance of an entrant in an Uruk-hai beauty pageant. A banshee cry surpassed even the noise made by the zombified freak as the woman charged from the other side, brandishing a chair like a WWE pro.

The metal back smacked into The Scorpion King's face, causing a tide of teeth, tongue, skin and chewed organ to erupt from its face. The woman stood by its kneeling form and delivered a fearsome forehand blow, sending the beast backwards. Another blood-curdling howl with the mother of all cracking sounds sent The Scorpion King flat onto its back.

Taking his cue from the woman's impressive chair work, Francis slung his chair to one side and launched himself through the air towards the fallen freak. Executing the perfect elbow drop, he caught The Scorpion King right on the throat. The force snapped its head against the floor, and as Francis landed, The Scorpion King's tail burst through its body, shattering bone and spraying purge fluids over Francis through his nose and mouth.

Claws scraped across the saw dust, trying to find purchase to fight onwards.

The woman stood astride The Scorpion King's head, with a "You were a shit film," she brought the chair leg down through its skull. The misshapen hands tapped each other gently and were then still.

The spotlight contracted. A clang sounded and the curtains fell, covering the rear area where the monster had come from. The tannoy sparked and crackled into life again…

TREVOR NORMANS PENNY GAFF
PRESENTS
DAISY AND VIOLEY QUEENSBURY
THE UNITED TWINS

THEY SING ! THEY DANCE !
DOUBLE THE ENTERTAINMENT
DOUBLE THE WONDER

IN FOR A PENNY...

'GRRR. HOW COULD YOU? HE WAS MY FATHER'S FAVOURITE. HE NEVER DID ANYONE ANY HARM. WELL NOT UNTIL HE BECAME ONE OF THEM ANYWAY. FINE. IF THAT'S HOW YOU WANT TO PLAY IT.

LADIES AND GENTLEMEN. BOYS AND GIRLS, OUR NEXT ACT COMES FROM BRIGHTON. THEY WERE BORN JOINED TOGETHER. THEY SHARE EVERYTHING. ALL THEY EVER NEEDED WAS EACH OTHER.

WITH TWO HEADS, FOUR ARMS AND FOUR LEGS, THEY USED TO KNOW HOW TO CUT THE RUG. WITH THEIR LOOKS, THEY HAVE TEMPTED MANY A SHOWGOER TO SHOWER THEM WITH MONEY AND JEWELS.

I GIVE YOU DAISY AND VIOLET QUEENSBURY.

THE UNITED TWINS.

THOUGH NOWADAYS, THEY MOVE IN QUITE MYSTERIOUS WAYS.'

"Quick, people, look around for how to get out of here. There has to be a way," Francis shouted, picking himself up and wiping gobbets of rank flesh from his face, and picking stringy pieces of tendon off his jumper.

"Hugh was looking for it, now look at him," a hysterical woman in her early forties shouted. "Is he still alive? Is my Hugh still alive?" The tie-dyed woman scurried along the sawdust drift and to Hugh. When she saw that most of his insides were now externally facing she let out a keening scream.

She stroked his blood-flecked hand, trying to ignore the assortment of organs which had been pulled from their storage. The spotlight flared once more; a loud clang rang through the captive audience.

Everyone turned to the stage as the heavy curtains peeled apart. From the abyss came two peculiar and opposite sounds.

The most noticeable was a solid slapping, the sound of flesh patting against wood. It was at a steady pace. Every fourth beat, though, was a clicking sound, like a pen nib striking a Formica desk.

The onlookers gulped as one. Birthed from the black chasm was a moaning in stereo. Eyes darted from the top of the gloom where they expected to see someone, or some*thing*, to the bottom, where two heads appeared. Lank hair hung like flex-covered wire, brushed over two grey faces, each the mirror image of the other, even in death.

The slapping and clicking picked up in pace as the prospect of a feeding became a reality. The Twins scuttled out on all fours like a giant, dead, two-headed zombie spider. Rags of fabric were wrapped round their bodies as if they were Egyptian mummies. The heads looked around independently of each other, eyeing up different people for consumption. Jaws snapped in anticipation.

Traversing the ground with no trouble at all, they scurried towards a group of three people. Yvonne and Terry Muller, both school teachers before the world went to crap, and their only child, Elizabeth Muller, ten and a half, who hid behind her dad. She glanced out at the abomination that stalked towards them on deformed human hands and feet.

One pair of hands and all of their feet were as expected, ending in familiar fingers and toes. The months of giving up the double bipedal life they had previously led had reformed their arms and legs to better support their new form.

As they rested, the conjoined twins sat on their legs like a dog crouching in the park, ready to lay a bag filler. This gave Daisy and Violet the opportunity to survey the area and work out what they fancied eating first.

The Mullers were top of that list.

With the slapping sound explained away, Francis and the others looked closer at the arachno-zombie as it inched towards the cornered family. The front pair of hands, which had borne the brunt of crawling around, had not fared well. The hands were missing, and the skin on their forearms was scoured away. Sharp triangular bone now served as crude stabbing implements.

It was with these that Terry Muller met his demise. Enthralled and repelled by the sashaying creature, he did nothing but four things:

The first was to emit a high pitched "'Huh?"

The second was to release the tension building against his bladder wall and create a puddle beneath him and his family. Nothing says I love you quite like a pool of piss.

Number three was equally useless as he raised his hands to defend himself from the incoming nightmare.

The fourth was to scream like a cricketer struck in the unmentionables without a box as a bone incisor stabbed him through the shoulder and down into his innards.

The force of the blow sent Daisy's pokey arm from top to bottom, coming out through Terry's left arse cheek. As she struggled to heave herself free, a trickle of blood and flesh became a torrent escaping through the hole. A look of exquisite horror plastered Terry's face as he collapsed to the floor; ichor was pumped out of the top and bottom holes as if he was a sachet of ketchup which had been squeezed in the middle.

Yvonne instinctively threw herself over her daughter. Violet raised her front arm and brought it down violently, and a shaft of savage bone cleaved through mother and daughter like a javelin through a misplaced watermelon.

Pinned to the floor, Yvonne screamed in agony, inches away from her husband who lay motionless on the floor. His face shuddered as Daisy thrust her arm blade into him again. A runnel of blood ran from his nose. Daisy bent her elbow and hooked the body. Tucking the arm towards their dual body, the lifeless corpse of Terry was reeled in.

As the corpse was carried towards their bosom he was slung within reach. With Violet still piercing the two women, their two heads leant down as one and started to tear at the hole created in his shoulder.

Unsatisfied with the first bite, Daisy snapped at Violet which caused the free arm to stab into Terry's back repeatedly, rending the skin from the bone and enabling the pair of heads to reach in and tear chunks of still-warm meat straight off the carcass.

Francis pointed in the direction they had all come into the arena. "You lot, start looking over there for a way out, *now*, or we are not going to get out of this. Blondie, you're with me." The woman released the chair which was still embedded within The Scorpion King's head. Black sludge had been forced out of the breach and ran off its face like a fat drunken worm.

Spectators who were not completely catatonic with fear ran to the entrance, trying to find a way out. Like Hugh, they came to a waterproof membrane which seemed to surround them like an Auntie's embrace. "I can't find a gap," a man shouted desperately; fingers scratched and pulled at the fabric, but made no indent or mark of egress.

"Keep trying," Francis shouted, as he and the blonde woman ran over to the stricken Mullers. As they passed Nathan, Francis glared at him to remain where he was. It was clear that the kid wasn't going anywhere.

Daisy and Violet tore and chewed their way through Terry's body. The left side of his torso and arm had all of the skin peeled off like an avocado. It lay to one side, curling up with nothing to hold onto. As they fed, their appendages twitched and pulsed. Each tremor made Yvonne and Elizabeth whimper in pain.

Having become bored of the body, the sisters wanted to sample some of the head before moving onto the next course. The claw tapped on Terry's skull as if it were a coconut. Trying to find a suitable point of entry, the bone rapped on his temple feverishly, and with one deft blow split his head open like a Chocolate Orange.

The skull pan cracked in four directions and the brain in two. A build-up of nasal mucus ran over the pink brain matter, covering it in a natural mustard. Its consistency was thick and it took a few seconds to cover the cerebral meat in a yellowy glaze. Using the claw like a hook, Daisy dragged Terry's body further beneath them, straddling him. The two heads bent over and started to devour the soft squishy ribbed meat.

Francis threw himself onto the broad back of the twins. The filthy bandages they were wrapped in were slick with dew and grime from their confinement. Brandishing the extended baton, he rode out the initial bucking and started to crack Daisy over the head.

Desperate to avoid being hit, the sisters started to shimmy wildly, unable to reach behind and grab the offender. As the front claws slashed blindly, they caught Yvonne and Elizabeth again and again. Blondie also jumped onto the twins' back, which caused them to finally collapse. Nodding to Francis, she linked her hands under Violet's throat, whilst Francis did the same with his baton under Daisy. "On three!" she shouted.

On the count of three, the pair pulled and rolled to one side. The momentum, and attempts by the sisters to lift themselves up, caused them all to lurch to one side. With Francis and the woman trapped underneath, the twins' arms and legs flailed and shadow-boxed aimlessly in the air. Francis grunted and, using his knees and forearms, bore the weight of the zombie spider. Blondie pulled herself free, taking care not to come within range of the pointy appendages.

Administering a few more blows to Daisy's skull, the last of which created a loud crack, Francis shimmied his way out. Taking a few steps back to get out of range, the pair looked down at the United Twins.

The filthy wrapping made both of the twins' bodies meld into one. Grey limbs floundered above their heads and body. Daisy's head had a flap of skull hanging loose. Francis delivered a quick punt which caused a cave in; black and grey sludge oozed from the smashed skull and Daisy started to convulse gently, teeth chewing the air.

As she died for the second time, the limbs down her side began to contract, like a spider in its death throes. The necrotic arms and legs closed in on the body. As Violet swung around, trying to work out what was happening, Daisy's jagged arm pressed against her searching head, catching her in the eye socket.

Violet instinctively snapped her limbs, which smacked Daisy's palsied arm through the eye socket and through the skull. Violet's head slipped off the spear and came to a rest against her sister's. The arms and legs on both sides pulled inwards and the pair died cheek to cheek.

Francis heaved Yvonne off Elizabeth and lay her next to her daughter. Yvonne was gone. In the frenzy she had been stabbed through the heart, killing her instantly. Elizabeth was no better off; her chest rose and fell sharply. She tried to speak but could only spit out bubbles of blood. Her eyes rolled upwards and she was no more.

Blondie put a hand on Francis' shoulder. "Hey, we did what we could, let's—"

From the other side of the arena, a woman screamed. Francis and Blondie looked across to see Hugh was sitting up. This time, though, he was the one who was eating.

His wife Shirley had been lying on his chest when he was reborn. In the process of sitting up, the half-chewed pieces of offal rolled off his clothing and onto the floor. Hugh's hand closed round his wife's hair. Holding her head like a toffee apple, he started to rip pieces of her face off in long ragged strips.

Francis bounded across to Hugh and coshed him around the head with the baton. His head rocked viciously to one side and a piece of his wife's face hit the canvas and stuck there momentarily, before slowly sliding down like a flesh slug.

Standing over him and with one foot on Hugh's throat, Francis repeatedly applied the baton to the zombie's head, until all that remained was a red lumpy paste and broken plate-like pieces of skull.

Shirley lay to one side. Her breathing was shallow; her face a mix of normality, red raw sinew, and lumps of crimson tissue. Francis picked up her husband's headless corpse and draped it over her legs, creating a ballast to hinder her movement, should she expire and follow her husband into zombiedom.

Standing in a swamp of gore he looked across to Blondie, who snapped off a chair leg, creating a metal shank. She caught his glance as she solemnly tipped the Muller women's heads forwards and drove the jagged piece of metal into their brains. As she stood up after Elizabeth, tears streaked down her face. Francis walked back to Blondie and pulled her into an embrace, trying to squeeze the sorrow from her every pore.

The curtains fell, the spotlight constricted like an iris having a torch shone into it and the tannoy fizzed into life once more…

TREVOR NORMANS PENNY GAFF

PRESENTS

SHARK BOY

HE IS DROP DEAD GORJAWS
THE DEADLIEST OF LAND PREDATORS
A MENACE IN A PADDLING POOL

'NOOOOO, NOT DAISY, NOT MY DAISY...YOU WILL ALL PAY FOR THIS. SHE WAS THE LIGHT OF MY LIFE. HOW DARE YOU TAKE HER AWAY FROM ME. WE USED TO HAVE TO DRUG VIOLET SO WE COULD BE TOGETHER.

YOU WILL ALL DIE!

LADIES AND GENTLEMEN, BOYS AND GIRLS, YOU TEST MY PATIENCE. I PICKED YOU ALL UP TO FEED MY MENAGERIE NOT TO KILL IT. WE HAD DREAMS YOU KNOW. DREAMS! AND THIS IS WHAT WE GET?

WELL, LET ME INTRODUCE YOU TO...SHARK BOY. HIS BACK IS DEFORMED WITH A FORBIDDING FIN, BUT IT'S HIS MOUTH YOU BETTER WATCH OUT FOR.

LINED WITH RAZOR SHARP TEETH, AND A KILLER'S INSTINCT, YOU WON'T NEED A BIGGER BOAT.

YOU JUST NEED TO DIE.'

"Thank you," Blondie whispered into Francis' ear. She wiped the tears onto her sleeve. Francis smudged his with the palm of his hand.

"Do me a favour, before the next act is released. We need to find a way out of here. Everyone else is not capable of dealing with them. See if you can use that and cut us a way out of here." Francis thumbed towards the gore-soaked metal spike. Blondie nodded and jogged to the back of the tent. She pushed people out of the way and started to try and cut her way through the inner shell and to freedom.

A wavering voice screeched from one side of the big top. "Mister Man, I think something's coming out for their noon feeding." The spotlight widened once more; the curtains were pulled up like an elegant dress in a curtsy, and a clang rang from the void beyond.

Francis walked to the middle of the chamber, pushing chairs out of the way, trying to make barricades for the remaining survivors. "You, keep a watch on her. If she turns, shout, okay?" he shouted at a man in his mid-twenties. He nodded slowly and edged his way around the blood-splattered tent to one side of the flourishing abattoir.

"What the…" a woman's voice trailed off. Francis looked for the source and saw a lady standing guard over an elderly couple and their carer. She held an umbrella like a club, and was transfixed by something emerging from the far end.

A wail was the first thing that signalled the arrival of the next zombified freak, followed by an extended upper mouth. It was like someone had opened up the head, stuck half a dinner plate in above the upper gum, stretched the skin over it and then sewn it shut. Below the growth was a large, tooth-filled maw; each one glistened in the light. It had no nose to speak of, save for two holes at the prow of the face.

Trading Standards could've received complaints from people about the term, 'Shark Boy', as the thing that stumbled out was anything but.

Francis estimated he must've been in his late teens when he added one to the zombie total column. His once muscly frame had withered since reanimation, but he still lumbered out with purpose and poise. His jaw never stayed closed, snapping and clacking at the array of food on offer.

Francis braced himself, picking chunks of matter off the baton. Before he had a chance to finish, an almighty yell drowned out the chattering of Shark Boy's jaws.

"Have this you wee bastard," the woman shouted, admonishing the beast with the closed umbrella. The woman was a blur of activity, weaving this way and that. No sooner had she twatted him from one side, she would duck under his lazy grab and attack him from the rear.

She had just manoeuvred herself back to the front and was trying to ram the pointy bit into one of his nostrils when her wards were showered with arterial spray.

The umbrella landed on the floor in a puff of sawdust, quickly followed by her arm, severed at the shoulder. The woman shrieked like a hedgehog on date night and clamped her free hand over the stump where she now had half an armpit and an unwelcome blood fountain feature.

Shark Boy grabbed her around the waist with both hands, tilting her towards him. He leant in and took a gargantuan bite. Shaking like a dog with a length of knotted roped, he yanked the woman's head off in one go.

Passing the severed noggin to the back of his mouth, he ground her skull with the pressure of a millstone. After a few solid crunches, he tipped his head back and swallowed the remnants of her bonce in one.

With his hands still clamped round her waist, it looked for all the world as if he was learning the cha-cha-cha with a headless mannequin. Though this dummy had a pulsating stream of blood being pumped out of the place the throat should be. Shark Boy, bored with his dancing partner's lack of finesse, released her and the body fell to the floor, the sawdust absorbing the abating liquid.

The monster trudged towards the elderly couple, Cyril and Tabitha Talbot of Eastbourne. They had survived to date through blind luck, a locked caravan, and Tabitha's food hoarding instincts. They had only ventured outside when their supply of butter beans and potato flakes had finally expired.

Promised sanctuary and a slap-up meal, they, along with Dana, their carer, and Harriet, the now headless woman, had accepted eagerly. The road was not the place to be for two old people who had the combined total of one birth hip between them.

Dana moved behind the couple, shouting, "Take them, take them, they're old and knackered, don't eat me Mr Shark, please don't eat me!" Once behind the octogenarians, she started to push them forwards, towards the thresher-like jaws of Shark Boy.

The monster grabbed one of the chairs that were barring entrance to his follow-up serving of skull. Between his dragging and Dana's eagerness to offer up the people whose arse's she had spent the last two years wiping, the way ahead cleared quickly.

Francis waded through the sawdust and tonked Shark Boy on the head. The beast looked around at his attacker; even bereft of emotional reflection, he looked a little miffed.

Swirling like an elastic band whirly thing, Shark Boy roundhoused Francis and sent him to the floor. In two minds, he turned back, his impulse telling him that two behind the chairs was worth one in the sawdust.

His jaw cranked open again. Lines of insanely sharp, blood-rimmed teeth loomed towards Cyril. Dana let out an almighty scream. Time slowed down as Shark Boy moved in for the kill. Falling back on his basic training for the Suez crisis, Cyril thumped the abomination right on the snout.

The monster reeled backwards, howling with primal anger. Dana, having finally grown a pair, shoved the old folks aside and went to seize the initiative.

"Hit 'im on the nose, kid. Sharks don't like it too much if you hit 'em on the nose," Cyril rasped through the upper set of his false teeth; the bottom half were currently on loan with his good lady wife.

Dana rolled up her sleeves and advanced on the zombie. It was stumbling backwards, yowling and bawling. "You stay away from them, you...you...you nasty man." She wound back her arm and let fly a fearsome right hook. Shark Boy had recovered from the blow. In truth, Cyril's jab had merely pissed off the few remaining impulses he had left.

As Dana's fist flew towards his face, he simply jacked open his jaw further still. She missed his nose and connected, tamely, with the rotting uvula at the back of his throat.

Shark Boy simultaneously bit down on her arm and vomited pieces of jaw and brain matter through his nose. Dana screamed, squeezing her arm, which was now missing the bit after the elbow, and covered in a viscous film of Harriet. Before she could try and break the world screaming record, the monster gorged himself on the top of her body.

His jaws locked around her shoulders. The scream still echoed within his vast mouth and emerged out of his wet nostrils.

He shook his prize like an eager apple bobber and her head and shoulders separated from the rest of her body. This collapsed with a dull thud onto the floor, adding yet more lashings of blood into the now soaked wood dandruff.

Shark Boy crunched his way through the mouthful he had torn off, the scream finally dissipating with a gurgle. A few chomps later and he again gulped back his catch of the day. Tabitha collapsed under the stress. Cyril knelt down and tried to pick up her skeletal frame. She felt like a lead weight in his hands. He managed to pick his wife up only for her to slip from his grasp.

Tabitha's unconscious body fell onto a chair, sending her and the seat careening over onto the stodgy floor. Cyril could feel that his back was wet. Slapping his hands around behind him, he felt nuggets of enamel and gum clamped around his waist. All of a sudden he felt a whoosh of air, and then he felt lighter.

For the first time in years, he could see properly; the indistinct details which he had long since given up on seeing now jumped into focus. He could make out the intricate hem on Tabitha's petticoat, the grooves in the chair leg, the plush faux velvet cushion, stitched with a golden thread. He chuckled in wonder and awe as he made out the bulge in the back of his trouser pocket where he always kept his wallet.

Wait a minute.

How was he seeing his trouser-encased butt cheeks unless…? Looking down, his suspicions were confirmed as he saw the teeth embedded in his guts. "Oh bugger," he muttered as Shark Boy tilted his head back and tipped the top half of Cyril into his mouth. He crunched down on him and felt the eighty-one-year-old matured meat slip down his gullet.

Francis pulled himself to his feet. His legs felt like he'd been doing the running in an eighties training montage. He saw the zombie freak tip back what was left of the old man into its gob.

Shaking away the grogginess, he girded himself and thought back to his school days. Ignoring 98% of it, he launched himself at the monster with a rugby tackle, catching him in the sweet spot at the back of the knees, he tumbled onto the monster's back.

The meeting of head against floor, whilst halfway through swallowing, was not the best thing. Half-chewed old man was spat out, covering Tabitha with her husband's squashed head and broken mangled arms.

Francis was overcome with pent-up aggression. Nine month's worth of biting his tongue and patience washed away as he started to pummel the back of the beast's head.

Divots of skin and flesh were gouged away with furious and frantic flaying. Through the grey skin, lined with coagulated blood-filled veins, he saw the shiny white of bone. Pressing fingers into the decomposing muscle and tissue of the neck, he reached in and grabbed hold of the spinal column, just below the skull.

With one hand pushing down on the neck bone, his other hand slipped up into the base of Shark Boy's skull. The beast began to shake and shriek, sensing that the invading things in its head should not be there. Pushing through chunks of gristle and nobs of bone, Francis felt a bobbly ridge of something that felt like a pastry-less pork pie. He squeezed his hand and pulled and clawed away at the brain. Shark Boy went up and down the octaves like a schoolboy learning the oboe.

Pushing the neck bone down further, Francis started to grab fistfuls of decaying encephalon and threw it behind him. To the casual observer, it looked like this madman had misplaced something inside the zombie freak's skull, possibly his watch, and was frantically trying to find it amongst reams of that weird Quaver-like packing material you get with electronic equipment.

Shark Boy's extremities quaked as if low-voltage electricity was coursing through them. Still, Francis pulled clumps of grey chunks of brain out. The twitching stopped and Francis mirrored the movement by ceasing his cranial assault. Panting with a surge of adrenalin, he looked over his hands.

As he studied the pieces of brain under his fingernails, he heard a munching sound. Looking over to the unconscious old woman, he saw the severed mangled head of her husband chewing through the back of her calf. A jet of blood flew through the air and added a swish to the messy puddle which had already formed. Francis jumped up and took Cyril's head on the half-volley, sending it through the air where it disappeared into the vacuum beyond the stage.

Like an alligator at feeding time, the curtains snapped shut and the spotlight concentrated its gaze again. Francis checked Tabitha's pulse. It was still strong, but time was not on his side. He pulled the belt from Cyril's trousers and lashed it around her leg as a tourniquet. He put her in the recovery position and dropped what was left of the old lady's carer over her legs.

Just in case.

"I'm nearly through," shouted Blondie. Francis checked Tabitha's pulse one last time and headed over to where the woman was.

"What the hell is this stuff?" Francis asked, trying to make the hole in the membrane wider.

Blondie wiped the sweat from her brow. "No idea, but it's one tough bastard."

Francis nodded. "Look, I can't keep referring to you as Blondie, or 'woman number three'. I'm Francis, you are?"

"I'm Zena," she said, picking the hair off her forehead, "and before you say anything, do not even ask if I'm a warrior princess, or I will fucking end you."

Francis chuckled. "No problem, sister. You carry on with that, I'm gonna get Nate, and we can—"

A burst of static belched from the PA system, the tannoy clicked and spat into life once more…

TREVOR NORMANS PENNY GAFF

PRESENTS

PEARL 'PRAYING' MANTICE

SAY NO TO A HUG !
ELEGANT, REFINED, A REAL LADY
MAKE SURE SHE DOESN T BUG YOU

'HE WAS AN ENDANGERED SPECIES. HOW COULD YOU DO THAT? WHEN FATHER FOUND HIM, HE WAS EATING SCRAPS OUT OF BINS BEHIND LA COSTINA. MAYBE THE ODD DOG OR CAT HERE OR THERE,

BUT HE WAS GOOD PEOPLE, MISUNDERSTOOD.

AND YOU COME IN HERE, AND YOU CARRY OUT THE CRUDEST OF LOBOTOMIES. I HATE YOU. WHY DON'T YOU PEOPLE JUST ADMIT THE TRUTH AND DIE ALREADY?

FINE. I NORMALLY SAVE PEARL FOR LARGER GROUPS, BUT YOU'VE LEFT ME NO CHOICE.

PEARL MANTICE WAS A REAL HIT WITH THE MENFOLK. BY THE TIME THEY FOUND OUT ABOUT HER AFFLICTION, IT WAS TOO LATE. I SAVED HER FROM INVESTIGATION.

HOWEVER, SINCE SHE CHANGED, WELL...LET'S SAY OLD HABITS DIE HARD.

UNLIKE YOU, YOU WILL ALL DIE EASY. LADIES AND GENTLEMEN, BOYS AND GIRLS, I GIVE YOU THE PRAYING MANTIS!'

"For the love of…" Francis moaned. He looked across to the chair corral on the other side of the Big Top. Two men stood wearily behind the flimsy barricade; an older woman cowered behind them. It was located between the remains of Hugh and Shirley and the hole that Zena was trying to make.

Francis bounded over to them. "Hey, guys, look. We have no idea how many more freaks of nature our host has for us. We have to work together now, or we're all going to end up like these poor souls." A wiry arm swept around the blood-stained circle of death that they were all inhabitants of, as if the point needed further labouring.

One of the men stood forward. He was tall and thin; a San Andreas baseball cap kept a mop of greasy hair in check. "Man, me and Chris here, we ain't fighters. We're just looking after our mum, ya hear? She's all we got left now," he stammered.

Francis placed a conciliatory hand on his shoulder. "Slim, look, let me lay this out to you. Everyone else in this chamber is either dead or dying. If you don't help now, then you, your brother, *and* your mum are going to die."

Chris comforted his mother and took a step forward so that he was standing by the other man's side. He was the same height, but his metabolism worked a little slower, adding a bit of filler to his frame. "Okay, pal. Me and Russ can help out, but we're not leaving our mum, deal?" He offered a hand to Francis who gratefully shook it.

"Good choice, pilgrim. I've got a plan. Zena is trying to get out the way we come in, but I got a sneaky feeling our friend here hasn't made it that easy. I'm going to see what lies beyond there." Francis nodded towards the parted curtains. "Don't point, don't point, there's a camera on the rail, he's watching us. I'm going to have to sneak around the side and under it to avoid him seeing me, which means…"

Russ pulled his cap off by its peak and ran his fingers through his slick hair. "You need us to keep this Praying Mantis busy, huh?"

Francis nodded glumly. "Afraid so, slim. You've seen pictures of lion tamers, yeah? Grab some chairs, keep her attention on you and keep her at bay. Hopefully that'll give me or Zena enough time to get us all a way out of here. Nathan, come here."

The child scampered across the ring to Francis. "Nate, this is Chris, Russ and their mum. I want you to stay with them, okay? They'll keep you safe while me and Zena try and find a way out of here. Stay with them, and listen to what they say."

The spotlight flooded the butcher's yard once more. A metallic clang sounded from beyond the parted curtains. Francis nodded and jogged back to Tabitha's still body. He pushed himself flat against the canvas and held his breath.

Russ turned to his brother, each of them picking up a chair and holding it so the legs pointed out, towards the forbidding entrance. "Hey bro, it'll be fine. It's only a bird. What harm could she possibl—"

The chair legs thudded into the floor as a six foot tall, lithe woman stalked out onto the wooden stage. She was wrapped in a tatty black silk robe. The only things visible were her cue-ball eyes and a band of grey skin. She seemed to float to the middle of the stage. The robe covered her limbs, but even with it, she had a strange allure.

Her head turned slowly, across to the caterwauling of Russ and Chris. Like an automaton, she glided off the stage and made her way towards them. "Come here, you bint!" shouted Chris. The brothers had regained their poise and were banging the chair legs together.

As she got closer, her head snapped to the right. Eyes like a laser-guided missile looked to the bloody corpses from the initial attack. Ignoring the name-calling and gesticulating, she slid across the floor towards them.

"Where am I?" Shirley groaned. The words came out all slurred, with a degree of surprise. She ran a hand across her tacky face. As her eyes took in the sight that greeted her, a sheet of coagulated blood and skin, she screamed. Frantically, she started patting her face. She couldn't work out why some of it was fine, and some of it was not open to the possibility of having salt applied to it.

"Whatsth happened to my thace?" she begged. Running a hand through her hair, she pulled out one of her husband's shorn finger nails, pink bit and all. Shirley held her cheeks in terror. Her fingers recoiled as she touched exposed gum and teeth.

"Helpth me," she pleaded. Looking to her left she saw two men and a couple of hidden figures gawping at her. No sounds were coming out, though they looked like they were trying to say something.

"Thank Godth, pleasth, helpth me. Theresth thomething wong with my thace, where's my Hugh?" She tried to stand up, but something was pressing down on her legs. Flipping over, she noticed two things, each ascended the horror scale.

The first was the sight of her husband's body, except where his lovely face should've been—the one she fell in love with, the dimples in the corner of his mouth, his furrowed brow and beauty mark on his temple—was a crater lined with ragged skin, a core of broken spine and a deep red meat surround.

Ordinarily that would've sent her into psychiatric care, if it existed, for the remainder of her days, which probably wasn't long given the prodigious blood loss she had experienced after being peeled.

The second, though, which trumped this, was the sight of a figure bedecked in what looked like a long black satin nightie. This at first was not the cause of consternation; perhaps it was a mere hallucination brought on by a mental imbalance caused by the desolation of her world.

No.

As the apparition got to within five feet, it cast a long shadow over her. Shirley kicked off her husband's body and stood up. Even with a slight hunch, she was looking up into the strange face of this newcomer. "Thave oo come tho elp thus?" she asked cautiously.

It was then that the mercury in the Horro-meter™ went volcanic and erupted through the top. Almost on cue, a thin ribbon parted, and Pearl stretched out her two arms, causing the black robe to slip off her dead body and float to the floor as if carried by cherubs. Shirley gulped and looked up into a mouth lined with razor-sharp needle teeth. This, though, was not the worst of it. This was reserved for what passed as 'its' arms.

They were bony and bent backwards at the elbow. Each hand looked like it had melted and formed a skin paddle. As they opened, the inside was lined with thick fused, jagged rows of bone. Pearl stood over Shirley, her modesty preserved by the same type of bandages as were bound around the twins.

The monster regarded Shirley as an alien might regard a giraffe. Shirley coughed and managed to squeak out, "Thello," before the two raptorial arms snapped out and caught her around her shoulders. As she let out the first chord in her scream, the Praying Mantis closed her arms together and jerked them upwards. The motion severed through skin and bone, juddering Shirley's body one way and her arms the other.

She slumped to the floor, blood bailing out of her body through ruptured arteries. Her arms slopped to the ground. With a gentleness her previous action belied, Pearl picked up one with her folded arm and flopped it around so she could feast on the wet end.

Shirley made a wet burbling sound as she flapped around on the ground like a beached haddock. The sawdust stuck to the gooey lines of raw flesh on her face, giving her a new texture to try out.

The thrashing subsided quickly and the only sounds were the slurping and tearing as Pearl ripped chunks of meat from Shirley's bicep, Zena desperately trying to tear a hole through the material, and the two brothers gasping in a metaphorical soiling of underwear.

"*He* wants *us* to keep *that* at bay with *these*?" Chris whimpered, dumbstruck at the sight of Shirley bleeding to death on the floor and her vanquisher nibbling on her bingo wings.

Russ pulled his cap down. "Well, mate, not as if we have much choice, is it? Dunno about you, but between that dead bird's screaming and our howling, it's a wonder the whole freakshow doesn't know we're here."

Chris nodded. Sweaty palms gripped the back of the chair. "Bring 'em on. Think I'd prefer a straight fight than all this dancing around."

The two brothers twitched as Pearl dropped the arm. Swallowing in unison, they braced themselves, only for the dead freak to pick up the other arm and start gnawing on it like a spare rib.

Zena had made a foot-wide hole in the material. It was like nothing she had seen. Perspiring with effort, she dropped the bent metal bar onto the floor and stuck her DM-covered foot into the hole. She then proceeded to pull herself up and use her weight to make the hole bigger. After several attempts, one of which nearly sent her arse over tit, a reluctant tearing sound signalled a measure of success.

With the hole made wider, she managed to pull herself up and bounced on the hole until it finally decided to allow her admittance.

She jumped off and peered through the gap into the hallway they had all made their way down, what seemed like three omnibuses of *EastEnders* ago.

"In for a penny..." she mumbled to herself, and in an act of reverse birth, clambered through the vulvic opening. Landing on the wooden walkway, she dusted herself off and felt her way down the corridor. The pitch black claimed her as its own. The only thing which offered any semblance of reality was when she looked over her shoulder to the tear back to the room of grisly death, and the voices in her head castigating her for taking a lift from a stranger.

She argued back that in the situation she was in, it wasn't much of a choice to make. The group she was with had been devoured whilst they slept; she had only escaped as her claustrophobia meant she had slept on the caravan roof.

After moments of blind groping she reached the entrance. The flaps were covered in what felt like the same material she had just spent the best part of ten minutes fighting through. Back then she had the luxury of being able to see what she was doing and an implement of some kind. A little irked, she turned around and made her way back towards the beacon of light, guiding her way back to the budding charnel house.

Shirley's other arm slapped her dead body on the back as it was discarded, as if it was congratulating her on having both arms ripped off at once.

Good show, old bean!

The brothers shared nervous glances and adopted the en garde pose.

Pearl kicked the cooling corpse in front of her. Seeming to lose interest, she turned to see what could be eviscerated next.

"Oh fuck! Here comes big bird! Try to stay out of range okay? Thrust and parry, okay?" Chris offered.

Russ looked at his brother with something amounting to disdain and ridicule,. "You're joking yeah? How about we just try and keep her from eating us, Mum, or the kid, yeah? The only game plan we have is along the lines of winging it and hoping that mental man or psycho bird get back here before Insect girl here tears us apart."

"You're such a dick," Chris mumbled.

Pearl stopped and looked at the cowering food. Her right arm snapped down and decapitated Shirley like a paper guillotine. With the end of one of her arms, she picked the head up by sticking the morphed fingers into the shiny meat, and brought it to her mouth like a Chupa Chups lolly.

Brain, sawdust, and blood flavour; fifth favourite in the zombie apocalypse.

"Man, she is dragging this out, huh?" Chris grumbled.

Russ turned to him. "As far as I'm concerned, she can take as long as she wants. I'd help her write an aria, ponder the vagaries of folk music or go on a sabbatical to the Ivory Coast, mate. Anything to stop her coming anywhere near us."

Francis worked his way to the parted curtains. Casting a curt glance through them into the ether beyond, he clenched the baton tighter and stepped under the camera and into the corridor.

In the confines of the gangway, the spotlight from the room cast splinters of light onto calloused metal bars. After a few seconds, his brain deduced that they were cage doors. Looking along the length of the corridor, he guessed there were ten in total, five on each side. His mind a whirl of what abominations might be lying in wait for him, he forced down his reluctance and inched down into the belly of the unknown.

The first pair of cages, opposite each other, appeared to be empty. They had the same dimensions, but aside from some discarded newspaper and crisp bags, they held no nightmares.

As his fingers grasped the next set of bars, the door creaked open. His heart jumped up from its usual home to somewhere around his inner ear. Calming himself, he realised that this was the residence of one of the things they had been murderously introduced to recently.

He cast a furtive glance within the cages, and clocked small piles of bones within each. Pieces of rotting meat clung to them like Garra Rufa fish giving them a buff up. The next pair of cages were equally furnished. Some of the longer bones had been snapped in half in one cell, whilst the other had segments of jawbone and eye-socket lying around like modern art installations.

The next cage was firmly shut. Inside, he could hear something stir. A moan warbled out as if the owner had a cleft palate. Looking down beyond the cages, he saw a line of light like a goal frame on its side and covered with glow in the dark paint. Sticking to the middle of the walkway, Francis tiptoed towards the light…

Pearl chomped through Shirley's head as if she was oblivious to anything else in the entire universe. Lazy bites had reduced the meat-pop to a leering gore-smeared skull. The eyes had been one of the first things to go; the nose had also followed quickly. With a pointed tongue which matched the things masquerading as hands, she teased the meat and brain out through the freshly created cavities.

Russ sighed. Both brothers had decided that, given the delay in proceedings, they might as well have a bit of a sit down. Chris was playing I-Spy with Nathan, though given the array of body parts and visual stimuli, each round was taking longer than normal.

Their mother remained in a sedentary state behind the lot of them. With her arms hugging her knees tight to her chest, she stared unblinking at the dead thing carefully picking out morsels through Shirley's gaping eye socket.

"Hi guys, no dice." Zena's words came out of the blue and raised the scaredy-cat alert level from white to brown. "What's she doing?" Zena pointed to feeding time at the non-petting zoo.

"Been like that for five minutes. Seems quite happy chewing on that bird. No disrespect to her, but she must taste damn good, and it's keeping her occupied. Oh, hang on." Chris shoved Nathan behind him, elbowing his brother and picking up the chair again. "Looks like we got some action."

The remainder of the head, now a bloody skull with a mop of hair on, was discarded like a stale bread roll. Pearl stood motionless for a moment, before leaning forward and sicking up all that she had just devoured onto the arena's positively rank floor.

It would take a bulk order of sawdust and Magic Tree's to remove all trace of the wretched hive of scum and villainy that now befouled the onetime harbour of glee and astonishment.

As a shimmering pole of rust-coloured fluid linked Pearl to the floor, she pulled back up to full height and surveyed the room. Dead orbs locked onto the brothers baiting her with chairs as she turned and skittered towards them.

"Mum, stay low. You too, kid. We're all over this," Chris predicted confidently. Zena darted back to the ripped fabric to retrieve her lucky shiv. The zombified human-mantis closed the range with surprising ease considering the lack of beating heart. Chairs jabbed out at her, fending her off.

"Ha ha ha, look at her. She don't know what to do. Hey? Come on then, let's be 'aving ya, you dead bint. I've seen scarier things—"

Chris' analogy was cut short as a crooked bone-spiked arm flicked out and snipped his head clean off. His body remained upright, refusing to accept the absurd notion he had been bested so easily. The head slid off his neck backwards and landed upside down in the deep floor covering.

His mother screamed as her eldest son's eyes met hers. His inverted smile came across as that of a glum, moody bastard. Lava-like blood ran down the neck and onto his face from the rather nasty wound.

Hands admitted defeat first, the chair dropping to the floor and onto his feet. His body then collapsed in on itself like it had been the subject of a controlled demolition. Russ looked down at his brother with panic and shock. "Bro?" he spluttered. He bent down instinctively to tend to him, even though he knew there was no chance he still lived.

Having your head lopped off is one of those terminal things that you just can't come back from.

This act saved him from joining his brother in returning to stardust, as Pearl's left arm shot out and clacked shut where his head had been nanoseconds earlier. Fuelled by maternal rage, their mother leapt at the monster like a coiled viper. Unclipped talons slashed at Pearl's sallow flesh, tearing chunks of what looked like grey plasticine free and sending it via air mail to distant areas of the amphitheatre.

Her wailing was akin to a snubbed harpy. She clawed at her son's killer's face until huge divots of dead flesh were missing. Pearl seemed to not even notice what was happening; she placed an arm underneath the frenzied woman and flicked her off like a stringy bogey. She cartwheeled through the air and smacked into the canvas wall a few feet away. Flouncing across the floor like a ballerina, the Praying Mantis was upon her before she had a chance to even see stars.

Pearl tilted her head sideways at the stricken woman, as if examining the woman who had the audacity to struggle against her. As the victim got up onto her knees, the spiked arms shot out and severed her horizontally at the neck and waist. With a gurgling, she splatted to the ground in three pieces, oozing blood onto the floor, which was, quite frankly, getting a little pissed off with it all.

An arm lashed out and pierced the torso through its ribcage. Picking the body up to her mouth like a corn on the cob, Pearl began to nibble at the exposed flesh and dangling internal organs.

Francis stood to the hinged side of the door. He crouched and, using the tip of the baton, gently pushed the door open. With no annoyingly formulaic creaking of the door, he crept into the room. The Ringmaster sat with his back to him, looking at a crackly, static-lined television, showing a fish eye view of the auditorium and the mayhem within.

In one hand, he saw their absolute asshat of a host was clutching an old-school handled microphone. His other hand stroked the screen. He was emitting a purring sound. From a small set of speakers, Francis could just make out the strains of 'Freak On A Leash'. He edged closer. The purring grew louder. Francis tensed his hand round the baton handle.

"MUUUUMMMMMM," hollered Russ. Holding the chair by its seat, legs sticking out, he charged the monstrosity.

The charge caught Pearl in the middle of the back sending her crashing to the floor mid-bite. The torso remained attached to her appendage. Russ followed through with his attack and pinned the zombie freak to the floor. The legs dug into the mulch either side of her arms. She lay face down against the bloody pieces she had just prepared.

Russ sat on the chair as Pearl tried to right herself. "Hang on!" Zena bellowed and jogged over to the seated revenge-fuelled man.

The chair began to rock as Pearl scrabbled around on the floor, trying to find a way to push her body up and out of the contraption which bound her. Zena reached the pair as Pearl had got her opposable arms under her torso and was trying to use them as a jack. "Push down," Zena commanded, and Russ followed her orders.

A Doc Marten stepped on the top of Pearl's head, robbing her of any momentum. Before she could resist further, Zena slammed the jagged piece of metal through the back of the zombie's skull. As the unlife went out of her, the tannoy fizzed into life…

"OOOFFFFF, WHAT THE…WHO WAS…NO, NO……

IT'S YOU"

An ear-piercing shriek reverberated through the PA system before falling to deadly silence. Russ dropped to the floor next to his butchered family. Tears ran down his face and his eyes were red and puffy. Zena stamped the bar of metal into the freak's skull and knelt down to console him.

The silence was broken by a pleading from the tunnel the zombie monsters had been shepherded down. "Please, please mister. Don't hurt me, I didn't mean no harm."

Francis appeared from the back of the tent holding the handle of an animal catcher pole. Attached to the other end, with the loop firmly pulled around his neck, was the master of ceremonies, Trevor Norman.

"Looks like our host here has been doing this for a while. There are cages and these poles out back in his little viewing den," Francis reported, stamping into the theatre of death, dragging the reluctant Ringmaster roughly. "Nathan, come here."

The kid unfolded himself from under a chair and walked over to Francis. As he reached him, Russ shook off Zena's embrace and stormed towards them. "Let me have him," he growled, fists balled. Tears flew off his face in his wake.

"It wasn't me, sillies, no it wasn't me! He made me do it! He made me!" Trevor's protestations were met with a fierce right hook. A loosened molar flew out the side of his mouth and joined the multitude of human pieces lying around in various states of sunder.

Francis yanked the man to one side and squared up to Russ. "I know you're hurting, slim, but we can't do what you're thinking."

Russ' eyes were aflame with venom and anger. "Look at what he's done! Every-fucking-one here is DEAD because of him. He deserves to die," he snarled. Gobbets of spit flew as he spoke.

"A society is judged by how it deals with those who choose to destroy it, slim. If we kill him, you're no better than him, no better than the zombies," Francis countered, trying to keep Trevor from his clutches.

"Fuck that, man. You haven't just seen your brother and mum killed because of this motherfucker. You haven't had to try and pile the hacked up pieces of the person who brought you into this world into a heap so you can bury them more easily. Huh? No. I'm going to ask you nicely. Step. The fuck. Aside." Russ was in Francis' face; the heat from his breath and cheeks burned like a stoked furnace.

Francis stood firm. "No. I'm sorry, slim, but I can't do that. There has to be another way, we're *better* than this."

The two men, who from a distance looked like they were on the verge of tongue jousting, bored holes into each other's eyes. Russ nodded gently. "Fine. Fine, but we have to do *something* with him. We can't just let him go."

"Please, don't hurt me! I didn't mea—"

"SHUT UP!" Russ bellowed and lunged at Trevor. A wild swing connected weakly with his jaw. The Ringmaster held his face theatrically and mewed.

"We could put him in with the last freak?" Zena's voice came from the cage tunnel.

"There are *more*?" Russ asked incredulously.

Francis yanked the pole, forcing Trevor to his knees. "Yeah, there's one more out back. I don't fancy our chances much with him, though."

Zena coughed. "Doesn't matter. There's something you guys need to see."

She led the small procession down the row of cages, into the monitor room. A door in the far wall, next to the TV table, jutted into the room. "Through there," she said. "I'll keep hold of him till you get back."

She took the handle off Francis and pulled it violently, causing Trevor to gag on his own tongue.

Francis pulled the door open and looked into a large tent. As he walked into the new room, he noticed that the canvas was a dark green. He recognised it as the tents he saw from the hill, the ones which were stuck to the back of the Big Top like a chimney.

Russ shuffled in behind. His mouth dropped open as he saw what was within. "Holy fuck, man, look at all this stuff…"

Trestle tables ran in neat lines, leading off to the far end of the room which was shrouded in gloom. Stacked upon the tables were piles of belongings, sorted by type and the date they had been obtained. Francis rifled through a pile of assorted hand weapons; clubs, machetes, hammers of all kinds lay in a spreading heap; torches were on another table, sorted by size and battery type. There were whole sections devoted to clothing, broken down into women's, men's and children's. Francis felt his hackles rise.

Another row had food neatly stacked and faced up. Soup was alphabetically arranged, pasta stacked by type, Pot Noodles, bags of crisps, teabags sorted by brand. There was even a table with packets of cigarettes and booze. Francis felt the room spin; Russ staggered round like a drunkard in a town centre.

"So what should we do with him now, huh? Give him a fucking medal? He's been doing this for months, probably since this started…he can't be allowed to do this again," Ross said softly.

"Let's go get some answers," Francis uttered bluntly and made his way back towards the monitor room. Russ followed close behind.

"*GAHH, GAAHHHH, GGAAAAAHHHHHH,*" was the sound they were greeted with as they stepped back into the room they had left Zena and Trevor in. Both of them were still there, but not in the same place they had been left in.

Zena stood cross-armed, resting against the table with the TV stuck on something which resembled the *Outer Limits* intro. The voiceover, though, came from Trevor, who had both of his hands clamped round his throat. He had tried, and failed, to prevent the blocky rectangular microphone, and the top three inches of the stand, from being shoved down his throat.

Between his spindly fingers and gag reflex, he was trying to eject the foreign object from his throat. The two men looked at Zena, who shrugged. "Don't look at me. He wanted to make an announcement, must've tripped when I wasn't looking and accidentally swallowed it. Looks mighty painful, eh?"

Trevor collapsed to the ground, his face ashen, his moustache made bolder by the colour being drained out. His eyes were taking on the same appearance as an eight ball.

Russ stood over the suffocating man, staring down with pure unadulterated hatred. He turned to the others. "Fuck him, let him die."

CHAPTER SIXTEEN

Eva shone the penlight into Bartholomew's eyes. The pupils contracted as the beam flicked from one eye to the other. "Excellent, looks like you should make a full recovery," she purred.

Bartholomew nodded groggily. "Thanks, Doc. I appreciate everything you've done, really."

A click turned the light into dark. Chopper slipped the torch back into her pocket and walked over to the sink. "I'm still a little puzzled as to how someone of your physique happened to be beaten to within an inch of your life and left out there." She poured a jug of water over one hand, squeezed liquid soap into the other, and combined them to wash her hands.

"I don't really remember what happened. I was travelling with someone, and they mentioned this place, so we headed here. We were walking up the road towards the gate and that's the last I can remember. You say someone saved me?" Bartholomew asked quietly.

Another slosh of water over her hands cleaned the suds off. "Yes, he even fought off some chompers who were intent on having you for brunch. I wonder if he could be—" her words were cut off as Andy, Steve, and Thomas entered the makeshift medical bay.

"He's awake, least that's something. You looked in a pretty bad way when I found you, mate. Hell, you won't be pretty, but you're breathing at least," Thomas said, noticing that the man's face still had a yellowy-purple complexion.

Bartholomew offered a shaky hand. "I guess you're my saviour. Thanks, really appreciate it. If you hadn't come along, I—"

Thomas took the hand and shook it. "Think nothing of it, mate. You've survived this long, wouldn't want you going out like a bitch. Now, if you fellas don't mind, I better go and make myself useful. Heads Up is it Andy?"

Andy nodded once, and stood to one side of the doorway. "Jackson and Coates are out there, or they should be. Go join them. The three of you should be able to deal with whatever is out there. If it's quiet, make a bonfire will ya? The west side is getting a little whiffy." Thomas grunted in the affirmative and left them all to it.

"So, Bartholomew is it? My name is Steve. I'd like to ask you a few questions, if you don't mind of course?"

Andy piped up, "I'm going to leave you all to it. Just something I need to check on, if you don't mind?" Chopper and Steve shook their heads and turned their attention to Bartholomew.

Back on the factory floor, he picked up his pace. He looked across to see the exit door on the far side being pulled shut. *Least he's not going for another piss.* He started to jog across to the door; his jaunt was interrupted by his name being shouted. He turned to see Grimm marching down the steps from The Gaffer's office.

"Andy, we have a situation, *he* needs you, *now,*" Grimm grunted. The act of walking down the stairs had taken its toll and his leaden legs plodded slowly across the expanse of the factory.

"This better be good, Grimm. I've got other things to do right now," Andy called out and continued on his path to the door.

Grimm coughed and shouted, "You need to grab a weapon and get up to The Gaffer's office *now*. Some little toe-rag has got the drop on him."

Andy froze. "Fuck's sake. Okay, mate, gimme a minute," he said, and ran off to the armoury.

"You don't have to do this, mate, you know? You walk away now and nothing will happen to you, you have my word." The Gaffer's voice was level and calm. His arms rested on the arms of the chair usually reserved for his guests. He looked down the barrel of an old Webley service revolver. Up until the recent dead rising from death predicament, it had last seen service in the trenches of the Second battle of the Marne in July 1918.

"Shut up, just...shut up..." Tristan stammered. The gun felt heavy in his hand. He could feel the trigger was all hot and sweaty from his finger resting against it; the weapon swayed in his heavy grip.

The Gaffer raised his hands and crossed his legs. His right calf rested on his left thigh. He began to idly pick at the ragged hemline at the bottom of his grey trousers. "Well, isn't this a fun way to spend the afternoon? Tell me, son, what exactly do you think this little stunt will achieve, hmm? Why don't you just give me the shooter, and then you can be on your merry way."

Tristan wiped his sweat-drenched brow with his free hand. "You think you can just do what the hell you want, don't ya? Hurt these people who are scared and just trying to do the jobs you give them. You think you're our fucking god or something. Well, you hurt my friend, he's barely said a word to me since he got out of the chomper box the other day, after your 'Remedial'."

"From what I've heard, mate, you aren't exactly the gregarious sort either, huh? Steve tells me that you've said the exact amount of words as a monastery full of Trappist monks. Your pal fucked up, he knows the rules, same as everyone here. You fuck up, you get a strike. It's the only way to keep order. Now, I'll ask nicely for the last time. Give. Me. The. Fucking. Gun." The Gaffer enunciated. He pulled on his tracksuit top, emblazoned with MB on the right hand breast.

The gun shook some more, like it was the last autumnal leaf to fall, but was afraid to do so. "I don't think so. I think I'm going to just..."

A shout from the doorway bludgeoned through the tension. "Tristan, don't do it!" Andy shouted. He had a glock raised and pointed at him. He inched into the office. The Gaffer had his back to him, while across the table and in the large plush leather Queen Ann chair where he normally resided, sat Tristan; a slight man who seemed to be constructed solely from skin and bone.

"Andy? What are—" Tristan began to stutter. His sentence was punctuated by the sound of a crack. He slammed back into the chair, which enveloped his scrawny frame; a small round smoking hole was stamped into his bone white throat.

It throbbed from within and a globule of blood expanded from the crater. In shock, Tristan pressed his hands over the wound. The revolver clattered to the floor. The noise of someone gargling on their own fluids was the only audible sound. "Chopper, get up here!" Andy shouted into the vacuous factory, before rushing over to the bleeding man.

As he ran past The Gaffer, he saw a smoking Ruger .22 pistol pointed at the chair and window beyond. In the slabs of meat that lay claim to the title of hands, it looked like a cap gun.

Tristan slid off the chair and fell onto a grubby ruby red rug, Andy had to push the chair aside to get to the stricken man. "Hang on, mate, just hang on," he repeated, though he could see that the wound had already given Tristan a sopping red bib over his once white shirt.

He knelt down and looked into a pair of desperate eyes, eyes which were pleading with him for help. Blood was pumping from the wound, between his fingers, and creating a crimson lake on his horizontal throat, his Adam's apple a receding island of flesh.

"Gaahh…gahhhh….!" Tristan gasped. He reached a bloodstained hand towards the fading face in front of him, pawing at some unseen phantom.

"CHOPPER, GET HERE, NOW!" Andy bellowed. He could hear frantic footsteps up the stairs, but when he looked down again, he saw that they would be too late. A pathetic hand wafted at his face once more; blood-soaked digits reached out.

Tristan belched blood which made a waterfall of viscera pour from his throat, and was then still. His hand dropped and tapped his head.

Eva barged Andy to one side, but took one look at Tristan and closed her eyes. She reached into her shoulder bag and pulled out a long thin stiletto blade. She roughly tilted Tristan's head to one side, placed the point inside his ear, and jammed the blade upwards and into the skull. The handle was the only thing visible in the ear. She gripped this tighter and stirred it quickly. As she pulled the blade out a trickle of blood, crushed bone, and lumps of brain dribbled out through the hole.

She stood up, shook her head, and trudged out of the room. Andy was still looking down at the lifeless body when he felt a familiar grip on his shoulder. "Nice one, my son. Pretty sure he shot first, he had me bang to rights," The Gaffer's rich voice said, cloying in Andy's ears.

"What the fuck happened, Gaffer? How...wh...just how, that'll do for now?" he muttered.

The Gaffer pulled up to his full height and motioned to two of Grimm's guards, who were stood idle by the doorway. "He came in and said he wanted to talk to me. I went to pour him a drink, the next thing I know I'm looking down the business end of his gun. Luckily for me, he didn't know about Mister Twenty Two in my pocket and you managed to distract him. Cheers pal," The Gaffer said. He pointed at the body, and the two guards walked round the desk and grabbed an end each.

"Burn it with the chompers. He don't deserve anything more. He don't get to go on the wall, neither," The Gaffer ordered. The guards picked up Tristan's body and pigeon-walked their way out of the office.

"Gaffer, no disrespect, but we coul—"

A large hand silenced Andy. "Coulda, woulda, shoulda. Some prick *should* have been on guard. Then they *could* have stopped that nutter just fucking waltzing in here with a gun. Where the fuck did he get that from anyway? Don't look like one of ours. See, then I wouldn't have had to do an emergency tracheotomy on him with my Ruger, *would* I? No."

The two men exchanged glances.

"No Gaffer, you wouldn't," Andy agreed.

"No harm, no foul, Andy. It's not your fault. You've been busy with our new arrivals. I trust they're settling in okay?"

Andy distractedly looked at the puddle of blood which was struggling to soak through the dirt and grime and into the rug. "Fine, Gaffer. That one who was beaten is back up and running. The other, Thomas, there's something not quite right about him. I'll keep an eye on him."

The Gaffer nodded. "Good. That's why you're here, Andy. Go on, I'll get someone to sort this out, you get back to it."

CHAPTER SEVENTEEN

A funereal hush wreathed the group as they sat in a loose circle in the dusty storeroom. Even Anton looked shell-shocked from the events of the last few days. "Okay everyone, so you all know the terrible news about Tristan. This is why we do this. He wasn't strong enough to cope with what he went through, was ill prepared to deal with the way the world is now, and…and that's why he did what he did," Steve ventured.

Matt shook his head. "Patches and Dad are gone. I haven't shot anyone."

"No, you haven't, Matt, but remember, you told us all your story last week, didn't you? Sharing helps people deal with the horrible things that they've been through, especially since all of *this* happened," Steve replied.

Dee blurted out a "Bullshit," which was met with more floor-gazing.

Sylvia looked across to her. "You know, Dee, there really is something familiar about you. It's like we've met before, I just can't remember where. You were in the police, do you say? But you couldn't have dealt with…my situation, you know, with Donald. When he was. Hmm. No. Couldn't have done."

Steve cleaned his glasses, scratching a particularly stubborn piece of dried-on grit with his thumbnail through his t-shirt. "Well, Dee, perhaps you can tell us about yourself. What happened when this started. From what I've been told, you were there when it kicked off in Man—"

"SHUT UP!" Dee shouted, covering her ears with her hands. "You can't judge me. None of you can. We did what we had to, the only thing we could. There was just so many, and we couldn't be right all the time. It was war, bad things happen, okay?"

"Shhh, it's okay Dee. You should know by now that we aren't here to judge you, or make you feel bad. We are a conduit to help you deal with the things that have happened. Why don't you start from the beginning, yeah? I think what you have to say could help everyone. You have seen so much, th—"

Steve was interrupted by a thunderous "Fine!" He slipped his glasses back on and opened his notebook.

"Dee, take your time, please…begin."

SURVIVOR

TALES FROM THE ZOMBIE APOCALYPSE

The NETZACH'S Series

ISSUE #3 LET THE BEAT CONTROL YOU

NARRATED BY DEE ROBINSON

LET THE BEAT CONTROL YOU – PART I

So, right, it's weird isn't it? How sometimes in life, things can come down to a simple decision. At the time it seems so innocuous, something that ninety nine times out of a hundred turns into nothing of note.

Sometimes it's as simple as going left instead of right, or hitting snooze and staying in bed. Do you think that in some parallel universe there is a you who got up that morning when the alarm did? Instead of opening the door, late for work and seeing the aftermath of the crash, in that other universe you'd be the body sprawled on the floor in a puddle of your own guts and brain?

Do you ever think that?

I do.

Every single fucking day.

Me and DK were seeing each other on the sly. Never shit where you eat, that's what me mum used to say. When you're in our line of work, that goes double. I had pals who didn't follow that advice. When *that* call came in, you see them double over, howling like a fucking trapped animal. You know there's nothing you can say to make them feel better.

Nothing.

But no, not me. I thought that would never happen to me. We'd be different, we'd be careful, no way that would happen to us.

We were both in the Tactical Firearms Unit, part of the Greater Manchester Police department. We were on the afternoon shift, clocked in at five, and bored shitless by half past.

It was about ten to nine and my parallel universe moment was that I went to make a brew. That was it. I didn't walk under a ladder, piss off a black cat, break a mirror or open an umbrella indoors. I made a cuppa.

The call came in. By the time I got back, DK and Mick were just heading out the door. I sat down and read through Brief, some article on us lot which had been doing the rounds.

All I can think of now is what would've happened if I had been there instead. Gone instead of him, or even *with* him. Would it have made any difference?

No, I doubt it, but at least then what happened to them would've happened to me and I wouldn't fucking be here, stuck telling people I don't even fucking know my bloody sob story.

We didn't even know it had begun, none of us did. The call they had gone to was some domestic down at the hospital. Said some people were getting a bit frisky with some of the staff; some of the nurses had been bitten. We were laughing about it, then the second call came in. By the time we were Oscar Mike they were building up. They said Alpha One could deal with the city centre. We were sent out to Altrincham Ice Dome, said there was something strange going on, people attacking people, biting people.

Then we got outside to the Land Rover and saw the sky. Me and Bloater just stood there. I mean, who had ever seen *that* before? Seen a red sky at night, but this was different, this was…well, *fucked*.

Bloater does the driving. The calls are still coming in. As we're heading out into the sticks, it feels like there's this noose tightening around the city. We could feel it. Don't think we said a word to each other the entire time. I tried DK but got nothing. That wasn't good; it didn't make sense, none of it.

Just as we rock up to the Ice Dome, we can see this group of people surrounding someone in the car park, just standing there. They see and hear the blues and twos and move out of the way. I got out and went to see what the hell they were doing while Bloater calls in the ambulance.

They parted like I was Moses, and there it was, the Red fucking Sea, that sure as shit didn't part. His body was just lying right in the middle of it. Never knew someone could have that much blood inside them, ya know?

I ask the crowd what happened, and about five people start jabbering away at once. Something about someone in a gown attacking this poor bastard and then wandering off inside, like he just got bored.

I called it in and knelt down to have a look at him. He was gone, you could fucking see it a mile off. His throat was all ripped and torn. The poor sod had this look on his face like he was gasping for air. His eyes were all mad and open, like he was trying to scream but couldn't get anything out. Just so much blood. It was only when I stood up I realised I had stood in the bloody lake.

Sorry, pun unintended.

I grab some names from the witnesses and can hear the ambulance siren. I look over to the Ice Dome and can see this wave of people moving towards it, like ambling, real slow. Thought it was a bit odd as the match would've finished at nine, they should've been coming out, not going in. But then nothing seemed to be making much sense so far that night.

The ambulance turned up, we had a quick chat, told them that it was too late, and left them to it. Me and Bloater got our HK36's, spare mags, and headed off to the entrance. Most of the crowd we had seen before had gone. There were a few stragglers, but they were just bumbling around, like they were pissed.

We got to within, what, fifteen feet of them, when we heard a scream behind us. The crowd of vultures who were still by the dead body scattered, like someone had just dropped one. I brought my scope up and saw that one of the paramedics was hitting someone who was lying on the ground. I looked closer and my fucking heart stopped. The paramedic was punching the man we'd just seen was a DOA, what, two minutes ago. You could see the poor bastard's collarbone through the bite mark. He was leaning over one of the medics who was sparko on the ground.

I was about to head back when Bloater yelled out a stop command. I turn around and there's five of them.

They just looked *wrong*, you know? Like when you open the fridge and get the milk out, even before you take the top off, you just fucking know that it's gone off; slight discolouration, a separation of good and bad. They were like that. Their skin was just…all grey, slack, it was hanging off them, no energy to them, you know? And then as they got closer the smell hit you, like a punctured piss bag on a radiator, made my eyes water.

This big lad was lumbering towards us. His chubby arms were reaching out to Bloater.

He had lost a couple of fingernails, and underneath the others there was bits of, well, *stuff*. His pals weren't far behind. Bloater shouted again, telling him to back the fuck off and get down.

Like fucking *now*.

Nothing.

You get told what to do, it's ingrained into the fabric of the uniform every time you put it on. It becomes your mantra. Fire, assess, fire again if necessary. *You* decide when to shoot, no one else. It's your nuts on the block if you fuck up, so you always make sure it's the only option left.

You aim for the biggest target, the main body mass, less chance the round goes through and takes out Mr or Mrs Civilian behind them. Same reason you don't go for the arms or legs. It could go through and take out a civvy, or worse, nick an artery and then you're playing find the fucking end of a raggedy ass vein inside the poor bastard's groin.

I guarantee that you won't get it in time, and then in addition to being covered in their blood and piss, you'll find yourself in the shit too.

Bloater shouts again. Tells him it's his final warning. Fatman is about eight foot away now, and we're both backing off, trying to buy ourselves some time. He says nothing except that fucking moan that they bring out all the time.

Just once, you want something different you know? Like a moo or a woof. Hell, just one fucking word would be nice, instead of that god awful moan.

The first round goes through Fatman's chest, just to the left of the sternum as we're looking at it. He doesn't even flinch. The only way we knew Bloater had fired was the hole in Fatman's Led Zep t-shirt.

No blood.

None.

Not a single fucking drop or spatter, just this black goo dribbling out.

Fire.

Assess.

Fire again if necessary.

The second round clips fatty in the guts, around the liver I would've guessed. He just keeps on coming, so do his pals.

Fire.

Assess.

We assessed alright, we were fucked. However, the one good thing that al Qaeda *ever* fucking did was to change what to do if the first shots don't work. Go for the head. Standard anti-terrorism measure. We were always told 'shoot to neutralise'. If you don't bring 'em down one way, you bring 'em down another.

Bloater's third shot hit porky just above his right eye. He noticed that alright, ding-ding, NO SALE. Fucking went down like a ladyboy on payday. His pals are getting closer. I let off a round at the closest one, square in the chest, nothing. Second shot goes in the head, down he goes.

We didn't fuck around after that. The others got one each, job done. Bloater gives me the eye after the last one drops. I can see it, the *what the fuck just happened there* look. I don't even know it but I'm giving him the same look back.

About then we hear the screams. Must've been too focused on our little situation. It was like I could hear for the first time. The sound was coming from everywhere, but the loudest was coming from the Ice Dome entrance in front of us. We didn't hesitate, we just went in.

LET THE BEAT CONTROL YOU – PART 2

We'd barely got to the turnstile when we saw another group of those bastards. They were crowding around this lad on the floor. He wasn't moving but their mouths were. Poor sod. They had made short work of him; all you could make out was his face and feet. Everything in between was in the process of being pulled apart.

Yes. The fucking Z word. Bloater said it then in the hallway. I told him it was bullshit, but I knew, just didn't want to believe it I suppose. Not as if you wake up in the morning, munching on your cornflakes with a to-do list in your head, shower, get the paper, get some shopping, shoot fucking zombies who are eating people, like right in front of you.

Not what I had planned at all.

Anyway, the group were too involved in eating the lad to notice us. We pulled out our Glocks and put a round in each of them.

Yeah, *course* we did. Not going to fucking shout a warning, were we? They were eating him, not engaging him in an in-depth chat about glacial fucking erosion were they?

Prick.

Course, we already fucked up then didn't we? Chaos theory, that ol' son of a bitch. Well that came back to bite us in the ass on the way out.

The screams inside are still going on, but they sound fainter. Either less people were screaming or they were getting further away, we had to choose.

Do we go for door A, or do we risk all the prizes we had won so far and go for door B?

Those dead bastards made our mind up for us. They came out of both. It was a trickle at first. Before we even knew it we had taken a corridor each. Pretty sure I got off easier. So for the next fifteen minutes I hear precisely three things.

Screaming, unintelligible words, begging, pleading, I heard swear words that I never even knew existed.

The moaning. That fucking sound came from everywhere, especially in that corridor. You'd turn around thinking they were right on you, but nowhere to be seen. You'd turn back, just in time to see one bearing down on ya.

All the while, though, one sound was above both of those. Crack. Crack. Crack. By the time I got half way round the corridor my pistol had run dry. Changed over mags and began again. I had one thought: *as long as I can hear Bloater shooting, things are going to be okay.*

I stopped hearing him shooting just as I got to the other end of the dome. There was a set of double doors which led to a bar. The screaming had pretty much petered out by then. I got to the door. I had five rounds left. I tried to look through the glass but it was covered in blood. That was a good sign, I thought.

Not.

I kicked the door in and there was this couple standing there. I almost pissed myself with laughter. They must've been in their fifties, I guess. This guy was standing over one of the deadheads, and was smacking him in the head with this hockey stick. You should've seen him.

His missus was stood back-to-back with him, and she was leaning over another one and smashing its face in with a leg brace.

A fucking leg brace.

Oh my days, I swear, as long as I live, I will never, ever, see anything like that again. They finish up and look at me. You could see that he was working out if I was one of them.

I hold my gun out and tell them I'm a copper and here to rescue them. Ha, her face, never forget what she said. "You're here to help *us*? We're doing alright on our own, thank you very much."

He turned to her and said, "Hey hun, I'm just like Jack Reacher." I took out a couple of stragglers coming from the other doorway, and that was it. For the first time in twenty minutes, there was near silence. Which was both a relief and the scariest sound ever. Where was Bloater?

I asked the couple if they were alright, they said they're fine, and asked what was going on. I told them all I knew, which wasn't much. They didn't even know what a zombie was. I'll tell you this, though, they sure as hell knew how to finish one off. I looked around and they must've taken out a dozen, maybe more. They were thorough, too. By the state of the bodies, there was no way they would be getting up again.

Anyway, Karen and Bruce from Manitoba said thanks and that was it. Told them to go the way I had come from, and wished them all the best. He tipped his hat and they were off. I felt genuinely sorry for whatever deadheads they ran into. Those two weren't going to take any prisoners.

I tried getting Bloater on the radio. Nothing. I couldn't get hold of anyone. I had three rounds left in my pistol, but nigh on three full mags of my carbine. I had to get to Bloater, couldn't leave him to those fuckers.

No fucking way.

You what? How should I know? They left, never saw them again. By the time I got outside, they were long gone.

There weren't that many first off. The odd one here and there. Most were working their way through some poor unfortunates who had been caught. Never forget this one girl. Must've been sixteen, tops. Poor cow was still alive as this deadhead just scooped his hands into her stomach and pulled out lumps of…meat…guts and that, I guess.

After I took the deader out, she looked at me. From her chest up, it was like she was resting. She just said, "Thanks," and I shot her in the head.

She was…she was the first *real* person I had killed. The others I had shot in that place, you knew they weren't people, not any more. Something had gone from them; they were just machines, no soul left, no spark. Nothing. *Her* though…

No, I'm fine. I said I'm *fine*.

Cheers, though.

I still see her face. It's always just before and then just after, like the world's shittest flipbook. One page, she's there, a slight grin on her face, life, hope, opportunity, the other page has her head smacked against the floor as the round hit, her eyes still locked onto me, even though her head is facing the other way. Her grin is still there, the blood running from the corner of her mouth.

She won't get to go on a date, get stood up or let down; she'll never get to try out all the things that we took for granted. Even the shit stuff, the stuff that we do at the time because we think it's a good idea, but run home crying to your mum about. She'll never have kids, get a job or get married.

And she's not alone, huh? How many do you think we've lost? How many of us do you think are left? How the fuck are we going to get back all the stuff that we had?

From *them*, those dead fucks.

I fucking *hate* them.

So, right, that shot has emptied my Glock, and still nothing. I get through the next set of doors and I swear my heart actually stops. I can see a booted foot sticking out from this mass of deaders.

BA-BOOM

BOOM

I lost it. I actually lost it. One minute I feel nothing, then I hear my heart play the downbeat.

Next?

I'm breathing so hard I think I've just crapped out my lungs. I look down at my hands and all I see is two red sticks of meat.

I'm still clutching my Glock. I know I have no rounds left. I look down and see this sea of bone, ripped skin, chunks of meat, and the floor slick with blood. In amongst all of this, like a new-born fucking baby, is Bloater. He's still alive.

They overwhelmed him by the looks of things; his Glock is off to one side. The mag was ejected, so figured it was when he went to reload. If it wasn't for his vest, he'd be like that poor lad we saw on the way in.

He's in a bad way, though, don't get me wrong. He's covered in blood, and I know some of it is his. One ear was gone, right down to the side of his head. Looked like Mr Blonde had just done his 'Stuck In The Middle With You' moment. Fingers are missing, and how the fuck they didn't chew through his head must've been sheer bloody luck.

But he's still there, alive, just, he's looking at me like I'm the patron saint of saving asses. I switch back to logic. Got to get him outside, the first aid kit in the Landy, or the ambulance at a push.

I pull off a couple of belts from the remains of the deaders I've just pistol whipped, well, pistol smashed the fuck back to death. Tie them together and loop them through the back of his vest.

Like a goddamn action movie, I drag Bloater back through the building. There's a few milling around. Some are the actual ice hockey players, which was weird.

I get back to the lobby and set Bloater down, tell him I'm going to get the first aid kit, or a medic, and I'll be back for him.

A minute.

Tops.

I promise.

I get outside and you can see that we have company. There are nurses, taxi drivers, every fucking kind of normal sod you see every day. All of them are fucking dead. So are the paramedics. I saw one of them walking off towards the Tesco down the road. That was where the screaming was coming from now. They didn't even bother to look at me.

I grab my kit and head back in, and there he was. That lad. The one who had been feeding the deaders. What was left of him was slopped over Bloater. He finished off what the others had started. He was like those eel things.

Lampreys? Yeah, them, with the circular mouths and sharp teeth.

Just stuck on his face, chewing. His legs, or what were left of them, were still where we had left him; this trail of blood and guts all over the floor and smeared over Bloater's body like a snail on a period.

The downbeat again. I tried to stop it, tried to calm myself.

BA-BOOM

BOOM

It didn't work.

LET THE BEAT CONTROL YOU – PART 3

Three, two, one, and you're back in the room. Except I was in the driver's seat of our ARV. For some reason I've got Bloater in the seat next to me. Thank fuck that some part of my brain was smart enough to put his seatbelt on.

He's like the bloody Alien, jaw trying to snap at me; his face is just, well, a mess. He'd have a hard job getting on the Undateables, let's put it that way.

In addition to no nose, how does he smell I hear you ask. I would say terrible, but that's also how he looks. One of his eyes has a chunk bitten out of it. It looks like a deflated football hanging out of its socket, still on this bit of fleshy string.

If you say so pal, I ain't a fucking doctor am I?

I've also had the foresight, or dumb luck, to put my seatbelt on, which I found out when I looked through the front window and see I'm heading towards a crowd of people running past Boots. Slammed the brakes on just in time. I work out I must have been heading back to HQ. I'm only like five minutes away?

It was bedlam out there. So many people, you couldn't tell who was a deader and who was just trying to get the fuck out.

They say it's why Manchester went so quick, ya know? All those pissheads out in town on a school night. Well, that and the fact that, unlike the South, we were spread thinner than a hotel portion of Nutella on toast.

Bloater, or whatever the fuck he was now, he wasn't gonna get me, so figured I'd just head back, quick as you like. Even from the bottom of the street, you knew it was bad. Must have been about half eleven now, proper night time. The orange glow from the fire in the station lit up the entire road.

Still had nothing from DK; he was gonna be my next stop. Parked up out back, the barriers were down and no fucker was manning them. Got inside sharpish, headed towards the armoury.

The Sarge was there. Must've had the same idea as me. Gave me the biggest smile I've ever seen, told me that everything's gone to shit. Could've told him that myself. So, get inside the armoury, get a bag, and grab handfuls of mags, grab myself a Remington 870 shotgun, a couple of vests and we go. Sarge isn't trained, but he's keen enough. He doesn't even ask me what I'm going to do, he just followed me.

Ha, poor bastard got a shock when we got back to the ARV. Completely forgot to tell him about Bloater, thought it'd be an ideal opportunity for the Sarge to break his duck. Gave him the Remington, told him all he had to do was point and shoot.

I knew Bloater was gone. The man I knew was fucking lying down dead in the entrance to that ice rink; that thing I pulled out and watched have its head turned into puree sure as hell wasn't him. Sarge didn't even blink, which was mad as him and Bloater were close.

We were halfway to the hospital before he spoke again, asked me what I'd seen that night. I've never sugar-coated anything, so I told him.

All of it. He went a bit pale, but said he was fine. That was good enough for me. Two were better than one right now, that much I knew.

It was a crap idea going there. I thought seeing that poor girl was bad enough, but the night had saved its best for last. We pull into the hospital car park, we can see their vehicle parked up, the doors are open, they must've got out fast.

The place is a mess, there's shit everywhere, like someone had got every single bin from every single house in Manchester and just thrown it into the street. Crowds of people milling about in the half light, no idea if they were deaders or real people.

Ha.

Real people.

Right.

And then…there he was.

He was over with this nurse. She had blonde hair, which was all tied up. Guess you have to if you work in a hospital. Petite girl, too. She was dead pretty.

She was also pretty dead.

They were side by side, crouching on the ground, pulling at something. I got out of the car and walked closer to see what they were doing, not that it mattered. The fact that he was as dead as she was didn't even register.

It was Mick. DK had pulled his arm off and was eating it like a chicken drumstick. Ha, there was even this bit where he licked his lips. It was mad, just like when we went to Nando's after shift.

At least I knew. That's what I told myself then. I know now, I can move on. Out of the side of my vision, I see Sarge stomp off to them, cock the shotgun.

BOOM.

Blondey doesn't have to worry about tying her hair up anymore, cos she's got no head left for the hair to be attached to.

The next bit goes by in super slo-mo. I know what Sarge is going to do, and I've got these two voices in me. One is going, 'Good, blow that fucking deader away, better him than us.' The other is shouting, 'Are you gonna let him kill DK and do nothing about it?'

Saw the expended shell get ejected, it twirls around in the air like a coin being flipped, felt like shouting Tails.

Sarge had already called Heads.

No Matt, not a real coin, it's a metaph—

Oh forget it.

I heard the click, and watched the barrel vomit fire and sparks. DK had clocked him by then. He was still chewing on Mick's bicep; must have been a stringy bastard. Then just as the first tiny ball of shot hit him, time went back to normal, and DK's head gets torn into pink gooey ribbons.

After that, we got back in the ARV and left. We stopped to help people out when we could, but we couldn't do much. By about four in the morning we were knackered. We knew what we had to do, just couldn't believe we were going to do it.

We stopped at mine first, then dwent round his. Sarge was living in this little bedsit in Salford, never thought we'd make it out of his digs alive, got pretty hairy. By then, though, we had ditched the uniform and the ARV. We got some water and food from the shop, then we left.

My family was abroad, and Sarge, well, he said he hoped the deaders would eat his soon-to-be ex-wife, but you can tell when someone's bullshitting. His eyes were all red for starters.

Took us a few hours to get out of the city, but we figured we'd head south. The government would look after them better, more likely to vote for the pricks in power than us lot. We helped when we could and ducked out when we couldn't.

We just kept going until we got here.

The.

End.

CHAPTER EIGHTEEN

Steve's pen stopped scratching in his notepad. "Dee, thank you, I th—"

"Why don't you tell them the rest, Dee?"

The group turned around instinctively to see who the intruder in their session was. The Gaffer stood there, the atypical immovable object. He was wearing his sheepskin coat, the collar was pulled up around his thick corded neck.

Dee simmered with barely checked anger. The Gaffer pushed himself off the doorframe and strolled into the room, running a finger over a dust-laden shelf. He pulled his finger away and dropped a flaky brown caterpillar of filth, which floated lopsidedly to the floor.

"Go on, if you were such a pillar of the community, why are you here? Everyone knows why Matt is here, for instance." A slab of a hand fell onto Matt's shoulder. He looked up with a beaming grin.

"Is it cos I managed to go poo-poo in the bucket today?" he asked with an infectious enthusiasm.

"Ha, no Matt, though good job on that. Matt is here as he has the intellectual ability of a pencil sharpener, which was not helped in any way, shape or form by having to smash a rotary line through his dad's head. Or witnessing his dead dad's dick and realising it was still bigger than his, eh champ?"

Matt grinned even more. His face looked like it was unable to deal with the continued strain. "Whatever you say, Gaffer. I liked telling my story. Though I still miss Patches."

The Gaffer pointed a marker pen of a finger at an empty chair. "Tristan there, you should've heard how my men found him. Bordering on feral, by all accounts. Didn't say boo to a goose for three weeks. Some people thought he was deaf and mute, others thought he was a touch retarded. One look into his eyes, though, you could see what he went through."

"So, come on, Dee. Now you're sharing, why don't you tell these nice people why you're in here, and not out there, considering your background, hmm?" The Gaffer asked, resting his frame against a drainpipe.

Dee glowered at him. "Like you're some kind of fucking saint? You run this place like—"

"LIKE WHAT?" The Gaffer boomed, his eyes wide open, burning with a passion and intensity which, if left unchecked, would burn up all the dust in the room. His demeanour softened. "Like what? Anyone here can leave at any time. Everyone knows that. They will get no problem from me or the men that guard them while they sleep. You take your stuff, food for a day, whatever weapon you came in with, and you can go. This isn't a prison, Dee. You, of all people, know this."

Dee crossed her arms, still incandescent with rage. "But what about the Remedials, eh? Mister fucking big man, aren't you? Getting Grimm to beat people, lock them in that crap-hole or have them lashed up to the angel outside.”

The Gaffer held his arms out. “Yes, we have to. Without rules, we have disorder. Without rules, we have chaos. But what use are they if they are ignored? You need a punishment, you need a deterrent. If someone stole from you and got away with it, how would you feel?”

He walked behind the circle, like a shark monitoring the shoal. “If someone beat on you, and you got no justice, would you feel safer? If some piece of distended rectum fell asleep while keeping a watch on you when you were at your most vulnerable, would you want them to get off Scott free?”

“No Gaffer, I wouldn’t. Dad always stood up for me when I got sent home from school for things. Like when I went wee-wee in the bin in class, cos Mrs Copping wouldn’t let me go to the toilet. I told her I needed to go, but she just said no. I didn’t want to make my new shorts all wet,” Matt rattled out.

“No, Matt, we wouldn’t. So I make the hard decisions, so you don’t have to. The world, unless you haven’t been paying attention, has very much gone to shit. I am responsible for the safekeeping of forty eight people. You, Dee, are barely responsible for one, especially after what happened,” The Gaffer continued. “So, Treacle. Are you going to tell them why you’re here, or shall I?”

- 128 -

SURVIVOR

TALES FROM THE ZOMBIE APOCALYPSE

The NETZACH'S Series

ISSUE #4 A LOCAL SHOP FOR LOCAL PEOPLE

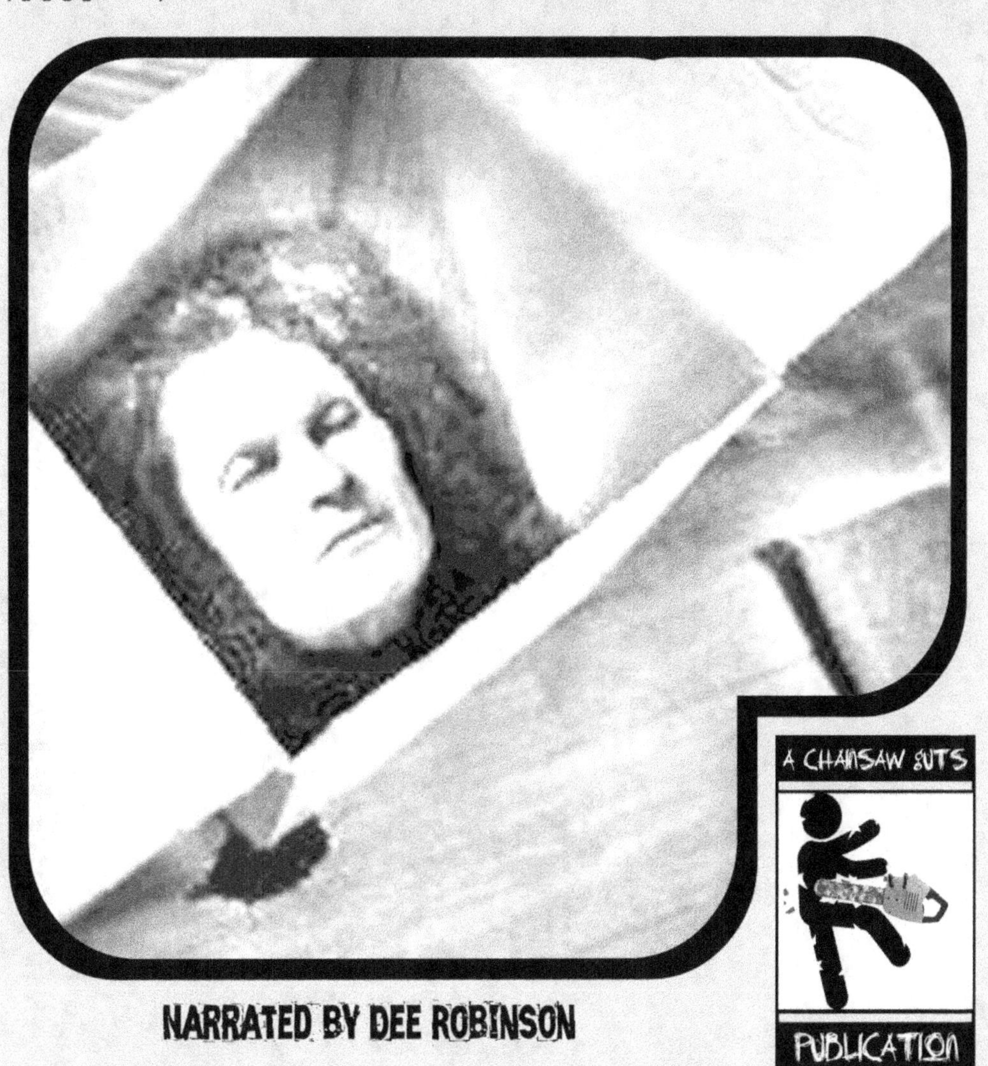

NARRATED BY DEE ROBINSON

A LOCAL SHOP FOR LOCAL PEOPLE

Fine, so me and Sarge meet up with this complete bellend, yes, *you*, somewhere outside Oxford. We'd been travelling for a few weeks. Some days we managed to get a few miles down the road before we'd come across another roadblock, run out of fuel, or stop to try and help folk.

Everything had gone to shit by then. Gave up listening to the radio, same old crap they kept spouting. We were *out* there, we saw it all. Most survivors were holed up in their own gaffs, keeping their heads down, making sure the deaders didn't get wind of 'em. A few times we had to intervene to help out, nothing major like.

So me, Sarge, prickface over there, and a few others, we find this place after a bit. We could see the potential, even if the size of the place was a bit daunting. Didn't even have to kill anyone to get it. Within a few weeks, though, with every supply run we'd do, or recce around the area, we'd get more and more people. He who shall not be named, Grimm and some of his pals, Matt—

Yes, hi Matt.

Along with some others, we start getting a proper little community going.

We knew by then we needed regular supplies, but it was all about risk versus reward. The supermarkets, especially the big out of town ones, were an obvious target, but me and Sarge found out the hard way that those places were more trouble than they were worth.

For one, every other fucker had already thought of this, so most of the good stuff had been chaved already. The power was pretty much gone by now, too. And on one run we did, we ran into both of those lovely groups that we now spend so much time avoiding.

Deaders and bandits.

Yeah, yeah, Romero would say that they were going back there from some sense of memory, or some emotional link to that place.

Bullshit.

They were *hungry*. They are *always* hungry. They knew people were there cos one of them, could've been days ago, saw a live one.

That deader moaned at the fucker, stopped doing what they were doing and followed them. That moan attracted other deaders, who also stop what they're doing and follow, and before you know it, you've got a band of them walking in the same direction, following their lunch.

It was the only time so far I was glad to see those dead wankers.

We'd got into the warehouse out back; there was next to nothing there, though. Before we had a chance to take what we had, this bunch of pricks with baseball bats and god knows what had surrounded us. Sure, we had guns, but we could have got two, maybe three of them before their mates would be doing the Riverdance on our twitching bodies.

So, it's like The Good, The Bad and the fucking Ugly. We're eyeballing each other, waiting for someone to make the first move.

This is going to end, *badly*.

Then the deaders strolled in through the doors. With all the commotion they just walked right in amongst us. It was mayhem. I don't reckon the toe-rags even knew we were there when their mates were being snacked on. We left them to it and legged it out back.

So from then on, we stuck to the little newsagent shops, the Tesco Metros of the world. Sure, they'd been hit up, too, but not as much. You knew if you found one, you would come out with enough stuff to last a few days. We got a map of the area, and every couple of days we'd head off on bikes, fill up the trailers, and get back. In the early days a good run or two would feed us all for a week.

Then we started having to go further and further.

Yes, alright, I'm *getting* to it.

Fuck me, you really do want to rub my nose in this, eh?

Prick.

Me and An…I mean Sarge, used to do the runs up until a few months back. I had the Remington and Sarge took the Glock. We only had them for emergencies. He had that fucking sword by then. I preferred the subtlety of my knuckle dusters.

Bit more personal, y'know?

Find this little One Stop on the outskirts of some village, some weird name, Curry Fartpants or something. What is with those stupid names?

I go in first. Sarge is watching the street, making sure we get no surprises. Some of those little places look dead, literally, but the amount of times we came out of shops on a run and have a meet n' greet waiting for us wasn't even funny.

After a bit of a poke around, it looked pretty safe to me. Started loading up a basket. There wasn't loads there, but some stuff we hadn't had for a bit.

Got some Vanilla Hob Nob Creams for one. I nearly pissed myself with joy when I found those at the back of the shelf. Got some fags, too. Camel Lights, but when you're desperate…

I drop the basket by the front, tell Sarge I'm just gonna do a sweep of the storeroom and head back in. The storeroom, though, well, it was pretty much bare. Some nappies and some of those piss-pads for men. Contemplated getting some for you Gaffer.

No?

Fine, fine, I'm getting to it.

Fucking hell.

I'm just about to head out, call it a day, when I see this rug on the floor. It just looked wrong, y'know? Really out of place. I gave it a bit of a kick and there's this trapdoor under it. Felt like I was Tintin or something. Just needed a Snowy.

Got the door open, turn my Maglite on and mosey on down. The smell hit me first; smelt like spoilt meat and shit. It had been one bouquet we had gotten used to on our journey down south. The amount of times we kicked in a door hoping for a place for the night only to be greeted by that smell. If your luck was really out, it would be followed closely by a moan.

Guess my luck was out too when I got into that cellar.

Smell.

Moan.

Like some sick director bastard had done it on purpose.

I shine my light round and I find where most of the food is, stacked up against one wall. As nice as finding that was, the fact I hadn't seen the deader who was making the sex noise wasn't filling me with happy-happy-joy-joy thoughts, y'know?

See this wall of boxes halfway down. Again, doesn't look right. Too neat and tidy. Just as I'm about to give it a nudge, a box of Quavers hits me on the head. The moan gets louder, and as sure as wiping follows a shit, this grey arm is fumbling around trying to give me a cuddle.

Thing is, he ain't alone down there. Can see more movement behind him. I bring up the shotgun and I'm just about to fire when I notice that he's got this metal collar round his neck. He's reaching for me, but there's no way he can get to me.

Time to have me some fun.

I move the boxes out of the way best I can, and can see four of them, two men, two women. They were proper rotten, looked like they had been melted, their skin was all saggy. So, I start laying into the first one, work the legs first, get him on the floor, on his back. They can't do shit then.

Get my knife out and start taking his fingers off, one at a time.

Ha, it's mad what you can do to them. Just stick the blade in above the knuckle and flick it, finger comes right off and they don't even scream. The moan was the same. I'd done both hands and had started on his toes when it happened.

Thought the boxes were empty. They didn't feel like they had anything in 'em at all. I was kneeling on the deaders back, had my ass to the others. They were on a tighter leash by the looks of it. Either way, they weren't any nearer to me.

Then, I feel this pain in my calf, like something's pressing down on it. I look down and there's this fucking zombie head. Its teeth were trying to chew through my combats and have a little nibble. I freaked, kicked out, and it went flying off into the dark. Heard this crack and this slurping sound. I'm wired now, I get that feeling again.

BA-BOOM.

BOOM.

BA-BOOM.

I try to breathe slower, and I think that's nipped it in the bud.

Just like in that movie, *Se7en*, I shouldn't have looked in the boxes. The nearest one was for Monster Munch. Ironic, really. Opened it up and there's half a dozen chomper heads all looking back at me, packed in real tight.

The one that got to me, though, was this young girl. Her head had been lopped off at an awkward angle, sort of diagonally through her jaw. What was left of her mouth was going at it like she was coming up on a pill.

BA-BOOM.

I drop the box, my knife hits the floor.

BOOM.

When I came to, the lightbulb above me was swinging. Ha, fuck me, even when I'm gone, I can still find the light switch, eh? The room is like an abattoir; there are bits of brain everywhere. Looked like at one stage I had an eye fetish as there were rows of them. Must've played conkers with them, as some were smashed to fuck. This jelly stuff was, like, everywhere.

Looked like it was an hour after waking up on Christmas Day as a kid. Open boxes everywhere, but instead of Lego and Barbie, there were piles of caved-in deader heads. There were loads; it was like a preparation room for the Khmer Rouge.

My boots were caked in blood, and skull, and stuff I didn't even know the name of. Even the deaders at the back were lying around in a hundred different pieces now. I found an ear in my pocket later on, when we got back and…

Yeah, I'll skip that bit. *You* can tell 'em if you want?

Whatever.

I get some food which isn't covered in all the colours of the blood rainbow and climb back up the ladder.

Standing there at the top is this old couple, clutching each other real tight. They ask me what I've done.

I didn't say anything at first. Wondered how the hell they had got there. Turns out they were upstairs the entire time. I tell them that I was in the basement and ran into some deaders, but it's okay. I'd taken care of it, so they were safe.

That old bat screamed like I'd set fire to her saggy tits. She came flying at me, calling me all sorts. I ain't taking shit from anyone, whether they carry a bus-pass or not. Hit the bitch when she got into range. She fell to the floor, got up, and did it again. The *noise* on her, fuck me.

Repeat.

She's on the floor again, rubbing her jaw. Must've cracked something. She ain't happy but it did shut her the fuck up.

Which was nice.

The husband, at least I *think* that's what he was, picked her up and said it'd be okay. Then he looked at me and asked me what I'd done to the village. I said I hadn't done anything to their village; I'd just took some stuff from the shop.

He squeezed the old bird and took a step towards me. Only then did I notice that his trousers were crusted with dried blood, and not just a little bit. It was like he had gone fly fishing in Blood Lake.

He then proceeds to regale me with the story about how they had kept everything tip-top, even when the dead came back.

How they kept the village together.

For the greater good, he said.

When they turned, they took care of them, took their heads off and stored them in the basement. Turns out the deaders down there had been their two sons and their daughters-in-law.

Aww, isn't that sweet, I thought. Fucking chop everyone else's heads off, but keep your own family in one piece.

Turns out that sometimes they didn't always wait until they were dead, either.

BA-BOOM.

I had cocked the shotgun before I even knew it.

BOOM.

Sarge was the next thing I saw. I was in a room I didn't recognise. Turns out I'd offed Mr and Mrs Natural Born Killers and gone upstairs, where other upstanding members of the community were hiding out from the looter—me—downstairs. In that state, I didn't know any better. There were four bodies lying on the floor in a neat row, all had their backs to me, all of them missing something important.

Their heads.

One of them had blood caked all over their crusty jugular.

An—

Sarge got up the stairs just as the last one finished begging and started pissing blood following a sudden meeting with a twelve gauge shell, and piss from his, well, normal place. He said that I almost took him out too.

So there. That was the last run I went on. You happy *now*, Gaffer? Make you feel better?

Anyway, we got back here. Andy told The Gaffer here what had occurred. I got a week in the coal scuttle.

That really fucking helped.

Thanks.

I'm being sarcastic by the way.

CHAPTER NINETEEN

"You know why you got a week out front, Dee. Don't pout and give it the big 'un. Self-defence is one thing, offing people without provocation is not really what we're trying to accomplish here, is it?" The Gaffer's beady eyes glared at her.

She met his stare. "No. I guess not," she growled back.

The Gaffer clapped his gloved hands together. "Ha, excellent. Seems like you're all making real progress here, Steve. What do you reckon?"

Steve continued scribbling as he looked around the room. "We're making progress, for sure, but it's still early days. Losing Tristan didn't help. We need stab—"

"We lost Tristan because he tried to introduce me to my maker. It was unfortunate. Ultimately, if you had done your job better, perhaps he would still be here," The Gaffer replied.

The scratching stopped, the room held its collective breath. "My job? My job is long gone, as is my family, and every single thing that I valued or held dear. Most people these days who are still alive, which is the minority I'd like to add, have seen more horror than the average person can cope with in a lifetime. Pretty much every person I've met in the past three months is suffering from some form of PTSD."

Scratch.

"You included."

The room gulped as one.

Scratch.

Scratch.

"You're the Doc, *Doc*, now, if you don't mind, I've got things to do, a camp to keep running, people to keep alive." The Gaffer pulled his trousers up and thudded out of the room.

"Steve?" Matt asked with a squeaky voice.

"Yes Matt?"

"I need to go wee-wee now."

MAY 14TH 2014

20:22

The monitor crackled and died, stealing the grainy image into an inky black void. Francis and Diane held hands even tighter.

The doctor broke the silence. "I'm really sorry, he's…your baby has died. We need to talk about what the next steps are, but I want you two to take a moment. If you need me, I'll be outside, okay? If not, I'll pop back in ten minutes and we'll go through what happens next. I'm really sorry for your loss."

The doctor trudged wearily out of the room, the door closing with a soft click. The sound seemed to be the signal for the outpouring of grief, as Francis and Diane grabbed hold of each other and set free the mountain of emotions that had been building up since the ultrasound had shown the baby, their baby, not moving and with no signs of life.

"H…he looked like he was just sleeping. His little thumb was by his mouth…" Francis gasped through waves of tears and sobbing.

Diane held him closer. "I can't believe it. How long did we try for? When that test came back positive, I thought it was a *miracle*. He was our miracle. I just can't—"

"It'll be alright, love. We'll get through this. We have each other; we'll try again. When you're ready," Francis said through judders and spasms of crying.

Diane convulsed as if wracked with electricity. "I want him, though, Francis. I want *him*."

CHAPTER TWENTY

Daffodils waved in the gentle breeze, sticking through the gaps between the railway sleepers, another indication that Mother Nature was taking the power back. "First sign of spring," Francis said, pointing to the scattered flowers.

Nate looked at them with as much interest as a vegetarian eyeing up a bacon sandwich. "Are we nearly there yet?" he complained.

Zena chuckled. "Not far now, Nathan. Just round that bend." She pointed to the near horizon, where the train tracks took a stern right turn, disappearing behind trees teeming with blossom. She took in a deep lungful of the early evening air, laced with natural perfume and damp concrete. "Rain's coming in. Only a shower. Always remember that smell as a kid. Never leaves you eh, Francis?"

Francis trudged alongside the woman. In the past week, since surviving the Penny Gaff of Death, he'd been glad of some grown-up company. "You're not wrong there, sister. It's up there with creosote, petrol and exhaust fumes." His mind flitted back.

"Petrol fumes? That's an odd one," Zena quipped. She climbed the rail and endeavoured to travel as far as she could without falling off; an amateur trapeze artist in practise.

"Ha, my dad had this blue Cortina. We never got to spend much time together, what with him being away in the army. When he got home, I used to be like a limpet. Wherever he went, you can bet your life I was there with him. He used to take me out on these little drives. Never too far, perhaps into town to get some sweets, or off to camp on Bonfire night. It was the trips to the petrol station that always stuck with me."

Francis pulled a bottle of water from a side pouch on his rucksack and took a swig. He offered it to Zena, who politely refused. "I'd be allowed to sit up front, the window was wound down, and I'd watch him fill the car up and watch the world go by. Petrol smelt good, but it was always when he had paid and we pulled away, window still open, those fumes would roll right in. Used to breathe them in deep. Ha, guess that's what you do when you're a kid. You do what feels good, rather than being too bogged down with doing what is right." He screwed the cap back on the bottle and slid it back into its home.

"What about him?" Zena shielded her eyes from the dropping sun and nodded towards the solitary figure thirty odd feet in front of them. Russ looked like he was a Scalextric car, on a fixed path equidistant between the rusting metal rails. Baseball-capped head looking down, hands tucked into the shoulder straps, he crushed the delicate spring flowers with no compunction.

Francis sighed. "It's gonna take some time, I guess. Sure would be good if he would say something, though. He's not said a peep since he watched that fella choke to death."

"I'm not that surprised. Not long after that, when he caved his head in to stop him coming back, he picked up what was left of his family and buried them, remember?" Zena replied, staring into the distance.

"We offered, sister. It was the least I could've done to take that burden off him. I know I would have wanted someone to…"

"What?"

"Nothing, doesn't matter. How far to go?" Francis asked, changing the subject as quickly as possible.

Zena stumbled off the rail, ruining the chance of breaking her twenty year old personal best. "Well, the station is only half a mile away. I think, Rontey is another ten, maybe twelve miles after that? I do appreciate it, you know? Not many people would do this."

Francis coughed and wiped his bristly beard with the back of his hand. "Hey, it's the least we can do. It's only a slight detour for us. After everything that's happened, I know I'd feel happier about you getting there in one piece."

"Well, it's taken me this long to get to here. The closer I get, the more scared I get," Zena confessed.

"What do ya mean?"

Zena shoved her hands into her pocket. "When this all started, I was in Oslo for work. I never thought for one moment I'd make it this far. Nearly didn't make it off the ferry. Then by the time we finally got to the port here, well, you remember what it was like in those first weeks. If *they* didn't get you, some opportunistic prick would. When you measure the distance first off in hundreds of miles, the notion that you will ever get back to something, anything that is 'your area', well, it seemed impossible."

Francis looked across to her and waited for her to continue. She fished out a Lego Boba Fett keyring; a single brass key hung from the metal hoop. "I never thought I'd get to use this again. Sounds stupid, but even something as monumentally mundane as putting a key in a lock, and stepping into your house, well…it's gone from being a pipe dream to being on the verge of reality. Of hopefully seeing Tom again."

She shoved the key back into her pocket. "Our first date, and where we're heading to, is two stops down from here. Every place I've lived, everywhere I've ever worked, exists up and down this train track. I've sat on trains rolling up and down these tracks after the best of times, and after the worst." Zena stepped onto the rail again, teetering as she edged along it.

"Except now, when I think back to those days, you know the *bad* ones, I can barely remember what the hell was so awful. Not just because of how crap everything is now, just…it's all so *impermanent*, eh? The person I am now would tell the me back then to shut the fuck up and get on with it. Robert Young was never worth crying over, or that job going door-to-door selling fucking discounted dinners at some new eaterie was as shit as it sounded."

Zena concentrated as she wobbled after an overstep. "Phew. So now, I'm not getting the train down these tracks, I'm walking down them, which is odd, admittedly. But I'm scared. I'm here. I'm here despite everything I've gone through, for over *nine* months. What if he's not there? What if he's been evacuated? What if…what if he's dead?" Zena let the words hang in the air as she tried to regain her balance. "Balls," she uttered as she fell off.

"Honestly? I can't say what we'll find when we get there, if anything. If I believed in some higher power or being, I'd probably be able to comfort you and tell you with a sure heart that we'll find him there. All I can do is hope. That's all I've got now. Well, that and keeping that little tyke alive." Francis nodded over to Nathan, who had taken his turn to balance on the metal track.

"Hope? Think that's a commodity Russ is lacking right now. What do you do when everything you love is gone?" Zena said.

Francis looked across to her. "First you go a little mad. The rest? That's up to you. You can't live with sorrow flooding your heart, it'll destroy you."

Zena stared into Francis' deep blue eyes. "Speaking from experience?"

"More than you know, sister," Francis coughed. "More than you know."

"Hey Francis, look." Nathan pointed off to a small station sitting amidst the overgrowth. It looked like it was squatting there, unloved and unwanted.

Francis and Zena broke their gaze. "Good find, kid. We'll be spending the night here. You should have some reading time before bed if you're lucky."

Nathan pumped his fists in the air like Rocky and ran off to catch up with Russ, who plodded on like a human monorail.

The three stragglers climbed the ramped end of the platform. Russ stood waiting for them, leaning on a sign proclaiming they were in;

The painted veneer was chipped and scaly, revealing the rust-coloured metal meat under the outer skin. The last smudge of sun lingered, just about to fall off the edge of the earth for another day, before the night would usher in the cadaverous embrace of nightmare-filled sleep.

"What's in this place? Anything of note?" Francis asked, pulling his bag off his shoulders and easing the tension out of one of them with rough pinches of skin.

Zena shook her head. "Nope, nothing worth stopping for. It was only a two horse town before this all started. I doubt either have stayed around since it all kicked off."

The platform had weeds sprouting through the joins between the large concrete paving slabs; clumps of dandelions swayed annoyingly. A rectangular building housing a small ticket office, waiting room, and lavatories ran two-thirds the length of the structure.

Newspaper had been stuck to the inside of the windows with Blu-Tack. Judging by the lurid headlines, they had gone up just after the dead had started wandering around, nibbling on folk:

THE DEAD WALK !

It was one of the more bleeding obvious exclamations, though Zena did look at the closing date on a voucher for Paintballing in Wiltshire.

"You guys hold up a minute. I'll go check inside, make sure there isn't anyone waiting for the train to nowhere." Francis flicked the baton to extend it to its full bashing length.

Holding a small Maglite in his free hand, he sidled up to the door and tugged on the handle, fully expecting resistance. It opened with a pathetic PFFFTT.

Switching on like a baby monitor, he motioned the others for silence. He pulled the door open as gently as possible. Once it was wide enough, he planted a foot against the door like any good double-glazing salesman and crept into the gloom.

The light from outside was sparse. Through the paper-covered windows, it gave the effect of a mock dusk. Zena held the door for him, holding a wrench in her hand which had been liberated from the weapon stash back at the Penny Gaff.

A thin rod of light stabbed through the air and flashed around the interior. Symmetrical rows of uncomfortable metal benches stood idle, some covered in mouldering food packaging and more newspapers.

A Perspex wall with a circular metallic grille looked out over its kingdom, with a rectangular hole cut at the bottom for the transaction of tickets for money. It looked like a gormless robot. The torchlight slashed through the particle-laden air; flakes of dead skin and fragments of hair drifted aimlessly around, disturbed from their kip.

From behind a bench at the back came the scuffing of boots and a stifled belch. Francis sighed and reluctantly skated slowly through the rubbish-strewn floor to the origin of the sounds.

He rounded the bolted down bench and shone the light onto the back of a crouched figure. A mottled grey hoodie was a snug fit on the man. Matching grey combat trousers ended a few inches above the ankles, which were covered in pulled-up white sports socks with pale brown Chelsea boots.

The man was leaning over the slightly steaming remains of an elderly fellow whose checked shirt had been torn open. The figure's blood-soaked hands rummaged through the assortment of guts, stopping from time to time to extricate lumps of meat.

"Goddamit," Francis muttered under his breath. He pulled the baton over his shoulder and inched forward, ready to administer a bit of old-fashioned justice.

As he got to within striking distance, the figure spun around. Mad, startled eyes looked up at Francis. The torchlight shone into the back of his retina, giving his ocular orbs a reddish tint.

Between chewing on strips of pancreas, he waved his gory hands. Droplets of blood were shaken over Francis and the poor geriatric laying very dead on the floor.

"Hhmhhmmhh nnaaaaahh!"

Francis looked at the man with a furrowed brow. He peered into his eyes and noticed a lack of tell-tale infection. "What the hell are you doing, slim?" he demanded.

The man sheepishly pointed to his mouth, indicating that he might be a cannibal, but he sure as hell was a cannibal with impeccable eating decorum. Francis lowered the baton and waited for the man to finish. Zena, Russ, and Nathan were now in the room and were staring at the scene with equal parts disgust and confusion.

The cannibal ran a finger around his gums, he fished out a nugget of clotted vein from his teeth and flicked it behind him. After reverently placing the hunk of digestive organ on the old fella's shirt, he rubbed his hand against the dead man's trousers before holding it out to Francis, gibbering, "Wait, don't hit me. Oh you haven't. This isn't what it *looks* like.

"Honest."

"So, erm, yeah, this is going to sound a little crazy, but I kinda found him here like this, so…I…erm, well, you know…"

"You ate him?" Zena finished, glaring at the man with a look that suggested she was about to stove his head in.

You know the look.

That one.

"Well, not at first. I'm not a savage. I stuck the screwdriver in his ear first." The man elicited a nervous high-pitched laugh. "Look." With a grip usually reserved for shoddy care home workers, he cranked the dead man's head ninety degrees to the side.

The shaft of a long reach screwdriver protruded from the old timer's large flappy ear. A skin of dried blood like the kind you find formed on the top of cooling rice pudding, split, releasing a tidal wave of crimson liquid over the dead man's liver-spotted face.

"Oops."

"I didn't want him coming back, so, you know, took the necessary steps to stop him doing so and eating me."

Francis interjected, "Whilst you were eating *him?*"

The man wrung his hands and let out another nervous laugh. "So, I guess I'll just be on my way…" he said, and peered behind the group looking for the exit.

Francis crossed his arms over his formidable chest. Even with the apocalypse, he still possessed an imposing demeanour. "I don't think so, slim. Let me ask you something. How did you know he was dead? Did you check?"

"Ha ha ha, of course I did. I did that thing, you know? With the pulse. And the breathing check, that one too, nothing. I think. My fingers are pretty cold. So I…"

"Rammed a screwdriver into his head, tore his clothes open and started eating him," Zena growled. She took another step forward; the wrench wavered in time with her anger-infused body.

"Look. If it's any consolation, there's still some good stuff left. I haven't gotten down to the gristle and bone yet. Urgh, who wants bhat, eh? No? I'm not getting the cannibal vibe from you guys, to be honest. You're not…you're not *straighters* are you? You know, those people that only eat food from the last age, before the fall of man. Shit. Well, okay, how about I take this one with me? He's only going to stink the place up and I'll just go, no harm, no foul, yeah?" The man gave them a salesman's grin, even going so far as the wink and the dual-finger pistols.

"I'll give you to the count of ten. If you're still here after that, I'm going to introduce your head to your insides, via your rectum." Zena spoke with a Zen calmness. The wrench, however, added a violent undercurrent.

"Well, hold on a minute, that's not fa—"

"One…"

The man gulped and looked from face to face, hoping for a dissenting opinion he could play on.

"…two…"

A hand grabbed the screwdriver handle and twisted out of the ear canal it had violated. As the stem was retracted it pulled a wad of wax, brain, and drying blood with it. "Oops."

"…three…"

"Fine, fine, but you crossed the Ralston-a-tron tonight. What goes around, comes around, you feel me?"

"…four…"

The man slid the screwdriver into the hoodie pouch and barged his way past the group and out of the door, casting one last hungry look at the carcass as the door closed behind him.

Zena sighed and the adrenaline, held back in reserve, flushed itself from her blood stream. "Man, that guy was an arsehole. We should really take care of him. Who's to say he won't come back and 'check to see if we're dead' in the night?"

Francis knelt down by the dead body and started to push the spilled offal back into the body cavity it had until recently resided in. With as much shoved in as his bile duct could muster, he buttoned the shirt up. The blood soaked into the thin cotton shirt; red bloomed across it like a well-played game of Plague Inc.

"He won't come back. We'll keep a watch out tonight anyway. Let's take him outside, clean this place up a bit, get summat to eat and rest. It's your big day tomorrow, sister. You need your zeds," Francis said as he worked. Russ appeared at the feet of the cannibalized body, waiting to help take it outside.

CHAPTER TWENTY-ONE

"STOP"

The RV door swung open as if it contained a tempest. Malky's gigantic form jumped out of the cab and landed on the cracked tarmac. He shot an acidic look at the driver. "You're going too fast. If you go too fast, we'll lose them. We are too close now for some idiot to fuck this up."

The driver's brain instantly sent his sweat glands into overdrive. A sheet of salt water coruscated down his forehead; his armpits turned a deep crimson. "S…s…s…sorry, Malky," he stuttered. His words were met with a barely noticeable shake of the head. The door thundered closed, and the driver's sphincter released slightly.

Malky walked to the back of the blocky vehicle. The latest cage-dweller was a sullen mass of tears, blood, and faecal matter. "Shhh, have some self-respect. Go out like a man. Not a mewling pathetic worm."

Devin appeared from the other side of the vehicle. "They're not too far behind. They will catch up shortly. We are still on target, see how Her flock has swollen over the last few days. There will be more than enough to overwhelm the non-believers. This could be the biggest one we've created yet."

A few hundred feet away ambled a sea of grey, interspersed with the odd flash of colour from disintegrating clothing or gore-stained limbs. The collective moan rumbled across the distance to them, chopping through the trio like a jacked up sub-woofer. A pitter patter from between them signalled further loosening of their captive's bowels.

"Six more days. This is the moment where we need to exercise caution. The other chapters being where we need them to be are vital in order for this to work," Devin lisped.

"They have not let us down yet, your Grace," Malky replied flatly.

Devin looked back at him and held up his fiery charcoal red arm. "I think they let me down once, wouldn't you say?" he countered.

Malky nodded. "Of course. I meant no disrespect. I still hold myself to account for that day. Just say the word and I will offer you my heart and swell the flock."

"Don't be so dramatic my friend. If it weren't for you, then *he* would have made sure there wasn't anything left of me for you to find. I am grateful to you. Your single mindedness showed me my weakness, and granted Ishtar the chance to guide me anew."

"I hear the words, your Grace. But they do not make me feel less remiss in my duty."

A fingerless blob of a hand rested on Malky's shoulder. "Fret not, we are here today, and we are ready to continue with the purge. As long as everyone does their duty, we will…we *cannot* fail."

"Y…y…you're *mad*, both of you," a gentle voice ventured.

Devin and Malky turned to regard the source of the words. The half-naked man was slumped in the gently swinging cage, his skin growing paler with the steady loss of blood from his slashed feet.

"What will you do when there's no-one left? Kill yourselves and join this f...fl...flock of yours?"

Another moan resonated around the two stopped vehicles.

"Thought not. You are worse than those monsters. They're purer than you will ever be. They were created the same way that we were. You two are b...bastards of evil. Mummy and Daddy never show you any love? You d...d...dis...disgust me. You'll get yours, make my words, y...you'll get yours."

Malky swatted the cage with a balled fist, causing the contraption to move backwards. The man receded into the depths as far as he could; the goliath's hands caught it on the back swing. "Good. You do have some fight left in you."

Devin peered at the man, who seemed repulsed by the fearsome visage in front of him. "You know nothing of what you speak, penitent. We have been chosen by *Her*, she foresaw this day, only we had planned for it, only we were—"

"Bullshit," the man rocked forwards in the cage and launched a wad of thick pasty spit. It hit Devin in the ruin of his sliced up eyeball.

"This isn't a prophecy you fucking fruitcake. It was the probe that came back, the thing that *we* built, everyone knows that. The stuff it brought back from that meteor caused this, not some fucking bullshit text or whatever the h...h...hell you're basing your madness on."

Devin let the ball of bubbled saliva slide down over his split iris. It paused slightly on the lip of his eyelid before dripping onto his boot. His mouth curled in one corner.

"Don't you remember that night? When the sky went red? This is just shit luck, that's all, nothing else. But no, you fucking nutjobs u...u...use it as a basis for this? What sick fucks are you? You're scared little men, and one day, people will stand against you, and no matter what you do, they will prevail, and your light will go out of this world."

Devin's remaining fully-functioning hand slid slowly around his back.

"And when it does, I hope to fuck they let you come back. Just so they can kill you again. I hope they c...c...cu...cut you up into pieces and leave your diseased, fucked-up brain till last. Cos once you go, it'll be a symbol that evil fucks like you are nothing but—"

The curved knife whistled through the bars and slammed deep into the man's right lung. The force pushed him back against the frame of the cage. The man's fading eyes looked from the hilt of the buried knife and back into Devin's face. His face creased in agony as Devin slowly rotated the blade. A cruel smile had birthed into life; the crease of it met the face-long scar which gave him the appearance that his skin had cracked into three.

Clammy hands slapped against Devin's. With the last reserves of strength, the man hauled himself towards Devin, whose hand sunk further within the man's chest. Blood-flecked lips pulsed, desperate to force out one last thing.

"—cowards."

His body shuddered. Viscera-covered hands fell slack and rapped the side of the cage. His eyes rolled upwards into the recesses of his sockets. With some trouble, Devin dragged his hand back out through the man's ribcage. A broken bone sliced through the webbing between thumb and forefinger.

Another moan, seemingly in mourning, bounced down the road; the distance from sender to recipient had been greatly reduced.

"Get him out of there, Malky. See to it that he does not violate the flock with his seditious soul. We'll drive a little further and prepare the next penitent. We'll save the bleeding until the sun falls."

Malky nodded, unlocked the cage, and slung the lifeless body to the ground. As undead claws sought to gain purchase on the ground, Malky brought a steel-toe-capped boot arcing down through the temple and into the parietal lobe. The scrabbling ceased. The foot raised and fell like a piston, spreading pieces of brain and shards of skull across the road.

CHAPTER TWENTY-TWO

"Man, today is full on slow, eh? Guess we'll be out on a run tomorrow, though. Better than sitting around here on sentry duty. No wonder people fall asleep eh, Deano?" Paul said, punctuating with a bored sigh.

Dean flicked his wrist and the seven of hearts spun through the air and hit the rim of the bucket. "Bollocks."

Paul walked over to the receptacle and picked up the cards which littered the roof. "Three nil, mate. Looks like I'll be keeping my crown for another night. What did you make of the other day?"

"Tristan?"

"Yeah, bit odd, huh? How he just changed like that. Still, figure we're better off with The Gaffer than without. Remember what life was like before we found this place?" Paul reminisced, he trotted back to his fold-up chair and passed a handful of cards back to Dean.

"Mate, don't even get me started. We did alright for the first few months, but we were having too many close calls. Do you remember Dunstable? Fuck, barely got out of that church with both testicles attached," Deano agreed.

"Well, to be fair, we were being dicks. No way we should've gone into a town that size; we were bloody lucky when you think about it."

Dean turned the card over to reveal the Jack of spades. He aimed and flicked the card at the target. "Take a bow my son. True, but we were getting desperate. You know what those times called for mate."

Paul spun the three of spades through the air. "Balls, pretty close though. Yep, just glad we found the poster. Dread to think where we'd be now if we hadn't."

"Shh, did you hear that?" Dean asked. He jumped up and grabbed the rifle which was resting against his chair. The two men looked in the direction of a clatter.

Paul gestured to Dean and slunk off into the murk. The corrugated iron roof clanked and popped, even with his careful steps.

"Whoever is there, best tell me now before I fucking shoot ya," Dean hissed.

"Woah there, tiger. It's me, Thomas."

Dean squinted through the darkness of night and recognised the man they had saved. "Paul, it's alright. It's Tommy. Can I call you Tommy?"

"No."

"Oh."

"What the hell are you doing, Thomas? It's the middle of the night, you should be in bed, not creeping around up here," Paul said angrily. He could feel his heart-rate slowing back to normal.

The two sentries walked back to their seats and set down their weapons. "Whose turn is it?" Dean asked.

"Bet you can see for miles if it was a bit lighter. Never been up here. Couldn't sleep so thought I'd have a look. Don't mind, do ya lads?" Thomas asked.

"Knock yourself out, mate. My turn, Pauly. Watch as the comeback kid kicks your ass," Dean said, safely bunkered in his chair.

Thomas walked to the corner of the rectangular plateau of the roof, before it fell away to a steep fall down to the guttering.

"Fuck, the *wind*. That one was going in when it took it away," Dean whinged.

"Shut up, mate. My turn now. Just need to…YES, get in! One all, everything to play for," Paul wooted.

"Guys…" Thomas said softly.

"And…it's….fuck, that card was bent, you've given me the shit cards here, Paul."

"A poor workman always blames his tools. That's what your missus used to say anyway. *Zing*, I went there."

"*Guys*, look over there," Thomas hissed, finally managing to get the mens' attention. They reluctantly shuffled their way over to him. "Look, just over there. One o'clock. That light keeps flickering; must be going through the trees." Thomas pointed to the gloom and took a few steps back.

"Where? I can't see any—" Paul started to say.

Thomas edged forwards quietly, his hands rubbing together.

"Ah, there it is. Good spot, man," Dean finished.

Thomas blew warm, stale breath into his hands. "No bother. Wonder who it is?"

Paul walked back to his chair and grabbed his weapon. "Let's go have a look. Dean you stay up here. Me and Thomas will go check it out, cool?" Dean nodded and continued to peer into the night.

"I can't see anything now. Where were they?" Paul asked. He was scanning the horizon through his rifle's scope. The barrel was resting on the links of the gate. With no moon and no light, he couldn't see much at all.

Thomas was kneeling by the middle of both gates. He saw the coal scuttle, but beyond that it was all a blanket of black and grey. A glint of light stuck out like a football fan in the wrong end. "There Paul, right hand side, near to where you found me."

"Oh yeah. Only looks like one person. They're being cautious, could be injured?" Paul ventured.

"Or they could be scouting this place out, seeing what the defences are, sizing us up, working out our—"

"Oh, he's waving to us. Yep. Hi mate. Okay, so that answers that then." Thomas waved back limply. "Keep an eye out, yeah? I'm going out."

Thomas pushed the rusting gate open, checked the area, and cautiously walked towards the still waving man. As he got closer he could see that the man was in pretty good shape. He was wearing army fatigues, and had a rather hefty backpack, which he seemed to bear with little to no consternation. When he got to within ten feet or so, the man ceased his waving and walked towards him.

"Tom."

"Tom?"

"Thompson."

"Tom Thompson?"

The two men were now within poking distance. "Yes, my name is Tom Thompson. How do you do? Was going to hold off introductions till the morning. Most people don't really appreciate doing this at night, but once I saw you, thought it best. You know, in case you thought I was a muncher, or a scout or something for some big, bad war band," the militarily-dressed man said.

"Well, are you?"

"Am I what? Tom? Yes, that's my name, I—"

Thomas massaged the bridge of his nose, *this is going to be a long night.* "No, I know your name, you told me. Twice. I meant are you a scout for a big, bad war band?"

Tom laughed. "Ha, no. Mind you, if I was, I think it unlikely I would divulge this information to you so willingly, eh?"

"True. I'm Thomas. We might have to call you something else with you having a similar name. Tom Two or…I dunno, Duane or something? And Tom Thompson? Your parents didn't like you very much, huh?"

Tom laughed louder. "I get that a lot. So are you the Big Cheese here?"

"No, not in the slightest. Only got here myself a few weeks back. Tell ya what. Let me check you for weapons and let's continue this discussion the other side of this fence, yeah?" Thomas said, conscious of the fact they were stood on a road, with a dark, sinister forest just beyond their visual range.

"Sure thing, Thomas. I've got my Glock and this hammer. You're welcome to check me if you want, but…"

"What?"

"Well, just be careful. I'm pretty ticklish."

CHAPTER TWENTY-THREE

"Wow, this place is pretty cool. Shame they don't do the biscuits anymore. Used to love their Chocolate Crunchy Crème's. Well, until it transpired that the chocolate content was as low as a diabetic's blood sugar levels." Tom took in the vast space of the factory.

Firm metallic clangs sounded from one end of the building. The Gaffer, dressed in a red and silver tracksuit, emblazoned with MB on the front and 'Guildford Goblins' on the back, got to the bottom and walked towards the visitor. In one hand he held a steaming mug of tea.

"'Ello my son. We don't normally get visitors this late. I doubt you're out trick or treating?" he asked, blowing into the mug which sent whirls of steam spiralling into the frigid air.

Tom shot his hand out, which The Gaffer took firmly. "Pleased to meet you, Mister Gaffer. I'm Tom Thompson, and no, unfortunately I'm not out trick or treating, though I could murder a Twix right about now."

The Gaffer raised an eyebrow and a smile appeared on his face. He gestured towards his office. "Cheers, Thomas. I got this. Just let Andy know what's happening and get one of Grimm's chums to make sure we're not interrupted, okay? C'mon son, let's go have a chat upstairs. I can make you a cuppa and we can have a proper chinwag, deal?"

Tom nodded vigorously and walked towards the stairs, taking two at a time. He had to wait at the top for The Gaffer to catch up.

The leather covering the Queen Ann creaked as The Gaffer's bulk filled the chair. Before he sat down, he had honoured his agreement and provided a cup of tea with milk and three sugars, in a Thunderbirds mug.

"You do not know how good it is to have a warm drink, Mister Gaffer. Been a good couple of weeks. At least. Thanks, much obliged." Tom held the mug in both hands, using it as a mitt radiator.

"Good. Now, as we're friends, would you mind telling me what the fuck you're doing sneaking around outside my gaff at stupid o'clock at night?"

Tom sighed, placed the mug down on an unopened envelope on the desk in front of him, and pulled his backpack round from the side of his chair to his legs. "Do you mind?"

The Gaffer sat back. His hand slipped to his trouser pocket as he shook his head. "Be my guest, Tom." His finger slipped the safety off the Ruger.

Through a whirlwind of unclipping and loosening of drawstrings, Tom plunged his arm into the backpack and rummaged around in its bowels. His tongue slapped around his lips and philtrum in deep concentration. "A-ha, here we go. Always the same, eh? Got loads of the bloody things, but just can't find them when you need to. Have a look at this, Mister Gaffer."

He held a pamphlet in his hands. After a brief attempt at straightening out some stubborn folds, he passed it across the desk and picked up his mug again. "F-A-B, Gaffer," he said, with his best Virgil Grissom accent.

The safety reapplied, The Gaffer's face went from one of concentration, to one of a monkey been given a new swinging rope toy. "What's this?" he asked.

Tom took a gulp of tea, coughed as it went down the wrong way and managed to splutter. "It's a Survival Guide. My friend Phil wrote it. Well, we all helped with some bits, but *he* wrote it. It's not just a guide though. We've been trying to meet up with other survival groups, spread the word, tell people that they're not alone. You know? Reach out."

Thumbs the size of fig rolls rifled through the sheets of paper. "This guy spent a lot of time on the 'Weapons to fuck things up' section, eh?" He flicked back to the front cover. "Thirty four safe zones?"

"Yep. Well, it was at the time we printed it. I've been on the road for…eight weeks now. A few others are also out doing the same thing. I've come across six decent sized camps so far, but yours looks the biggest. You've got a nice little gig here, Mister Gaffer," Tom said, taking in the detail of the office, looking at the night sky through the large window which framed his host.

"Thanks, I think. So you guys actively go out and meet people? Survivors I mean. What for?" the Gaffer asked, his voice soft and anxious.

"Well, don't you think that we need to work together to survive this thing? You know we're not the dominant species anymore. The only way we're going to get through this is by finding likeminded people. Though not everyone thinks that way, it would seem," Tom replied.

"What do you mean, Tom?"

Tom took another mouthful of tea. "Well, of the six camps, one was…not very keen to help. They locked me up for five days; thought they were going to kill me at one stage."

"What happened?"

"They let me go in the end, gave me a bit of a pasting first off, but it didn't matter. Not when I crept back in the night after and slit their throats while they slept before burning their bodies." Tom leant back blissfully. "Man, this tea is *good*."

The Gaffer chuckled. "I almost believed you then. There's no way you would…"

Tom sat up and looked across the table. "Mister Gaffer, I assure you, I'm telling the truth. Just before this kicked off, I had just gotten through…special training. I may look like a bumbling idiot, but if I wanted to, you would be dead before you managed to shoot me with the pistol you have concealed in your left trouser pocket. Good choice putting the safety back on, by the way."

An unconscious look down made The Gaffer laugh again. "You know what son? I like you. So, tell me about this group of yours."

A beaming smile greeted the question. "Sure thing. We headed out to Rhayader in Wales on Day One. Complete blind luck I went with them to be honest. Not complaining, though. We got things set up just the way Phil said we would. He's a pretty sound guy, bit quieter these days, especially after what happened, but isn't everyone? We've all lost someone, people that were your entire world. Just now, it's all about how we deal with that loss and what we do to try to keep the light burning. These are dark times. Though I don't need to tell you that. Your little memorial wall downstairs tells me that you already know."

"So, what do you want?"

"If you don't mind, I'd like to stay a few days, give me a chance to sleep in something which isn't hanging from a tree. Some hot food would be brilliant, then I'll be on my way. I'll leave you guys some of these, and, if you don't mind, when I get back, I can add you to our network. When we have a plan and some numbers, we can then get everyone organised," Tom said.

"Have I missed something? Organised for what?" The Gaffer asked, confusion reigning supreme.

Tom looked across the table like a cat glancing at a light reflection. "Erm, so we can take back what is *ours* of course? I'm sure at some point you would like to go back to living in a world with running water, electricity, Wi-Fi, proper food, and all without the risk of being eaten alive by one of the undead?"

The Gaffer's eyebrows rose in surprise. "You know what? I never even thought we would do that. We've spent so long just trying to survive, getting through one day at a time, never even thought about what we would do in the long term."

"Then I'm glad I found you, Mister Gaffer."

"As am I, Tom Thompson. As am I. This place will be your home for as long as you want. I'll tell my men to make sure you're treated as our guest. Thank you, Tom. You've given us something I had forgotten about."

Tom gave a quizzical look.

"Hope."

"Think nothing of it. I'm glad of two things. One, that I don't have to sneak back in the middle of the night and slit your throat. You're quite a big so-and-so."

The Gaffer laughed. "And the second?"

"You sure as hell make a kickass cup of tea."

CHAPTER TWENTY-FOUR

The fire crackled. The light drizzle caused it to hiss and spit out gobbets of flame and sparks. Tom Thompson pulled his coat in tighter, cradling a mug of tea. Sleeping inside the factory over the last couple of days had revitalised him. He felt as if the near-constant dampness within his skin had finally evaporated.

"What is it like out there now?" Dean asked. He looked up to the heavens, searching for a respite from the autumnal shower.

Tom took a sip and held the mug to his chest. The heat seeped through to his skin. "It's pretty much the same as it has been since the early months. Most of the undead seem to be in the cities. We steer clear of them. As it was before, it's always the living that are the worst."

Paul threw some soggy twigs on the fire, causing it to rasp with disgust. "Sounds to me like we've got it pretty good in here," he ventured, ducking back from the *woosh* of heat expelled from the additional kindling.

"I reckon so. Mind you, as dangerous as it is out there, I kinda like it. Think it's the whole 'lone-wolf' thing. Look after myself. Though it has its downsides," Tom replied, taking another mouthful of tea.

"You must have some crazy stories," Paul said, rubbing his forehead to check if his eyebrows were still intact. He sighed with relief when he felt them.

"Room for a little one?"

The trio turned as one to see Andy stalk through the fine mist. "Do you mind, lads? Could do with a bit of a break."

The group shuffled around on their folded-up blankets, allowing Andy a gap to slot his frame into. He nodded thanks. "What are you guys up to anyway?" he asked, trying to reinvigorate the enveloping silence.

"New guy here was just gonna give us a little tale from the apocalypse. Go on, mate." Dean gestured towards to Tom, who wiggled himself into a position of comfort and begun;

'Well, this was a few months back now, not long after we got to Rhayader, actually. Philip asked for some volunteers to go out and find other groups like ours. I raised my hand faster than you could say *boo*. Was kinda cool, you know? Being out there, meeting people, seeing if I could help out.

I headed east. One of our guys, Jay, we hadn't heard from him since he went off to find his family. Figured I'd head that way and see if by any miracle I could find him. Long story short on that, no, just hope he's alright, whatever he's doing.

So, I get to Kidderminster, which is now better than before the zombies started eating people, if you can believe it. Actually one of the more organised places I've been to. Small pockets of survivors everywhere, banding together, helping each other out. A real sense of community which is severely lacking nowadays.

At the risk of getting on my soapbox, you'd think the fall of society would make us all want to put aside our differences and work against a common threat. Nope, Kidderminster is an exception to what life is like out there now, believe me.

A group gave me a heads up on some larger camps, so I headed out to them, bit closer to Birmingham. Reports from there are not good. The RAF firebombed it quite early on; all it did was put *them* into the ascendency.

The directions took me to a little village, proper picture-perfect place, thatched cottages, pubs which look like they were built when Shakespeare was supping on mead. They were supposed to be holed up in the church there, St Martin's I think. Got to the bottom of the lane and you could tell that it was gone.

For one, I could see that the doors were open. Not exactly the sign of a fortified base, huh? A few of the dead were milling about, took care of them pretty easy. Stragglers are okay. It's when you get the groups, that's when you know you have to bug out.

Thought I'd better check the place out. Wouldn't want to leave anyone up a creek without a paddle. Can't really go on about helping people if I don't actually do it, huh?

Took me twenty minutes to clear that place. The pews made things nice and orderly, though. Reckon most of the village was in there. Men, women and children, some were in their Sunday best, too. Weird thing, though, was that some of them had gunshot wounds. It was like they'd almost been intentionally killed just so that they would come back.

I'm rambling. Sorry, that's not the weird thing.

So I'm walking out of the village, cleaning the assortment of weapons used in culling the local zombie population, and I hear this metallic rattling sound.

I'm looking around, trying to work out where it's coming from and then, from this petrol station, this family of five come trudging at me. They're moaning like they've just sat through a five hour talk on Solipsism at the local hall, so I know they're not going to invite me in for some Horlicks and Digestives.

See the upstanding father first, arms out front, looking like he's pushing an invisible shopping trolley. Around his wrist, though, is a length of chain, which has shackled him to his wife, and she's linked to their eldest son in the same manner. He's linked to his younger sister and, in turn, she's linked to her baby brother.

Thing is, the youngest kid is dead-dead, and the four of them are dragging this body around. Must've been for a while, as if it wasn't for the Pokemon pyjamas hanging off the body, you'd think it was just an animal or something.

Not much left of the poor little bugger, either; his arms and face were scoured down to the bone. Even with the dragging, they were moving at a fair old rate. Barely had time to sort myself out before they were onto me.

Figured I'd start with the bloke and work my way down the chain-gang. Seemed the best way of doing stuff.

So I step up and slam my knife into the guy's head. He goes out like a candle. Then the 'unique-ness' of the situation kicks in. The old man drops to the ground, but he's still linked to his family. Before I get a chance to take care of his missus, they starting to wrap round me like they wanna welcome *me* into the family, work out when we should go camping in the summer.

The kids start pulling on my gear with multiple pairs of hands, teeth trying to work their way through my clothes. The woman is on a slant as she's got the joy of dragging her husband.

I manage to stick the knife up through the wife's mouth. Could see the blade in there, you know? Gave it a twist, which made her eyes go up and then she fell slack.

One of the kids manages to find the divide between my trousers and top and starts chewing on my hip. I know that if I don't take care of them quickly, I'm gonna go out.

I brought my elbow down on the boy's head, which took a bit of a chunk out of my side, but least he wasn't connected to me anymore. Their mum, collapsing to the floor, yanked them off to one side, probably what saved my life I reckon. By the time they regain their footing, I've managed to get the other knife out and took care of them.

Took no pleasure in that, poor bastards. Did make me wonder if the same thing that happened to the churchgoers befell them too. Started checking the bodies, but couldn't find any gunshots, which was something.

However, I did find a small plastic box taped to each of their chests, the bottoms of which were blown out and scorched. You could see through the container and into their bodies. It was sick. Took me an hour to dig a hole to bury them; figured for all they had gone through, especially in the last moments, that it was the least I could do for them.

Goes back to what I was saying earlier. You'd think that people would want to work together now, but as always, in every bad situation, there are always people that want nothing more than to make something out of it.

I'd guess that for every three camps I've found in the last few months, there is one that has been wiped off the face of the earth. Sometimes you can tell that it was just bad luck. Others, though…I saw the same thing as I did back in that church.'

MAY 14TH 2014

20:57

Francis lay down on Diane's lap. His eyes were red and puffy. Diane stroked her tummy bump with a gentle reverence.

We were going to call you George, after your Grandad. You never knew him, but you would've liked him.

Her hands caressed the taut skin of her belly. The ultrasound gel had given her skin a waxy surface, shiny and gleaming.

We were going to buy a house in the country, a little cottage or something, away from the town, a big garden for you and Daddy to play football in.

Fingers splayed over her distended belly button, a mound of knotted flesh on top of her stomach hill.

On Sundays, we'd have a roast dinner, and then after, we'd all go for a walk around the fields, perhaps head into the forest and feed the ponies.

She traced a line from the crest down to the pit of her breasts.

On your first day of school, we'd pick you up and take you out to wherever you wanted to go for dinner, treat you to pudding afterwards, too.

Your favourite.

Her fingers ascended to the summit of her tummy again.

And when you grew up, I'd vet all your girlfriends, make sure that only the best would do for my Ge—

Diane's hand stopped moving. Francis bolted upright, his face white with shock. "Did…did…did you just…"

Diane nodded and placed both of her hands on top of the baby bump. "George just kicked. H…he…he's still *alive*."

CHAPTER TWENTY-FIVE

"Bastard must've come around after and carted him off in the night," Zena said, looking at the depressed area of long grass where they had dumped the old man the previous night. "Told you we should've dealt with him."

Francis shrugged and headed off down the train tracks. Russ had resumed his daily plodding and was a little way off already. "Just because you *can* kill someone without legal consequences, doesn't mean you *should*. C'mon kid."

Nate looked from the man to Zena and then to the train tracks. He huffed and started to hop from sleeper to sleeper.

The track wound its way through the countryside like an irrigation channel. With no speeding metal snake travelling down the line for the best part of a year, nature had taken the opportunity to claw back some of its territory.

The tall grass verge had crept from its borders, across the mud and gravel no man's land either side of the railway, and taken first dibs. Patches of thistles and dock leaves made new homes amongst the flourishing grassy path. In scattered patches the track was almost completely covered.

Birds tweeted and chirruped in the branches, unseen. The fresh verdant reclamation now provided ample sustenance for them approaching mating season. The sounds of human commerce were being forgotten, relegated to a historic time period.

"Without meaning to sound like a damp squib, how far into town is your house?" Francis asked Zena, stepping over a pile of rabbit droppings which he had to stop Nathan from eating, thinking they were Maltesers.

Zena laughed as Nate rubbed his hands down his trousers, smelling his fingers, his nose wrinkling with the smell of shit. "From the station, there's a hill which leads to a bridge and a row of houses. We're up there, number thirteen."

She handed the kid a bottle of water to wash his hands. "We hated living so close to the station sometimes, especially early morning. The sound of them going by, you got used to. It was when they sat at the station and then moved off. The bloody sound of them, especially after a few bottles of wine the previous night." Francis smiled and looked a little relieved.

"Don't worry, we won't have to fight our way through town to get back to my place. Look, there's the bridge." Zena pointed.

Russ had stopped in the middle of the tracks. Looking back to the others, he pulled his cap off and ran a hand through his hair. Zena turned the key around in her pocket, feeling the warm metal rotate between her fingers. "All looks the same, but different, does that even make sense?"

"It does. Some places, you leave a piece of you in. You can go back after years, and even though things have changed—different shops, new buses—the feelings you had are always the same," Francis said, rubbing his beard with his hand. His dry skin rasped against his bristle like hair.

They climbed up onto the platform, which was even more spartan than the one they had stayed at the previous night. A graffiti-scratched, mossy, plastic shelter looked pretty depressed. Its sole companions were a blistered and decrepit ticket machine and signs welcoming people to;

Francis pulled Nate up as he had tried, and failed, to scrabble up the sheer wall where trains once sat, waiting for people to get on or leave; engines ready to grumble loudly, waking up the hungover residents living nearby.

Russ walked through a set of metal barriers designed to stop cyclists from bombing down the hill and taking out the returning pensioners or pissheads. A few feet away lay a badly decomposed body. Bones were strewn around.

Wispy grey hair waved in the mid-afternoon breeze. A worm slid through the neighbouring eye sockets, their contents long since pecked out and fought over by gulls.

The group walked through another set of barriers at the top of the hill. The climb was short in distance, but made up for it in steepness. As they neared its peak, each of them was panting and looking forward to some respite.

Standing on the road, just shy of the bridge, Zena was doubled over, hands on her knees, trying to suck air into her lungs. "Gimme... a...minute. Bloody....hill...always...hated...it," she wheezed. "I'm good...let's...go..."

A waist-high brick wall, broken up by squares of wrought iron, ran off towards the bridge, where it ended. The other side headed towards the town, disappearing round a corner.

None of the gardens they passed were going to win any awards. Even those who had painstakingly removed all greenery had surrendered it back to rebellious weeds and strands of invading ivy.

A few houses before the bridge, Zena stopped by a faded blue gate. Shaky hands fumbled for the latch. It opened with a rusty creak and came to rest in a nettle bush. She nervously withdrew the brass key from her pocket, looking from it to the house in front of her. It, like the rest of the abodes, looked deserted, stripped of life and motion.

"I...I'm scared..." she said softly. A tear tracked down her face, pooling on her jawbone before falling to the floor.

Francis lay a comforting hand on her shoulder. "It's okay, take your time, it—"

Zena's head darted to the living room window. A large single-glazed aspect, divided in four by thin metal. "Did you see that? The curtains moved, someone's in there. It's *Tom*, it must be.”

She fought to get the key into the lock. Pausing momentarily as she heard it click into the housing it was made for, she turned it slowly. “I’m home.”

CHAPTER TWENTY-SIX

For a moment, Zena was swaddled in a supernova of emotion and memory. The door swung open and the light faded away. She looked to the hallway table where a few unopened letters lay in wait. A takeaway menu for 'Pearl River', the local Chinese restaurant, sat underneath them like a Kanji printed carpet.

The old style telephone sat on the cradle, its numbered faceplate looked back with a surprised expression. Tom's muddy football boots still sat on an old copy of the Metro. Zena made a mental note to have a quiet whinge about them a bit later on. The floorboards were polished and looked immaculate, like they had been scrubbed just for her arrival.

She stood at the bottom of the stairs and looked up. A vase of fresh flowers sat on the windowsill, halfway up the ascent.

Aww.

She walked down the hallway, her shoes click-clacking on the hard floor.

The doorway to the kitchen was open and she could hear the kettle whistling away. Her South Park mug sat on the worktop with a teaspoon resting inside it. The smell of toast and bacon wafted down the corridor. She closed her eyes and breathed it in.

It had been so long since she had eaten properly cooked food, she thought she might never have gotten to savour such sensations ever again.

The living room door was pulled to, and from beyond she could hear the strains of Kim Deal singing 'Here Comes Your Man'. Her heart beat faster. She had to put a hand to her chest, as at one point she was sure it was about to be propelled from her insides. She placed the palm of her hand on the door and gently pushed it open.

Inside, the curtains were still closed, but the room was lit by hundreds of church candles. Little bobbles of melted wax ran from the top, forming lumpy scars which slid down to the base.

And there he was. Tom. Standing with his back to her, peeking through a crack in the curtains, on the lookout for her, no doubt. She stifled a snigger. *He's wearing his bloody Rick Grimes cowboy hat again.*

Zena closed the door behind her gently, seeing her chance to repay Tom for all the times he had sneaked up on her whilst she was doing the washing up and scaring her half to death.

She tiptoed her way across the thick brown carpet to him. He was still wearing his knackered jeans, the ones with the hole in the gusset. she could see the top of his leg through the tear. Even with his back turned, she knew he was wearing his Ramones t-shirt; the dried specks of magnolia paint on the collar gave it away.

She snuck up behind him and wrapped her arms around his torso, pulling him into her. She savoured the moment her head had told her so many times would never happen.

She nuzzled into his neck and whispered into his ear, "Hi T. I'm home."

CHAPTER TWENTY-SEVEN

Francis stood back and let Zena enter the house first. He wanted to give her as much time as she needed to deal with the fact that she had made it home. As he crossed the threshold, the stench struck him like a flyswatter. It was spoiled meat, sour milk, bacterial spores having had free reign for too long and creating their own kingdom in the absence of cleaning products.

He looked down at a table where stacks of unopened mail lay strewn across its surface. Government leaflets imparting next to useless advice were the crest of the mound. Paper mulch hill was covered in a thin film of dust and dead insects. Flies lay on their card thin backs, wings neatly tucked back and legs pulled together as if they were hogtied.

At the foot of the stairs, Francis looked up and saw thick brown smears along the walls and on the carpet. Dried puddles of blood sat on top of the pile like plates of basalt. At the top of the stairs, through the balustrade, a grey shrivelled hand hung in the air. It looked like someone was waving to him. Francis shuddered.

Zena, though, appeared to pay none of this any heed. She seemed to float around the grime and gloom like it was some spellbinding archaeological discovery. He could hear her tutting in surprise and amazement.

The kitchen door was open, and this appeared to be the main source of the overpowering aroma. The fridge door was ajar and stuck out into the room. Even from distance, Francis could make out a bloody handprint on the face of it. Trickles of liquid had dribbled down from the impact site, giving it the appearance of red string attached to the fingertips.

Zena had stopped by the living room door. Francis patted her shoulder and walked to the kitchen. As he reached the doorway, he saw the desiccated husk of a person, gender unknown. The skin and clothing had sunk into the skeletal frame, almost like it had melted over the bones. A large browny-red stain had become one with the floor tiles, spanning the width of the kitchen.

On the worktops, amongst the rotting food and broken crockery, were piles of soiled tissues and tea-towels. The window which made up half of the back door had capillary cracks spreading out from an impact in the middle. His search was interrupted by a man shouting, "HEY!" from behind him.

Nathan was standing just inside the doorway. "Close the door, Nate. Keep on the lookout, okay?" Francis wheeled down the corridor to an open door where the shout had come from.

Inside he could just about make out three figures. Russ was standing inside the room. The smell from within was even worse than the one bathing the rest of the interior. This was the epicentre – Stink Central.

Russ was standing, braced, holding a crowbar, which he had chosen from the weapon stockpile. As his eyes grew accustomed to the murk, Francis could see that nearly every scrap of flat surface had nubs of melted candle on. Tiny burnt-out wicks were the noses in glossy faces of wax. Discarded pizza boxes were sown over the rancid carpet. Silhouetted through a chink of light between the curtains were Zena and a man.

Zena screamed. Russ leapt to the window and heaved a heavy curtain down its runner. With every agonising inch revealed, the room took on an even more disturbing vibe. There was dried blood sprayed everywhere; over the curtains, the floor, the ceiling. It looked like the room itself had been slashed over and over again, bled dry.

A dead body was stuffed headfirst through the flat-screen television, its grey skin crispy like old leather. Its hands were caked in yet more dried blood. Strips of skin hung from broken fingernails like fly paper.

The silhouetted man was a grey waif of a revenant; dead eyes looked out over saddlebags of sagging skin which made up his face. One arm was wrapped round Zena's waist, while the other hung slack at the side. A grievous wound on the front of the shoulder had left the bone and rancid meat exposed. It swung listlessly as the zombie tried to manoeuvre to get a better hold.

Zena held a bloodied hand to her ear as she fought to escape the unrequited tête à tête. Russ, with his fist still clenched round the crowbar, punched the zombie square in the face as it loomed in for another bite. The sound of breaking bone overrode the sound of screaming, and the zombie staggered backwards, coming to rest against the now revealed window.

Zena took a step or two back. She glanced wildly around the room, as if she had just been brought out of a trance. She stifled both upchuck and the scream which threatened to envelop them all.

The crowbar was pulled back over Russ' head. With ruthless dedication, he brought it down repeatedly against the stunned cadaver. Splatters of thick black ichor and shards of bone showered the window and surrounding area with each strike.

The zombie's face had a huge crater in it, right down the middle. The sides of his eyes were on show as the crowbar was pulled from the impact site with a gut-wrenching slurp.

The signs of unlife started to waver within Tom. The brain, or at least the remaining slop which was still connected to the central nervous system, tried to send signals to tremorous limbs, none of which responded with any real alacrity.

A final hearty crack put Tom out of his misery, and the ruined remains of his skull slid down the window. As it squeaked against the glass during his final descent, it left a smear of black lumpy goo, splinters of bone and nodules of putrescent meat.

"Are you okay?" Francis asked. He pulled out a clean handkerchief and pressed it against the side of Zena's head, trying to staunch the flow of blood from the bite.

She nodded sheepishly. "Yeah, I'm fine…just…it all looked like it used to be. Like the last time I was here, it was like a dream, or something." she looked down at the brutalised remains of her husband and started to well up. "I made it back, T. I'm sorry I wasn't here for you."

Zena crouched down by her husband's body and wept. Russ, still wired from the confrontation, stood immobile. Strands of black gunk ran from the end of the crowbar and onto the floor.

Nathan hugged the doorway, impassively studying the grisly sight. "I'm hungry,

Francis," he muttered, before disappearing back into the hallway to read his comics.

CHAPTER TWENTY-EIGHT

"Well, hello again, everyone. Hope you are all well? Been quite an eventful few days, hasn't it? What with our little guest. Really has been quite the fillip. Just goes to show that not everything is doom and gloom. Not sure if any of you got a copy of the Survival Guide he brought with him, but I've got a copy if anyone wants a read?" Steve looked around the group with an off-putting sense of optimism.

Dee looked across at him. "Have you been smoking something, Steve? You seem a bit…well, fucking *annoying* if I'm being honest." Anton let out an abrupt chuckle.

Steve looked at her in a daze. "No need to smoke anything like that, Dee. Not when you're high on life."

Dee fell about laughing. She was on the verge of blacking out from the lack of oxygen she was taking in due to her hysterics. "Whatever, Doctor Steve, you sap."

Scratch.

"Fucking stop it now Steve, okay?" Dee warned.

Steve stopped scribbling, slid the pen into the metal binder, and turned the page around to face her. A large phallus and hairy balls had been drawn onto the page. "Not even you and your borderline psychoticism can bring me down today."

Dee chuckled. "True, but my foot up your ass might."

"Tease," Steve simpered. "So, campers, today is the day we all thought would never happen. Anton here is the last to go. Take your time, please, begin."

SURVIVOR

TALES FROM THE ZOMBIE APOCALYPSE

The NETZACH'S Series

ISSUE #5 THE GREY WORM

NARRATED BY ANTON KOVAC

THE GREY WORM – PART 1

When you die now and come back, do you reckon you know? I know what you're gonna say: no. And that's fair, I guess. I thought that, but after what I went through? I'm not too sure anymore.

Ha ha, guess that's why I'm here with you lot.

Fair play.

Before all this I worked loads of jobs. Labourer, painter, office monkey, pulling pints, you name it, I've probably done it. Left school with grades that spelt one in French and what else you gonna do?

Never done anything that lasted too long. Think roofer was what I did the most, and I utterly hated it. Still, got money for it, and that's all I wanted.

All *we* wanted.

She was the most beautiful woman in the world. About my height, long brown hair, all the bumps and lumps the right size. For me, at least, but each to their own, huh?

Jennifer.

That was her name.

I'd do anything for her. I did. We met when we were eighteen at some party. Love at first sight? Thought it was bollocks until I met her.

Within a month we were engaged. Ha, all our friends and family said we were too young. Laughed at them at the time. They were right, though. You haven't had time to live by then. Need time to grow. Find out how shit works.

Like yourself.

Casey came along a few years later. We were living in some one bedroom flat in the middle of town. Unplanned. Mind you, who plans having a kid? I mean *really* plans it? We barely had enough money as it was, and now on top of everything we had to buy all that stuff. I look back on those days and wonder how the hell we didn't kill each other. You could see it was playing over her eyes some nights.

Do me while I'm sleeping, then drown her and Casey after. She told me that once, a few months back. When we were still holed up in that craphole. Seemed to be the story of our lives. Holed up together. The things that had brought us together, they'd long gone. We were together because of Casey. No use pretending otherwise.

I was 'in-between' jobs when the world went to pot. Just got my social and we were skint already. Casey was a few months off five years old. We were going to have this party for her and her mates. Looking at the cash in my wallet, it was going to be a pretty shit one. Still, one thing though, we always found a way. Whenever we got brassic, somehow we'd find something to get us through.

Two days off payday once and skint. Bumped into her folks in town who gave her a fiver. We had the choice between food or fags. No choice at all. Life without one would've ended up in more arguments. That was our life. Constant triage.

Yes, I know what triage means. Don't judge a book by the cover.

Ha, yep, unless you cover another. Good one Steve.

We didn't even know anything had happened. Casey was in bed by then. We were watching crap telly. Woke up the next day still none the wiser. Casey was crying about having gone off milk with her Coco Pops. I pulled some clothes on and went down the shop. Anything to get out. Any excuse. I once went out to check whether it was raining down the pub.

Serious.

We lived on the fourth floor, so you get to walk past all the other flats. The microcosm of society right there. Old folks with 'Good Morning' on too loud. Potheads on the floor below, the smell of green under the door and XBox through the surround sound.

Except this morning, every door I walked past had the same thing blaring out. The News. That stupid bollocks jingle they play before the headlines? That. All the way down through a mix of speakers. Was like the shittest club in the world.

Outside was just as weird. People would've gone to work by then. I hated going out around eight with them lot leaving. Made me feel like shit. The streets were just filled with people though. Packing up cars. Kids screaming. Horns honking. Sirens. Endless sirens.

I get to the shop and it's like the Wild West. The cashier is lying on the floor in the foetal position. Don't look like it's been too friendly in there. People are filling up their baskets like it's Christmas.

Twelve pints of milk? Check.

Four loaves of bread? Check.

Novelty jar of chilli olives? Well. Okay, I didn't see any of them. But you get the idea, yeah?

I'm not one to look a gift horse in the mouth. Pull out my folded Bag for Life from my pocket. Seriously. Never leave home without one. Especially these days. Bag For Looting I call 'em now.

I waltz out of there feeling like a goddamn king. Think someone must've been capped. Racially motivated incident? Perhaps it's a terrorist attack or something? I ain't fussed. Free food. Plus even got some fags and a bottle of Jack. Today was my lucky day.

That's what I thought then anyway.

Get back to the block and there's still people *everywhere*. The roads are clogged. Worst I'd ever seen it. Even when they have the half marathon on and close the streets off. Bump into a few people who don't even bother to check if I'm there.

Wankers.

I've never been so glad to get back to mine before. Well, not since before Casey was born. Kids change everything. Thing is, everyone tells you that, but like a twat you think it'll be different for you. Like you're something special. We weren't. Hadn't been for a long time. Jenny was different, though. That bit they got spot on. She was born to be a mum.

I get back and Jenny and Casey were sat in silence watching the telly. Not CBeebies. The News. I know. I was shocked too. Those reports just kept going. Some of the things they showed, though. Not sure Casey should be watching that. What was I going to say, though? Jenny would've just got the hump and then the prison would've been hell.

Again.

People eating people. Think that needs to be said out loud once in a while. What a messed up sentence, huh? You heard it from time to time back then. To be fair, mostly from Germany where some guy puts up an online advert.

Yeah, you remember that, too?

Mad.

Thing is though, at least that implied consent. Those reports were something else. Animalistic. Primal. Fucked up.

We watched it until lunchtime. Casey had gone off the idea of Coco Pops by now. Wasn't entirely sure she'd ever want to eat again after seeing that reporter. Yeah, that one. Always wondered why the cameraman just followed the body dropping. You notice he didn't lift a finger to help? Recorded the whole time.

You can bet your arse if we had internet now, the full length clip would be on YouTube. Wonder how long it was until the reporter got up and ripped the cameraman's throat out. Thing is. Goes back to my earlier question.

Do you think he knew?

Did he do it because;

A. He's a zombie.

Or

B. To get the disrespectful prick back for filming instead of fighting?

I'm not sure anymore. But for a while, she sure as hell convinced me that it was B.

Not yet mate. This is called background. Context. You lay the foundations before you build the house yeah? Patience. Where are we in a rush to go anymore anyway?

Chill.

Now I'm not much of a survivalist. Not much of a talker, either. Yeah. You guessed, huh? But I do listen, and I take in a lot of pointless shit. Remembered a mate talking about what to do in an apocalypse. Not tape the windows up shit. They were the undead, not a nuclear blast wave. Filled the bath and sinks up with water. Got the candles out from the kitchen drawer. Anything else we might need. Got it all to hand.

Then we just sat there and watched the world burn. In amongst the zombies eating people of course.

THE GREY WORM PART-2

Like most normal city folk, we never met our neighbours. Sure as hell had names for them. The Old Fucks opposite us. Potheads and Star Trek Tennis Porn below us.

Eh? Oh, you used to hear it at night. Just as you're trying to get to sleep. You know the sound of the transporter in the old Star Trek? Well you got that interspersed with:

UH

UHHH

UH

UHHH

If he got into a pattern with that, by day five it would go on for twenty minutes or so. Must've been yanking his dick red raw by then.

So. Single White Female and Estate Agent Cock on two. Pingu and Pervy Old Bastard on one. Then Gary Glitter and an empty on the ground floor. No. Not the real Gary Glitter. Just this guy. Well. He had a look of the paedo about him, that's all. We were worried that someone would firebomb his flat in the night and we'd go up, too.

Heard this big commotion and go out onto the landing, can see the single bird downstairs dragging a suitcase out of the door. She'd been crying. Red eyes and that. Looked a right state. Sounds like Pingu was also getting out of Dodge too.

Pingu? Have you seen the cartoon? You know the sound? Yeah, that matched the exact pitch of his voice. You couldn't have a conversation with him. Not without checking to see if he was squeezing his balls at the same time anyway.

Went back inside my flat. We had one of those chains for the door. Never used it before. Sure as hell did from then on, though. Our kitchen had this big bay window. Useless if you fancied a quickie. That had ended years before anyway. But it was handy if you wanted to watch what was going on outside. It was madness. Single White Female got into her MX5.

Took her twenty minutes just to get let out of where she parked.

That was that. We spent the rest of the day watching people trickle slowly out of the street. By night time it was pretty quiet. We went back to watching the news. Casey was bored of it by then. Was grateful for that fact. She went onto her 3DS.

Cooking Mama I think, Matt. Yeah? You too? No I never tried to cook proper food on it.

It—

It doesn't work that way.

No. I'm not surprised you got food poisoning.

We went to bed late that night. Jenny was really quiet. I woke up in the night and she was just staring at me. Was really freaky. Worried I'd wake up with a carrier bag over my head and look up into her face. With the red Tesco logo stretched over it.

That became our life for a few days. Aside from the news, we never actually saw one of the zombies. Nope. Guess they were hitting up the roads and that. Supermarkets, hospitals, all the places they say to avoid in crises.

First one we saw was a few doors down. The kitchen window was our second telly by then. Not much was happening. But the fact nothing was going on was equally as fascinating. This car screeches up the road and brakes real sudden. Two guys jump out and are kicking in the door of this house a few down from us. Looked like they knew where they were going. Didn't look random.

About three or four minutes later they saunter back out. Real casual like. One gets in the driver's side and starts the engine. The other, though, he stops to light a fag or a spliff. Something. See this shape behind him.

Just. Lunges.

Even from where we were stood we saw the blood. Sprayed everywhere. The car was white. A poor choice in hindsight, eh? The smoking guy falls to the floor and the zombie follows him to the ground. He's clawing at the guy's throat. It was like he was sorting through all the veins. Looking for one in particular. He must have found it as he pulled on this bit of purple string. *Whoosh.* Another fountain of blood. The driver must've seen it, but just like the cameraman. Does nothing about it. After a minute, he's done one. Gone.

We just stood there and watched the zombie. The other man was alive for a bit, but with the amount of claret all over the place, not for long. It was weird. The zombie was eating him. But didn't really seem that fussed. He was chewing. But looking into the middle distance, like he was thinking about what he had for tea last night. After ten minutes and having torn the man's arm off and nibbling on it a bit, he got bored. Got up. Threw up. Then staggered off down the road.

The other guy lay there for ages. When we came back later, though, he had gone. Just this big patch of dried black blood. And his arm. Looked like a rolled-up doormat lying in paint from our window. Over the next few days there were more and more. It was like they had been cooped up somewhere. And then someone had just set them all free.

Estate Agent Cock tried making a break for it at the end of the first week. Jenny and I had a side bet on whether he'd make it to the end of the street.

That cigarette never tasted so good.

Poor bastard barely made the third lamp post. Think he might have had a chance if he'd travelled lighter. Dunno what he was thinking about when he made the decision to take his golf clubs.

Well, hardly aerodynamic, are they? The bag just kept banging against his back. Interesting factoid. Golf clubs are shit against zombies.

Yeah.

We saw it alright. He got taken down. But we saw his smug bastard grin. Pulled out his driver and swung it at the closest one. The club head broke off on contact. The zombie's jaw was a bit fucked but he was left there holding this metal stick.

No. Don't think there was enough of him left to come back. Least the dick closed the front door.

Few days later we lost Gary Glitter. Stupid bastard. Must've seen the schoolkids go past. Didn't check their vitals though. They checked his alright, by chewing through his jugular. When he was going, though, all these kids over him, biting, I'll never be sure if the look on his face was pleasure or pain. Sick fuck. One thing for sure though. He had the biggest grin.

Everyone else hunkered down. For now at least. No one left their flats. Star Trek

Tennis Porn man went into overdrive. Don't think any amount of Vaseline would put his dick back together again. Three hours was the record. Must've been an old VHS tape. A T-60 I think. Had to rewind it once it was done. Could hear it over our telly it was that loud.

Then a couple of weeks in. *Boom.* No more television. Food wise we were okay. Well in the sense that we had enough frozen fish fingers to last until the second coming. We would have to do something. But not for a week or so.

The telly was a bummer, though. Meant we had to communicate with each other. We compromised. We sat in the kitchen longer. A few days later, that's when we heard the shots.

We used to hear the odd boom when the exercises were on the plains. But never a gunshot. Too far away.

We looked at the end of the street. The goddamn cavalry was here. We thought that it would all be over in a few hours. A day at most. Sure the council would have to clean up the blood and body parts, but at least things would go back to normal.

Fuck. I'd even do that job. This steady trickle of soldiers walked from right to left. Down the hill. You could see the muzzle flashes. Even Casey tore herself away from her 3DS to see the 'soldier men'.

THE GREY WORM PART-3

The stream of men stopped. You could hear the crackle of gunfire, though. It was mad to think that it was happening in our city centre. All the shops we had gone in. All the places we had bought stuff from. The battle was going on amongst it all.

As night fell so did the amount of shooting we heard. They somehow seemed to be entwined. Casey fell asleep on the sofa in the living room. We put a blanket over her and maintained our vigil in the kitchen.

Any minute now, we thought. We didn't know what would happen to signal it being won. But we knew it would be *something*.

Something *big*.

Poor Jenny flaked out about half three. The shooting now was pretty sparse. Either it was far away or worse. There weren't as many soldiers as there had been.

You know when you fall asleep on the train? And you wake up and you've dribbled on yourself? You look around and see that it's a completely different time to you last remember?

That.

I woke Jenny up and I made a cup of tea for us. She grunted a thanks. It was then I realised I couldn't hear anything. No gunfire. Nothing. That was it. We had won! I was so happy I nearly kissed her. One look at her face, though. That told me it wasn't an option.

I'm about to get up and get changed. I'd turned my pants inside out so many times that it was like a runway on the fabric. Then I saw him. He was dressed in army camouflage. Limping badly. I couldn't see that he was carrying a weapon. He was going back the way they had come from the day before. He crossed the road, and I remember he stopped and looked back.

We saw them first. This mass of bodies. All flailing arms and snapping jaws. They looked like they were one great big grey maggot. Then the sound rolled up the street to our window. That moaning. The army guy looked away and disappeared up the road. The grey worm just kept on coming.

That's when I knew. This wasn't going to end. Not now. Not ever. It was me, Jenny and Casey. Forever. In this stupid little flat.

Fuck.

I don't know what depressed me more. Looking at her showed me that she had just had the same thought as me. We smiled like idiots at each other.

Fuck.

Fate usually has the temerity to kick you in the balls. And that it did. The electric went a few days later. No freezer. No oven. No ability to recharge Casey's batteries for her 3DS. Things became even more strained. I knew that within a day or so, we'd have to go out *there*. Get food. Something. And then it happened.

Another nugget of advice you get when you become a parent? You need eyes in the back of your head. The little devils get everywhere they shouldn't. Casey had stayed content so far. But when her 3DS died. Well. Never thought anyone could moan that persistently for so long.

I was in the kitchen, trying to work out where I would go to look for food. And how I would get past the zombies. Part of me thought why bother? Would it be so bad coming back as one of them? I wasn't exactly setting the world on fire so far, was I?

Jenny had just told Casey to stop whinging. Again. She was in the toilet. Shouting about how it wasn't flushing. Great. Summertime in a little flat with overflowing faecal matter. Sounds like heaven, doesn't it?

Next thing. I hear this giant bang. A crash. A thud. A whimper.

Rush into the living room to see Casey in a heap against the window. The sofa should've, in theory at least, arrested her accelerated journey. All it did was spin her through the air. I look across the room and see a fork embedded in a plug socket. This little wisp of smoke was coming off it.

Ha. Reminded me of Willo The Wisp. Do you remember that?

Creepy. But good.

We reckon she was trying to get electricity out of the socket. Get some out to put into her batteries. She had her doll's trolley with them in it next to the plug socket. Turns out that even with the power out, sockets hold some residual charge. And when you're four and ten twelfths, that charge is enough to propel you across the room at breakneck speed.

Bad choice of words. I know. It may sound like I didn't love them. But when you've seen them grow up from a grainy black and white picture on a bit of paper, into a proper little girl, then…then when you see them *lying* there. And you know there is absolutely fucking NOTHING YOU CAN DO ABOUT IT.

I tried to wake her. She was groggy. Not with it at all. I was frantic. Jenny came in. I've never heard any animal make a noise that even closely resembled the sound that came out of her then. It was a mix of every human emotion. She took Casey's hand, and it was all burned, this little line stamped down the centre of her palm. Like it was her life line. But it wasn't. That line went from top to bottom. Palmistry would've said a long and bountiful life.

Casey left us five minutes later.

Jenny was born to be a mum. I've said that. I know. She held Casey for ages. I knew we had to do something. At some point, soon, Casey would come back. But it wouldn't be her. It would be something else entirely. I thought about going outside again. Let myself be added to the grey worm.

I would've done. But Jenny said otherwise. She lay Casey down on the sofa and went into our bedroom. We all had to sleep in one room. She came back with Casey's skipping rope. Tied one end around the radiator pipe and the other around Casey's arm. She yanked it to make sure it was tight enough.

Much like the night which ended with all hope walking injured back up the hill, we watched our dead daughter. Waiting for the sign. Waiting for her to come back.

At twenty three eleven, on my watch, the thing that now lived in her dead body came back. Jenny started crying. Tears of joy I think.

I cried too. I know mine weren't the same kind, though. She wasn't my daughter. That thing was not of my making.

Jenny tried to hold Casey, but her little mouth kept snapping at her. She put her puffa jacket on and held her again. Those little teeth tried to chomp on Jenny's arm. Her dead eyes couldn't work out why she wasn't getting through. Jenny sang her a lullaby. Did fuck all use, though. Well, not on Casey.

I fell asleep and awoke to find Casey straining at the end of the skipping rope. Trying to bite my wrist. Jenny was in the kitchen. Nothing for breakfast, she said. Tell me something I don't know. For the past god knows how many weeks I had told her the same thing.

Nothing for me, she says.

Nothing for you, she says.

Nothing for Casey, she says.

I skirt round the My Little Zombie in our living room. Jenny is as calm as I've ever seen her. She tells me that Casey is still there. She's changed, she says. But she's still our little girl, she says. I try to explain to her that the thing in our house is no longer our daughter. She said one thing.

You'll see.

You'll see like I do.

THE GREY WORM PART-4

I had an epiphany. I'd go into the flats that were now empty. They were bound to have food, supplies, whatever. I wouldn't have to get eaten by the worm. I'd be the good guy for once. I told Jenny my plan. She smiled at me. I barely recognised her face making that shape. It had been that long.

I thought I'd start at the bottom. Gary Glitter hadn't bothered to lock his door. His flat was like a time capsule. Turns out he wasn't a paedo. At least, I don't think so. His walls were lined with pictures of him and giant cheques. Money he'd raised for all these different charities.

I got my Bag For Looting out and went through his cupboards. Didn't have much. But bagged some rice, pasta, pot noodles and the like. Even had some bottled water. Carbonated. Better than nothing, though. I must've been gone fifteen, twenty minutes. At most.

Get up to our floor and see that the door opposite is open.

Bad things.

The old couple hardly ever went out. She was pretty much bedridden. We saw him from time to time, though, bringing the shopping back.

I put the bag of food by our door and went in their flat. I could hear Jenny's voice. It was soft and calm. Like when we first met. When we had everything open to us.

Their flat was the mirror image of ours. I got to the living room door. It was shut. I could hear Jenny on the other side and someone crying.

I pushed the door open and my heart stopped. Laying on the floor with a bruise the size of a fist on his head was the old fella. There's this big armchair facing the telly just behind his body. I can make out the back of the old woman's curly hair. She's sitting down, watching the blackness of the powerless telly.

She's the one crying. Jenny is stood in front of her. Being kind enough to not obstruct the telly I should add. She looks up at me and smiles, then down to the old woman again. I step over the man. He's still breathing. Which is something.

Buried in the old woman's lap is Casey. This bloody knife is lying next to the woman. Casey's delicate little fingers are rummaging around inside the old lady. You could see her little knuckles under the creased, yellow skin.

Knew you'd be proud of her, Jenny said. She didn't want to eat anything we had. So I remembered what we saw. Henry got in the way so I had to hit him. And try as she might, Casey couldn't get into the good stuff.

Could you?

No you couldn't.

After a starter of a few fingers, Mummy thought I'd better help you out. All I had to do was make a little cut and our clever little girl did the rest.

Who's a clever girl?

Casey isn't paying her any attention. She's too interested in cramming her little inquisitive hands into the innards of the old lady. Reminded me of Han Solo cutting open the Tauntaun in Empire Strikes Back.

You like Jar-Jar, Matt? Says it all really. No. I didn't. Why? Because he was a fucking twat. Do you mind? Yes. I guess I did interrupt your story. Sorry. May I continue? Cheers.

I'm not entirely sure what happened next. I think I blacked out. The sight of your neighbour being eaten alive by your dead daughter, having been prepared by your wife, is not something you can easily anticipate.

I wake up and I'm looking into the eyes of Henry. The old fella. Jenny has been busy while I've been out. The old man has got a sock for a gag and is tied up. He's proper frantic. His bruise is looking full on nasty, too. I was half expecting to find myself in the same predicament. To my surprise I find I'm able to stand up.

Casey has the same bored look as the man we saw. Chewing on some piece of meat. No idea what it was. If I had to guess, I'd say it was a bit of kidney. She stops chewing and then just barfs all over the floor.

Once she's finished, she shoves her little hands back inside the old dear. She was slumped forwards now. Either dead. Or very nearly dead. I tell Jenny that while it's great we still have Casey, I don't really want to spend my time living with a zombie old lady. She laughs. The last time I said anything that made her laugh was a week before Casey was born.

The first time she was born.

Properly.

Not when she came back.

Jenny checks for a pulse. Then, quick as you like, she grabs the old dear by the throat and slings her over her shoulder. Casey looks a bit miffed, but as Jenny lifts the body up, bits of stuff plop out of the hole. Casey lets out this little moan and got back to eating. She was always a fussy eater. Not so much anymore.

Never had Jenny down as a physically strong person. I always had to do the lifting. But she carries the old woman down four flights of stairs and into Gary Glitter's, no bother. She reappears a few minutes later. Flashes me a key which she stashes in her bra.

Why do women do that?

Anyway. We get back upstairs just in time to stop Casey starting on dessert. *Henry.* Jenny says that we need to space out the feeding. She pulls on the skipping rope and leads our little girl into their bedroom. She ties the end of the rope to the radiator pipe again, kisses Casey on the head, and then leaves.

I didn't sleep for two days. Jenny on the other hand slept like a log. When I did sleep I had the same nightmare over and over again. I'd wake up and find myself tied to the radiator pipe. Jenny leans over me. Smiles and then hacks away at my guts. She then steps back. Our little girl totters over and starts pulling out my insides like they're on special offer.

Jenny cuts off a length of my intestines which are lying on the floor. She ties one end around Casey's wrist and the other around hers. I wake up just as Casey's unravelled the lot and is tugging on my pancreas.

Jenny tells me it's going to be okay. All she wants to do is show me that our daughter is still alive. The same thing I'd seen tuck into the old bird next door. I was somewhere between desperate and shit scared. I know it's not much of an excuse. It's all I got. All I had.

What was I going to do?

I don't think I would have made it to the front door. Not before Jenny would've stopped me and turned me into a nice fricassee.

Five days after Casey's demise, Jenny says it's time to feed her again. She asks if I want to help. Given the fact that she was wearing an apron and holding a cordless electric knife. I opted to postpone the events of my dream manifesting in real life, and said yes.

Henry was still passed out on the floor. His breathing was soft. The bruise had gone down. But the lack of sanitary conditions had left him a rather unsightly mess. And smell. Jenny turned him over onto his back with all the care of an abattoir worker.

The look in his eyes. He had come to by then. She revved the knife up. Poor sod. She sliced into his side. Not too deep. Then she dragged him into the hallway by his shirt collar. We could hear Casey scratching at the door. Jenny told me to stand back. Opened the door and there she was. Since I last saw her, she had changed. Her skin was grey and lifeless. Her veins were blotchy lines of black.

Something else struck me, though. She was wearing different clothes. Jenny had obviously been back in and changed her. It didn't really do much. She still looked, well, like a zombie. Just a slightly smarter dressed zombie. With a pink ribbon in her hair.

Feeding time began. When Henry was on the way out, Jenny chopped off a leg to tide little Casey over. Then hauled him down the stairs and into the bottom flat.

That became our life. The stoners went next. They had loads of food. I was happy with that. Jenny lured them in with, well, herself. Never seen her act like that in a long time.

A month later, though, the flats were nearly empty. Except for ours, the now silent Star Trek Tennis Porn man and number one.

I thought I saw a change in Casey. Sure, she didn't want to play with her dolls anymore. But the more time I spent with her, you could see that something remained. Or so I thought.

Honestly? Looking back? I think I would've found a similarity to David Bowie if I'd looked hard enough. It was fair to say my mental health was deteriorating.

Five days after Star Trek Tennis Porn man had been added to the undead waiting-room downstairs, we were out of people. Jenny had eked them out as best she could. Even managed to get a few passers-by that she promised safety to.

Amongst other things.

She had become a bit more rambling by then. Said that she needed more connection with Casey. That it was no good just being her mum any more. She needed to be at one with her.

I should've seen the signs.

I'm asleep one night and woke up with a start. This searing pain is lancing through my skull. I try to get up, but I can't move. I'm pinned to the bed. And not in a good way. Not in a 'it's my birthday' kinda way.

I can feel my cheek is all runny. Out of one eye is darkness. The other is that half-light you get. The pain increases. It's then I realise that it's Jenny. She's trying to *eat* me. I've never hit a woman before. Hit a few blokes when they deserved it, but never a woman. My first punch is a testament to that. A mere slap. The second though, when it feels like she is actually going to rip my eye out, well, that one sent her flying.

I was up on my feet straight away. Half expecting her to fly at me. Arms pumping with rage and fury. Nothing. Do you know what I got? That moan. The one I heard from the worm. But this one was in the same room as me. Burrowing into my flesh. She flailed at me and missed.

My face was still hurting like a bastard. Could feel liquid running down the left side of my face. It ran into my mouth and I got that coppery tang. Jenny was dead. Gone. The veil had been well and truly fucking lifted. Nothing remains when you go. Nothing. No vestige of humanity. No spark of ingenuity or enquiry. No impulse to explore and expand your horizons.

Just a desire to feed. A desire to kill. In some respects you could argue that in those final few seconds we had together, the true Jenny was exposed. We'd grown so far apart. We were nothing like the people we once were when we met.

No chance to grow.

No chance to explore.

We had wilted together.

The relationship with the woman I met called Jenny died years before. I watched as she clawed her way across the bed on her belly towards me.

Since the power went I had this torch next to me. Proper full-on security thing. Cheap in Woolworths years ago. I don't remember picking it up. I don't remember bringing it down onto her skull.

Again. And again. And again.

I do remember seeing what was left of her after. I shone the light on her. With the blood running over the lens, she took on a peculiar hue. She had these little bite marks up and down her body. Guess that's the price she paid for insisting on changing our daughter.

I clock the bedside table. Her side. The bottle of Jack Daniels I got on Day One was next to a pile of pills. All the colours of the rainbow, must've been hoarding them from the other flats. She wanted to join our daughter. Do it properly. No fucking about.

I couldn't stand to see Casey again. Not like that. Not after what I had witnessed her doing. I got a length of tubing. Chose one of the cars outside. Drained enough petrol to fill a bucket that we used to put the mop into.

I lay a trail of it from number one to the path outside, lit a match, and watched them all burn. Grey hands pawed at the window. Scratching to get out.

I heard the worm scream.

I saw the worm writhe.

I watched the worm die.

I wandered for days. From one place to the next. Forever onwards. Surviving one day at a time. Trying to forget about my dead family. Eventually I bumped into a patrol. They took me in here. After a few clashes, though, my card was marked.

I don't mind. It's better to pick up dirty paper plates than kill *them* through the fence.

Plus. I have a new nightmare.

I'm on Heads Up detail. Walking around the fence, stabbing the zombies in the head with the end of this crowbar. Turn to face the next one and it's Jenny. Her head is all bust open. She doesn't moan, though. She just says, 'I'm disappointed in you'. As well as you can with half a head anyway.

I stab her through the face. She drops and turns to ash. I move onto the next one. It's Casey. But she's not a zombie anymore. She's that little girl I blamed for everything.

I'm crying now. I try to stop myself. But I can't. I smash the crowbar into her skull. She sinks to the ground. Her little hand holds onto the leg of my jeans. She starts to pull me through the fence.

So strong. Can feel my flesh getting all pinched. Then I get dragged like cheese through a grater.

My legs first.

Then my body.

My heart.

Lungs.

Arms.

Just as my head is being dragged through, I let out a scream. That tends to be echoed by the sound I'm making as I wake up.

I have only one reminder of those months. This lovely scar. This necklace around my eye. I never look in the mirror. I need no reminder of the things I witnessed.

Of the things I lost.

Not just now.

But all those years ago.

CHAPTER TWENTY-NINE

A stunned silence hung over the group. Dee broke the silence first. "Fucking hell, we're a bunch of checry souls, eh?"

Steve finished scribbling in his notebook, pulled his glasses off and rubbed weary eyes. "Thank you, Anton. I appreciate that must've been very difficult to talk about. I…we all thank you for letting us in. The first step to recovery is…"

"Sausages?" Matt asked enthusiastically.

"No, Matt, not sausages. Talking. The more you talk about something, the less of a hold it has over you. We don't speak just for ourselves, we speak to remember those we have lost along the way. Those who are no longer able to tell their story. You have all shared something which unites you. Loss. Grief. The stories you shared may be different, but the crux of them all remains the same. We call this survivor guilt. Why did I live when those we cared about did not? Why do I alone remain?"

Steve looked around the group. Matt raised a hand to which Steve shook his head gently. "It's not a question which requires an answer, Matt. It's rhetorical. I hope you can all see now that you are not alone. We will continue this work next week. There are some coping mechanisms we can discuss. Don't know about you lot but I could do with a drink."

Steve eased the glasses back onto his face and pulled a half bottle of whiskey from his jacket pocket. A stack of plastic goblets was retrieved from the other. He lined up the cups and poured a decent measure into each, before offering them around.

"To those we have lost, we remember them. And to those who survive, we salute them. Salut," Steve said sombrely, taking a brief moment of introspection before taking a sip.

"That tastes like gran," Matt said.

Dee coughed. "Shut up, you idiot. That nearly came out of my nose then."

Sylvia laughed, held the plastic cup in both hands and took a sip, before wincing. "Been a while since I had a drink."

There was a gentle rapping on the doorframe. "Steve, sorry to interrupt, can I just have a quick word with Dee?"

Dee walked over to Andy. "What is it Sar…Andy?"

The sound of plastic hitting concrete made everyone turn around. Sylvia was stood stock still, a hand clutched the empty space her cup had been. "You alright, Sylvia?" Dee asked.

"I…I…I'm fine, just lost my grip. I've got to go, excuse me." Sylvia put her head down and skittered out of the room, brushing shoulders with Dee on the way out.

Andy shot Dee an inquisitive glare. "Sure she still doesn't remember?"

Dee looked around at the sight of Sylvia disappearing into the factory, "She hasn't said anything. Sure she would've done by now. Anyway, what's up?"

"Just wondered if you'd be up for going on a run soon? Paul and Dean have cleared out anything half cop nearby. Going out in a couple of days, if you fancy it?"

Dee's face broke into a smile which threatened to destabilise the universe. "Do woodland animals crap in their beds. You bet I would, thanks mate, cheers."

CHAPTER THIRTY

The two guards rechecked the fuel canisters that had been prepared by their brethren. One said to the other, "Have you ever met The Apostle?"

"No, have you?" came the enthusiastic yet hushed reply.

Guard number one checked off the total from his list and shoved the notepad into his hoodie pocket. "No, he's rarely seen by anyone. More often than not he is amongst the unbelievers, making preparations. When he returns, he rests for a few days and then he's off again."

Petrol sloshed around within the containers as the pair loaded them into the RV, tucking them behind the door. "I heard that he was born of Ishtar herself, taught *Her* ways since birth. He is the epitome of our purity," his friend added.

"I've heard many things said of him, yet too often, I've heard the same story retold to make it even grander, more fantastical," came the reply. "There's one story of his that I believe, though."

After placing the last of the supplies in the vehicle, curiosity got the better of him, Checking to ensure they were not overheard, he replied, "Go on, tell me."

"This was when the end days began, before the Mass Rapture campaign started. He was captured by the despicable Lions of Gilgamesh outside of Runcorn. For fourteen days and nights they tortured him, hoping to learn the location of his Grace and his brother. For fourteen days and nights he refused to submit to their violence and threats. He said no word or made one utterance of pain."

The guard closed the door softly, checked the safety on his pistol and continued. "On the fifteenth morning, they went to wake him, to begin their assault anew, yet when they got to his chambers, it was empty. Even his sweat and blood, which had marked the floor and walls, was gone. It was as if he was never there. The Lions grew frantic. They searched high and low for The Apostle, some questioned whether they had ever captured him at all, for no sign of his incarceration or torture could they find."

He slid the pistol back into his belt. It nestled in the small of his back. "On the fifteenth hour, a great cry came from the sentries. One of the Lions had been found, crucified to a telegraph pole outside their compound. The Ascended were feasting on the fool. Before they could retrieve their kin, a second call sounded out. A horde of the Enraptured were bearing down on them from all sides. They yelled that a man was at the head of the host. The Apostle."

The second guard looked upon his friend with incredulity. "But how could that be?"

"It is said that The Apostle is able to command the Ascended, make them do his bidding. The army he summoned fell upon the vile curs and tore them asunder. None were allowed to Ascend and swell Ishtar's ranks. As the last of the accursed Lions was slain, his Grace arrived, summoned by Her to use The Apostle as the sickle in the coming harvest," his friend finished.

A clanking sound from the rear of the RV set both of them on edge. The pair crept round to see Malky closing the cage on the final penitent. They bowed respectfully and continued with their preparations.

The padlock closed with its customary metallic finality. Malky pulled on it a few times to ensure it was locked. "You should feel pride at being the last one. You will lead Her flock to the very gates of our enemies." He looked at the emaciated woman now incarcerated in its gore-splattered frame.

"You don't look very proud," he growled. He knelt down and slid the Stanley knife across the soles of her feet, and she whimpered.

"P…please, you don't have to do this you know? I have a family out there somewhere. They need me. Please just let me go," her reedy voice implored.

Malky slid the blade into its plastic housing and stood to full height. He had to look down at her; his silhouette blocked out the rising morning sun. "Your family is dead. When we took you from the supermarket, they were already dead," he snarled and went to turn away.

"You're lying! You didn't know where they *were*, you would nev—"

"Your husband and son were hiding out back. My men found them when we were looking for our volunteers. We were going to use him until he resisted. To demonstrate to him the error of his ways we peeled the skin from his face."

The woman gasped and tried to stifle her building tears. "You're lying…"

Malky's mouth broke into an approximation of a smile. "This was after we slit your son's throat in front of him. Poor boy, not so sweet sixteen, I think. There is only certainty now. There is no hope. No one will rescue you and no one is waiting for you. Ishtar delivered you unto us. Providence I believe." He walked away from the woman who broke down into a primal wailing. "Start the engine, we have a long day ahead of us."

Devin stood by the open RV passenger door. He took in the shuffling sea of grey on the horizon, and his chest swelled with pride. "Look, Malky. Look upon what we have amassed. *She* favours us indeed. Tonight they will break upon the non-believers. It will be another strike to the heart of those who still cling to the misguided notion that they are safe."

Malky stood to Devin's side. He too surveyed the wall of dead shuffling towards them; moans and feral snarls smothered them in a blanket of noise. "It is the biggest gathering yet, your Grace. The men know what to do. We will ensure none leave alive."

"Mister Mystery Man, are you satisfied with what you see?" Devin asked the figure in the RV, looking out through the back window.

"I don't care, just as long as you let me go in first. I have some unfinished business to take care of." he fingered the stub where his little pinky used to be.

"As you wish. We will grant you this. I think I don't need to tell you that we will not be waiting for you. Our agreement will be complete once the first of Her flock set foot within the perimeter. For your sake, I would make sure you take care of your business and then leave via the old railway line. My men will not impede you," Devin hissed. "We leave. Now."

MAY 14ᵀᴴ 2014

21:01

Francis burst through the door holding the doctor roughly by the upper arm. "Just check, doctor. You'll see, it's true," he said angrily.

The doctor was released from his grip and, whilst looking into Francis' eyes, tried to recall the number for security. He placed his hands on Diane's belly. He jumped back. "B...but that's not—"

Diane started crying, tears of joy this time. "Doctor, it's true, he's *alive*. Whatever it was, it wasn't true, he's still with us, he's still fighting."

Flicking the ultrasound back on, the screen bloomed into life, the doctor squirted gel onto Diane's tummy and grabbed the scanner. He wiped it to and fro across her skin, trying to get an image to appear.

Finally, with three pairs of expectant eyes locked onto it, a low-res image manifested from the static. "Look, there's his little feet," the doctor pointed out, and sure enough, there they were, gently kicking in the amniotic fluid.

Diane started pointing. "Look, there's George's head! He's moving, look Francis, look!"

The ghostly image appeared to look directly at its spectators; hands formed from the gloom and reached upwards.

Diane screamed.

The image waned but finally settled on a relatively clear picture of the baby. The doctor looked on in astonishment. "But, that can't be, there's...there's no heartbeat."

CHAPTER THIRTY-ONE

As the wind sucked in its breath and blew it back out, the gate hit the frame and swung out again, repeating the process over and over like a badly programmed machine. Bodies were spread out on the concrete as if they had been dispensed by a giant kid playing war with their toy soldiers.

"This is like that other place we went to," Nathan remarked, fingers gripping the chain link fence.

"You're not wrong there, kid. Looks like someone's got a bee in their bonnet about people riding this out in peace. Look, this chain was cut. The padlock is still locked at the ends." Francis prodded the length of chain with the toe of his boot.

Russ piped up, "So where now then? Dunno about you, but I don't really fancy going in there. All these dead bodies are what we can see, who knows what the hell is in there waiting for us."

Zena sighed, sinking to the floor and sitting cross-legged. "Well, we're gonna have to find somewhere to stay. We got a few hours of light left, at most. How far are we now until this Rhayader place?"

Francis pulled the map from his bag and lay it on the floor, placing rocks on the corners to keep it pegged down. "Well, we're here, which gives us another twenty old miles until we're at the border, then another forty odd till Rhayader itself, then another couple down the river to get to where Philip said the camp was, about… here." A thick podgy finger pointed out the places on the map.

"That last stretch will be on country lanes and through fields. Let's hope we get some good weather. The days are getting longer, that's one good thing. So, there's a golf club or something a few miles from here. Reckon we can get there before nightfall if we're lucky, hunker down there for the night and then carry on tomorrow, deal?" Francis looked around the group who nodded in agreement.

"C'mon, let's get out of here. This place gives me the creeps," Russ said, lancing a crawling, legless zombie through the head.

Boots crunched over the gravelled drive of the Bransford Golf Club. There were no parked cars, and with the lack of maintenance, the previously immaculate fairways and greens were going to wrack and ruin. After scouting the main building, skirting round the decaying remains of gaudily dressed golfers, the group huddled within the large dining room.

"Man, I am getting sick to death of tuna," Russ whinged, reluctantly fishing out chunks with a plastic fork. "Who's to say that this place we're going to won't be like that one earlier?" he added idly.

Francis chewed on a strip of Biltong, his by the virtue that no one else wanted it; even Nathan, who was far from picky, said it was like eating a coat. "We don't know until we get there. Could very well be, slim. It's odd that two of these so-called safe zones that we've found have been turned over."

Nathan had wolfed down his cold beans and was now engrossed in Merrick: The Elephant Man, a spin on the yarn, which saw the titular character take on the occult. "Look, Francis, it's like that man we saw at the circus, the one we left alive," Nathan said distractedly, pointing at the deformed character tearing his way through a gang of ne'er do wells.

Francis looked over at him, nodded, and turned back to Russ. "Regardless, we gotta go on. This is for him. Think of the effects this has on him. I know we've got it bad, but…"

Zena nodded. "Fair enough. To be honest, it's nice to have a goal in mind, something to aim for, takes my mind off…you know, Tom. Where's the next place we're heading to, anyways?"

"Philip marked out a milk distribution plant, just over the border. We should get there in a couple of days, I reckon. We're not exactly at the peak of our powers anymore, eh?" Francis quipped as he tore into another strip of cured meat.

"Speak for yourself, Grandad. I reckon I could still run a marathon," Russ chuckled, "mind over matter, just like everything else. Does anyone…"

The group turned and looked across to the man, "Go on," Francis invited.

Russ sighed. "I dunno. Does any of this feel a bit pointless to anyone else? Me, Chris and Mum had been in a few scrapes since this all happened, but nothing me or Chris couldn't get us out of. He always had a plan, you know? Even the times when it looked like there was no way out, he'd always find a way." He placed the can on the threadbare carpet. "When this all kicked off, we were all at home. Chris was staying with Mum after his wife left him. Me? Ha, well, I was a mummy's boy, never left home. She dropped these subtle and not so subtle hints, but I ignored them. Mum lived in this little two bed flat, we were glued to the news, just like everyone I guess. Dunno what happened, but there was this banging at the downstairs main door. We looked out of the window and there they were, this group of ten zombies all thumping on the building, trying to get in."

Russ opened a lukewarm can of Coke and took a sip. "We lived on the third floor, no fire escape, the only way out was through *them*. As long as they're outside, and we're in, we'll be fine, Mum said. Two days later, the group had tripled in size. The constant moaning must've driven Mr Talbot loopy. We heard this muffled shouting from downstairs, and we all ran to the window and looked out. There he was, Mental Talbot, being carried aloft by those things. They were tearing him apart, limb from limb. His screaming drowned out their moaning. Don't know which sound was worse."

He offered the can around the group, passing it to Zena. "Stupid bastard had let them in, though. The banging, which had been downstairs, was now on our flat door. Mum was catatonic, mumbling how we're all going to die, which was not helping in the slightest. I had a rolling pin and after piling furniture against the door, just stood there. Fucked if I knew what we were going to do, except starve to death or do a Talbot. To be honest, think Mum would've done that if we were in there for too long."

Russ took his cap off and smoothed his hair down. "Chris, though, he was on it. Told me to stop being a flid and give him a hand. We dragged the mattresses to the living room window. We still had power, so he got an extension lead and put a stereo on the furniture by the door, started blaring out 'Killing In The Name' full blast. We looked out and the stragglers were filtering into the building. He told us to get what we needed and kicked the window out. We slung the mattresses onto the pavement below and lowered me out, then Mum, and finally Chris."

Russ ran the rim of the worn cap around in his fingers. "We made it away just as the first of the dumb bastards heard us outside. We had to carry Mum, but they're not exactly Usain Bolt, eh? We just kept on the move from then on. It hit Mum hard, though, when that bastard drove past us and offered us some food and rest, we didn't have the heart to refuse. Mum was going Talbot man, I knew she was. She needed a break. We figured a show and some food would help her. We…I mean, why do people do that? Isn't it bad enough that we've got to deal with all of this, without these bastards making things worse? They're worse than the undead. I fucking hate them."

CHAPTER THIRTY-TWO

Thomas woke with a start. He tried to rub his eyes, but the rope hoiked his arm back: *fuck's sake*. He loosened the knot and sat up, easing the sleep from his eyes with his palms. The interior of the factory was cold. Small palls of mist were expelled from the rows of sleeping people. The odd cough or splutter was the only sound. He stood up and stretched out the kinks in his body. His bones cracked, demanding tribute for their lack of comfort.

He shuffled across the dusty floor to the toilets. Since the water stopped running, metal buckets had been shoved into the bowls. He blindly walked into the closest cubicle and began to relieve himself. The stream of warm, steaming piss bounced off the side of the receptacle, sounding like a distant dinner bell.

Out of habit he pulled the chain, which resulted in nothing more than a half-hearted arm workout. He buttoned himself up and waltzed back to his bed. Reaching underneath, he pulled out his coat and wrapped himself in it.

The door to the outside world groaned at the lateness of the hour and the unexpected user. Thomas breathed in sharply as the temperature au naturel was nippier than inside. He yawned and pottered over to the fence. Looking around the exterior, he could see the odd straggler, but nothing close by to cause him consternation.

The gateway to the road beyond stood like a giant, bored robot face. He flicked small icicles from the chain link fence. His mind was a whirl of the past few months: escaping from his work by the smallest of margins, the zombie missing him and grabbing hold of the girl behind him. He had been saved by her hood; that was the margin between life and death now. Similar occurrences had followed.

Having his surname fall within A to D meant he got on the first transport truck to the military safe zone. When they arrived, they all heard the frenzied radio reports from the hastily created camp they had just come from, not two hours before. The dead had swamped them. There would be no E to H coming. No more alphabeticised withdrawals.

He hated it there. No space to grow, no sense of control, always being told where they should be and what they should be doing. *HA*, he realised that this place was panning out the same way. Soon, though, things would change. He'd strike out on his own again. It was easier that way. No one to slow him down, no one to get in the way, no one to mourn when they died.

Everyone died.

These days it was like Mother Nature had arranged an outsource company to help speed the process up. She had a quota to meet, shareholders to keep happy, KPIs to aspire to.

Everyone died.

The problem was that they no longer stayed dead.

Was that a cough?

Thomas broke out of his thoughts and squinted. *Was that?* He cupped his hands and saw a flash of movement over by the ditch where he had found Bartholomew, beaten to a pulp and left for dead.

Discretion was never the better part of Thomas' valour. He slid the gate bolt and pushed the metal door, trying to stifle its protestations. He hunched over and crept towards where he had seen the movement. There was nothing there now, but curiosity was a bitch.

He made his way carefully to the drainage ditch, back to where he had found the man resting against a small brick tunnel which enabled rainwater to run off the road and stop the creation of potholes. He edged closer and peered off the road and into the ditch.

Nothing.

Ha, dumb bastard.

"You shouldn't have checked Thomas."

As he spun around he felt two needles jab into his neck, quickly followed by the long icy reptilian tongue of electricity which seemed to wrap around his throat. He collapsed to the floor in a heap of limp limbs and convulsed under the waves of electricity.

His vision crackled like Robocop getting a hard-reset. His back arched as the flow increased up and down his body, now pulled taut like a violin string. The smell of burnt hair filled his nostrils, his teeth gritted together like a broken lift door.

And then, just like that, he was released from its grip. His body relaxed but ached like it had been on a route march up and down Mount Snowden. The full moon looked down on him like a shocked mouth with a torch embedded in its roof. He flexed his fingers and toes to reassure himself that he was still alive.

A figure loomed over him. Thomas could only make out a head and shoulders. He chuckled, "Who the fuck are you, the Milk Tray man?"

The silhouette regarded him impassively. "No, Thomas, I am the last living person you will ever see. I have work to do, and you are putting me behind schedule."

Thomas laughed. "Man, you are such a drama queen. Why so serious?" The shadow leaned down. Cold, impassive eyes bore through Thomas. "Oh, it's *you*. Fucking typical. Well, get it over with will you? I've got things to do."

A fist like granite caught Thomas on the side of his face, slamming his jaw into the concrete. His head bounced off the road and he fell still.

"As do I, and you will be of some use to me yet."

CHAPTER THIRTY-THREE

Gloved fingers teased the door handle. The latch popped out of the hole in the door frame and the barrier let out a crack of light. Slowly, the hand pushed the door. When the gap was of a sufficient size, they edged into the room and carefully closed the solitary exit.

The sides of the room were shrouded in night. The moon cast a creamy marbley glow through the large window at the end, creating an elliptical arena of light. It looked like a Roman gladiatorial ring.

Facing the large window was a Queen Ann chair, looking out onto the front of the Netzach's complex, and the road and forest just beyond its boundaries. The leather-wrapped hand reached into the depths of a raincoat and pulled out a stubby sawed-off shotgun. The other hand came up and rested underneath the barrel, cradling it like a cucumber.

Dirty, filth-encrusted canvas shoes crept across the room. The gun aimed at the top of the chair: *slowly does it.* It seemed to take an age to make the voyage from the doorway to the visitor's side of the desk, but it was now complete. They took aim.

"Douglas."

As the intruder made to turn, on instinct from hearing his name, the parking meter smacked into the front of his skull. A crunch told both parties that the melee had started with a broken nose. Douglas flew back into a filing cabinet, clutching his shattered face. Hydrants of blood squirted into the air. The shotgun hit the floor and skittered under the desk.

The impact winded him and he collapsed to his knees. His body tried to take in extra reserves of air to replenish the batch that had been expelled with such force mere seconds before.

The Gaffer hefted the weapon onto his shoulder. "I told you last time, you are not welcome here. I thought I made myself perfectly clear. Do I have to take another finger? Perhaps something which you'll notice if you didn't have, hmm?"

Douglas fell forward onto all fours and coughed up a ball of blood and pulp. "I got the message, Mike. Just found some new friends. They'll finish the job I started last time I was here."

The Gaffer snorted. "You always were a complete coward. Always had to get other people to do your dirty work. When you wanted to be the football team manager, you just bitched to the other kids' parents, even tried to start that rumour that I was a Charlie Chester."

The parking meter slammed down onto Douglas' back, sprawling him over the floor like a specimen in an entomologist's display. Another crack rang out in the office. Douglas started gasping as if in a vacuum. "Sounds very much to me like someone's got a couple of broken ribs. Might well have a pierced lung, if your luck's out mate."

Douglas' arms tried to lift him up like a jack; his body rose a few inches before the pain knocked him back onto his front. The gasping continued unabated.

"Least you answered the question I had but never asked. Whether you let those chompers in here on purpose. You little fuck, I should've done this months ago. I shouldn't have exiled you; I should've fucking *gutted* you," The Gaffer grunted, pulling his weapon back onto his shoulder.

Douglas managed to catch his breath. "I...I...I just wanted to show th...the others how you couldn't manage y...you...your way out of a wet paper bag, if a few got eaten, so...s...so be it."

The Gaffer used his size twelve boot to roll Douglas over onto his back. Douglas winced with pain as his body pushed down on his battered frame. "No matter, I get to correct my oversight now." The Gaffer brought the parking meter above his head.

In stereo, both men looked towards the door and the factory secreted beyond. "What th—" was all The Gaffer could manage before a bony foot connected with the collection of squishy objets d'art in his pants.

He crumpled like a beggar diving for a dropped coin. The parking meter fell onto the floor with a clang, followed by its bearer, who was cupping his delicates. Douglas rolled towards the desk, ignoring the searing agony as each completed rotation ground the ends of his broken ribs against each other.

His hand patted underneath the desk for his gun. A finger clipped the trigger guard and he pulled it out from its resting place. Douglas stumbled across to The Gaffer, who was still prone on the floor trying to squeeze life back into his bruised meat and two veg. "Don't hold 'em, Mike, count 'em," he sneered. "How did you know I was coming?"

"We had a visitor recently. Told me about some of the camps he had found, that they had all been picked clean, warned me it could happen here. I've been waiting, didn't expect to find y—"

Both men looked again, trying to work out where the sound was coming from. The Gaffer took advantage of the distraction and executed a near perfect leg sweep which made Douglas tumble to the floor once more. The gun bounced and slid towards the door. Both men glared at each other on the blood-spattered rug.

The Gaffer crawled over to the stricken man, ignoring the dull sensation in his pelvic region. Douglas tried to get to his feet. His attempt was met with an uppercut, which sent fragments of chipped teeth into the air.

Douglas tried to recall what day it was, his brain seeking an anchor in reality again. His vision was swamped by The Gaffer's large skin-covered skull. Using his weight, he sat on Douglas' chest, which sent a new battalion of pain from his broken bones into his nerve cluster.

Knees which wouldn't have looked out of place on a baby elephant pinned Douglas' biceps to the floor. "This is for the ones you killed, Doug," The Gaffer panted as he placed ham hock hands around Douglas' neck and began to squeeze.

"This is for Mary..."

Strands of spittle, peppered with blood, spooled off The Gaffers lips and onto Douglas' face.

"...little baby Rick..."

Thumbs dug into the trachea.

"...Ethan..."

Spots swam across Douglas' vision, giving The Gaffer the appearance of someone afflicted with the pox.

"...Kev..."

His trapped hands tried to get some momentum but just bounced back limply from the wrist joint.

"...Bethany..."

His legs had gone numb. He could feel his circulation start to wrap up their travel plans.

"...Clive..."

His bowels, in one last act of one-up-manship, voided. The Gaffer puckered his nose, but merely increased the pressure. The hyoid bone cracked under the onslaught and the tongue slapped out to one side.

"...Sarah."

Douglas fell limp in The Gaffer's grip; a wet gurgle signalled his end. The Gaffer stood up on wobbly legs and walked over to his weapon. He dragged it along the floor to the body of his one-time coach and friend. He lifted it above his head. "This is for me."

CHAPTER THIRTY-FOUR

The cable-tie rasped like it was blowing a raspberry. Rough hands shook the body to make sure it would stay attached to the gate. He put the one sleeved coat over his shoulder and made his way through the gate, heading towards an old metal ladder affixed to the side of the building's entrance.

The moisture from his sweaty hands stuck to the freezing rungs. He hauled himself up like a monkey with a rocket up its jacksy. The ascent took him to the flat canopy which was below the main roof. The giant Netzach's sign looked out into the night sky. The metal frame of the angel, Netzach's logo since its inception, stood immobile. Metal panels had been blown off after the factory shut, giving it a piecemeal appearance.

He could see the two guards, sitting back to back in the cold, looking out to each side into the surrounding forest. His heart skipped a beat as he saw a face looking his way, but it made no attempt to warn anyone of the intrusion. As he got nearer, he could see that his eyes were shut and he was lightly snoring.

A long thin stiletto blade slid from its place on his belt. He crept towards the two men. Kneeling down by the closest, he jabbed the blade into the man's heart. Eyes opened wide with shock, but the life soon drained out. His nap pal barely stirred as he was dealt with in the same way. He made his way across the felt floor and started climbing up the ladder which would take him to the main roof.

"Oohhh, nearly there, mate. Looks like another night of being a loser, Deano," Paul chuckled. He walked over to the bucket and started the laborious process of picking up the cards.

"Yeah, well, whatever. If the one thing in life you're good at is chucking cards in a bucket, then my fr—"

The hatchet thunked into Dean's spinal column, severing the connection between the upper and lower halves of his body. He reached around to his back, trying to locate the cause of his sudden lack of toe wiggling ability. Like a back itch that couldn't be scratched, his arms flailed around as a trickle of blood ran from the corner of his mouth.

Paul stood up, impotent with surprise. The cards he had collected fluttered to the ground as a shuriken whistled through the air and hit him in the throat. Like a bee stinging him, he slapped his throat with his hand, pressing the metal further inside. "Honestly…who actually uses throwing stars?"

Dean was still trying to find the object that had rendered his dancing days done when a boot met the hatchet handle. With a sound akin to someone splitting wood, his spine cracked in half and a ridge of knobbly bone was pulled out into the cold night air. Steam rose from the wound. He gargled and collapsed to one side, spasming on the lumpy iron roof.

Paul had slumped onto his arse. Blood was pumping out of the wound in his neck as if he were a boat taking on water. He looked at Dean's lifeless body a few feet away and then up at the man who was trying to yank the axe from his mate's spine.

"Bartholomew?" Paul gasped.

Bartholomew shook the hatchet. Droplets of blood and marrow sprayed over the playing cards which were scattered over the roof. "Hello, Paul. Bartholomew is one of many names I have. I am the Apostle of Ishtar. I am the blade in the night. The enemy in your midst. The tentacles of fear."

The Apostle spread his arms out, revelling in his power. "I am doom incarnate."

"You're a dick, more like." Paul winced and pulled his hand away from his throat. It was covered in blood. He knew it had severed something which would make staunching the flow unlikely.

The Apostle placed the hatchet into a small rucksack and floated over to Paul. He knelt down by him, reached out a hand and dug the shuriken out of Paul's throat. The flow of blood increased and Paul gave up trying to stop it. "Well, this is going to put a bit of a dampener on the evening."

Paul cocked his head to one side. "Seriously, who is making that noise? Don't they know it's night time and people are trying to sleep?"

"You'll be one of them soon, Paul. You'll ascend and be a part of *Her* flock. You should rejoice in this. Embrace it," The Apostle said softly, slipping the shuriken into a pouch on his belt.

Paul heaved himself to his feet and tottered towards Dean.

"He's dead, Paul. He has had his Rapture, and he will return soon, though I fear he won't be getting around very easily," The Apostle said, happy with his work.

"I changed my mind, mate. You're not a dick…you're a deluded *psycho*, a complete and total thunder-cunt." Paul walked backwards from Dean's body, blood still oozing from the gash in his neck.

"And if you don't mind, I've got better things to do than be a part of your fucking gang. In case I don't see you, may something really unpleasant befall you, hopefully involving spinny things and fire." Paul gave him the Agincourt salute and, with arms outstretched, fell off the roof backwards, relying on Newton's Law of Universal Gravitation to back up what it espoused.

CHAPTER THIRTY-FIVE

The RV engine whined to a halt by the junction. Devin jumped out of the passenger side and onto the frost-mosaicked tarmac. "Malky, tell the men to take their positions. We'll park just on from here. We'll track through the forest back to it once *Her* flock is through the gates. Remember. No one leaves there unless they're in an ascended state."

Malky bowed and gestured to the semi-circle of waiting armed men. They were identically dressed in red hoodies, black combat trousers and black army boots. They nodded as one and spread out to their assigned posts.

"I hate this bit," Malky grumbled.

Devin grinned at him. "But you're so good at it. Besides, I think the penitent is nearly expired."

"It's not them I mind, it's the need to carry them so close to the ascended."

"Get it done. I'll check to make sure the Apostle has prepared the way," Devin nodded and started to make his way up the side of the road, lurking in the shadows.

Malky moved to the back of the RV and unlocked the padlock to the cage. The wretch contained within fell out and into his arms, weak from blood loss and drained from the toil of the day.

He slung the woman over his shoulder as if she were an empty sack. He slapped the wheel arch and the RV moved off to the meeting point. As the engine noise dissipated, it was replaced by a wall of moans and fevered snarls.

Malky looked along the road they had come from and saw a moving, writhing mass of bodies. Arms, or in some cases, stumps of greying meat, reached for the sizeable meal a little way off in front of them.

Checking that the penitent was still breathing, he was content that they would survive for the time required. He stood and waited. When the horde got to within twenty feet, he turned and started the trek towards the factory gate. The moonlight lit the avenue like the Champs Elysees, just with less 'joie de vivre' and more zombies.

Devin slunk to the fence. For the past thirty seconds, he could see that something was awry. There was a figure by the gateway. Taking care not to cause any noise, he made his way cautiously forward. He got to the side of the road and let out a small chuckle. The figure wasn't guarding the gate; they were *on* the gate.

He ditched the stealthy approach and marched up to the offering. "I take it you met the Apostle?" The man's face had swollen on one side. An eye looked out from a purple and yellow letterbox, one cheek a criss cross hatch of grazes. A coat sleeve had been wrapped around the mouth to prevent them from making any audible noise.

Devin traced a cold, crusty finger down the man's shivering naked torso. "Despair not, friend. Behold your salvation." He stood to one side and lifted Thomas' face up with a hand under his jaw. Thomas tried to move, but was fastened too tightly. The only sounds were a rubbing of plastic against metal and desperate muffled expletives. Thomas took in the sight of an armada of walking dead, led by an emotionless giant of a man with a woman cast over his shoulder.

"Your Grace, looks like the Apostle prepared an aperitif." Malky smiled and placed the woman by Thomas' feet, which hung a few feet off the ground.

"This should steady the flow a little. This will work in our favour. Let's get the other gate open, and ensure that they may enter without any further distraction. We can then get back to the RV and make sure no one escapes," Devin commanded.

Thomas felt the other gate swing out. Looking down, he saw a bloodied woman curled up in the foetal position beneath his feet. He tried to say some calming words, but all that came out was, "Mnnh whhh, mh yhhg hgg."

The moaning was getting nearer. Again he tried to pull his arms and legs free, focusing on one appendage at a time, desperately trying to get some momentum to escape. The cable-ties, though, did not release him from their grip. The plastic sliced into his skin the more he struggled against his bondage.

The first zombie was now fifteen feet away. He cast his mind back to Sarah, the girl with the hood. He had seen her out in town in the months beforehand. He hoped one day to have asked her out for a drink, maybe even a meal. He stood the other side of the glass door as he watched the cleaner make a meal out of her; her hands patted and scratched against the glass.

He had just stood there and watched.

Watched as she was eaten alive. The blood had seeped under the door and soaked into his brown loafers.

Still he watched.

The zombie fell onto the woman at his feet. She put up no resistance as broken fingernails rent open her pale moonlit-infused skin.

He looked down into the sad dead face of what he guessed was a young woman, her lifespan frozen. Her once blonde hair was filthy and crawling with insects. Her eyes were cue balls with a black mark at their centre; her blouse was stained with the meals she had gorged on since her change.

"YNGGG, MHHHMMMM," Thomas shouted, trying to move out of her way. Cold fingers ran down his body. He flinched as they tickled his side. He started to laugh. The dead girl paid him no heed and pressed her fingers between his ribs. The skin bowed until it gave in and puffed out. The breach made, the other hand was shoved in the gap. Fingers wrapped around the bone and pulled like it was an emergency release. The skin covering his belly peeled off like a strip of thick wallpaper.

He felt something clammy and sponge-like around his toes. He looked down to see his internal organs, no longer bound by their wrapping, begin to avalanche out of their correct cavity and onto the floor. Beyond the girl was a child. He had Thomas' foot in his mouth and was gumming it. This tickled him too.

A crunch destroyed the tender moment as the kid came away with a chunk of meat which had two toes and a section of foot with it. More and more hands reached for him now, pawing at him like he was a good luck charm. His vision was fading as more and more key body systems were removed by untrained operatives.

He took in a large gulp of air as he felt and then witnessed one of his lungs being first squeezed, and then pulled free, of their usual dwelling. He couldn't make out the woman beneath him anymore. He was surrounded by his own fan club. Those who couldn't get an invite trundled through the empty gate and towards the factory beyond.

Thomas felt light, as one of his legs was chewed through. He dropped three feet as an arm was nibbled free, the remaining sinew and ligaments unable to support his weight anymore. He hung from his one remaining wrist.

I'm sorry Sarah. I should've done something to help you. I should've—

CHAPTER THIRTY-SIX

"Fuck's sake, why do people leave next to no toilet roll?" Dee grumbled to herself. She squatted above the bucket which had resonated with her ablutions. She looked around the cubicle to see if she could find any discarded sheets to complete the job.

BANG-BANG-BANG

Dee held her breath, before shouting, "Oi, fuck off! I'm having a dump in here. There's plenty of others, you know."

"Mind you, if you find any bog roll can you chuck some over?"

Silence.

BANG-BANG-BANG

"Seriously, use another one."

The door exploded in a flash of cordite, pellets, and shards of desiccated wood. Dee was slammed against the back wall. Her head struck the bottom of the cistern, making her chin crack against her breastbone. Her buttocks sank into the metal bucket which was buried inside the bowl.

The world felt like it had caved in. Dee struggled to lift her head. She could feel a ridge of bruising already rising on the back of her skull. There was a loud buzzing, which was not helping the freshly manifested headache in the slightest. She managed to look up to a figure which seemed shrouded in the gloom.

"Hello Dee," a gentle woman's voice cooed. "It took me a while, but I remembered in the end."

The figure stepped into her visual spectrum, the smoking shotgun barrel appeared first. A small hand gripped it halfway down. Sylvia followed shortly after; she raised the gun and aimed at Dee's face.

"Wait…" Dee mustered through a fat lip and a few broken teeth. She raised a hand towards the woman.

"I can't believe I didn't remember that it was you that broke into our new home. That it was *you* that shot and killed my husband. My Donald," Sylvia said calmly.

Dee tried to push herself up, but was firmly entrenched within the bucket. She could feel a drip-dripping from the back of her hair onto the toilet seat.

Feeble hands slipped off the edge of the bucket rim, and she raised her hands in defence. "It was after that other place. I was…I was still in shock. I didn't…didn't *mean* to. He was a deader, though, he was—"

Pieces of porcelain, bone, and a jet of blood sprayed over the confines of the toilet. Sylvia thumbed the release; the expended shells landed and rolled along the floor, coming to a rest against the toe of Dee's scuffed boot. A gasping and desperate slurping was the chorus to the shotgun verse.

A howling came shortly afterwards as Dee clutched her leg; cold fingers pried into the ruin of it, disappearing into the tattered remnants of her kneecap. The skin and muscle had been shorn away by the blast; chewed up veins spat blood into the air.

Sylvia slowly reached into her trouser pocket and pulled out two more shotgun shells. "He was my husband, Dee. He was my Donald. We were doing fine on our own, thank you very much. I read to him, he even helped me with my puzzles. He was perfect. Just like he used to be."

The first shell dropped in. Dee tried to stem the bleeding. Making a ring with her fingers above the remains of her knee, she squeezed. "FUCK," she bellowed. Gritting her teeth merely dislodged another molar.

"Then *you* came along, and in a few seconds, you took away everything that I had left in the world. Everything that I loved and treasured. My Donald was no angel, but he was still mine. He was all I had. You had no right to take him from me, to kill him."

The second shell slid into place. Sylvia cracked the breech shut. Content that it had closed properly, she lifted the barrels up to Dee's chest.

"Plea...pl...please *Sylvia...*" Dee coughed. "...I didn't mean..."

Sylvia placed the hot barrels' point against Dee's skin, a few inches below the base of her throat. "Don't worry, dear, I'll let you come back. You deserve to be dead, to live in purgatory for what you've done."

Both barrels catapulted Dee back the last few feet against the wall; her head once again smacked into the base of the cistern. A loud crack heralded broken vertebrae. A large smoke-filled crater took up most of where her chest used to be. The smell of burnt meat and flash-boiled blood filled the air. In a wide arc around where she sat was a pool of liquefied flesh and bone.

Dee's body sunk into the bucket further. Her legs tucked up against her body. As they rose, the bottom half of her destroyed leg hung on by tendrils of skin, before the earth called dibs and it dropped to the floor, oozing blood onto the white tiled floor.

"What have you done?"

Sylvia span around and looked into Andy's distraught face. "You *knew*. You *knew* what she did, and yet you covered for her. When I was lying in that bed after you brought me back here, I couldn't remember what happened. I *asked* you, and you said that my Donald had died. It didn't feel right, but I couldn't remember, so I took you at your word."

Andy was still looking at the crumpled body in the toilet. "She was all over the place that day. She went into that shop to try and redeem herself, that's what she said. Before I knew it she had shot him. You came tumbling down the stairs. Dee…she…she nearly shot you there and then. We got you back here, to look after you."

Sylvia wiped a hand across her face. Droplets of sticky blood smeared across her pale skin. "I DIDN'T WANT TO BE LOOKED AFTER. Not by you. Or *her*. I wanted my Donald. He was the only thing I ever wanted, and *you two* took him away from me. That's why I did this." Sylvia grabbed her left sleeve and yanked it up, revealing a four inch scar running inside her forearm. It looked like someone had sewn a skewer under her skin.

"LOOK AT IT! This is what I did, this is what you two made me do. I didn't want to come here. I wanted to be left alone with my Donald. You're as bad as her, aren't you?"

Sylvia levelled the gun at Andy, who raised his hands and edged out onto the factory floor. "Please Sylvia…please d—"

CLICK

Sylvia smiled slyly. "Bang."

Andy, who had shielded his face with his arms, lowered them slowly. "Hang on, that's one of the guns from the armoury. How did you get it? There's always a guard stationed there?"

Sylvia started to reload. "There were no guards there a minute ago, I saw your girlfriend come in here so thought I'd pay her a little visit. Make her into one of them."

A thud announced Dee's rebirth as she landed on one good knee and one ragged stub. The partially-filled bucket hit the side of the Formica cubicle with a loud clang. Unable to walk, her arms worked their way out in front of her broken body and started trying to pull her toward the humans. She looked like a cross between Sadako and a snail with a metal shell.

Her head hung against her body, the neck a mass of broken bone. Hands slapped against the bloody floor trying to gain some purchase on the slick tiles.

The rapier slid from Andy's belt as blood-drenched hands ran up his legs. He turned Dee's head to one side with a boot and ran the blade through her temple. Dead hands patted the floor before the human zombie snail fell to one side, life extinguished.

Andy looked over to the corner of the factory where the armoury was. He couldn't see anyone. "But, how can there be…"

Heavy booted feet stomped down the stairs. Like the proverbial elephant in the room, The Gaffer stormed across the floor towards the main entrance. "Andy, you're with me. We have guests, and not the kind who bring biscuits and tea round with them."

Andy looked at Sylvia one last time. she seemed at peace, nonchalantly reloading the shotgun. "Gaffer, someone's taken out the armoury gu—"

"Mate, we've been royally fucked. A snake in our midst. Tom Thompson mentioned something the other day, but had no idea how they did it." The Gaffer pushed the main door open with the end of the parking meter.

"Fuck me," Andy uttered; mental checkpoints failed in their duty.

They were met with a wall of grey faces. Dead eyes locked onto them, jaws agape. Some chattered teeth in anticipation of a meal, others let out a deep moan to signal to their chums that a midnight snack was indeed served. "Very possibly, Andy, I think we've all been fucked. Rouse who you can. We will need as many people as possible…"

Andy nodded and turned back into the factory. "…even then, it might not be enough," The Gaffer finished, before he marched out of the double doors and stood before the undead flood.

The doors seemed to recoil in terror at the sight that greeted them and closed slowly behind The Gaffer. A semi-circle of zombies surrounded him. For as far as he could see, there were gore-covered faces; most were damaged in some way or other. Patches of skin had been torn off, eyes hung slack from sockets like pocket watches resting, mouths shorn of lips displayed rows of cracked, yellowing pegs of ivory and slabs of exposed gum.

The moaning was interrupted by a loud huffing and the sound of displaced air, metal slapping dead skin and cracking bones. A wild swing cleared a ten foot swathe in front of him. Row two surged towards him, some tripping over their broken brethren and smacking into the concrete.

The Gaffer was a small crustacean in an ocean of groping hands and vacant stares. Those at the back, sensing a wait, strolled past the entrance in search of other means of reaching the building and the buffet within.

A backhand volley took out another row of the dead. A small knee- high wall of crumpled, deflated carcasses formed a small, but completely ineffective, barrier between those without a pulse and the one with a quickening one.

"C'mon, you dead fucks! You can do better than this," The Gaffer bellowed. An overhead smash on the skull of a sneaky bastard trying to claw up his leg sent an explosion of rippled worms of brain and jigsaw pieces of skull in a wide arc.

Adopting the disposition of a spinning top, he whirled into the centre of the swarm. Broken bodies were cast aside as if they were animals meeting a tornado. His momentum came to a gradual halt. He looked back to see a trail of destruction leading from the doors and towards the gates, where the undead still ambled through.

The zombies paid their losses no heed. No sooner had a gap been created than they surged back into the void. They walked over their fallen kin, desperate to bring down the walking meat lollipop and feast.

He fended them off with short, abrupt swipes and jabs. His brain filled his tiring limbs with endorphins, trying to jack him up to superhuman means.

We can do this, we can survive.

"This one really is becoming tiresome," Devin sighed. He closed an eye and held his breath. His finger squeezed the trigger and the .308 round was discharged from the rifle. Through the scope he saw the bullet hit the man-mountain in the left shoulder. Poised to strike, his body rocked forwards with the momentum of the shot.

Devin's scabrous hand reached out and pulled the bolt back to reload.

"FUCK," The Gaffer yelled. It felt like someone had just rammed a white-hot poker into his body. He buckled up under the impact. Running a swollen hand across his brow, he lifted the parking meter again and swung with reckless abandon; the exertion caused blood to ooze from the wound.

The second round struck him as he completed his swing, side-on. The bullet tore through the back of his neck, spraying gore over his sheepskin coat, and he teetered to one side.

The crusty hand pulled the bolt back once more. "Just go down, make this easier on yourself," Devin muttered under his breath. He steadied himself on the rug lying on the RV's roof.

Okay, so that stung a little.

The Gaffer's body railed against his efforts to continue. He filed their protestations under 'Pending', and pushed himself vertical again using the parking meter as a crude crutch.

He uttered a guttural yell, and charged deeper into the horde, hoping for sanctuary amongst the throng. Fingers like clammy tentacles rolled over his skin; some managed to dig into the freshly created wounds, causing him to grit his teeth further. He spat out a sliver of his own spongified tongue as he bit it off.

He swung this way and that, trying to keep his flanks clear, desperate to keep them at bay, to make sure that they didn't overwhelm him.

Another distant crack sounded just after he felt the impact in his right bicep. The meter swung feebly in one powered arm. The zombies kept on coming, climbing over the ones that had been downed, yet still pawing at their new nemesis.

The Gaffer yelled in pain as a powerful jaw clamped onto his upper arm. The mouth slurped on the warm blood and bit deeper into his flesh. Eschewing his weapon, he punched the biter with his left fist. It took a number of blows before the jaw finally relented and let go of its prize.

The lull had swung the odds in the undead's favour, and they surged at him like a tsunami, formed of eager maws and grabbing hands. He reached into his coat and pulled out the sawed-off shotgun. He struggled to bring it to bear, but managed to aim it in front of him and pull the trigger.

Devin watched through the scope as a group of Her flock were blown apart at point blank range by the shotgun blast. Clumps of meat slopped to the floor. He could see that the man was fading, though. "You will soon be amongst them," he promised, and squeezed the trigger again.

The Gaffer's vision lit up, as if a flare had been set off right in front of him. The faces of his enemy were illuminated in such clarity, he could make out individual ticks and snarls. His breathing felt heavy and laboured. He clutched his chest and discovered a hole around the area where he guessed his lung should be.

He slumped backwards into the embrace of the undead. Uncaring arms slowed his descent, seemingly holding him aloft in recognition of his efforts. Then the biting started. Incisors started to chew through the tracksuit bottoms. Digits fumbled with his trainers and socks. Other luckier ghouls managed to pull at the wounds already visible and picked out lumps of meat and viscera.

The light faded back to black. He gasped and breathed like he was hyper-ventilating. His left hand fumbled inside a pocket. "Ai…ain…ain't going out like no bitch," he muttered.

Devin cocked the rifle and looked back through the scope. The target was barely visible within the gang of clawing, gouging bodies that surrounded him. "Good, he was a stubborn one, but Ishtar will—"

With The Gaffer at its epicentre, the shrapnel from the grenade tore through the grey, decomposing ranks with ease, shredding a ring sixteen feet in radius. Pieces of severed limbs and unidentifiable body parts were flung even further. Devin cowered from the explosion, even from his vantage point.

He looked down at Malky, who stood impassively by the RV. "Let's get this done; my patience is wearing thin."

CHAPTER THIRTY-SEVEN

"Grimm, where the fuck is your lot?" Andy shouted. He had pulled his sword from its scabbard and was frantically trying to stir people from their slumber.

"Two are dead. Their throats have been slit, dumped in the back storeroom. What is going on?" he shouted back. He pulled the hammers from his belt and strode towards the rows of stirring inhabitants.

Andy shook Steve out of his sleep and looked at the imposing figure of Grimm. "We've been done over. We need people up and ready now. We fight or we die. Only caught a glimpse when The Gaffer went outside, but there are loads of chompers inside the perimeter."

Grimm's mask rendered his emotional state unreadable. "Why did the sentries not alert us?"

Andy hurriedly pulled the rope off Steve's arm, still groggy and squinty. "I don't fucking know. It's not the time for questions, it's the time for action."

As if waiting for the magic words, the side door opened into the factory. The muffled sound of shuffling feet and moans cranked up a notch as the first of the undead staggered into the factory, eliciting screams from the humans within. Grimm turned to the intruders, and nodded towards them. Two of his guards ran over to deal with the uninvited guests.

"We need to seal the doors, befor—"

Just to underline the severity of the situation, another two doors were pushed open. The undead filtered inside, spreading out towards the cluster of cattle at one end of the factory. "Steve, get up. These people need to be helped. *Now.* Look for an opening and try to get them out of here."

Steve nodded dumbly and fumbled under his bed for his clothes and glasses. Another door slammed open and more zombies sauntered into the chaos within. From behind Andy, there came a growl. Matt sprinted past and clotheslined a pair of zombies that were ambling towards the lazier members of the camp. Some were somehow still sleeping, blissfully unaware of the severe turn of events.

Matt crouched down by one of the fallen zombies and started to smack it in its face. The force and number of blows caused the jaw to crack and break off. Matt plunged his fist into the yawning abyss. Andy looked across, dumbfounded, *What the hell is he doing?*

One hand held the thing's head against the ground while the other rummaged around for something to grab a hold of. Content, Matt pulled, and despite a few nibbles, wrenched out the thing's tongue in its grey-blue entirety. Taking a moment to view it, he then started to administer it to the zombie's head. With its lack of moisture, it took on the appearance and weight of a blackjack.

Matt thumped it repeatedly against the thing's head, oblivious to his surroundings. He was swamped by a mass of grey. As he disappeared into the coterie, above the sound of skin being torn asunder, a voice rang out. "Ha ha, it didn't work, Dee. Patches, I'm coming to see you boy, WOOF, WOOF."

All ways in and out of the factory were now clogged with the dead sauntering in, eager to get their rotting mitts on something good before it all went.

Steve had secreted himself next to a cupboard which contained all the disposable plates and cutlery. He watched as the zombies streamed in and dragged the struggling survivors to the ground.

Most of the inhabitants were barely out of their nightclothes; fewer still had armed themselves with anything. Anton was struggling to get himself out of his arm knot, when a very dead woman, dressed in a once-smart suit, saw him and homed in. Remarkably, the glasses she wore had been with her through death and rebirth, and aside from a few scratches and dried flakes of blood, seemed perfectly functional.

"FUCK, FUCK!" Anton shouted. The knot had tightened so much it resembled a shrivelled-up raisin. The more he fought, the tighter it held him. The woman bared rows of stained and chipped Hampstead's and lunged at him. A few feet from contact, a swish and blur of metal flashed before Anton's eyes.

Two arms, which had been lopped off just below the elbows, landed on the floor with little fanfare or attention. Their previous owner, Yvonne Tatchell, who had died while hiding in the storeroom of the office in which she worked on the first day of the apocalypse, looked down at the two stumps.

With no intellectual acuity to comprehend what this would do to her somewhat limited chances in her new life as a denizen of the undead masses, she growled again and fell on top of Anton, who was still fighting to get out of his knot conundrum.

Teeth snapped inches from his nose. He recalled the night when Jenny had managed to clamp onto his face with teeth in a little better condition than the gnashers currently on display.

The pressure was lifted off his chest as Andy grabbed her by her blouse collar and threw her to the floor. He put a boot on her chest and slid the blade in through her forehead. Yvonne died for the second time, with no chance of appeal. Andy pulled out the rapier and slashed the rope which held Anton in place.

Anton rubbed his arm, trying to massage some life into it. "Cheers, mate," he said, before looking past Andy. "Mate, watch out behind you." The warning barely had a chance to be fully interpreted by Andy's cerebral cortex before three zombies reached out and grabbed his jacket. He swung around and, although he managed to catch one, it merely took a chunk from its face, the moan told him that it wasn't going to be enough.

He fought against them, but three became five, which swelled further in even increments, until he fell to the floor screaming. Despite his wild thrashing, the zombies were very much like barnacles to his boat hull and would not be shifted.

Anton watched as the bundled masses tore and gouged at his rescuer; a pool of blood broke against his feet. The decision to flee was passed without the need for a second vote.

He grabbed his belongings from under his bed, peeled Andy's sword from the exposed buttocks of some unfortunate bastard who must've died in the shower, and headed towards the nearest door.

The factory now rang with the screams of those being eaten alive, the moans of those wishing they had put their best foot forward, and the war cries of the few survivors making their final stand.

Steve, though, had chosen Option Four. He tried to clean his glasses again. His hands shook with the ferocity of an aroused tectonic plate. He gave up and managed to get them back on his face. He peered around the corner of the cupboard and saw a violently-smitten zombie, lying in three sections on the ground. A cunning plan hatched in his brain; he crept from his place of cowering and moved towards the corpse.

This is totally going to bloody work.

He crouched down by the body. The smell hit him first. It was like a rubbish bin which had been left out in the rain, where the rain was sewage water and six months had passed. He gagged, but kept his supper of cream crackers and Ritz down. He slipped his hands into the section he labelled as 'probably the torso' and rooted around for something.

He pulled out a lump of tissue. He guessed that it was a kidney, but it was black and pus-ridden. Steve held his breath, squeezed the chunk of meat, which oozed black and yellow goo, and began to administer it to his body. He needed a few more parts before he managed to cover himself, saving a small collection of nut-like objects for his face. He contemplated whether Lynx would pick up this latest trend in aromatic sensations.

The bile he suppressed as he rubbed congealed blood and month-old stools across his face, and accidentally into his nose and mouth, suggested it would not be a winner.

Content with his work, and amazed that he remembered the scene from *The Walking Dead*, he rose to his feet and got into character. Turning a foot inwards, channelling Roger 'Verbal' Kint and the zombies from the aforementioned TV show, he moaned and stumbled towards the door.

This is genius.

He dragged his palsied limb past another feast, and was around ten feet away from the outside world. He had gotten used to the smell, and in some dark recess of his mind, he quite enjoyed it. Worried what Freud would make of this new predilection, he picked up the pace.

As he reached the doorway, a straggler knocked into him. The two things looked at each other. One was a man: Clive, who had been a plumber until a zombie had rather fancied tucking into his throat. The other was a therapist, who was covered in the decaying remnants of a zombie.

Clive sniffed him and seemed to recoil.

Ha, these aren't the droids you're OWWW WHAT IN THE NAME OF FUCK.

Steve shuddered as Clive sank his teeth through the undead paste and into his face, tearing off a cheek as if it were a filo pastry shell. Falling out of character completely, Steve flailed about and tried to fight off his attacker. Clive hadn't taken the mantle of 'last one in', though, and a posse of geriatrics took their chance and brought Steve crashing down to earth.

As shrivelled, grey fingers pried into the gap his face once covered, scores of gummed mouths fought to break the skin. Steve let out an annoyed gurgle and felt around for his glasses. If he was going out, he was going to go out with his motherfucking glasses on. He had spent the last six months trying to keep them together with scavenged Sellotape.

His filth-covered hands twitched and fell still. Around the factory, the last vestiges of

human resistance were crushed into human crumble and devoured.
Without custard.
Savages.

CHAPTER THIRTY-EIGHT

Life as a henchman in a Doomsday Cult was a pretty cushty gig. You got a snazzy red hoodie, especially as Reggie was part of the Big Cheese's cabal. None of those white robes, like the common Children of Ishtar got.

Nope, not for him. Crimson red, like blood, with a moleskin interior, ample pockets and water-resistant to a degree. It wasn't going to be much cop in a monsoon, but for early December in Southern England this was some nice attire.

Not only that, but you had some decent weapons to choose from. Having pillaged vast tracts of the Home Counties, they had amassed a large collection of weapons, from those preferred by keen enthusiasts right up to military grade hardware. Times were good. Not for his family. Obviously. Nope, they were probably dead. But Reggie cared not one jot for them.

They'd always held him back, stunted his development and growth. He remembered when he had managed to get his first girlfriend, Sabina, a German exchange student. Ahh, sure her command of the English language was basic, at best. Granted, she smelt of cigarettes and David Hasselhoff, and admittedly, her personal hygiene routine was…patchy, she was still categorised as a woman.

He was being cosmopolitan by French kissing a German, when his father walked in. Convinced that he was on the verge of completing the Immaculate Conception, Sabina was ejected from the house quicker than it took the Fifth Panzer Division to get through the Ardennes forest.

Nope, Reggie didn't care one bit that his family were either wandering around as one of *them* or had provided the undead with a healthy feast.

Fat bastard.

Sure, he didn't agree fully with all the doctrines of the Children of Ishtar, but they gave him purpose, reason, camaraderie and a bloody huge gun.

He remembered seeing this film as a kid. Couldn't remember the name, something about locks and stocks, some Financial Locksmith perhaps. Anyway this one guy had something called a Bren gun. He didn't remember much about that film, but the one thing he did was the sound it made.

When they rolled over an outpost in an old World War Two museum, he called dibs on his dream gun.

He called it Brenda.

Brenda the Bren gun.

Had a nice ring to it, he said. However, one thing being a henchman for a doomsday cult in the undead apocalypse, is that you seldom get a chance to loose off a few rounds. He'd had Brenda in his possession for six weeks now, and the closest he had come to shooting it was in a dream he'd had a few nights ago.

He closed his eyes and thought back to it. Sabina wrapped herself around him, pulling

Brenda into the fray in a ménage a trois. Her hairy legs entwined with his. She blew smoke rings to him which morphed into various erotic images.

Mainly boobs.

She pulled in closer and closer. The smell of the Hoff was overpowering his senses. He was ready to surrender, and then…

A twig snapped. He looked up to see a woman walking down the railway line towards him. She looked injured as she held a crutch or a broom under her arm.

Let no one out, except for Douglas. Only he shall pass.

His orders were clear enough, but what about this woman. She looked like no threat at all. "Hang on, love," Reggie called out. "You can't be out here, you're going to get shot, if you're lucky, if not, one of *them* will probably rip the purple rinse off ya."

The woman kept on walking towards him and the forest beyond. She had a coat pulled up tight to keep out the chill.

"Seriously, love. I've got orders to shoot anyone I see. Please, go back where you came from, and I promise I won't shoot you."

The woman hobbled to within six feet of him, her grey hair with a rhubarb top had small water droplets hanging from the curls, formed from the condensation of her breath.

"You're one of them, aren't you? Donald warned me about people like you." She swivelled the shotgun up to her midriff and let loose both barrels at Reggie.

He was struck in the chest and slumped to the floor. Brenda hit the floor with a clatter against the rusting railway sleepers. Sylvia walked over to his body, his chest rising and falling in time with a nineties techno beat.

"B...B...Brenda…" he rasped, trying to hold in parts of his body which had never seen such sights as the outside world before.

Sylvia reloaded, brought the gun up to his head, and pulled the trigger, disintegrating Reggie's skull into a thick soup of blood, fragments of bone, and brain croutons.

Sylvia reloaded and walked past his smoking corpse and into the forest. "Damn Poles. Donald was right, they get everywhere, they look just like us nowadays."

CHAPTER THIRTY-NINE

The cabin door swung closed and Sylvia leant against it to make sure it was shut. She'd walked for what seemed like forever. The forest was a never-ending maze of trunks and bushes. Just as the first hint of daylight broke out, she saw the log cabin.

She threw the bag onto the table and emptied its contents: a map, some food, the survival guide that the stranger had brought with him a few weeks back. She flicked through the pages and allowed herself a chuckle.

In the growing light, Sylvia took the chance to look around. It wasn't the biggest of places, but it felt…familiar. Not much remained of use in the kitchen, and the previous occupants must've used this as a temporary stop instead of a permanent base. A single camp bed rested against one wall; an unzipped sleeping bag lay on top.

Recollection jolted her. "I'm home, Donald. Sure it's not the little place we used to go to for our anniversaries, but it's good enough for little me, eh?"

She rested the shotgun against the bed and sat on a chair by the table. "So much, so soon, Donald. I don't know how I'm supposed to cope with it all," she muttered, rubbing the row of raised new skin on her arm.

"Hmm, I guess I could, Donald, but it all seems so very difficult right now. I'm tired. So tired, and…"

She looked down into her hands, covered in soot and mud. "…I miss you. I know you didn't mean to do those things to me. I know that I tried your patience and was so silly, no other man could put up with me, hmm?"

"No."

"Still, no one around now, no one to interrupt my journey." She pulled down her sleeves and flicked through her hair, getting it just right.

She stood up, pushed the chair under the table, and walked over to the bed. She kicked off her shoes, folded her socks into them and slid the set neatly under the bed. Sylvia then climbed into the sleeping bag and hugged her knees.

"I'll be your princess again. Where we'll be, everything will be okay. I'll be everything you wanted me to be."

She tucked the shotgun between her legs, and pulled the sleeping bag over.

"No more silliness, Donald."

"I promise."

She placed the barrels into her mouth; the metal clacked against her teeth.

Made sure the angle was just right.

Her thumb fumbled for the trigger.

Sylvia Clare Patterson found her peace.

MAY 14TH 2014

21:08

The doctor bolted out of the room, screaming for assistance. His cries disappeared as he ran down the corridors, frantically looking for anyone. Diane gritted her teeth, Francis clenched her hand. "It's okay baby. It's okay." He repeated the mantra over and over again.

"He…he's trying to get out…" Diane grunted through lockjaw. She let out another scream of pain.

Francis looked at Diane's belly. It rippled like a caterpillar trying to free itself from its chrysalis. Her skin puckered and rose as something within squirmed around. Diane let out another bellowing cry of agony.

"F…Fra…Francis…I lo…" Diane's head fell to one side, her tongue fell from her mouth and lolled like a cat's might under anaesthetic. A trickle of blood ran from one of her nostrils.

"No, baby, come on, stay with me," Francis pleaded. He held her face in his hand; it felt cold and clammy. Her pulse felt weak, as if he was feeling for it through a woollen jumper. From the corner of his eye, he saw something move.

The bump went from being a mound to a squat, squeezed tube of toothpaste. The thing inside was pulling itself from its natural cradle and up through its mother. Diane's body shuddered like a washing machine set to the spin cycle.

CHAPTER FORTY

"What's wrong with this picture?" Russ asked rhetorically. They stood in the car park of 'Daily Dairy', and it was littered with dismembered bodies, burnt-out vehicles, and the smell of overcooked meat. A thin tail of smoke rose through a sizeable hole in the roof of the building.

Nathan huffed and kicked a mouldering foot, which tumbled across the pock-marked concrete. "Not fair," he muttered, and sat down on the floor, sulking.

Francis ruffled his hair, which seemed to antagonise him further. "This is becoming a habit. Ah well. We'll just keep on going. Got to be somewhere we can stop before night-time. It'll be alright, Nate. It just means we'll be even closer when we wake up tomorrow, won't it?"

The words caused a smile to crack through his façade, and Nathan gave an eager thumbs up. Zena had already wheeled back through the ripped open gateway and was ambling down a dirt track towards panels of fields trimmed by monstrous hedgerow.

"You wanna talk about it?" Francis asked. He'd caught Zena up and the pair were causing a small dust cloud to form in their wake.

Zena grunted. "No, what's there to talk about? Tom's dead, and I'm left, and all that time I spent getting from Norway to here was a complete waste of fucking time, woo-fucking-hoo."

"That's one way of looking at it. The obvious way I guess." Francis chewed off a craggy fingernail and spat it into a tall stack of waving weeds. "As odd as it sounds, you got to say goodbye, you got to find out what happened to him. No 'if onlys'. Sure, the end result wasn't what you or any of us wanted, but you get closure."

"Again, I refer you to the woo-fucking-hoo," Zena scoffed.

Francis picked at the jagged ridge left on his fingernail. "We bumped into a fella a few weeks back. The one who put us on this little journey, as a matter of fact. He's going out now to look for his father, what, ten months after he went missing. You know why, don't you?"

"Illuminate me," Zena replied sarcastically.

"Because he needs to know what happened. Sure, in his heart, he knows that the father he had is dead, and is wandering around god knows where. He might be properly dead now, probably eating survivors like us, it doesn't matter to him, cos he has spent the past ten months having that doubt eating away inside him. I'm not saying for one minute that what happened to you was a good thing, but you got something that some people don't have anymore. Answers."

Zena looked from the dry dirt track across to Francis. "Well, I'm not completely sold, but some of what you say makes sense. Just…what do I do now? I spent so long holding onto the prospect of getting there, that I don't know what comes next."

Francis chattered on the little peaks left on the end of his finger. "Sister, who *does* anymore? We've got no home, got nothing but each other, all we can do is keep going and look out for each other. The rest? That'll figure itself out. No point in fretting about something you have no control over. We keep going or we become one of *them*, and I know which I prefer."

"Hey guys, is that a farm over there? Do ya reckon we could see if we can hole up, work out what we do next?" Russ shouted from behind them.

The smallholding, which lay beyond waist-high partially collapsed stone walls, was an eclectic mix of churned dried mud and wild, untamed greenery. The area was dominated by a large breezeblock barn, covered in rusting sheets of corrugated iron. A clapped-out tractor sat entrenched in a large puddle of mud, which had risen up the wheels, dried and looked like it had melded with the earth.

To the side of the barn ran a long narrow extension, half the height of the building. At the far end, a door banged listlessly against the exterior wall. Just behind the embedded farm machinery was a large patch of deep, lush vegetation. The top of something was visible in the waving grass bristles.

"What is that?" Francis wondered out loud, and walked off towards the object. Russ sat atop a small tractor wheel and rummaged around in his bag for something to eat which wasn't fish in origin. Like a cat at feeding time, Nathan watched him with eyes full of expectancy.

Francis' heavy legs waded through the dense undergrowth. Whatever he had seen still offered tantalising glimpses. It looked like it was a wooden board. Zena followed behind him, though failing to share the same level of intrigue as Francis.

He got to within six feet of the mysterious object when, almost on cue, the tall grass parted and revealed a mud-stained cupboard door. It looked like it had been pulled off a kitchen unit and someone had gone to town on the surface in a thick black permanent marker and atrocious handwriting;

Sharing one trait with felines, curiosity, Francis took another step towards the crude gravestone. His foot failed to connect with solid ground and instead he fell forwards through a flimsy and rubbish grassy net. As he fell he let out a yelp.

Then a dull, "OW!"

"Francis?" Zena shrieked. One minute the lumbering bearded man was there, the next he had been subsumed into the ground. Russ' and Nathan's gaze darted to the flurry of exclamations and the pair sprinted over to Zena, who was bent over looking into the straggly mass of grass, as if she had lost a fiver.

"Francis?" Zena squealed again, this time with an added level of franticness.

"I'm okay," came a muffled reply. "Be careful. There's an opening just before that wooden marker up there. Must be…aw man…gross."

Zena got onto her hands and knees and rooted round in the ground where Francis' voice was emanating from. She picked up a worm just as the words, "This is great," rumbled through the earth. Discarding the non-arthropod invertebrate behind her, she resumed her search. Her hands fell away in front of her, and she bid the others to stop where they were.

Tugging away at the grass, she began to reveal an opening in the ground around four foot wide and six foot long. The wooden graveboard sat on the far edge like a lonely brown tooth. Either side of the newly revealed chasm was a heavy metal lattice grate which ran the same distance.

"Are you okay down there, Francis?" Zena called out into the hole. She peered into the abyss and could just make out a pair of beady eyes looking back.

"Just dandy. It's an old slurry pit by the looks of it. I'm lucky it's not been used, as otherwise I'd have drowned in the poo. Hopefully the fumes would've killed me before that dubious joy, though," Francis hollered back. The others could hear dry-retching.

Francis looked up to daylight and the laughing heads of his travelling buddies. "It's dried up, which is something, though the smell is still on the ripe side."

"Are you sure you haven't added to that smell, Grandad. Looks like a long way down there?" Russ spat out through fits of giggles.

"Har-di-har-har, Russ, I think there should be a way out down here somewhere, a door at the end perhaps? Can you guys have a look around up there for a ladder or some rope, anything to get me out of this?" Francis shouted back. The smell of ancient manure and rotting vegetation clothed him in a stink wrap.

"Sure thing. Give us a minute, we'll have a look around. Keep fresh, Mister Stinky," Zena called back.

The three stood up from the lip of the shit pit. Zena barked, "Right, let's look around for something to put down there. Those things can be dangerous, so we need to get him out pronto. Have a look in that barn for something, okay?"

A gravelly voice from behind them rasped, "M'okay."

CHAPTER FORTY-ONE

The three above-ground dwellers turned slowly on their heels and looked upon five men who stood in a loose semi-circle around them. Each wore the front half of a human skull as a mask. Eyes circled with ochre made it look as though their ocular orbs were bathed in flame.

They all wore a waistcoat of packed together, brushed clean ribs, affixed with thick wire around a bleached breastbone. Three hefted human femurs, which they wafted menacingly like clubs, sanded down to an immaculate sheen, a handle woven around the thin end, fashioned from tendon and ligaments.

The other two held arm radius bones, which had been whittled into a vicious point at one end, and a handle at the other, wrapped in inch wide strips of flayed skin. The appointed leader took a step forward, jabbing the air in front of them with his makeshift shiv, "Dun't try nuffing or I'll stabs ya," he lisped.

Rough hands grabbed the group and dragged them away from the pit entrance and forced them to the ground. "Gwan and git their stuff yous lot," grunted the leader. Whilst two stood guard, the other pair pulled off the bags and weapons from the trio. Nathan was shaking like a shaved pig in winter.

Casting their belongings aside into a heap, the leader pointed at them. "Best gets them inside. I just hopes we got enough room fur 'em, specially little 'un. Likes the looks of 'im, I do," he drawled.

As the savages loomed over the stricken gang, a voice echoed out from the poop chute. "What's going on up there? You guys got anything yet?"

The leader gestured to the captives. They peeled off into two pairs, one grabbed Zena under the arms and started dragging her towards the door, which was still banging nonchalantly against the extension. Russ followed after, cursing and struggling, but to no avail. Nathan remained kneeling, eyes wide with terror. His brain told him to run, but his body was closed to submissions.

"Hey! Come on, you've had your fun, get me something to get out of h—"

A leering face, the top half of which was covered by a yellowing skull, glared down the canyon at Francis. "Ha, you stuck down vere silly man, I don't fink you'll be getting owt some'ow. Vere's fings down thar you dun't wunt to be coming across. Best being quiet, I's reckun."

The face grinned and then disappeared from view. Francis tried to find some gaps in the mortar, something to use as a handhold. Scrabbling around, he managed to prise fingernails into the minutest of gaps and start to climb up the sheer wall, to freedom.

From above, there came the sound of grinding metal, like a devilish robot eating household appliances. Francis had only made it a few feet off the floor; his own height and a half again of sheer breezeblock lay ahead.

A shadow waved above him. Looking up, he saw the face smiling back down at him, broken up into tiny squares. "No, don't you dare," Francis said through gritted teeth.

The leader let out a pleasured yelp and let the slurry pit cover use the full benefits of gravity and slam down into place. A kick and a squeaking of metal dropped the heavy lid into its housing.

"I 'ope that didn't wake up the uvvers. Vey is worse than us." With that, the skull-covered face vanished.

Francis could hear a smacking sound, followed by a kid sobbing. "I'm gonna get you, pilgrim," he bellowed. He scrambled for another divot above him, but in his urgency he missed and plunged back onto the dried faecal matter.

He lay on his back, panting and heaving with exertion. Through the sound of his heart thudding in his temple and the rage buzzing around his nervous system like a trainful of pissed off bees, he heard a creaking sound behind him in the gloom…

CHAPTER FORTY-TWO

The lantern swinging from the rafters cast a pale glow over the desolate interior of the barn. A loud clunk signalled the padlock snapping shut. The savage tugged on the chain to make sure it was secure. "Vat shuld holds ya," he sneered at Nathan, before strolling down back where they had come in, running the bone knife hilt against the row of metal cages.

"Hey kid, it'll be fine," Zena called over to the kid, who was snivelling in the cage directly opposite her.

"Ha, you reckon? This lot go for the little ones first. Say they're a rare treat," a man tucked in the recess of his cage cooed. "Ha ha, no way, it's *you* lot. Well, isn't this a turn up for the books?"

The cage forced anyone over four feet tall to scuttle around its straw-covered interior like some kind of bug. The man bum-slid over to the front of his cage. "It's you, the eater of old men," Russ said, as if he'd just sat in vomit-flavoured chewing gum.

The train station cannibal shot them a tooth-filled smile. "Much obliged to you for leaving him outside. Had to fight off a couple of feisty squirrels, but I managed to finish him off. Though he did repeat on me for a few days." He thumped his chest with a balled fist as the memory made his stomach turn.

"Nasty."

Nathan held onto the bars with chipolata fingers. He flicked his head around, taking in the musty barn; the smell of the previous porcine inhabitants scratched against the back of his throat. The roof was a black sky. Lines of brown rust ran up and down its flanks, with equidistantly spaced out lanterns throwing out light like orange dwarf stars on a pendulum.

As far as he could see, cages ran to either side of him. Some were empty, doors ajar like a sleeping yokel, others contained hunchbacked denizens of despair. Some rocked like a weeble in a perpetual motion study, others stared blankly from corners which they never ventured from. Worn faces, creased like fish-and-chip paper, open mouths with rows of soot speckled teeth and diseased meat for tongues.

In one cage, five down from Zena, he could see one of the captives had turned. Muck-covered digits probed a festering wound in his neighbour's back as he sat there. Like a malnutritioned kid being pestered by flies in a commercial for food aid, the man sat there nonplussed. Arms which were no more than folded bones hugged his pointed mountain knees to his barely moving chest.

"I'm scared, Russ," Nathan whimpered, trying to peel his eyes off the myriad of degenerate sights on offer, but finding that for every desecration he skipped, he settled on another, as twisted and obscene as the last.

Russ was in the cage next to him. Since their incarceration, he had spent the time testing the security features of his new living space. The bars, though they looked like they could barely contain an irate duck, were unyielding and tough. Several stern kicks to the padlock failed to provide freedom, and the weathered chain brushed off the assault with ease.

"Don't worry, kid. We just gotta find a way outta here. Keep a look out, okay? Let me know if any of those bone bastards come back, ya hear me?" Russ barked, before scrabbling in the filth laden straw beneath him, looking like a cornered rabbit.

He scooted from one patch to the next, certain that in the next plot there would be a weakness, a chink in the armour he could expose and extricate them all from.

The train station cannibal piped up, "Go ahead, man. Try, like none of us have done that, eh? Might as well just accept it and make peace with it. One good thing is that the food here is top notch. Just you wait, they wanna keep you big and strong."

"Russ, someone's coming," Nathan hissed, eyes widened with terror and trepidation as the sounds of heavy boots clip-clopped down the concrete floor.

"Oh, goody goody, I hope it's feeding time," the cannibal simpered, "...though it could be...nah, they only got fresh ones yesterday, even they can't have gone through that lot already." He chuckled nervously.

Russ scattered the pile of straw over the floor, wiping his hands on his jeans after, as if on autopilot.

"Looks at that one. He's a bit too fresh. Best makes sure that Dick takes care of him, never likes them biters me," rasped the voice that had accosted them outside. The footsteps began again, coming to a stop by the new arrivals.

The skull-covered face bent down and peered into Nathan's cage. Nathan staggered backward until he hit metal covered wall. "Free little piggies went to market, one wuz a runt wiv a stupid face," he looked down on Russ who was sitting calmly in the middle of his pen. "Ve ova was a hat-wearing city boy wiv a body ma would like to get 'er ands on."

The man grabbed the top of the cage and started to dry hump it, eliciting the appropriate grunts and warblings. After a minute, he stopped, unfulfilled, and turned to Zena. "But vis little piggy...well, papa said that gurls were sugar an spice an all fings nice. We don't get many do we, 'Url?"

One of the other bone-adorned savages grunted in the negative and started to pick off a piece of flesh he had missed from his knife.

"Nah, we don't. Still, it's the festival of the night, so we've got a liddle feast to prepare." The lisping savage stood up and re-joined his inbred brethren. From a leather loop on his belt, he untied a large ring of keys, all different sizes and, much to an OCD sufferers chagrin, not all around the same way.

He plunged a finger into his nostril and began to nose-mine, seemingly lost in his current 'To-Do' list. After failing to extract anything of note, he wiped his digit against his leg and fingered through the keys. He settled on a small silver one, before turning to address the rows of captives. "Url, Vints, get 'im and 'im, vey will do nicely."

CHAPTER FORTY-THREE

As a kid, Francis' favourite film was *Jason and the Argonauts*. In particular, it was the effects that dug their talons into him and won a place in his infant heart. Whilst he gazed in awe at the mighty form of Talos, it was the skeletons raised from the teeth of Medusa that dropped his jaw.

The sound that rang through his ears reminded him of Harryhausen's creations. He rummaged through his rucksack and dug out the torch. Clicking the power on, he swept the beam across the dried slurry pit.

The floor was a mottled brown colour. Contained within its mortar was straw, ragged flaps of polythene, pieces of broken masonry and many solidified liquids that he hoped to never find out about. The ground itself was like a beach; mainly flat but with dips and mounds. The light gutted out above the craters and cast long shadows in the distance against the rises.

The cracking sound rumbled through his feet, like a fracking drill on low speed. It unsettled him and caused his cheeks to wobble. The light shone onto a patch of dried filth about twenty feet away from him. The top layer split and formed into a feculent crevasse. Francis swallowed, spit with traces of ammonia slid into his gut, causing a surge in acid production.

From the fissure, a rigor-mortised hand rose. Fingers, bent and stiff like an arthritic claw, pawed the air. Francis rooted through the bag once more and found the metal hatchet he had picked up from the freakshow of death. Pushing the bag behind him, he shone the light over the limited horizon. The hand had ceased moving, as though it had done all it had meant to accomplish and was waiting to be withdrawn back to its display case, under the hardened animal waste and assorted farm debris.

"Ha," Francis guffawed.

The ground resumed its vibrations. The beam of light searched again. He spotted another rift forming to the left of the rather creepy human pincer. This time, a full blown human head, complete with rictus grin, rose from the underground.

It seemed to convince the talon that now was the time to finish what it had started, as the arm it was attached to appeared from its tomb and started to excavate the ground around it.

Not content with the other two having something to eat, for the first time since their lifeless bodies were thrown into the liquid slurry pit, Shrill, or *Cheryl* as she was known to her brothers, sisters and extended family, decided to exercise her woman's prerogative, and break free of her putrid shallow grave.

Aside from *Jason and the Argonauts*, Francis had also watched a fair few horror films in his time, and spent a lot of that time shouting at the television to either 'get the hell out of there' or 'finish them, off you idiot'.

Not wanting to add himself to a weird edition of the Darwin Awards, Francis gripped the hatchet and stormed across to Shrill. She had managed to free both of her arms and torso and was testing out her mouth by chattering at the thing which looked very much like food in her zombified brain.

Having been well versed in splitting logs for his grandparents' fireplace, he brought the axe down with a dull thud directly on Shrill's crown. Her skull burst open like the foulest-smelling, rotten meat-filled piñata in all of creation. Teeth stopped clacking together and her body fell back into the cold embrace of pig shit.

Jed, or 'The Claw', had managed to scrape away the hardened gunk from half of his body. A wan light filtered into eyes that had not seen daylight for seven months. The last thing his memory had stored was a pair of headlights hurtling towards him, headlights belonging to an out of control car.

If it had any ability to recall this memory and enjoy the simple things of human existence, such as emotion, Jed may well have remarked on the similarity of seeing another light shining into his eyes before meeting his maker.

Again. This time for keeps.

Francis smashed the axe down again, for good measure. With the amount of crap on top of the half-submerged shit-zombie, he wanted to make sure it was dead-dead. The axe head came out slick with black gore and thick strands of brainghetti.

Mick, though, well he was referred to by his nine brothers and sisters as 'one tough sunnovabitch'. With Francis busy administering a non-denomination approved series of brutal last rites, Mick had managed to rise from the crap fabricated barrow and, after shaking free a number of burrowing insects, turned to face the fratricide instigator.

Francis ducked beneath the lunging arms of the last shit zombie. As it stumbled on the follow-through, sheets and flakes of dubious origin fell off Mick. As his death shroud disintegrated, Francis could make out a large wound through his assailant's stomach. It reminded him of a cored Goldie Hawn from *Death Becomes Her*.

Strands of decaying flesh swung within the tatty crater. Mick turned with all the speed of a mobility scooter and lurched towards Francis once more. A hasty swipe shaved off the top of a shoulder, slicing it as if he were an eccentric butcher.

Like a zombie matador, Francis *Olé*'d the zombie and Mick ambled towards the patch of ground where Francis had made his rather unceremonious entrance.

Seeing his chance, he slammed the axe into the back of Mick's skull, and Mick sank to the floor like a mannequin on a hot tin roof. The shit zombie plunged face down, the axe still embedded deep within its manky head.

Francis tried to heave the weapon out, but it was stuck fast. Seeing it was still moving, he stamped on the axe head, which bit further into the soft liquefying brain mulch. Mick quivered like a cold Elvis impersonator and was returned to sender.

Thinking to himself about the ease in which he had dealt with these poor wretches, Francis turned his attention to removing the axe from the properly dead zombie's head. Despite a boot on the back of its skull, and his best Excalibur removing techniques, the axe held fast.

He punted the handle side on and heard a promising crack of bone. A few more meaty kicks later and he felt the shit zombie's hold on his weapon relent.

"You are one tough son of a bitch," Francis muttered as he knelt down to retrieve the axe. As he waggled it out of the cranium, his nose twitched in disgust. Before he could put two and two together, the hatchet was liberated, along with a pocket of bog gas which had been fermenting within Mick since his internment in the slurry pit.

The fog engulfed Francis and stole the air from his lungs. He reeled from the stench. Gasping for breath, he staggered backwards, and as he moved clear of the noxious fumes, his body shut down, starved of oxygen.

MAY 14TH 2014

21:27

Francis peered through the window into the surgery. A bevy of doctors and nurses, all dressed in blue, worked frantically around Diane's body. From his vantage point, he could just make out a monitor showing her vital signs.

Her heart rate formed shallow mountains and valleys, a topographical terrain which would have been easily traversed if made real. Francis slumped against the glass. A screech made him stare into the room. it had gone from orderly mania to unbridled hysteria.

The surgeon who had been leaning over Diane tried to pull back from the operating table, but something was holding him. He was trying to hit whatever was grabbing him. Ignoring medical protocol, Francis pushed open the door and walked into the room. It was like he had made the transition from reality into a fucked-up corner of existence, where only nightmares and the bogeyman lived.

A male nurse barged past him and through the door. He had sprays of blood down his blue smock. Francis floated up to the table, where Diane lay. He looked down into the space where, up until an hour ago, the prospect of a new life and fresh meaning in their lives had been growing.

Now he saw something which seemed the antithesis of birth. From an incision that had been made, a green-blue baby was poking out, his little infant digits were red gloves flecked with black lumps of congealed blood and tissue. They were holding onto the surgeon's gown. Tiny eyes, with a black imperfection at their core, looked up at the terrified man, still clutching the scalpel like a biro.

The infant was chewing on thin air. His gums were lined with blood, the previous owner a mystery. Amongst the screaming came a high pitched squeal. Francis looked up to the heart rate monitor and saw the gentle undulating line crash into a straight red line. Numbers at the side flashed zero, expecting urgent corrective action.

"Help them, for God's sake! Help them," Francis shouted, trying to shake the surgeon out of his inactivity. The scalpel freefell to the floor and landed with a metallic clatter. The man, eyes wide with terror, pulled off his mask and ran out of the room, smacking his shoulder into the doorframe as he went.

CHAPTER FORTY-FOUR

"But, you can't take me, I'm just like you," the train station cannibal protested as he was dragged unceremoniously from his pen. With a boot on his back, one of the bone savages clasped his hands together and cable-tied them. The plastic teeth rasped, followed by a yelp as it bit into his wrists.

Another padlock was unfastened and cast to the floor with the chain. "Git," the leader commanded. Russ removed his cap and shoved it through the bars to Nathan. With a nod of understanding, he shuffled out into the dank corridor that ran between the rows of cages.

"Ain't cha a good little lamb," the leader said, gesturing to his two accomplices. As they approached, preoccupied with fishing out another cable-tie from a pocket, Russ head-butted the closest one. The half skull covering his face absorbed some of the impact, but split down the middle, leaving the cracked plate hanging off by the string it was held on by.

The assaulted savage clutched his face with his hands, forgetting he was holding the knife, which in turn slashed his cheek. A jet of blood splattered his inbred brother in the face. Russ turned to the one who had just been sprayed and punched him in the gut, just below his bone bodice. He bent over double, the air stolen from his lungs by the blow.

Before Russ could press home the early advantage, a flash of movement out of the corner of his eye manifested itself in a lick of pain in his temple. He turned to see the leader wielding nunchuks made from a pair of clavicles, joined together with tightly wound ligaments and tendon.

Screaming with primal rage, Russ charged the boss, who sidestepped him easily and clubbed him on the head on the follow-through. Russ sank to the floor with an, "Oooofff," and after a scraping of cheekbone on the concrete, his resistance ended.

"Tie 'im up you useless fugwits," the leader ordered. The gut-punched savage hobbled over to Russ and restrained him, adding in a friendly punch to the kidneys for good measure.

"Vese two will do nicely. Ma and Pa would be pleased," the leader commented. "You two, let's go." 'Url and Vints grabbed hold of the men by the scruff of their collars and dragged them down the straw-covered runway to the rear of the barn. The sound of metal scraping against metal set everyone on edge; a brief pause brought relief, until the process was repeated in reverse.

"I'm scared, Zena. What are they going to do with Russ?" Nathan asked, his eyes heavy with impending tears.

Zena slumped against the side of her cage. "No idea, Nathan. I don't think we want to know. Cover your ears, okay?"

"Leave 'im vere." The leader pointed at Russ, who was released and did the worst caterpillar ever against the floor. He rolled to one side and took in the new room.

It looked like it used to be a large chicken coop, though from the looks of it, hadn't been used for that purpose in twenty odd years. The roof was lower, covered in the same rusting wavy sheets of iron that covered the containment area they were in previously.

Arranged side by side were four weather-worn troughs. Tracks of drying dark liquid ran from the lip down the concave body to the floor. Russ flung his head around. Part of him wanted to see what else was there, another part wanted to squash his eyes shut and yearn for a return to happier times.

A standing lamp was glaring down onto a large grooved metal table. From underneath, it looked like a shallow paddling pool, dipping in the middle with a three inch wide lip running around the top edge. This was where the cannibal had been dropped, face down. His wide open eyes met Russ as he mouthed one word: "Help."

One of the savages, the one with the split skull mask, kept watch over Russ. He looked a little crestfallen with the removal of part of his outfit. The other two were busying themselves around the cannibal. The leader passed a length of rope to the other, which had loops at either end, like a figure of eight.

The savage took this and headed off toward the end of the table. "Vere you go, Juhn," he slobbered. The leader tucked his bone nunchuks into his belt and headed off to a winch, which was positioned down the other end by Rope Man.

The leader, Juhn, pushed the winch closer, locked the feet, and pulled down a length of cable which ended in a hook. He fiddled with something unseen, and then nodded to his brother. He stood back, staring over at Russ and smiling as if he was on the verge of sharing some hilarious secret. "'Url, fire it up," he grunted, all the while looking at Russ.

A whine of spooling machinery rang out. The cable grew taut and the cannibal flinched and was pulled down from view. As the winch effortlessly worked, the hook appeared in sight again, connected to the looped rope which was firmly affixed to the cannibal's ankles.

Like the other shark from Jaws—the one mistaken as the killer—he was pulled into the air, where he dangled like a punching bag. When he was a few feet off the metal table, 'Url killed the winch and the whining and ascension stopped.

Juhn gave Russ a gummy smile. Running his bloated tongue over the remainder of his teeth for effect, he slid out his bone knife from its skin scabbard.

"No, no man! Don't! I'm like you guys! I eat people! Not him, and the others he came in with! They're all straighters, they aren't like us! They don't get i—" the cannibal begged.

"Shhhhh liddle piggie, it's okay. You're not like my bruvvers and me. You're a townie. Always taking the mick out of us when we go to the pub. Sayin' 'ow vick we urr and 'ow our ma and pa are bruvver and sithter." Juhn slapped the cannibal's face gently, leaving bits of shit covered straw stuck to his cheek.

Juhn laughed. "Well, fink Ma and Pa might be, but vat doesn't matter. We don't need anyfing from you outsiders." He turned his back to Russ and ran the knife across the cannibal's forehead, leaving red furrows.

"Please, pl—"

His words were replaced with strangled gasps and thrashing as Juhn grabbed hold of the cannibal's head with one hand, pulled it back, and drew the knife across the middle of the throat. Blood bubbles formed along the remarkably clean incision, and a cascade of gore washed over the cannibal's shocked face and pitter-pattered against the metal table beneath.

The trickle turned into a torrent. The throat opened up like a Pez dispenser and the cannibal's protestations turned into a gentle warbling. Juhn swung the hanging body round and cut the cable-ties. The arms fell and tickled the surface of the blood pond beneath him.

Open eyes covered in sticky red liquid gawped at Russ, who felt every fibre of his being clench.

Nathan was in the corner of his cage. Arms pulled his legs up so close to his body that not even a Higgs Boson particle could exist between. A prod on his arm brought him back to the room. "Hey kid." Nate turned slowly. As he looked into the man's face he screamed and shot across to the other side of his enclosure.

"Stay away from me, stay away from me!" he shouted.

Grotty fingers ran around a series of scars surrounding his eye socket. "Ha, sorry kid. Sometimes I forget I have this. Mirrors aren't too popular these days, eh?" he offered. "Where are my manners? Anton. I'm Anton, pleased to meet you."

CHAPTER FORTY-FIVE

Francis came to. The smell of sulphur and rancid shit lingered, but only as an after-taste. He rubbed his head and hauled himself to his feet. The murk had a green tinge to it, but Francis knew he had to get out of there. Like *now*. Who knew what other creatures of the deep had been cast into this pit and were waiting to get out, like extras from the *Thriller* video.

Patting the ground around him, he came upon his torch. Checking it still worked, he scanned the recesses of the pit again, looking for a point of egress. "Quickest way is up," he surmised, and ran the beam of light up the breezeblocks he had attempted to climb first time round.

It looked like the people that had built it were no master craftsmen; chunks of mortar had already been pulled out through his first climbing attempt. Using the axe, Francis began to chip away at the surface and form some proper foot- and hand-holds. The grate looked down at him with a forlorn appearance, as if reluctant to lose the one inhabitant that could conjugate verbs.

After several attempts, many of which ended with him being dumped back into the dried slurry with a solid thump, Francis had managed to get to within touching distance of the pit lid. Digging his feet into the loose mortar as deep as he could, one hand held onto a breezeblock while the other pushed the axe up against the lid.

With Herculean effort he managed to displace the grate from its slot and slide it to one side. Using the axe as if he were climbing a glacier, he hooked the head over the edge and hauled himself free from the den of poo, and out into the coolness of a spring evening. The farm smell was still not the most pleasant, but as he panted on the ground, looking up at the tiny pinpricks of light forming in the sky, he allowed himself a small chuckle.

Francis crept along the side of the barn extension. The flapping door was still rocking back and forth at the end. He took off his bag, tied up the end, and set it against the doorframe. He pulled his sleeves up, exposing wiry ginger arm hair, which bristled in the evening air. Cradling the axe loosely in one hand he ducked into the building.

The extension was nothing more than a long corridor. Along the walls hung farm tools in various states of disrepair. Old chest of drawers, clinging onto life with rotten doweling pins and corroded screws, looked back with busted open drawers. They were filled with filth-covered extension cords, cables and wires which their owners didn't have the heart to throw out, 'just in case'.

At the end of the corridor there was an old-school gas lamp, its feeble light flickering and gutting over some*thing* hanging on the wall. To the side of this, at the end of the clapped out furniture, was a closed door.

Stepping over mouse droppings and discarded shoes, Francis inched his way to the door. The far wall came into view.

A man in the mid stages of decomposition was crucified to the wall with metal marquee stakes, bent over at the end to stop his putrefying body slipping off and bursting like a water balloon on the floor.

He had been stripped to his underpants. Another stake had been hammered through his skull to prevent reanimation. His body was a patchwork of nicks and slashes, though it was a lucky omen to mark it as you passed. Above his corpse hung an old flaking sign;

Beneath that, someone had added the following tagline in blood:

PUTTING THE 'BATTER' BACK INTO BATTERY FARMING

Francis held the axe tighter and pushed the door open with the business end. Peering into the innards, he saw rows and rows of cages.

CHAPTER FORTY-SIX

A plughole in the middle of the table carried away the drained blood. 'Url carried a milk urn, which had collected the fluid, to the side of the room where a number of other receptacles waited.

Juhn pulled a trolley along the floor carrying the tools of his macabre trade. First off he used a meat cleaver to finish hacking through the exsanguination hole in the throat and pulled the head clear of the body.

The three brothers worked like a choreographed dance troupe. No sooner had the head been removed than Vints had picked it up by the hair and took it across to a corner of the barn where a sheet hung down from the rafters. As it was pulled to one side, Russ saw row upon row of sallow grey heads. With little ceremony, Vints stuck the cannibal's head on a spike and twisted it so it was held firmly in place.

Festering zombie heads welcomed it to the neighbourhood with gnashing of teeth and clicks of dislocated jawbone. Vints smoothed down the cannibal's sticky hair just as it budded into unlife. Eyes rolled down and looked around at its new home. Seeing the human in front of him, he joined in on the chomping chorus. It sounded like the testing facility at a castanet factory.

Juhn had moved on to a handsaw, and was hacking through the arms and legs like a possessed woodsman. Ochre mixed with sweat ran down his face, giving him orange streaks. As each appendage became separated from the body, 'Url snatched them up, worked a hook through the palm of the hand or meat of the foot, and set it to one side. He caught Russ staring at him. "Fur the smokeowse," he grunted, and a trickle of drool ran down his chin at the thought of oak-smoked thigh.

Discarding the saw, with tidbits of meat stuck to its teeth, Juhn picked up the bone knife and sliced down the remainder of the ragged throat to the top of the sternum. Digging his fingers in, he peeled the skin aside and, using a claw hammer, dug out the Manubrium, the chunk of bone which sat at the top. Having removed this, he tore the skin some more and threaded some fishing wire under and around the sternum.

Tying a knot, he ran off a length and tied the free end to the hammer's head. "I loves vis bit," he drooled. Juhn rested the hammer on the torso, and moved to the end of the dissection table. His brothers stood either side and held the slab of meat down. Grabbing hold of the hammer and bracing his feet against the table legs, which were embedded within the floor, he pulled back.

Much like filleting a fish, the skin relented and the sternum was pulled free. Each rib popped as it was disconnected from the central column of bone. As Juhn picked the chunk free from the wire, the two brothers each grabbed a flap of skin and yanked their sides open.

Deft fingers picked the ribs out and put them to one side, no doubt to create some new line in the human bone clothing range.

Juhn put the hammer back on the trolley and picked up two buckets. The three of them then fished around inside the limbless body and allocated organs to each bucket. One was marked 'GUUD' the other 'BAAD'.

As utterly repellent as it was, Russ had to admire the efficiency and rhythm that they had shown; a real demonstration of teamwork over individuality. It was only when the buckets were carried off to the milk urns, the stripped carcass flung into a trough, and pairs of eager eyes turned on him, that Russ realised that he was next.

"Balls."

CHAPTER FORTY-SEVEN

"How long have you been here, Anton?" Zena asked, fingers pinching the cage mesh.

Anton shuffled. "Sorry, dead leg. You'd think you'd get used to them. A few weeks, I guess. I've just been wandering around after the last place I was at. Living day to day. Saw the farm and thought there'd be some food inside. Little did I know that the food was, well, *this* lot…" He gestured to the other cages.

Zena shuddered. "But how have you stayed alive so long?"

"They give us these scraps of meat. You don't want to know what it is, and this homemade bread. But if you've got an image of a nice white bloomer in your head, you're mistaken. It has the consistency of trifle and tastes like feet." The thought of it made Anton heave. "Man, the first time…anyway, every few days or so, they come in to get another one of us, take them out back, and you never see them again, well, not anything of them you'd recognise."

"You mean?"

"Yes, they're a friendly bunch of inbred cannibals. I'm sorry to sound like a bastard. But your friend? He's going to die. If he isn't already. Sorry." Anton shrugged.

"Hey, Zena, is this party invite-only?"

The man's voice startled them all. Standing in the walkway was a man with mad auburn hair and matching beard which threatened to engulf his entire face. He was clutching a metal hatchet.

"Francis!" Nathan exclaimed excitedly. "I knew you'd come back for us."

Francis nodded and walked toward him. His face was a river of anger and relief. He did a mental count. "Where's Russ?"

Zena pointed to the doors at the end of the jail-block. "They took him. They're gonna…" Her fragile voice broke off and was replaced by the subjugation of crying.

"Okay, okay. I'll get him. How many are there?"

Nathan stuck up three fingers. "Though there were five in total outside."

"Fine, I'll deal with them. You guys need to get out of here, though. We just need…" A lightbulb moment lit up Francis' face. "Hey, Nate, you got those paperclips still?" The kid looked at him as if he had just asked him his name in Japanese.

Francis sighed. "The metal faces? You still got them?"

Nathan's expression changed from general bemusement to acknowledgement, and he thrust his hand into his trouser pocket and after, picking out balls of fluff, he passed the paper clips through the bars to Francis.

With dextrous fingers, Francis bent the metal to an approximation of the lock. After a few moments jiggling it around within the chamber, the clasp opened up, Nathan let out a muted cheer. "I wasn't always a security guard, you know."

He passed the bent stick of metal to Zena. "Get those who can still move free. I'm gonna go get Russ and we can get the hell out of here."

Zena nodded furiously and started to pick the lock. Francis bent down by Nathan. "Whatever happens, kid, you make sure you stay safe. If something don't look good, get out of there, okay? Your mum would be proud of how brave you are. You're a good kid." He finished by ruffling Nate's hair before standing up and walking towards the closed sliding door.

Nathan stood up and called out. "You are coming back, aren't you?"

Francis sagged, turned and said, "Everyone comes back these days, kid," before storming off towards the end of the barn.

Francis peered through a crack in the frame and saw Russ lying trussed up on a metal table. His feet were tied together by rope, which in turn led to a winch. He could hear Russ speaking, cursing at the three men surrounding him. One stood by the winch, pulling the cable taut. He was the man who had trapped him in the pit. Another was cleaning items on a tray, while the third stood with his back to him, patting Russ on the head.

Grabbing hold of a pitchfork which he found standing up against the wall, he formulated a plan. Checking that the door was off the latch, he rested a foot against it. From inside the room beyond, he heard the sound of a winch grinding and frenzied shouting. With a mighty push, Francis pushed the door open and charged into the room.

The pitchfork met 'Url square in the guts as he turned to the sound of squeaking metal. Francis twisted the implement like a door handle and, with one foot resting on the bone armour, yanked the weapon free.

'Url screamed in agony as his stomach and intestinal tract were ripped out. They slopped to the floor in a steaming pile. Francis swung the pole around and caught him on the side of the face, sending him to the ground. A rope of intestine linked the offal pile to its owner, who was now convulsing on the floor.

The winch continued to whirr and Russ' body, up to his waist, was now dangling in the air. Vints was caught in two minds between manning the winch and stabbing to death the intruder who had eviscerated his kin. The indecision allowed Francis time to close the distance. With his broken skull discarded, Vints looked like he had applied fake tan to his cheeks.

Whirring ceased as the winch hauled Russ up to full height. Vints growled and fumbled for his weapon. Francis swung the axe down and it carved off the side of the savage's face, from the corner of his eye diagonally down through the middle of his mouth and through the jawbone.

Frantic hands tried to hold his face together, but to no avail. Holding one bit meant that another segment was neglected. Whilst trying to hold his jaw together, and stop teeth from falling out, his eyeball bulged through the wound and swung across his face, hitting his nose and coming to a rest.

As he instinctively went to catch his eye, he let go of his jaw, which swung downwards and broke off, landing on the floor with a dull thud. Francis lashed out and caught the eye in his free hand. Squashing it in his palm elicited animalistic howling.

Like a ripcord, Francis tore it free and cast it aside. Vints collapsed to the floor. Blood seeping from his disfigurement, he lapsed into unconsciousness.

"Uh uh uh."

Francis turned to see Juhn grabbing Russ' head by his greasy hair, exposing his throbbing jugular, against which was held a blood-flecked bone knife. "Easy pal. You put that down, and I guarantee you can walk away from this," Francis said calmly, holding his arms out as a symbol of acceptance.

"New as suun as I seen you, that you wood be trubble. You slain ma kin, vink it only fair I call you on that," Juhn grunted, a smile bloomed on his face.

"NOOOOO."

As Francis dived over the table, Juhn ran the edge of the knife across Russ' throat. Like a bag being unzipped, it opened up, spraying blood in a wide arc. Francis tackled Juhn to the ground and, in a cloud of fury repressed from the events of so long ago, he pummelled his fists into the savage's face.

The skull mask chipped and fractured; the ochre-lined eyes burst with blood vessels and turned purple. All the while, amongst the sound of skull smacking against concrete and fists striking skull, was the sound of cackling.

Francis looked down on the misshapen face he had formed with his anger. From behind, he heard a gasping gurgling sound. He leapt up and put an arm under Russ' hanging head. "HELP ME, SOMEONE, HELP ME!" he bellowed.

"Stay with me, slim." Francis looked into Russ' fading eyes. Tributaries of blood had run down his face like melted wax. Russ moved his lips. "I can't hear you, slim," Francis said.

Russ closed his eyes and huffed. He rolled his eyelids open and through wet gurgling he mustered, "I'm going home." Upon utterance of his words, he fell slack in Francis' arms.

"Behind you," came a call from within the barn.

The warning came too late. Francis felt something slide into his back, pushing ribs aside and cracking one as an icicle of pain burrowed into his body. He released Russ, who swung gently, liquid still pumping out of him, tip-tapping against the metal like a leaky pipe. Francis looked down to see a section of sharpened bone sticking out through his skin and clothing. Then it was gone, along with the pain, only to appear again a moment later. He saw the spear of bone jutting from his chest, a cackling the soundtrack to his assault. Francis clutched his front and fell to the floor. A boot rolled him over onto his back. He could feel his top growing wet. He felt cold, his legs felt numb, he looked up and saw the bruised visage of Juhn looming over him. "Aww, looky here. Looks like you're bleedin' out bad, Mister."

The knife was waved in front of his eyes, seeking out the next place to desecrate. Having decided, it was pulled back from view, and Francis braced for impact. He didn't care anymore.

Instead of the expected stabbing sensation, he heard a solitary crack which ended the maniacal laughter at once. Juhn fell on top of Francis, a claw hammer embedded in the crown of his skull. He felt the deadweight being dragged off him and then a child's face appeared in his vision. "I got him, Francis, just like the *Red Mask from Mars.*"

Francis softly wrapped his arms around Nathan and pulled him to his chest. "Great kid. Don't get too cocky now, you hear? Remember... stay...safe..."

MAY 14TH 2014

21:32

The room was deserted, save for Diane's body, and the baby which was pulling itself free of the cavity in her torso. It plopped onto the side of the table with a wet slurp. The umbilical cord tethered the infant to its mother. On unsteady podgy arms, it started pulling itself towards Francis.

"George…my son," he gasped. The boy crawled through a puddle of slime and blood towards him. As the child lay a bloodsoaked hand on top of his, Francis recoiled. Then another hand, one he was intimately familiar with, was slapped on top.

"Diane?" Francis asked dumbfounded. The woman he had spent the past eight years with sat up slowly. As her torso stretched, a number of organs took the opportunity to escape and slopped out through the incision.

A low moan rumbled out of her diaphragm, causing Francis to stumble backwards. Dead eyes looked at him. Mother and child reached out for him, eager to grab hold and resume the unholy communion.

"No…please…this is just a dream, please," Francis begged out loud. He bumped into an oxygen tank as he backpedalled from the couple. He looked down and knew what he had to do. He picked the tank up and held it above his head.

"All I wanted was for us to be a proper little family. We'd spent so long planning for this moment, but this…this is not what was supposed to happen." A tear ran from the corner of his eye and soaked into his moustache.

"I love you both," he said softly, before he brought the tank down again and again, until no more murderous hands reached for him.

CHAPTER FORTY-EIGHT

"Where are the others?" Zena asked. Anton ran a finger across his throat and shook the blood from the end of the axe. She nodded and looked back to Francis, who was lying down on a pile of hay bales. His face was white. Around his body, lengths of bloodsoaked rags were wrapped, ripped from the bodies of those who no longer needed them.

His eyes flickered and opened slowly. He looked as if he thought he was somewhere else. "Where's Diane? And George? I thought they were right…right here, with me…" he mumbled. Zena held his hand and stroked his hair.

"Francis?" Nathan asked.

"Hey kid…how did…no matter. I ain't got long, can feel it, gonna be a time real soon where I won't be there to look after you. I done my best to get you this far…I…" Francis' voice rose and fell as waves of pain wracked his failing body.

Nathan squeezed Francis' hand so tightly that the skin turned white and yellow where they met. A tear bulged in the corner of his eye and trickled down his face. "Please don't go, Francis. I don't want to be on my own," he begged softly.

Francis closed his eyes to ride out the latest pulse of agony. When they opened again, he seemed relaxed, calm. "You won't be, kid. I ain't much for believing in God, but I know that as long as…as long as you remember someone, they're always alive." He tapped Nathan's chest. "In here. Your journey goes on, kid. I gotta stop here and get off, but these folks here will look after you now, won't you?"

Zena nodded gently and continued to stroke his hair reverently. Anton stood over him. "You bet we will. You guys saved me, I'll look after him. You have my word on that."

"Hmm, good. You better, pilgrim, or Zena here will end you." He let out a chuckle. "Keep going to Rhayader. There's a man there called Jim. Tell him that…that we saw his brother in the factory. You should be safe there. You should all be safe there. Another thing, when I go, one of you will have to make sure I don't come back. It won't be easy or pleasant, but I don't want to come back as one of *them*, promise?"

Zena nodded. "Of course Francis."

"Good." Francis looked into Nathan's eyes. "I've seen things people wouldn't believe, entire cities on fire, burned to the ground, turned to ash and dust. I've witnessed my family die and come back, and had to…kill them. I'm glad I found you, kid. You saved me from myself that day, and I will always be grateful for that. You gave me peace. Don't mourn me when I'm gone. Get to safety, stay safe, get through this, cos it will end, but most of all…"

Nathan leant in closer. "What was that, Francis?"

Francis coughed, his eyes rolled back. "…live."

Crudely-formed gravestones, fashioned from broken cupboard doors, were hammered into the fertile land at the head of two mounds of freshly piled earth. The spring air felt crisp, but not cold. The morning rain had made the task of excavating the earth less back-breaking, but Zena had longed for the toil.

Anton stood behind the pair. He stood as a solemn guard, feeling almost like an intruder into their grief. "I'm gonna leave you guys to have a moment," he said, laying a comforting hand on their shoulders before turning and heading towards the yawning gate.

Zena bowed her head. "I'll look after you, Nathan. Both of us will, at least until we get to this place, then we'll see what the future brings, eh?"

Nathan pulled Russ' cap down to shield his eyes from the low sun. Having had to already pull the band as tight as it would go to make it fit, he nodded glumly. Zena saw a glint of silver flash in his hand. "What you got there?"

The child held up a watch. The time stuck at 7:27. "Francis told me that when his Grandad died, the watch he was wearing stopped at the exact time he passed away. That at the time he stopped living in one way, he became something else, energy again. I always thought it was one of those stories that grown-ups tell kids to make things seem easier. This was his watch, and it did the same."

Zena knelt down and pulled Nathan into a bear hug. "It'll be okay, Nathan."

The kid hugged the woman and then pulled away. "I know, Francis will always be with me. In here." He tapped his chest.

"With mummy."

The pair took one last memory photograph before turning from the graves.

CHAPTER FORTY-NINE

Most of the inhabitants in the RV were asleep. The past few hours had rolled by like a slug on sandpaper. Devin looked through the morning fog, focused on getting back to the mill as quickly as possible.

The Apostle rubbed dirty fingers around the inside of his mouth. He pulled out a chunk of broken tooth and flicked it out of the window. "Next time, Malky, can you go a bit easier on me? I lost two teeth last time. You may have noticed the lack of adequate dental care these days. I would appreciate keeping them for as long as possible."

Malky huffed and looked down at the man. "If I recall, I was reluctant to strike you. You made some unnecessary comments about my mother, and the origin of my true father."

"You can be such a sensitive soul, can't you? Regardless, at this rate I'll be needing to start checking corpses for dentures in a few months." The Apostle wiped his dribble-covered fingers on his trousers and put his feet up onto the dashboard. "Where to now, Your Grace?"

Devin stared ahead. "We rest for a week, replenish the men we lost and resupply. Then we head towards the next haven of falsehood."

"We need some penitents, too. They are becoming a scarce commodity," Malky growled.

"The other chapters have been on the lookout for more. Don't worry, my friend. Your cage will soon be full again with pathetic whelps," Devin sighed as the fog became denser.

"In the land of the dead, the one eyed man is king."

CHAPTER FIFTY

"I spy with my little eye, something beginning with…S," Otto said, sounding as bored as a child during Mass.

Huw looked around. The raised platform bolted to the cabin roof offered decent views of the valley, though the blooming forest canopy now hid the ground from prying eyes. Beneath them was the general hubbub of people going about another day of surviving.

Campfires hissed as water bubbled over from boiling pots; children grumbled at another breakfast of porridge made from water or day-old bread, toasted to within a speck of its existence.

"Sky?" Huw offered.

In truth, they had been playing the game every time they were on sentry duty, so they had long since exhausted every viable thing, from branch through smoke, and onto water.

"Amateur," Otto quipped. He whittled away the end of another arrow, adding it to the pile of pointed sticks, ready for fletching by someone infinitely more able than him.

Huw pointed out to the track which had been trampled through the countryside, from the water's edge to the camp. "Survivors, look, coming out of the trees."

Otto cupped his hands over his eyes and smiled. "Been a while since we seen some of those." He looked down into the milling people, before shouting, "JIM, MAIN GATE!"

Jim kissed Sophie on the head and ran to the gate, gesturing to the two guards to get ready to open up. "Keep your eyes open, lads. Been some weird reports coming in recently." The guards nodded in agreement and drew their weapons; one was a near unmanageable claymore while the other patted a solid steel mace in gloved hands.

The gate was fabricated from row upon row of felled tree trunks, lashed together, though they could open up like double doors. These days, most incoming and outgoing trips necessitated only the one mighty door to be in use.

Jim stood in the gap, flanked on either side by the lightly armoured guards. Down the trail they could make out four people, moving swiftly up the dirt track. "Get ready, they might have some stragglers after them, the speed they're moving at," Jim warned.

A child was the vanguard of the group, his legs pounding against the ground as fast as they could. Each step sent up puffs of dust. He reached the open gate and pulled off his cap, running his sleeve across his sweat beaded brow. "M…mmmm…mister," he stammered through burning lungs. "Please help."

"What's going on?" Jim asked sternly. The kid stood there panting, out of breath, his hands resting on his aching thighs.

"We need help. This man, he's…he's hurt," the child blurted out.

Jim looked back at the camp, to where a crowd of people were forming. "Fine, you two follow me," he said, and ran off to the three people stumbling up the makeshift path, the gate guards in tow. The kid followed suit, though at a far reduced pace.

As they approached the trio, the man in the middle collapsed to the ground. The others sank to their feet and were checking his vital signs. Jim reached them and looked at the group. One was a woman. Her blonde hair was tied back and she wore a pair of DMs that were on their last legs.

The man attending to their stricken companion had a carpet of hair on his head, made into no style, just stuck to his head with sweat. As he looked up at Jim, he noticed a ring of small scars around his left eye socket.

"Please, mister, we've come a long way to get here. Me and Francis met someone called Philip at a factory and he—"

Jim held up a hand. "You *saw* him? When?"

The boy gave a French shrug and continued. "He said to come here, that we would be safe, to ask for Jim."

Jim knelt down by the boy. "Well, kid. That would be me. You mentioned Francis? Where is he? I never really got a chance to thank him properly."

The kid looked to the ground and shook his head. "Francis is dead. He died saving us from these bad men in a farm who wanted to eat us."

The guards moved Zena and Anton aside and checked over the wounded man. "Are you all together?" Jim asked forcefully.

"Us three are. Him….we found him on the water's edge. Someone obviously took a disliking to him, he's been beaten half to death," Zena said, pulling strands of loose hair from her face. Anton stood by them and offered Jim a hand, which was shaken.

"And what about you son? what's your name?" Jim asked the boy.

The kid looked up and said softly, "Nathan, pleased to meet you."

Jim shook his hand and pointed to the open gate. "Why don't you lot get inside. If you're quick you might be able to get some breakfast, a cup of tea at least." The trio nodded wearily and trudged towards the fenced community. A number of good intentioned men and women streamed from within to help them inside.

"How is he?" Jim asked the guards, moving down the path to look at the man. As the guards parted he saw that someone had indeed given the poor fucker a helluva pasting. His left eye was swollen, and crusted blood clung to his nostrils and lips, which were cracked from dehydration. The one good eye burned with bare embers, staring at the three men standing over him.

"What's your name?" Jim asked.

The man coughed up a wad of coagulated blood and stringy phlegm. "…Thaddaeus…my name is Thaddaeus," he whispered, before lapsing into unconsciousness.

Jim sighed. "Get him inside. Let's hope Doc can work his magic again. This guy is gonna need all the luck to get through, by the looks of it." The guards nodded and picked the unconscious man up under his armpits. They dragged him back up the rise and into the compound.

Feeling the morning sun tingle on the back of his neck, Jim looked from the ground where the man had been lying to the growing community living behind the tall wooden fence. "Thaddaeus? What kind of name is that?"

TO BE CONTINUED...

ABOUT THE AUTHOR

Duncan lives in Chippenham, within the county of Wiltshire in Southern England, with his wife Debbie and their two cats, Rafa and Pepe. The furry faced ones would like to say hello, but their words come out in a rap, the meaning of which he cannot discern.

When he's not writing, Duncan can often be found traversing the town on a tandem bicycle on his lonesome, looking for Mr Dead to join him and help ascend Monkfish Hill. The biscuit shop is at the top, and he does long for the day when he is able to reach the summit, and have a nice cup of tea and a custard cream.

Go gently now into this world, for if you should happen to stumble, you can bet that someone has videoed it and will upload it for public viewing.

Get in touch with Duncan via;

Facebook –
https://www.facebook.com/duncanpbradshaw

Website –
http://www.duncanpbradshaw.co.uk

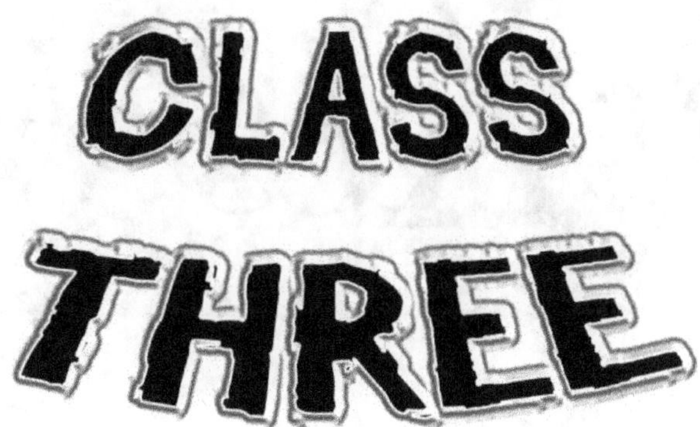

Hungover, dumped and late for work.

On an ordinary day, one of these would be a bad morning, but today Jim Taylor also has to contend with the zombie apocalypse.

Follow Jim during twenty four hours of Day One, as he and his zombie obsessed brother deal with the undead, a doomsday cult and maniacs in their quest to get to their parents, win his girlfriend back and for them to instigate 'The Plan'.

Worlds will collide and fall apart in a Class Three outbreak.

"A perfect blend of humour and horror."

- Scream Magazine

"*Class Three* does a lot of interesting things that seemed quite clever. I loved how seemingly random unrelated chapters would down the line make sense and have bearing on the plot, revealing secrets that give those chapters deeper meaning."

- The Rotting Zombie

We are all made of stars.

When an ancient Inca ritual is interrupted, it sets in motion a series of events that will echo through five hundred years of human history. Many seek to use the arcane knowledge for their own ends, from a survivor of a shipwreck, through to a suicide cult.

Yet...the most unlikeliest of them all will succeed.

"Hexagram is a visceral journey through the dark nooks and crannies of human history. Lovecraftian terror merges with blood sacrifice, suicide cults and body horror as Bradshaw weaves an intricate plot into an epic tale of apocalyptic dread."

- Rich Hawkins, author of The Last Plague trilogy

"So much more than just a horror novel, this one really makes you think. I like books that make me think, and books that present, and pull off, an original idea. This is that book and it's very much a must-read."

- Castle Macabre

PRIME DIRECTIVE

Some things are better left undiscovered.

The crew of the first manned mission to Mars, are in the final days of their expedition before they head home. Shamed by a lack of discoveries and humiliated by her colleagues, geologist Dana Fischerman heads out to the Galle crater, eager to find something to make her own legacy. What she uncovers will not only threaten the safety of her colleagues, but also everyone back on Earth.

"A perfect mixture of sci-fi and horror this story plants the seed of fear in your head and makes it grow and grow until you close the book."

- Confessions of a Reviewer

"Prime Directive is filled with some fantastic comic situations and a premise that will rock your socks off."

- 2 Book Lovers Reviewers

It's the thirteenth annual Lou Gehrig awards. Four B-list celebrity virologists vie to claim the Locked In Syndrome cup and get mulched down to form their disease for mass distribution.

A disease hipster takes centre stage on a night when a blast from the past threatens to turn his ordered, pus filled life upside down. In order to blow open a deep rooted conspiracy, he must team up with a disgraced one time child star who wants another shot at the big time, and clear his sullied name.

Together, they're going to show people the real meaning of a meltdown.

"I have never read anything like this, and don't think I'll ever encounter another writer with the ability to write like this. This book is the very definition of the word 'metaphor', is very clever, and totally hilarious."

- Kayleigh Marie Edwards, author of Bitey Bachman

"Remember, you've now willingly plunged yourself into the mind of Duncan P. Bradshaw. You're completely at the mercy of his strange imagination and all the eccentric oddities that his curious mind can conjure up. Indeed, it quickly becomes apparent that the only way you'll be able to wade through the veritable quagmire of lunacy is by simply succumbing to the madness."

- DLS Reviews

CHUMP

Eight stories which take a different look at these reanimated denizens of death:

CURE WHAT AILS YA - When a snake oil salesman rolls into the Wild West town of Lobo, both he and the inhabitants are unaware of what is about to crawl out of the desert, hungry for brains.

1984 - Finally, after years of being subject to official censure, the true story as to why the Eastern Bloc countries boycotted the 1984 Los Angeles Olympics, is revealed.

RED SABRE ONE - An SAS team are tasked with extracting a high value target from their world famous home.

SENSELESS APPRENTICE - Step inside the mind of one of the undead, unable to do anything but watch on as his body acts on primal instinct.

DEAD DROP - A novella following a courier in the apocalypse. Ceepher's motto is simple; never look inside the package, and always be on time. His latest delivery will put both on the line.

CHARITY BEGINS AT HOME - Whilst out collecting for H.O.A.R.D. (Helping Orphans Affected by the Reanimation Disease), Sadie stumbles upon a middle age couple, who seem to have survived the apocalypse with their pristine house intact.

GONE FISHIN' - Bored, a son pleads with his dad to tell him, again, how his parents got together...one summers day on the lake.

WHACKOS - After 'Reclamation', a radio host and his sound engineer, follow a clean up team, as they confront the after-effects of the zombie apocalypse.

BEFORE YOU GO

I just want to say a big thank you for buying and reading this book, 'they' say that the zombie genre has been done to (un)death. Personally, I believe that as long as there's an interesting story to tell, that will shine through.

Ultimately, you've either taken a punt on this or read Class Three and decided to see what happened next in the world that I created. Whilst there are zombies in it, I believe that they are part of the background, on par with the Netzach's factory or the Penny Gaff which turned into a bloodbath.

Either way, I hope you enjoyed the ride, there are two more to go in this series, and who knows what else I may add as time goes by.

Before you go, if you have the time and inclination, I would really appreciate it if you could post a review on whatever website you bought this through.

These days EVERYONE has the power to inform, YOUR opinion is valid, and either praise or constructive feedback is a writer's lifeblood.

Thank you once again and until next time, take it easy.

Dunk
23 May 2015

www.ingramcontent.com/pod-product-compliance
Lightning Source LLC
Chambersburg PA
CBHW082146130726
47910CB00013B/2595